PROLOGUE

THE DAY THE MORTALS discovered the afterlife, the sky opened up—and it never closed again.

That day, a black fissure appeared across the Underworld's pale violet sky, like someone had torn a hole in the very fabric of the universe. There was nothing beyond the tear but darkness—a black veil, dividing one world from the other. The rupture in the sky remained, like a scar—reminding any immortal creature who glimpsed it that their home would never be a secret again.

Haben hadn't been there when it happened. He had not yet arrived in the Underworld, nor had he received his eternal sentence. But he knew what it meant, the first time he saw it. Enlightenment had come at a price for the mortal world. *That* he'd seen: decades of violent infighting. Ruin beyond redemption. For all their intellect and technological prowess, the humans fell on their own sword. Sometimes, Haben thought they deserved it. They'd reached for something they were never meant to grasp. Underworld dwellers had always been able to cross to the other side and observe the mortal world, but the opposite was forbidden. There was a reason the humans were left in the dark: They were greedy. Selfish. Their simple minds couldn't absorb the truth.

Haben was glad to be rid of the mortal world at first. But that was before he understood the meaning of his new life, before he understood what it meant to be a demon. Before the torture began.

He glanced up at the rising sun and the jagged black rock face that loomed before him. He only had a few more minutes to reach his destination. The dark fissure in the sky, the mortals' window to their world, would soon align with the cliff above him. He knew sending a message to the other side was hopeless; the mortals didn't watch the Veil anymore. All the demons knew that. But it didn't stop them from trying.

Haben grasped a craggy foothold, hoisting himself up onto the cliff. The sleeve of his tattered robe shifted, revealing two identical black tattoos snaking up the length of both his arms. He was always startled, even after so many hundreds of years, to catch sight of them: diagonal lines, originating at his elbow crease, crisscrossing down the pale flesh of his forearm toward his wrist, creating the appearance of a cage on his skin. He couldn't help but think, as he always did, of their resemblance to shackles. Dohv marked all his servants this way once he claimed them.

As he climbed, Haben remembered the first time he had observed his immortal body in the sunlight, how horrified he had been when he realized he could see straight through the flesh on his arms if he looked hard enough. Dohv, Lord of the Underworld and Keeper of Life, had given him a new encasement for his soul, different from the body he'd had in life. His ashen skin housed organs, organs that circulated blood—blood that would never run dry, so long as the universe endured. He had been made this way for a reason, so he could still experience whatever physical pain Dohv wished to visit upon him.

Haben had only seen his reflection once, in the dark, mirrorlike floor of Dohv's palace. He was struck by the face of the man staring back at him. He had not aged, but he was gaunt. Sallow. A husk of his former self. His eyes, lively and green, which had suited his face so perfectly in life, bulged disproportionately above his protruding cheekbones. His hair had thinned to wisps. He dared to hope he could still glimpse the man he used to be, underneath it all. But he hadn't looked at himself even once since then.

With an exhausted grunt, Haben pulled himself up over the edge of the obsidian cliff. As dawn crested the horizon, the rupture in the sky inched toward the spot where he stood. Haben caught his breath, gazing across the enormous stone slab before him, at the hundreds of thousands of crude etchings that had been carved into it. He plucked a shard of rock from the ground and clutched it in his shaky fist. Even though he knew it was useless, even though he'd tried it so many times to no avail, he found a small, blank space and began to write:

I . . . Am . . .

Haben wasn't sure what lay on the other side of that fissure in the sky, but he knew the humans weren't watching anymore. Not since the war. But still, he longed to tell them . . .

I . . . Am . . . Sorr . . .

At that moment, he dropped the stone and doubled over with an agonized growl. He felt as though he'd swallowed a knife that was stabbing him from the inside out. He collapsed onto his side, bracing himself. *Here it comes.* Here was his punishment from Dohv. Here was the hunger.

Whenever Dohv's curse reared its ugly head, it took Haben by surprise, even though it had been happening for centuries. He would languish, starving, until he finally accepted his fate: to cross to the other side and consume his sacrifice. He would eat his fill, destroying, bit by anguished bit, whatever was left of his mortal soul.

The second hunger pang hit Haben like a tidal wave and forced him to draw his legs to his chest. He gnawed on the top of his knee to keep himself from screeching like a tortured animal. This was the breaking point for a living being, the moment a starving person would succumb to death. But for Haben, there would be no release. There would be no death.

As he writhed on the ground, he mouthed the words he was unable to finish writing:

"S-sorry. I am . . . s—"

But he knew he'd soon give in. He always did. And even as he howled and cursed Dohv's name for such a gruesome sentence, he knew he deserved every moment of it for the crimes he had committed. He had earned this terrible, endless fate.

CHAPTER ONE

SEYCIA HADN'T REACHED the pit yet, but she already knew: tonight's victim would be a child. The autumnal sacrifice had been a woman, with silver hair and chipped, yellow teeth. Seycia had been close enough to see her, the last time—though she'd closed her eyes for the worst parts. But because the last offering had been an adult, she knew General Simeon's next victim would be much younger.

A frigid breeze whipped her mane of dark, untamed hair across her face and into her eyes. She tied it into a knot behind her neck and shivered as the day faded to cold, foreboding twilight. Twice each year, a fearsome windstorm rattled Khronasa for three days. On the third night of the storm, the Savage would come to claim its sacrifice. That night was tonight.

"His name's Henshaw," a small voice piped up. Seycia spun to face her brother, Miko. He'd been silent up until then, shuffling along a few paces behind her. It was a long walk to the city center from their cabin on the hillside—he was probably getting tired.

"Where did you hear his name?" She didn't need to ask who he was referring to.

"Last night. You must've been asleep already. There was a lady crying, down by the river. She kept saying his name." Miko lowered his voice and added, "I think he's from the hill."

"Hmm." Seycia absorbed the news with a frown.

"You always said we were safe up here."

Seycia stole a glance at her younger brother, wondering how to respond. He was nearly twelve summers old. She wouldn't be able to shield him from the truth for much longer.

"General Simeon controls all of Khronasa. Including the hill," she replied. A moment passed as she watched Miko for a reaction. He pulled a shaky breath, then nodded.

"So we're not safe anymore."

"We've never been safe."

She regretted the words as soon as she said them. She'd spent years trying to convince him that the world was only dangerous for those who couldn't protect themselves. She'd been so careful to empower him. But with each passing season, with each sacrifice, it became harder for her to keep the fear to herself.

Woosh! A tiny dart sliced through the air.

Miko bounded over to a patch of brush and produced a rabbit he'd just shot with one of his poisoned darts.

He picked it up by its ears and dangled its paralyzed body in the air. The red-feather tip he'd attached to the tiny weapon stuck out of the animal's neck. "Enough for dinner?"

"Sure," Seycia said. "He's a big one. Let's cut him quick before the poison wears off."

Miko dislodged the dart from the rabbit's flesh and wiped it on the sleeve of his frayed deerskin tunic. From underneath the collar of her coarse gray shirt, Seycia pulled an animal's fang on a cord and used it to slit the rabbit's throat.

The fang was both her most valuable weapon and most treasured heirloom, a trophy her father had claimed after killing the Black Beast eighteen years ago. She'd been little more than an infant at the time, but her father had retold the story of the kill so often that she swore she'd been right there with him. The fang's surface was smooth and whiter than a pearl, a perfect half-moon shape with a jagged tip, about the length of her own hand. She often thrust it between her second and third fingers, brandishing it as though it were a talon that had sprouted from her fist.

Seycia drained the rabbit's blood and handed it back to Miko, who shoved the carcass into a leather pouch he wore on his back. Then from his belt he pulled a hollowed-out tree branch and a walnut shell filled with gummy red paste—his homemade tranquilizer.

"There's another one, over there," he whispered, pointing to a rustling bush on the other side of the path. He coated the sharp end of his dart with poison.

Seycia tiptoed behind him as he ventured off the path, stalking their prey through a labyrinth of fallen trees. They came to a clearing, where the skeleton of a once-great temple lay in a heap. Years ago, the sparkling white tower had been a place of worship devoted to Dohv, Lord of the Underworld and Keeper of Life. Now, it was nothing but a pile of marble shards on the ground. Seycia heard rumors of Khronasans who hid scraps of its shattered columns under their beds, but nobody dared to worship at the foot of its crumbled remains. Not since the arrival of General Simeon and the Coalition.

Miko clenched the hollowed-out stick between his lips and fired off another dart. But the second rabbit was quick, having learned from its partner, and hurried off. Miko sighed.

"I think there's a burrow nearby. We should try to find it," he said as he ran off to fetch the fallen dart.

"One's enough, Miko," Seycia hissed. "We'll be late for the sacrifice."

"Wait! Come look over here!" Miko called out to her. A reluctant sigh escaped her lips as she followed him behind the temple ruins.

A wedge of silvery metal poked out of the earth, likely the corner of something larger buried beneath the surface. Miko was already digging for it with his bare hands. The forest beyond the city was filled with mysterious odds and ends that Seycia and Miko used to collect as children: Shiny silver discs, cracked into jagged shards. Scraps of worn metal, warped with age. Echoes of a world that once existed, a world that had disappeared before their own had begun.

"Miko, come on. We don't need any more junk," Seycia grumbled.

"Just let me see what it is, then we'll decide if it's junk."

Seycia watched as Miko pulled a rectangular metal object from the ground. It was cracked and discolored and had an unfamiliar white emblem on the front. The emblem looked like a piece of fruit someone had taken a bite out of. He frowned, pawing at the artifact, and realized he could pull the edges apart, like a book, revealing a shattered, reflective surface between the two sides. He breathed an excited gasp.

"I don't have one like this!" he said, examining the ancient treasure. He held it up to Seycia. "How old do you think it is?"

"I'm not sure."

"But it's definitely from before the war, right?"

"Mmm," Seycia murmured in agreement, then set out on the path again, encouraging him to follow her.

He turned the mysterious object over in his hands as they walked, straining to see in the dim light. "It's not fair that we don't know what this is. It's probably really useful, for someone who knows what it does," Miko chattered on. "Doesn't that scare you, a little? To think about all the things and people in the world that nobody remembers?"

"There are plenty of things that scare me more than that."

At that moment, a small, childlike voice rang out from the thick of the woods. Seycia and Miko both slowed down and glanced over at a parallel path that would soon converge with their own. The shadows of three figures drifted into view: fellow foragers from the woods. Seycia realized the child among them was singing. It was an old song—one she knew well:

His tongue's black as coal from the souls that he's swallowed;
When you walk home tonight, be sure you're not followed.
For if you've been guilty of treason or theft,
The Savage will feast on what life you have left.
He sends evil to Earth, such mischief he makes:
The famines, the floods, the wildfires, the quakes.
He acts out of fury, the hunger he feels;
So, child, stay in line or you'll be his next meal.

The family of foragers met up with Seycia and Miko at the place the two pathways became one. As they passed each other, Seycia peered at the young husband and wife, holding torches and wearing mismatched deerskin. Their frail, barefoot daughter continued humming to herself as she kicked pebbles out of her way. The little girl looked up at Seycia with a fierce, starving blankness, and Seycia inched away, as though the girl had smelled the fresh meat they were carrying. She'd learned long ago not to share. Food was scarce enough.

Seycia and Miko reached the edge of a gray meadow, where the muddy pathway widened and became a gravel road that led to Khronasa's central square. These roads were neat and straight—a newer development. Seycia heard a distant rumble and pulled Miko to the side of the road for safety. Two Coalition vehicles with darkened windows streaked past, into the rough terrain of the woods. She took it as another sign that their shelter on the hilltop might not be as safe as she'd once believed. Seycia choked on the putrid, greasy exhaust they left behind and remembered the first time she saw one of the Coalition's monstrous vehicles. Nobody had ever seen anything like it. She'd panicked, wondering if the Black Beast had somehow resurfaced.

As she and Miko walked on, a city of crude cinderblocks and rusty red rooftops loomed before them, interspersed with twisted towers of rusted metal: relics from whatever world had perished before theirs. They followed a set of ancient steel tracks, stuck deep in the dirt and overgrown with weeds, as it wound through the city and led them to the central square.

A considerable crowd had already gathered there, abuzz with anxious chatter. In the middle of the plaza stood a covered platform of polished marble, flanked by six huge pillars. Seycia noted the ancient silver gong situated at the front of the plaza platform, which had been engraved ages ago with images of her people's demons and gods—a relic the Coalition had stolen and reclaimed as their own.

Just below the stairs to the platform was the pit—the same pit Seycia's forefathers had dug to establish their village. Now, General Simeon's servants surrounded it, clutching buckets of water, squinting through the round, black goggles they wore that made Seycia think of overgrown roaches. They were busy splashing water down the steep sides of the hole in the ground, making sure the muddy walls were slick and impossible to climb. Seycia had never wanted to be close enough to the hole to peer down into it, but she was sure it was incredibly deep. Nobody ever climbed out.

Most of the villagers had already queued up in front of a barricade of stuffed burlap sacks, where a sallow Coalition woman with hair like stiff, yellow hay was handing them out. Seycia and Miko took their place in the line. Each spectator would receive a sack of grain on their way to watch the chosen boy march to his death. General Simeon could ensure everyone's attendance by distributing sustenance; the woods and the hilltop produced no crops. Seycia would have gladly subsisted on berries and scant scraps of rabbit for the rest of her days, but Miko was still a child. Miko needed to eat.

The Coalition woman lifted her dark goggles and fixed them on top of her head as twilight crept across the plaza. Seycia was thankful she could always identify her enemy. Coalition members all wore protective eyewear and multiple layers of clothing to shield themselves from the oppressive sun they'd avoided for so many years. Their eyes were a pale ice-gray, like dirty day-old snow, and Seycia swore she could feel a chill every time one of them met her gaze.

Long ago, Seycia and Miko's ancestors braved the elements and joined forces to breathe new life into their war-ravaged world. But the Coalition took refuge below the surface, hoarding their riches and knowledge as they rode out the storm. As the Khronasans learned to live again, they couldn't have imagined the evil lurking beneath their feet, an evil that would one day rise to face the sun and devour everything they held dear. An evil that spread like a plague across the land where they'd danced for their gods, taught their children to walk, and buried their dead.

"Thank you, sister," Miko grunted as the yellow-haired woman shoved a bag of grain into his arms. Seycia didn't even make eye contact as the woman distributed her reward.

"Thanks," Seycia muttered.

"Thanks, what?" The woman snorted.

"Er . . . thanks, sister," she corrected herself with a grimace. She hated admitting that they needed the grain. Even the smallest reminders of the Coalition's strength sparked an uncontrollable fury inside of her that she didn't know what to do with. She knew she'd taken a risk, being rude to the woman. But she couldn't help it.

She met Miko at the far edge of the plaza, a good distance from the pit. Before the Coalition arrived, Seycia had never attended a public sacrifice. Back then, the ritual was done in private, and only criminals were offered to the Savage. Never, ever children. She always wondered about the people who pushed their way to the front of the crowd, the ones who desperately wanted an unobstructed view of the helpless victim. There were quite a lot of them. She didn't understand it. It was as though they'd convinced themselves that what they were watching wasn't real.

The gong rang out—an ominous, metallic moan. And that's when she saw him.

General Simeon entered the square. A team of bodyguards slung with heavy black machine guns walked in step with him across the cobblestones. He was, at a distance, little more than a snip of a man in a red military uniform, with thinning blond hair and an uneven gait. He wore a small pair of black spectacles that became transparent whenever the light faded, and his gray eyes were tense and narrow, as though he were constantly struggling to see what was in front of him. But Seycia knew not to be deceived by his appearance. Since the night of the occupation, it had been his eyes that spied on her from the darkness in each and every one of her nightmares. She shuddered as the general approached, unable to keep the chilling memories at bay . . .

At sunset on the day Khronasa was invaded, her family's hunting dogs had started howling in a blind frenzy. They burst out the door, never to be seen again. They had heard the march of the army in the distance like an impending thunderstorm. Nobody else had.

Seycia remembered exactly where she'd stood in her family's pasture, calling out to the dogs, when an explosion rocked the entire countryside. Seycia's father, Oskar, yanked her back into the house and told her to hide under her bed. She watched her neighbors streak past her window, fleeing in terror. It wasn't long before the flames from a second blast devoured their cabin. She, her parents, and Miko, just five summers old, bolted from their home.

They raced for the hills, mounted on their two horses, but they didn't get far. A line of Coalition soldiers halted them, positioned like a fortress on all sides of the village, each of them holding . . . What was it? A long, black staff? Seycia had never seen a firearm before in her life.

General Simeon stood at the center of his militia, barking orders to his men in a strange language. Then he changed his tongue. He addressed her family and neighbors directly: "The first man to flee into the woods does so with a bullet in his back," he had said. What was a bullet? Nobody knew . . .

A man who lived nearby ignored General Simeon's threat and drove his horse through the line of soldiers, toward the hillside beyond. *Then* the Khronasans understood what a bullet was.

It was all a feverish blur after that. Seycia hadn't seen it happen, but she'd heard it: one of General Simeon's bullets hit her mother square in the neck. She hardly had a moment to process where the deafening *crack* had come from. Her father caught her mother in his arms as she sank to the ground, drenching him with blood. It was over fast. She didn't even scream.

Oskar was wearing the Black Beast's fang around his own neck that night. He didn't have any other weapons on him. As General Simeon kept his gun fixed on their helpless family, Oskar lunged toward him, brandishing the fang like a dagger. Terrified, Seycia watched them struggle. Oskar knocked the gun from Simeon's hand and swung at him with the fang. But instead of landing a fatal blow, Oskar plunged the fang deep into General Simeon's left cheek and twisted it—carving a hole into the side of the wretched man's face.

As Oskar pulled the fang from Simeon's cheek, a soldier standing behind him took aim and fired. Seycia's father was gone in barely a breath, asleep forever on a blanket of moss and trampled leaves. It was early summer, and the ground was covered in white blossoms that had fallen from the trees like a soft, fragrant snow. Seycia would always recall how deeply red her father's blood appeared against those white flowers in the moonlight.

Seycia leaped to her feet as the general lifted his head and blood cascaded from the hole in his face. He looked at her—he gazed right into her eyes—and he *smiled*. It was the wickedest thing she'd ever seen. He smiled at her, his butchered cheek gruesomely off-kilter, as if promising her that this was only the beginning.

She grabbed for Miko as he wailed, desperate to stay with their parents. He didn't understand what had just happened to them. She peered down at her father's body in despair, and spotted the fang in his lifeless fist. She grabbed it and scrambled to mount an abandoned horse that streaked past. As Seycia hung the fang around her neck and helped Miko up onto the horse, the general locked eyes with her again. *He was still smiling*.

Holding together his mangled cheek, he hissed at her, "I'll give you a head start for being so pretty." She remembered the way her stomach lurched when he said those words.

She and Miko stole away toward the hilltop as the fighting quieted and the night wore thin. They found an abandoned hut deep in the forest and made it their home. She'd been lucky to spend her childhood learning the secrets of the woods alongside her father. She knew they could survive, but quickly doubted whether survival was enough. Seven years later, she still doubted it. And whenever she caught sight of General Simeon, she doubted it even more.

Simeon was close enough to the pit now and Seycia could see his repugnant scar. His face was fixed into an eternal scowl, lip upturned at the left cheek, skin pulled taut to cover the hole in the side of his face. It was hard for her to remember exactly what he'd looked like before her father mutilated him, but she relished the idea that he'd once been a handsome man who'd been turned into a monster—as foul as the one who would come to claim its sacrifice tonight.

The boy, Henshaw, trailed behind General Simeon, surrounded by a team of four bodyguards. He was shackled from head to toe and couldn't have gone very far if he'd tried, with or without the guards. He shuffled down the gravel walkway, eyes pinned to the ground, as night descended and the gas lamps surrounding the pit flickered to life. Seycia remembered seeing him once or twice before. Freckles dusted the apples of his two youthful cheeks, and his sun-kissed skin was the color of warm honey. He'd been one of the healthier-looking children from the hilltop, but no longer. His face was drawn and grim, caked with mud and tear stains. He couldn't have been much older than Miko's twelve summers. She wondered how he'd been chosen. She wondered that every time.

Unnerving silence rippled across the crowd as General Simeon and his bodyguards led the boy to the pit and clamped a weighted shackle to his foot. Seycia squeezed her eyes shut for the next part, the part she hated the most: When the silent victim would break down and plead for mercy. When they'd scream. They were always ignored and tossed into the muddy pit—an end without dignity.

As Henshaw's plaintive whimpers echoed across the captivated crowd, General Simeon stepped forward to begin his blessing. Seycia bit down on her tongue, nauseated by his voice as he led the ritual he'd stolen from her people. Everything else about the old Khronasan ways had been banned—except the sacrifices.

"We are the mortals. The frail. The selfish. The ones who failed you—and failed ourselves." He spoke slowly, gazing up at the sky before making eye contact with each spectator in the front row. "In the years since we breached the Veil, we have learned a great lesson. War has reminded us how weak we truly are. We come to you, great Keeper of Life, in supplication. We know why you send the Savage. We know how he hungers. We are here to satiate him."

One of Henshaw's guards snarled and struck him in the back with his boot. The boy tumbled into the pit with a howl that took Seycia's breath away. Then there was a low rumble of thunder. The stars above them vanished as Simeon hit the gong again. She shuddered in the cold, clammy air as an enormous black storm cloud ebbed across the sky. The Savage was on its way.

The rain was quick and ruthless, as it always was. Seycia braced herself as the storm swept across the plaza like a ghost and water flooded the pit. Henshaw screamed. Seycia stared at her feet, flexing her bare toes in the freezing mud. She wanted to run, but running was forbidden. They would wait until the boy had drowned—until the Savage had come to claim him.

The Khronasans began to hum a simple tune, swaying in unison, as rain pelted their faces and filled the pit. Henshaw kept screaming, but the chorus overpowered him. The people in the front were always the most enthusiastic, making sure General Simeon could hear their impassioned effort. Seycia hardly participated. Nobody would know she wasn't humming along. She closed her eyes, gritting her teeth through the cold. She lulled herself into a trancelike state as the minutes passed, swaying back and forth. Even with the supernatural intensity of the rain, it would still take time to fill the pit.

She was forced back to reality when Miko suddenly yelped and lost his footing. Annoyed, she opened her eyes and stifled a gasp—his nose was bleeding. She pulled him close and whispered, "Miko, are you—?"

"Get away from me!" Miko turned and hissed at a figure lurking behind them.

A teenage Khronasan boy with matted brown hair and thick, meaty arms burst forth, grabbing for Miko's leather knapsack, the one that held their dinner and provisions. Miko dodged his grasp, and the boy struck him a second time. Miko sputtered, wiping blood from his nose and mouth.

Seycia wasn't sure if it was because of the boy's petulant snicker or the rage she'd been bottling up all day, but she was thirsty for a fight. Miko tried to hold her back, but she was too quick. As the Khronasans kept humming and swaying in the downpour, Seycia butted between Miko and the boy and elbowed him in the eye. He kicked her right back, square in the gut, but adrenaline was on her side. She clawed at his face with her sharp nails and wrapped him in a chokehold. As she tightened her grasp . . .

"Brother Henshaw," General Simeon continued his blessing. The pit was nearly full now.

"Brother Henshaw," The audience echoed. Seycia was still squeezing the boy's neck.

"May your flesh appease the wicked one. May your blood protect the earth," Simeon went on, eyes to the heavens.

Again, the audience replied, in monotone: "May his flesh appease the wicked one. May his blood protect the earth."

The boy wriggled free and threw Seycia down into the mud. As he turned his attention back to Miko, Seycia sprang to her feet, tore the fang from under her collar, and swiped the boy's arm with it, drawing blood. Then, she pointed it right between his beady eyes.

"May your sacrifice be remembered," General Simeon concluded his remarks.

"His sacrifice shall be remembered," the audience responded.

The boy's nervous gaze shifted from Seycia's scowl to the razor-sharp tip of the fang. Finally, he held up his hands and retreated, weaving through the crowd like a frightened deer in the forest. Seycia caught her breath and wiped the mud from her face, surveying the scene. She hadn't realized how many people were watching them. Her heart stammered as General Simeon lowered his head and returned his gaze to the audience. In a panic, Seycia dropped the fang back down the front of her collar. She was frozen to the spot, unsure of her next move. She hadn't meant to draw so much attention to herself. Had General Simeon seen the fang? What was the punishment for carrying a weapon to the sacrifice? She cursed herself, sure she'd broken a rule of some sort. There would be repercussions. She swallowed hard and did her best to blend in with the crowd, avoiding Simeon's stare . . . when a woman's bone-chilling shriek sent shock waves across the shivering crowd.

General Simeon spun to face the pit, and Seycia grabbed for Miko with an awestruck gasp. For there, peering over the edge of Henshaw's watery grave, were two enormous, hungry yellow eyes, piercing the darkness with a phosphorescent glow. A deep, fearsome snarl rattled the earth beneath Seycia's feet.

"S-Seycia. Is that . . . ?" The words stuck in Miko's throat. He held tight to Seycia's hand.

All at once, Seycia forgot about General Simeon and the fang. They were staring into the eyes of the Savage—for the very first time. In years past, Seycia might have been too frightened to look directly into the pit, but she was certain the creature had never shown itself before.

The villagers clutched one another in terror. Some of them kneeled. The woman down in front kept screaming. Why had the Savage revealed itself? What was happening? But the creature vanished as quickly as it had come, back into the depths of the pit.

A hush fell across the plaza. Seycia and Miko exchanged a stricken glance . . . before a ferocious thunderclap shook the city and all the water in the pit rose up into the air, hanging above the crowd like a menacing black rain cloud. This, Seycia had seen before. This was the beginning of the end. There was Henshaw, hovering helplessly in midair, as sickly green and yellow lightning fractured the sky. Then, the rain cloud took the form of a face, dark as smoke, with its enormous mouth hanging agape. Seycia held her breath. This was the moment.

If Henshaw screamed, nobody heard it. The night sky swallowed him whole. The Savage was satiated . . . and the boy was gone for good.

CHAPTER TWO

HABEN HADN'T MEANT to show himself. He always took care to stay hidden whenever he crossed over to claim his offering. He couldn't bear to imagine how people would react to him. But tonight, he'd been distracted. He'd seen something just beyond the pit that forced him to stop and stare. *What was it?* He couldn't remember. He couldn't think. *Not now.* Not while the drowned boy was in his clutches. Relief had come at last—he could almost taste it.

He heaved his weary body out of the passageway, dragging the lifeless boy behind him as he returned to the Underworld. The glossy black puddle on the ground, slick like oil, was his door to the living. He scanned his surroundings: red desert sand, far as the eye could see. He preferred to consume his offering in the depths of the cave network, but he couldn't always control where he ended up after the ordeal. It was all a dark, dizzying haze. His ragged breath was not his own. He stumbled across the coarse sand as the Underworld's violet sky deepened to sapphire blue, pulling the boy along by his ankle, face down. It was better not to look.

Since the hunger struck hours ago, his pain had physically manifested. He transformed into the thing he hated most—the thing the humans called the Savage. His shredded black robe had fused to him like a second skin. His jawline had expanded in size, and two scaly, grotesque wings jutted from his shoulder blades. His eyes narrowed to serpentine slits and shone with a sinister yellow luster. The transformation left him catatonic with pain every time, but there was something about it he enjoyed. He became something fearsome, something deadly, something he could have never imagined becoming during his earthly years. He hated the Savage only after it was over—after he had consumed his offering.

He collapsed to his knees and tore into the boy's flesh, right there and then. There might have been other demons nearby watching him, but he couldn't bear to wait. He wouldn't feel the shame till later. As he sank his monstrous teeth into the back of the boy's neck, tasting his flesh for the first time, his heart began to race. His bony fingers trembled and tears flooded his furious yellow eyes. He knew what would happen next, but he was helpless to stop it. When he consumed the flesh of the humans, he also absorbed their misery. Their sickness. Their terror.

He was dizzy with dread—dread the boy must have felt in those final moments. He cried as he gorged himself on the entrails, choking back sobs as he swallowed mouthful after mouthful. There was nothing lower than this. This—*this* was hell.

Hours passed. Haben lay in the blood-soaked sand, feeling his muscles quiver and twitch as his body returned to its human-like form. He stood and breathed a desolate sigh, massaging his shoulders. The wings were gone. He grit his jaw. His teeth were his own again. It was over. But the shame had just begun. He shuddered then, certain he was being watched. He glanced around, but the vermilion moon up above was his only companion.

He gathered his victim's bones to cast them into the River of Past Lives, as he always did. As he shuffled across the desert, he spotted the distant shadows of a dozen demon vagabonds in the bloodred moonlight, blindly clinging to one another, inching over the dunes as one. They might have heard him consuming his offering, but he knew they hadn't seen him. The vagabonds were sightless. He was sure they were being punished for something, but he'd never cared to find out what.

Haben crossed the desert, making his way toward an oasis where the River of Past Lives intersected the parched landscape. As he cradled the bones in his arms, his skin prickled and he spun around, still sure someone was spying on him. The sightless vagabonds had marched to the other side of the dune. He was alone again. But he couldn't shake the feeling. Part of him knew it was his own shame playing tricks on him, burning in the pit of his full belly.

He wished, as he always did, that he could overpower the Savage and consume something else in those horrific moments. But the monster wanted only one thing, and he had no control. One night, he'd thought to take a bite of his own flesh instead, but it turned to hot ash in his mouth and made him sicker than he already was, if that were possible. If only his tenure with Dohv had begun before the war—before the mortals had discovered the existence of an afterlife and Dohv felt the need to send them reminders of his strength. If nobody knew about Dohv, then Dohv would have no need for messengers, and there would be no need for Haben's curse. He would be free. But freedom was a dangerous, fleeting desire. He knew better than to allow the idea to seduce him.

Haben reached the river's edge and paused for a moment to watch a daisy chain of foggy, nebulous figures skim its inky surface, like a cobweb of arms and legs undulating in the breeze. There were so many Soulless in the river now, more than there had ever been before: millions of mortal lives, shed like husks. Their spindly limbs crested the water's surface, as though the river had become crowded.

As he tossed the boy's bones into the water, he suddenly recalled the ordeal at the pit, before he'd taken his sacrifice. Why had he looked out at the crowd in that moment? He watched the bones sink below the surface, and the memory materialized. From the depths of the pit, he had glimpsed a bright white light up above, like a beacon. He'd been drawn to it, as though the light were calling to him. When he peered over the edge of the pit to get a closer look, he realized the beam of light was emanating from the hand of a girl in the crowd. Was she carrying some kind of magical torch? Why did it entrance him so? And why didn't any of the other humans seem to notice it? He'd been so distracted that he'd even forgotten about his hunger for the briefest of seconds. He'd forgotten who he was and what he looked like . . . until he heard the screams.

As he turned to follow the river out of the desert, an earsplitting cry pierced the vacant silence. *Caw. Caw. Ca-CAW!*

Haben's breath caught and he turned in a circle, looking for the source of the odd sound. He glanced up into the sky, where a winged creature, silhouetted by the moon, was circling directly above the spot where he stood. Had Dohv sent it? Was *that* what had been watching him?

He stared at it as it continued to circle him, over and over, 'round and 'round. What was it? Some sort of bird? It didn't appear to have feathers. He squinted in the moonlight, but the mysterious creature was already retreating. As it disappeared from view, it released a final, earsplitting *caw*. It had seen whatever it had come to see. Haben shivered.

He hobbled off toward the cave network beyond, eager to take cover and end this long, strange night—eager to hide in the darkness till the Savage struck again.

"Let me clean him! I want to rip the guts out!" Miko hovered over the silver catfish Seycia was preparing to slice open. A rickety slab of wood balanced atop a flat crate stood between them, which passed for a kitchen table.

"Wash your hands first."

Their kitchen was piled with ancient, repurposed odds and ends they'd rescued from the forest ruins: Chipped concrete bricks surrounded an indoor fire pit. An old steel pipe sticking out of the ceiling collected fresh rainwater from outside and dispensed it into an empty paint can on the ground. Two rusted wheels with a metal pole fixed between them made for a functional cooking spit.

Miko bounded over to a misshapen cauldron filled with water hanging over the fire pit. He plunked his hands in and yanked them back out with a howl. "*Oww!* Why didn't you tell me it was hot?" he snapped.

"It's over the fire. Of course it's hot."

He sucked on his scalded fingertips as he shuffled back to the table. He grabbed for Seycia's fang and pointed it at the belly of the fish.

"Now, just make sure you're slicing in a flat, sideways motion—"

But he'd already cut a perfectly straight incision. He smiled, finished gutting and cleaning the fish, and wiped the blood off the fang before handing it back to Seycia.

"I know how to do it."

To supplement the fish, Seycia made a soup from the rabbit Miko had shot earlier. She stirred in a few wild mushrooms. Their sacks of grain sat untouched in the corner of the little log hut they called home.

"I'll make bread tomorrow," she said flatly.

She and Miko drank their soup out of hand-sculpted clay bowls and listened to the rain *pitter-patter* against the walls of their windowless wooden refuge. They were always silent during the rain after a sacrifice. Seycia got up a few times to move various bowls and buckets below the leaky spots on their ceiling—extra drinking water for later. The roof, constructed of old metal panels they'd scavenged from the woods, a patchwork of muted colors strung together with rusted wire, wasn't reliable in bad weather. The dirt floor of their cabin often turned to sludge on rainy days.

Finally, Miko spoke up. "You've never seen the Savage before, right?"

She shook her head. She hadn't wanted to think about what happened at the sacrifice, and she didn't like that he'd brought it up. They had enough to be afraid of.

"So he's never shown himself. This is the first time anyone's seen him."

"We don't know what we saw," Seycia corrected him, if only to calm his nerves. She was sure they'd both seen those eyes peering over the pit.

"Do you think he was trying to tell us something?" Miko asked, quieter now.

"If the Savage has something to say, I'm sure he'll let General Simeon know," she scoffed, and took a long sip of her soup. Miko did the same.

After supper, Seycia lined Miko's hammock in the corner with a warm, sheepskin blanket as he undressed and put his dirty clothes in a burlap sack in the corner. She insisted upon a clean home, even if it was a home without a proper floor or roof.

Tucked beneath the blanket in his hammock, Miko pulled out the mysterious silver contraption he'd found in the woods and started unscrewing the panels. His favorite pastime was taking apart every artifact he dug up, trying to decode its inner workings.

On the other side of the room, Seycia lit three handmade candles and kneeled beside a mural on the wall—a crude painting she and Miko had created years ago, when they first took up residence in the abandoned cabin. The mural depicted a forest, in varying shades of faded green, punctuated by red blossoms. *The Forest of Laida.* Miko had made many of the blossoms by dipping his tiny thumb into red paint. She could still see the whorls of his fingerprint among the tree branches. As she reverently bowed her head before the mural, Miko piped up from behind her:

"You know, when I cut that fish up tonight, I thought about something. Do animals' souls have their own trees in the forest? Or are the trees only for us?"

Seycia gazed at the mural, lost in thought, as Miko chattered on. "Like, is the soul of that fish the same as the soul of a person, so that fish might be a man someday? Or a woman? What did people say about that?"

The Forest of Laida loomed large in her memories of the old faith, but she and Miko rarely spoke of it. The mural was enough of a touchstone. The mere mention of it flooded her with sadness. It reminded her of her parents and the world they'd lost.

Seycia turned to face Miko, still kneeling on the ground, pondering his question. She felt guilty for being short with him earlier that night, when he'd asked her about the Savage. His curiosity was a good thing. "I don't think we ever considered the souls of animals. That's not to say we didn't respect them, you know? But I never thought about their souls returning to trees in the Forest of Laida after death, the way ours do."

Miko nodded and made himself comfortable in the hammock. Seycia studied him as he furrowed his brow. His glittering hazel eyes, wide and expressive like their mother's, didn't conceal secrets the way hers did. She always knew when he was trying to work something out in his head.

"Do you think people were scared, when they discovered the Underworld way, way back? When they found out where their souls really came from?"

"Probably. Especially if they had other beliefs about it."

"How were they able to see what was down there? Why can't we?"

"I wish I knew. But maybe there's a reason we can't. Maybe there are things we aren't meant to see."

"Like the Forest of Laida."

She nodded, and her voice went soft. "But we can imagine it. Father once said something like, *Think of a forest with no breeze, no birds, no voices. You've never been anywhere so quiet. And it's big, bigger than anything any human could ever comprehend. A tree for every soul on earth.*"

"So . . . it's big and it's quiet. What else?"

Seycia shrugged and started snuffing out the candles. "I guess that's part of the adventure of getting there. You wouldn't want someone to spoil it for you."

Before she extinguished the final candle, she added, "But I'm glad to know it's there, whatever it looks like. It means nobody's ever really gone. Every tree grows new leaves. Every soul comes back for new lives."

"But that's the problem, isn't it?" Miko pointed out. Seycia noticed his voice sounded deeper all of a sudden. More grown-up. "Bad souls come back for new lives, in new bodies, just like good ones do."

"Is that what you think? That there are good souls and bad souls?"

Miko shrugged. "Look around, that's how it is," he said, then paused. "I wonder if a bad soul is bad to start with. And if that's what you got stuck with, a bad soul, I wonder if you can ever become a good one. You know, after you've lived more lives?"

Seycia frowned, then shook her head. "I think the bad ones were always bad, and they stay that way. It's like you said, they just keep coming back."

Miko nodded, even though he might have hoped for a different answer. As Seycia moved toward her own hammock, he spoke again, quieter this time. "That's the worst part, isn't it? There's no way to stop them from coming."

"Maybe not," she replied. "But we don't have to share our world with them if we don't want to. It's up to all the good people to fight them."

"But they don't. Not here, anyway," he said. The cynicism in his voice struck Seycia—because she recognized it in herself. Miko held her stare, but said no more. He was done asking questions. He leaned back with a yawn and pulled the blanket up to his chin. After a moment, Seycia stood and blew out the last candle. "Get some sleep."

"Tomorrow, can we go back to the spot where we found the silver box?" Miko asked in the darkness, gently placing his newfound treasure on the floor below his hammock. "I want to see if anything else is buried there."

"Sure, if it's not too hot outside after the rain stops." She passed his hammock and touched two fingers to her heart, then her lips, then his forehead. He did the same motion back to her: a loving gesture passed down from their parents. She remembered her mother doing the same thing to them both every night before bed.

"Goodnight," she said, cocooning into her own hammock. She rolled onto her side, but did not close her eyes.

She always stayed awake as long as she possibly could before surrendering to sleep. She tried to keep watch, to listen to the woods outside their cabin for any intruding footsteps. This was the time of day, and usually the only time, in which she yearned for even an hour without responsibility. She wondered what her days might feel like without that constant pang of worry in her chest. She thought about someone else's story, about a girl who didn't wear a fang around her neck and didn't live in fear of losing the only loved one she had left. But those thoughts were always silenced by fatigue. She never had time to dwell on them for long.

It was only a few minutes after her body gave in to sleep that Seycia started stirring again. A dog's mournful cry echoed across the woods. She woke with a start, her heart already thundering, and rolled out of her hammock. As she crept toward the door, she touched a fingertip to the fang around her neck, a tactile reminder that she was carrying protection. She paused before opening the door, glancing over at Miko. He was sound asleep, snoring with his leg dangling over the edge of the hammock. She would only be a moment. He wouldn't even notice she was gone. She opened the door and stepped out into the thick blackness of night.

They were far from the city, miles from the Coalition's streetlights. The fractured moonlight through the trees would be a traveler's only guide at this hour, but the rain clouds had obscured it entirely. Seycia squinted into the forest but she couldn't see a thing. Instead, she closed her eyes and listened.

She mentally combed through the sounds she heard: an owl, the rain tapering off, the rush of the river up ahead. *No barking.* She turned back to their hut, thinking she must have been dreaming of their old dogs, when—

Crack! A branch snapped. The sound was deafening. This time, she knew she hadn't imagined it. She froze for a second, weighing her next move. To wander into the woods could be fatal. To do nothing could put them in even greater danger. She turned and walked a few paces. One, two, three, four steps. Then she stopped again and listened. Nothing. Five, six, seven, eight—

She heard a rustling of leaves, then another snap. She whirled around and came face-to-face with a pair of black eyes glistening in the darkness. Seycia breathed a sigh of relief. The eyes belonged to a tiny fawn. It had probably been separated from its mother.

"Get out of here before someone makes a meal of you," Seycia hissed. But just as she broke her gaze with the timid animal . . . There it was again. A dog, snarling. Too close for comfort.

Seycia's heart leaped, and she turned around just in time to spot a sleek silver dart, zooming through the air out of nowhere. It breezed right past her ear, prickling the hairs on her neck before it lodged itself into a tree trunk right next to her. The fawn squealed and bolted away.

Seycia turned and stared at the dart, wondering if it was one of Miko's, but no . . . It wasn't handcrafted of wood. It was a long, metal needle, probably filled to the brim with some dangerous chemical.

Seycia sprang to action, yanked the fang off her neck, and wielded it like a talon in her fist. The dog howled, wherever it was. She couldn't see an inch in front of her face. She barreled toward the sound, into the blinding darkness, fang drawn.

As she ran, she caught the blurry outline of a male figure just a few yards ahead. Broad shoulders. Red military jacket.

Another dart flew through the darkness, grazed her shoulder, and landed right behind her. Someone was aiming at her, but not to kill. If they were, they would have been shooting bullets—though she wasn't sure this was better.

She thundered toward the man with her fang thrust in front of her. She was close now, and she knew he'd caught sight of her as he shot one more dart from what she could now see was a heavy black firearm. She dodged the needle by mere inches and flung herself at his looming figure, aiming her fang at his throat.

But before she could make contact, the Coalition spy grabbed her shoulders and kicked her hard at the knees. Her legs buckled as he grabbed her around the middle and whirled her around, holding her from behind, before she threw her weight forward, taking him along for the ride. He careened over her head, crashing to the ground.

Seycia felt her shoulder dislocate as the man flipped over her head, but this was hardly the time to focus on pain. Leaping over his limp body, she sprinted toward the cabin. She would need to grab Miko and run. Maybe they'd swim across the bay so the dog couldn't track them. Her head spun, wondering why they'd been targeted. What had she done wrong? She remembered the boy she'd fought at the sacrifice. Had she invited danger to their door by giving in to her violent urges? Was this her fault?

A piercing sting suddenly spread from the back of her knee toward the tips of her toes. She'd been hit. Her legs gave out. She stole a weary glance over her shoulder and saw the fallen soldier aiming his dart gun right at her.

This was no ordinary venom, not like the kind Miko made from the poisonous red Strychnos fruit that grew near their house. This was something toxic, something potent. She tried in vain to pull herself up, but it was as if her muscles had turned to liquid. The rain from above reminded her of tiny diamonds, tumbling in slow motion. She panicked. Was she dying? Why would they kill her so suddenly? The general's men rarely killed without dragging out torture beforehand.

With her final scrap of strength, she hung the fang back over her head and tucked it into her shirt. She silently prayed that she would escape whatever was to come and get home before Miko even woke up. Then her wrist went limp, and the world around her capsized into nothingness.

CHAPTER THREE

THE HOWLING WIND rattled the stained glass windows of General Simeon's stately mansion up on the hill. The streets of Khronasa below were slick with silvery rain. Simeon pulled an ancient bottle of liquor from his sturdy oak cabinet and refreshed his drink. These hours were usually his most treasured—the rain, his drink, his moment to revel in the success of another sacrifice.

But tonight, he was troubled. Tonight's ceremony had taken a turn. Not only had he gazed into the eyes of the Savage for the first time, but he'd also glimpsed the weapon that had destroyed his face years ago. He was sure of it. He caught his warped reflection in the window and heaved a sigh, pressing his fingertip to the canyon of scar tissue that was once his left cheek.

A girl had entered the square—a striking, slender, black-haired young woman with filthy clothing and bare feet. She was a pretty thing, but that wasn't what caught his eye. There had been a scuffle, and she'd pulled out a weapon. It was a fang, about the length of her fist—white, iridescent, glistening in the lamplight. He had recognized it instantly.

The man who'd wielded the fang the night of the occupation had been shot. Simeon had seen it happen. But the man had two children, a boy and a girl. He had let them go—why, he couldn't recall. He might have had some fleeting, sadistic plan for them, a plan he lost sight of the moment the battle intensified.

Those children had been in the plaza tonight, and the girl had the weapon that had mutilated him. He wanted her and he wanted it. He wanted her brought forth to him, bathed, groomed, and wrapped in satin so he could mangle her the way her father had mangled him all those years ago. He had given orders to have her followed after the ceremony, but no news had come of her whereabouts. Yet.

He listened to the rhythmic march of heavy boots outside as his guards changed shifts. A muffled salute—"Our fate in his hands!"—followed as one troop passed another.

Our fate in his hands. Simeon always enjoyed a private chuckle at the irony of the Coalition's slogan. Ingrained into the minds of the masses over the years, it had finally managed to trump the simple fact that Emperor Caius was a *man.*

Simeon was born in the darkness, but stories of the surface burned bright in his mind's eye. Every night, he dreamed of the world he would one day inherit, a world of divine color and light that would be his for the taking. He was among the first to brave the sun again after the war. He and his cohorts formed alliances with other underground powers—a coalition of societies that were still intact. Together, they had one objective: to restore order to a lawless, broken world. To do that, they would have to eradicate the root cause of the war's devastation—religious conflict. Discovery of the afterlife had had irreparable consequences, so the Coalition abolished the notion of gods, fate, and prayer, worldwide. And yet, people worshipped the emperor now. Their proverb promoted the very thing they had destroyed: blind faith. But General Simeon knew a mortal idol was always a safer choice. Mortals were knowable, unlike whatever lurked beyond the Veil.

When Simeon first arrived in Khronasa, he realized how similar worshipping a figurehead was to worshipping a god. He could easily swap one for the other if he maintained just one thing: fear. He knew he was bound to the Coalition's rules and that death was the penalty for practicing the Offenses, but when he learned about the Savage and the sacrifices, he couldn't help himself. It was the perfect way to keep the people in line.

Seven years later, the Khronasans still clung to the tradition of the sacrifice, despite what it had become. Anyone could be next. The simple-minded villagers would do anything Simeon asked to keep their loved ones safe from the pit.

There was only one element beyond his control: the demon itself. Since he was young, the Coalition's laws regarding religion were the only laws he'd ever known. He had refused to consider the demon's existence. He didn't believe any of it was real . . . until the first time he oversaw a sacrifice for himself. Just the thought of it made him shiver, even after all these years.

That night, he and his soldiers planned to pull their prisoner from the pit and burn his remains after everyone had left. But when it started to rain and the sky turned black, they realized they were in over their heads. Simeon would never forget the first time he saw his victim rise from the pit to be devoured by the hungry dark maw above. *All of it was real.* He remembered crumbling to his knees in awestruck horror. What would they do, now that they'd seen it for themselves?

Simeon swore his guards to secrecy, promising gruesome torture and eventual death if they revealed what they saw to anybody outside Khronasa. He was fortunate that the village was so remote; it would be difficult for word of the sacrifice to reach Emperor Caius in the imperial city. He could never know what they'd done. They'd broken the law by tangling with this society and their superstitions. But Simeon was already in too deep. What would happen after the next windstorm if they didn't leave a sacrifice for the Savage? He knew they'd have to do it again.

He became voracious for answers about the world beyond the Veil. If he was competing with mystical forces to govern this society, he knew he ought to get in good with them, and fast. He hoarded whatever confiscated Khronasan literature the Coalition had not yet burned. He studied the remains of the temple they had destroyed months earlier. It wasn't long before he built his own shrine to Dohv, Lord of the Underworld, in the basement of his mansion. He locked it down and forged only one key.

In the general's study, the clock struck midnight. He swallowed the last of his drink and placed the glass down with a definitive *clink*. It was time for his invocation, time to give thanks to Dohv.

He paused, making sure he heard no footsteps down the hall. To be safe, he dead-bolted the door to his study. He then produced the solitary key to his shrine and made his way to the basement door. It looked like little more than a locked closet to an outsider. He lived in fear of prying eyes and loose lips. He slid his hand to his holster and wrapped a finger around his pistol's trigger. He grew sick with paranoia each time he approached that door. He unlocked it, slipped through the entrance, and quickly shut it behind him.

He crept down the stairs and lit a ceremonial candle on a nearby shelf. The golden light illuminated the artifacts he had confiscated from the oblivious Khronasans over the years—amulets, worry stones, statues of Dohv in all shapes and sizes. He paused to gaze at one of them, sculpted of glistening white stone.

The Khronasans represented Dohv as an imposing human-like creature, tall and slender like a tree, whose face was concealed by a heavy shroud. He was posed holding two tiny, naked mortals, one in his left hand, and one in his right. His fingers were flexed, as though he were about to crush them. Simeon couldn't help but shudder as he stared into the figure's faceless void. *That* was who would control his fate after death. He'd never glimpsed the Keeper of Life for himself; the technology to do so had been lost in the war. In fact, he wasn't even sure *how* his ancestors had done it. But the Savage had given him all the proof he needed. Dohv was real, and he needed to pay his respects.

Simeon reached the bottom of the stairs and unrolled a carpet onto the cold, concrete ground before kneeling. He then produced three animal bones from a crude leather pouch on the shelf. The banned Khronasan literature indicated that there were certain creatures from the Underworld that occasionally wandered into the land of the living. If anyone was lucky enough to gather their remains, they could use them to communicate with Dohv as part of the ritual of prayer.

Years ago, he had threatened a decrepit Khronasan mystic for her pouch of bones, the ones he now spread in front of him. The woman assured him that the bones were the ribs of a Creeback, one of Dohv's favorite pets. Simeon never had a way to be sure, considering he did have a gun to her temple when he demanded the bones of her. But he figured her tears might be proof of their authenticity.

As he kissed the bones one by one and placed them on the carpet, his thoughts wandered to the girl with the fang. He'd often wondered if the fang had come from a similar creature. The piercing sting of the puncture wound was unlike any pain he had ever experienced. Worse than taking a bullet—or so he imagined. He'd been lucky in that regard so far.

Once the bones were arranged just so, three ends touching so they formed a triangle, he bowed his head and began his incantation: "Praise be to Dohv, Keeper of Life and Lord of the Underworld. Tonight, I once again send you thanks for preserving your promises. I shall never tire of cultivating power for you. Your river will deluge with death."

Simeon was nothing if not a shrewd negotiator. He had read that there was a connection between calamity in the mortal world and Dohv's power, specifically as it related to the mythical River of Past Lives. Times of great chaos on Earth were of immense benefit to Dohv; the more deaths in his river, the more power Dohv could generate. Simeon saw an opportunity to strike a deal with the immortal.

He began to ask Dohv for protection against assassinations and uprisings, both for himself and for Emperor Caius. In exchange, he and the Coalition would provide him with a steady stream of death for his river as they conquered a broken world.

Simeon closed his eyes and finished his benediction. "Tonight, we have satiated your messenger, the Savage, with another sacrifice. Build up our strength, and we shall build yours."

With that, the candlelight flickered, and the floorboards beneath him rattled as a thunderclap burst outside. A cold breeze from an unseen source swept through the chamber and sent a chill straight through his skin. Every time he finished his invocation, he'd receive the same ominous, silent reply. It gave him comfort—and it terrified him.

As he collected the sacred bones from the floor, he heard a knock from upstairs, on his study door. He knew he'd dead-bolted it, but the sound still made his heart skip a beat.

"General Simeon? The sentries have returned," he heard a young servant boy shout. "They've brought the girl."

Simeon stood, caressing the scar on his cheek, and he smiled. Indeed, someone had been listening to his prayer.

Pink. Pale, shiny pink was the first thing Seycia saw as her eyes fluttered open.

As her vision cleared, she realized she was staring at her own knees, curled up to her chest, draped in pink satin fabric. She stretched and winced. Her dislocated shoulder had been reset, but she was still covered in bruises. She examined the dress she was wearing with blank curiosity. It was dainty and girlish, taut at the bustline. She couldn't remember ever having worn anything like it in her life.

She sat up with a start when she realized her fang was no longer hanging around her neck. Who had taken it? Had they destroyed it? She clutched her chest as her panicked mind raced, and noticed her nails were painted the same pale pink as the dress. She had never even considered the idea that fingernails could be painted. She touched her hair, arranged in delicate waves that fell across her back. When had all this happened?

She took in her surroundings. Soft, golden light enveloped the room, radiating from two bronze floor lamps and a dimly lit crystal chandelier hovering above her head. It jingled in time with the footsteps in the room above her gilded holding pen.

The sofa she lay on was made of polished leather the color of rust. A thick, patterned carpet spread across the floor, a collage of blue and cream. It was a far cry from the cabin she'd been abducted from. Exquisite stained glass hung in each window, each boasting a different abstract design in blue, red, purple, and gold. A bookcase lined one of the walls, and a sword with a bejeweled handle was propped up inside a glass case beside it. Several golden plaques were arranged on the shelves, all of them bearing the seal of Emperor Caius's Coalition—the black silhouette of a rampant lion with two white rifles crossed in front of it. Seycia grimaced. She was not among friends.

At that moment, the door creaked open. Seycia sat up straight and winced, head still spinning from the twilight sleep she'd been in. The bookcase obscured the doorway, and she was not able to see who had entered right away, but the stranger had a gentle tread—soft footsteps filled the silence. She'd been expecting thumping boots and the cocking of a rifle. She caught sight of the scar on the face that had just become visible in the lamplight. General Simeon smiled at her. His left cheek dimpled and turned in on itself, creating a gruesome fold of flesh underneath his eye.

"Hello," he said, a grin still spread across his face. "I'm very glad you're here."

Seycia froze. Silent. What could she possibly say in return: *I'm certainly not glad*?

She held still as a stone and watched as Simeon crossed to his liquor cabinet and removed two glasses. She gaped at the inside of the cabinet: bottles of every shape, size, and color lined the shelves, at least a hundred of them—maybe more.

"I'm going to finish this one off, if you don't mind." He held up a bottle half full of dark red wine. "Unless you'd prefer something different?"

She held her vacant stare on him until she realized he was waiting for a response. She just shook her head.

"I think you'll like this one. It's a rather good year. Seven years aged, as a matter of fact." He poured the wine into the two glasses and put the empty bottle back in the cabinet. "I like to save the bottles when it's a special occasion."

He approached, offering her a glass. With no other choice, she cautiously took it as he sank down beside her on the sofa and draped his arm across her back. Seycia shuddered, clutching the glass in her anxious, viselike grip.

"Go ahead, drink. You're a guest here. Your mother must have told you it would be rude not to."

She stared at the contents of the glass. It hadn't been freshly uncorked; it could easily be poisoned. She took a small, polite sip and released it back into the glass in the same mouthful. She lifted her gaze to him. He hadn't noticed.

"I found this outside, by the way. Is it yours?" he asked with affected interest as he pulled her fang from his pocket. She felt as though the floor had dropped from beneath her, and she had to stop herself from yanking it out of his fist right there and then.

She caught his eye, trying to focus on anything but his repugnant scar as he dangled the fang before her, playfully twisting its cord between his fingers.

"Just because I gave you a head start didn't mean I wouldn't catch up eventually," he whispered.

She froze as he dropped the fang in a glass vase on the table nearby. She heard a reverberant *ping* as her weapon hit the bottom. Her gaze darted to all corners of the room, taking stock of her escape options: *Windows—how high up were they? Door—were there guards right outside? Sword—could she break the glass case?* Her focus was diverted when she felt his fingers in her hair. His long nails scraped against her scalp, and she winced as he stroked her like a house cat.

"You didn't think I'd forget about you and your family, did you? How could I? I think about you every time I look in the mirror." He chuckled. Seycia's gut twisted.

"Let's discuss your future, shall we?" he said and tucked a strand of hair behind her ear. "I know you and your brother live in squalor, bathe in the river, and only eat what you kill. You deserve better, don't you think?"

She could think of nothing else to say except, "We're all right."

She realized she hadn't spoken until that moment. All her courage had flown from her. She was locked in a room with the nightmare himself.

"But you don't even know what you're missing. Why bathe in the river when you can have a heated pool? Why walk with holes in your shoes when you can drive? The Coalition is at the forefront of progress. Soon we'll have access to luxuries not seen since before the great war." He went on, "I can give you and your brother everything you need to live comfortably for the rest of your lives. If you promise not to run."

Ice-cold fear rose in her throat that would have manifested as a scream if her voice wasn't so utterly crippled. *If you promise not to run.* And what would *he* get in return? She didn't dare imagine.

"You don't say much, do you, Seycia?" He leaned on her now, forcing her to sink onto her back.

She pressed against his chest, shoving him away as he slid his weight on top of her. She spied a silver medal dangling around his neck, right underneath his shirt. She could get out; she could fight him—as long as he wasn't expecting a fight.

"Y-you . . . you say . . ." she began, trying her best to appear timid yet convinced. She stopped pushing him away and let her hands fall to her sides. "You say you'll help us?"

He grinned at her and slid his hand under the small of her back, drawing her closer. She could smell sour wine on his breath as he grabbed her chin and pulled her face against his. His scar was a pale hollow of deflated, dead skin that looked even more horrendous up close.

"Such a pretty face," he remarked, stroking her cheek. "Suppose I cut it off?"

She could not afford to wait. She had to act. Now. Now, now, now . . .

He moved a hand up the side of her leg, then underneath the satin lining of her dress. He chuckled as he murmured into her neck, "I've been looking forward to destroying you." He turned slightly, reaching for something from his pocket—shiny, silver, sheathed. A dagger.

She lunged forward and snagged the medal hanging around his neck. She flicked her wrist and twisted it until it was taut around his throat, then yanked it upward in one swift motion. Simeon flailed his fist around, trying to draw the dagger as he struggled to breathe, and tumbled off the sofa. His spectacles fell off his face, and Seycia stepped on them with a satisfying *crunch* as she jumped to her feet.

She kicked over the vase on the table, shattering it to bits, and hung her precious weapon back around her neck. Her courage had returned in spades, but Simeon was already staggering to his knees . . .

She turned to thrust the fang toward his gut, but before she could take aim, she felt his hand ensnare her ankle. Seycia crashed to the floor as Simeon dragged her to him. Clawing at the carpet, she felt shards of the broken vase scrape her bare shoulders. He pinned her wrists to the floor as a fragment of glass burrowed deep into her skin.

"I thought we agreed you wouldn't fight," he snarled.

He smacked her across the face, bruising her eyelid with his heavy ring. Then he relented for the briefest of seconds, just to unclasp his belt—a second that was about to cost him. She had one free hand . . .

As he turned back toward her, the pointed end of Seycia's fang greeted his face. All she had to do was hold it up; he impaled himself on it. His accompanying scream was deafening as Seycia twisted the fang around inside his unscarred cheek before yanking it out, drenched in blood.

She leaped to her feet, inspecting her gruesome handiwork. She had drilled a hole in the right side of his face, a mirror image of the one her father had carved on the left side years ago. She could hardly believe the gory coincidence as the general pathetically crawled across the carpet, a river of red gushing from his wound.

As he clutched his butchered face, he sputtered, "You're fodder for the Savage, you filthy bitch. Make no mistake."

The hell she would be. Simeon curled into a ball on the blood-soaked carpet, losing consciousness. She loomed above him, holding the fang to his exposed neck. She'd slice it wide open and let all the life drain out of him. But before she could make contact—

"General Simeon?" an anxious voice cried out from the hall.

His bodyguards must have heard the scream. Seycia loosened her grip on the fang, knowing to leave him alive was to leave herself, and Miko, too, forever in danger. But she'd be shot on the spot if Simeon's bodyguards caught sight of the horrific scene. She flung the fang back around her neck, grabbed a plaque off the wall, and glanced at the stained glass windows. They were her only way out. She hurled the plaque through one of the windows with all her strength, shattering it to bits.

She hoisted herself up onto the ledge, peered outside, and sighed with relief when she saw they were only on the second story, and the outside wall was covered in thick, green ivy.

She climbed through the hole in the glass, tearing the seam of her long skirt. As she stretched out her arm to grasp the ivy and use it to climb down, the door to the general's study flew open.

"There, the window!" a bodyguard shouted.

She drew a deep breath and jumped, rappelling down the wall with a fistful of ivy as the guards gathered at the window.

"Shoot!"

She jumped as the loud crack from the guard's rifle echoed across the night.

Though a clump of bushes in the garden below softened her fall, she felt her right wrist collapse under the pressure. She cradled it in her left hand, knowing she'd probably just broken it, when another gunshot rang out.

She bolted off through the mansion's backyard, navigating a labyrinth of perfectly manicured hedges. Beyond a stately marble fountain lay a lush rose garden. She ran toward the fountain, desperate to take cover, horrified to realize how exposed she was. Lights inside the mansion's windows flicked on one by one; word of the violence in the study was probably spreading through the house like wildfire.

She crouched to the ground and crawled into the rose garden, gritting her teeth as thorns raked across her skin. Up ahead, she spotted a wrought iron gate that separated the property from the forest beyond. She heard another gunshot, one that sounded like it had come from outside the mansion. She slid toward the gate, keeping low to the ground, and dug underneath it with her bare hands like a dog. *Too slow, too slow.* She'd be there for hours trying to escape. She rose to her knees and fought back panicked tears.

There were voices now, and the sound of footsteps in the gravel just beyond the garden. Desperate, Seycia glanced up at the gate and spied a heavy iron lock securing the latch. It was a flimsy hope, but it was all she had: she drove the pointed end of her fang inside the keyhole and twisted it around, trying to pick it open. The lock suddenly grew hot in her hand, and she felt the fang vibrate. Instead of prying apart the lock's inner workings, the fang *split the lock in two*. Seycia gasped as it fell apart in her hands. She never knew her weapon could do something like that. How had it happened?

But she had no time to think. The guards were seconds away from entering the garden. She kicked the gate open, threw the broken lock over her shoulder, and stole away into the darkness of the woods. She wished she could scream with relief and fall to her shaking knees. But she had to keep running.

It was hours before she could see the hilltop in the distance. The fiery blush of dawn painted the sky as she finally paused to rest her aching body against a huge, mossy tree. She examined the fang, still stained with blood, and was shocked to discover it wasn't at all bent or chipped from splitting open the lock. Her father had always told her the weapon was powerful. He'd said the Black Beast was an Underworld creature who had found its way to the mortal world. Was it true? What else was this strange trophy capable of?

She shuddered as she slipped the fang back under her collar and pressed onward, back to their cabin. She prayed Miko would be exactly where she left him, sleeping with his leg dangling over the edge of his hammock. They'd need to pack their things and run as quickly as possible . . . But where would they run to? She'd heard the closest city-state was called Ellita, just south of Khronasa. Maybe they'd swim across the bay, where Simeon's tracking dogs couldn't follow their scent. Maybe the people who lived in Ellita would offer them sanctuary. Maybe it was safer there. Maybe . . .

But as Seycia approached their hut, she realized even the most carefully laid plans wouldn't save them. The door hung wide open, creaking in the breeze. The house was silent.

Miko was gone.

CHAPTER FOUR

NEVER ASK FOR a favor or you'll owe one in return. Never reveal your weakness. Never knock on a door if you don't know who lives behind it. And if you follow rules one and two, you'll never need the third.

This was the advice Seycia had taught Miko to live by—advice she'd taught *herself* to live by. There were other people living on the hill, people who could have helped feed them when they were hungry or protect them when they were in trouble. But Seycia didn't trust anyone else. All she and Miko needed to survive was each other. But now . . .

She forced herself to forget her years-old mantra as she sprinted up the hill, brow weeping with sweat. She tore her long pink skirt to ribbons as she navigated the steep switchbacks; she'd forgotten she was still wearing the dress.

At the top of the hill was another hut, similar to her own, where she'd seen a girl and an old man—*perhaps her grandfather?*—tanning animal hides outside. She wasn't sure why, but this house was the first place she thought to go for help when she realized Miko had disappeared. She and Miko had never been separated like this before. She'd never *needed help* like this before. There'd been a knot in her throat since the moment she saw the door of their hut hanging open, and it tightened with every passing second. She swallowed hard, pushing down the panic, as she approached the strangers' cabin.

She knocked, just once, quick as a blink, and held her breath. She knew she'd have to do better than that. If there was anyone inside, they hadn't heard her. She knocked again, twice this time, and harder. After a moment, the girl who lived there opened the door just an inch, just enough to meet Seycia's fierce dark eyes with her own. She could feel her studying her bruised face and the bloodstains on her tattered dress.

"It's very early," was all the girl said. Her voice was low and soft, but she had a peculiar sort of accent, like the end of each word was hopping up to meet the beginning of the next. If Seycia hadn't been in such a state, she might have enjoyed listening to her voice. Something about it soothed her, even though she could tell the girl was a few years younger than she was.

"I know. I'm just . . ." Seycia didn't know where to begin. The girl still hadn't opened the door all the way. "I live down the hill. With my brother. And he's—"

Vrrrrrooom. Seycia's blood ran cold as the distant rumble filled her ears. Coalition vehicles. She was sure of it. They'd gone off the road and up the hill. And she knew why.

"You want to come in," the girl said. It wasn't a question. Seycia shifted her weight, uneasy. *You don't know these people.*

"I don't. I mean, I don't have to. I just want to know if anyone's seen my brother. He's missing. I thought he might have come looking for help, once he saw I'd been—" She stopped herself from finishing the rest. The girl stepped aside and opened the door all the way. She had thick, matted hair down to her waist and long legs that stuck out of her short deerskin pants, as though she'd recently grown out of them.

"I haven't seen a boy," she said. "But maybe we can help you look."

The roar of the approaching vehicles grew louder, tearing through the trees, snapping fallen branches. Seycia shivered, imagining those wheels rolling over human bones, crushing them to pieces. She froze in the doorway, averting her gaze from the girl. *Where to go, what to do?* Finally, the girl grabbed Seycia by the arm, drew her inside, and slammed the door behind them.

The cabin was dark aside from a small fire in the burnt-out hearth, made of old concrete blocks just like theirs was. In the corner, Seycia recognized the elderly gentleman she'd seen with the girl, perched on a stump that grew out of their floor, shaving with a hand-sharpened stone. She noticed he only had three fingers on his left hand. He struggled to hold a bowl of water as he shaved with the other hand. He glanced up with a questioning grunt as the girl led Seycia inside.

"She's looking for her brother. I thought we might help."

"We're about to go hunting," the old man replied, peering at Seycia with narrow eyes.

"Maybe on the way, then—"

"What have I told you about answering the door to strangers, Minari?" He glanced over at Seycia with a weary sigh. "I'm sorry. But we don't—"

"We don't know each other. I understand," Seycia said, inching back toward the door. She'd see herself out . . . just as soon as those Coalition vehicles were on the other side of the hill.

It was then that she realized the engines had quieted. Where had they gone? Had they stopped?

Rap rap rap. A knock on the door—not with a hand, but a harder-sounding object. *A rifle?* Seycia's heart dropped to her feet. The girl, Minari, grabbed her by the wrist and pulled her over to a dark corner of the cabin, where a stack of firewood sat. "Hide," she whispered.

"Minari!" the old man hissed. "This isn't how it's done." *Isn't how what's done?* Seycia's mind raced. Who were these people? Were they any safer than whoever was on the other side of that door?

Rap rap rap! Seycia took cover behind the firewood, looking around the cabin for a way out. There wasn't one aside from the way she'd just come in.

She heard a voice from outside, "Open up, in the name of His Imperial Majesty Emperor Caius!"

The cabin was silent. Seycia held her breath. Despite the power she'd just discovered in her weapon, she knew the fang was no match for a gun. She peered at Minari and the old man through the cracks in the wood. Minari cast him a pleading stare, but the old man reluctantly shuffled toward the door and, to Seycia's horror, he opened it.

"We're searching for an escaped prisoner. We have reason to believe she might have come up the hill," one of the two soldiers growled. Seycia made herself small, gripping the fang in her trembling fist—if only for comfort. "Young woman, about eighteen. She's a forager, like you. Uses an animal's tooth as a weapon."

Seycia heard the old man sigh as he led them over to Seycia's hiding place. It was barely audible, but she was sure he whispered, "I'm sorry," before the two soldiers came into view. Seycia pulled a breath and rose to her feet, trying to focus on Miko and whatever leverage she had left. She steeled herself and stared into their pale, bloated faces, knowing their cold gray eyes were leering at her behind those black goggles. She met their pointed rifles with the sharp end of her own weapon.

"I'll come with you. I won't fight. If you take me to my brother."

The shorter of the two soldiers laughed and grabbed Seycia by the wrist, the one she'd broken. She howled as he pulled her out from behind the stack of firewood, but she still had the fang in her other hand. When the second soldier lowered his weapon to take it from her, she kicked him in the chest like a terrified wild horse. As he fumbled with his rifle, cursing under his breath, Seycia whirled back around and swiped the shorter soldier's neck with the fang. She heard Minari gasp from the other side of the room. It wasn't a deep cut, but it was enough to distract him. Blood pooled underneath his collar.

Seycia wrenched her burning, broken arm from his grasp and bolted toward the exit. But before she could yank the rickety door open, a gunshot rang out, shaking the walls of the tiny shack. Seycia took to the floor as she grappled for the door's latch, but she paused when she realized there'd only been one shot, and it hadn't gone off in her direction. She glanced behind her, sure either Minari or the old man had just taken the bullet. But they were still huddled together in the corner by the tree stump. It had been a warning shot.

"You go out that door and your chance to save your brother goes with you," snarled one of the soldiers in the darkness. He inched closer to her, brandishing his rifle. Seycia froze, feeling as though a hand had just seized her throat.

"W-what do you mean?" she stammered.

"He's being offered up to the Savage. Tonight," the second soldier replied through grit teeth, clutching his bloody neck.

"The Savage only comes twice a year," Seycia scoffed, doing everything she could to conceal her terror. Could it be true? Or was it just another one of Simeon's manipulations?

"The Savage will come if the general calls him. This is a special occasion."

A moment passed. Seycia chose her next words carefully. "General Simeon doesn't want my brother; he wants me."

The two soldiers exchanged a glance, and silence fell across the room like a storm cloud. Seycia's breath came in shallow gasps as the truth took hold. This had been their plan all along. They knew she would offer herself in exchange for Miko. *General Simeon* knew. And they were right. She thought of her parents, of the promise she'd made over their broken bodies seven years ago. She was Miko's protector. She couldn't fail him. Not now. She couldn't risk running if they were telling the truth, if General Simeon was really going to call the Savage tonight . . .

She shut her eyes before she whispered, "Take me instead."

The two soldiers shared a muted snicker before slapping a pair of freezing cold shackles onto her wrists. She didn't fight them, though she wondered if she even could. The burst of courage she'd had moments before was gone. She was numb to the bone and rigid with dread.

As Simeon's soldiers shoved her out of the little shack, Minari called out to her, "What's your name?"

"Seycia," she heard herself say. She felt like she was floating above her body, past the treetops . . . far, far away.

"Seycia. We will remember you," Minari said, solemn beyond her years.

Seycia glanced over her shoulder at the girl and the elderly man. Their faces were motionless with shock, but she could see the tears glistening in the old man's eyes.

Let them cry, Seycia thought as the soldiers escorted her back outside. The sun cowered beneath a blanket of heavy fog. *It's someone else's turn. I've cried enough.*

Haben lay on his back with a vacant stare fixed on the black stone ceiling above him. Only a thin, fractured beam of light shone through the rocks. Not a soul was in sight.

After eating his fill, he had returned to the cave network and ventured through the tunnels until he found the most private chamber he possibly could. No one would bother him here. He could admonish himself in peace.

He remembered the first time he ever took his prey back to the Underworld, the first time he'd succumbed to the unbearable hunger, and recalled the triumph he'd felt as he dragged the corpse through the Veil. But the thrill evaporated the first time the Khronasans left him not a dastardly criminal in chains, but a child. He hadn't wanted to take the young sacrifice, but he wasn't in control—the hunger was. After it was over, he wept. He had not shed a single tear since his death centuries before. He'd often wondered if he still possessed a soul at all. That day, he understood the complexity of Dohv's punishment, and he remembered it each time Khronasa left him an innocent victim.

The wind whistled through the crevices in the cave like a low, mournful song, lulling Haben into a distant half-sleep—the only escape he had. But seconds later, his eyes snapped back open. There was another sound—a deep, metallic rumble. *The gong.* He sat up. It was the signal from Khronasa, the one that told him an offering was on its way. But why were they giving him another sacrifice? He had just taken one. What was the meaning of this? He lay back down, sure it had only been a dissident note in the cave's somber song.

But there it was again. There could be no mistaking the way it made his temples quiver and his head ache. He rose to his feet and stalked out of the tunnel the way he came. Yes, he *had* just taken a sacrifice. But what a shame it would be to let an offering go to waste . . .

Hunger crept into his veins like a slow poison. His remorse, so palpable only moments before, faded with every step he took. He was a slave to the sound. Everything else melted away.

He emerged at the Shore of Awakening, a vast turquoise sea situated beside crystalline white sands. No vegetation surrounded the shoreline, and no creatures swam in its waters. It was a gracefully uncomplicated patchwork of violet sky, white sands, blue sea, and black caves. Haben scanned the area for the nearest passageway as the ringing between his ears grew louder and louder.

He spotted a black crater in the sand, his entry to the mortal world, and bolted across the beach on quaking legs. The nerves inside his shoulders began to spasm; his demonic body knew what was coming.

But when he reached the passageway, he paused, searching himself. He didn't think he could withstand consuming an innocent child two days in a row. This was a sacrifice he did not need. He swayed back and forth at the edge of the Veil, weighing his options. Maybe he'd forgo this unexpected sacrifice if he saw it was another child. He'd just drop in and see who they'd left for him. That would do. But even as he bargained with himself, he knew resistance was useless. The gong rang out again, calling to him. He was pulled to the sound. It hypnotized him. It *owned him*, body and soul.

As hunger wrapped him in her cold, harrowing embrace, he let himself tumble into the inky blackness of the passageway at his feet.

His heart pounded and his grin spread of its own volition as he crossed the Veil to the world of the living. Whatever promises he'd made to himself, the Savage wouldn't remember them. And the Savage was in control now.

CHAPTER FIVE

"GET UP. TIME to go," a voice growled in the darkness.

Miko inched forward, toward the bars of his bleak holding cell, where a heavyset Coalition bodyguard stood on the other side clutching a lantern and a rifle. His stomach turned as he wrung his sweaty hands to keep them from shaking. The night before, when Simeon's henchmen snatched him from his hammock, they hadn't told him where he'd be going or what would happen to him. But now, he knew. He'd just heard the gong outside.

"No need to start pissin' yourself," the guard said with a scowl as he unlocked Miko's cell. "You've got company up there."

Company? Miko didn't want to ask, but he couldn't help himself: "Where's my sister?"

The guard gave no reply as he snagged Miko's wrists and pinned them behind his back. As he bound them with a heavy rope, he muttered, "This way."

The guard escorted Miko down a long, dank corridor. Telltale white scratch marks marred the concrete walls. Cold understanding flooded him. *I am going to the pit. I am going to die.*

He bit down hard on his lip, holding back a scream, and tasted blood. He swallowed, as though he could wash down his terror along with it. His vision blurred with tears, but there was a voice in his head telling him not to let the fear show. It was probably Seycia's. It was always Seycia's.

For some reason, he thought of their home and all the things they had left behind: signs that they'd been there, that they had *lived*. Would someone loot his collection of ancient treasures? Would another boy wear the deerskin shirt Seycia had made for him? There was still leftover soup, sitting in a pot over the cold, black ashes of their fire. He imagined feral dogs scratching down their door for a morsel of whatever remained.

As the guard yanked him up a crumbling concrete staircase, slick with mud, he could hear the restless Khronasans gathering in the square. They were probably all wondering why another sacrifice was happening the night after Henshaw's death—and he was, too. There hadn't even been a windstorm first. He knew they were all holding their breath, waiting to meet him: the unexpected offering.

Miko emerged from the subterranean prison as the stormy sky devoured whatever daylight was left. He shivered, unable to control his quaking legs as he inched forward. He knew every beat of this ritual by heart. He'd never dared to imagine it from the prisoner's perspective.

The nervous chatter of the Khronasans quieted as Miko stepped onto the walkway that would take him to the plaza, and then to the pit. He focused on the bright yellow wildflowers lining the cobblestone path instead of people's faces. He remembered that every other victim had done the same thing; nobody ever made eye contact.

As Miko and the guard turned a corner and approached the plaza, he saw her. Seycia stood on the marble platform beside the silver gong. Four Coalition soldiers surrounded her in a semicircle. He wanted to run to her, to call out her name, but something wasn't right. Her face was a blank, emotionless mask, and he noticed her hands weren't tied behind her back, like his were. Had she come willingly? What was happening?

As he moved closer, he could see she was no longer wearing the fang around her neck. She'd given up her weapon. His heart thundered in his chest.

"Seycia!" he shouted, and his small voice cracked. She shook her head at him. She gave him their mother's old greeting: two fingers to her heart, then her lips. She held her palm out to him like she was touching his forehead. He wanted to cry again.

Miko's bodyguard led him to the place where she stood and positioned him right next to her. He gazed up into her face, never so relieved to see anyone before in his life. But it was as if she were having trouble looking back at him.

"When this is over, I need you to get as far away from here as you can," she whispered. "Don't try to be a hero. Live a little longer so you can become one when you're older."

He just stared at her, at a loss for words. *When this is over?* But he knew how this would end. He knew what would happen after the rain fell.

Before he could question her, Simeon emerged from a back entry to his mansion, his face covered by a sheer black cloth draped from his military helmet. He was an eerie sight, like a faceless ghost spying on them from the shadows. As Miko fixed his hateful stare upon him, he couldn't help but wonder why Simeon had his face covered up. Everyone already knew how ugly he was.

Simeon reached the place where they stood and stopped, chuckling from beneath his black veil. He lifted it, exposing his face, and a gasp erupted from the audience. Miko bit down on his tongue. At least a dozen stitches crawled up the side of Simeon's cheek, holding his raw, yellowed flesh together. His skin was pulled so tightly that his bloodshot left eye now bulged from its socket. Miko peered over at Seycia and swore he could see the tiniest hint of a smug smile as she stared at Simeon's monstrous injury. He knew then: *she'd* had something to do with this.

"It's time," Seycia said to Simeon as he loomed over her. "Let him go."

Miko's mouth hung agape as he realized what was about to happen. Seycia's eyes riveted to his and he shook his head with a horrified, pleading stare.

"No," he whispered. "Seycia, don't—"

But Seycia and General Simeon both ignored him.

"Did you hear me? Let him go," Seycia said again, lifting her head so she stood face-to-face with Simeon. Miko thought she might lunge for his neck like a cornered animal. But Simeon's guards were one step ahead.

Seycia yelped as one of the four sentries surrounding them tied her hands behind her back. "Stop! We had an agreement!" she howled at Simeon. He just smiled.

"You agreed to my terms. Your mistake was thinking I'd agreed to yours."

Miko felt Seycia's scream in the deepest part of him. He hadn't even noticed he'd started wailing along with her until one of the security guards clamped a hand over his mouth. As the black sky above them swallowed the final trace of sunlight, Simeon addressed the crowd.

"Our fate in his hands!" he greeted them. Miko gazed out at their faces. Nobody looked directly at him. But he'd been expecting that. What he hadn't expected was how it made him feel: Cold. Forgotten. *Already a ghost.*

"I know we were here last night. But, in light of yesterday's events, it appears we must gather a second time." Simeon paced back in forth in front of the anxious crowd. "The Savage is dissatisfied. I've long suspected it. We've been plagued by drought. Food is scarce, even in the heart of our great city. Nature has not been kind to us. The Savage has been trying to communicate his displeasure, but we weren't listening. But last night, we stood eye-to-eye. And we finally understood each other."

Miko felt the first raindrops fall, stinging with the promise of the nightmare that lay ahead. He glanced over at Seycia. She mouthed, "I'm sorry," over and over again . . .

"I fear the misfortune the Underworld may visit upon us if we don't double our efforts," Simeon said with finality, peering at Miko and Seycia. Miko screamed again, but the bodyguard's hand was still covering his mouth.

Miko squeezed his eyes shut as two of the guards roughly spun him in the opposite direction, toward the pit. He shuffled forward, nauseated with terror, as he heard Simeon begin his ritual blessing, "We are the mortals. The frail. The selfish . . ."

A horrible shriek pierced the solemn stillness, and Miko's eyes snapped open. Simeon stopped delivering his remarks. Miko spotted one of Seycia's escorts crumpled on the ground, cradling his bloody thigh. A hand-carved arrow, tipped with a red feather like his darts but twice as long, stuck out of the guard's leg. Miko held his breath and glanced around in all directions. From the treetops came a second arrow, and then a third. Then another, another, and another. Miko tried to shield himself from the deadly storm, but he quickly realized that whoever was shooting had impeccable aim—and they weren't aiming at him.

Chaos exploded across the plaza as Simeon's guards hit the ground one by one. The ones left standing fired their guns into the treetops, but it was hard to tell where the arrows were coming from in the darkness. Miko knew there had to be more than one shooter, in several different trees. Simeon took cover behind the gong as a few loyal villagers created a barrier around him. One of the bodyguards clutching Miko's arm took an arrow to the back of his neck, and he pulled Miko to the ground with him. Miko managed to wriggle out of his grasp and leaped to his feet, scanning the melee for Seycia. He fought against his restraints, twisting his wrists, trying to loosen the rope. The repeated motion burned his skin.

He spotted Seycia on the other side of the pit and took off running in her direction. She hadn't had the same luck as him—her three escorts had been injured, but not fatally. They held her down on the muddy ground as she struggled to break free: one secured her legs to keep her from kicking, and the other two gripped her arms.

"Seycia!" he howled as he raced toward her. But before he could reach her, a hand grabbed his bound wrists from behind. He whirled around and met the wild, dark eyes of a Khronasan girl with long legs and matted hair that reached her waist. She held a small dagger in her fist. As she sliced through his restraints, a gunshot rang out from beside the pit. Miko's heart stammered.

"Take cover. I'll be right behind you," the girl whispered, then bolted back toward the pit with her dagger drawn. Miko's head swam. *Who was she?* Nobody had ever tried to rescue someone at the sacrifice before . . .

He fell to the ground to shield himself, inching toward the grove of trees beyond the plaza. Through the rain and muted lamplight, he spotted his strange rescuer and two other Khronasans wearing dark animal hides, circling the spot where Seycia lay pinned to the ground. Another gunshot, and one of the girl's companions went down. Seycia met Miko's gaze across the plaza as she struggled to break free. He could tell by the resigned way she shook her head that she knew the truth—and he did, too. Only one of them was going to survive.

"Run," Seycia mouthed at him.

But he didn't want to run. Not without her. This was what she'd wanted. She'd given herself up for him. But what about what *he* wanted?

Another reverberant *crack!* rang in his ears, and he made himself even smaller on the ground. What he wanted didn't matter. If he was going to make it out alive, he had to go. Now.

On his hands and knees, he turned back toward the woods as tears and rain streaked his muddy cheeks. He couldn't believe he was doing it. His movements didn't feel like his own as he scrambled away, low to the ground on all fours. He had nowhere to go, and he didn't know how long he would survive on his own. But surviving would have to be enough.

He stole away to the shadows of the forest, holding his breath to keep the tears inside. A staccato of gunfire echoed across the distance as the rain came down in sheets between the trees.

Stop! You can't leave her, his mind screamed. But he already had.

Seycia watched Miko disappear behind the trees with a pang in her chest. She exhaled with relief, even though he didn't have much of a head start. She could hear the rumble of a dozen angry boots on the cobblestone—backup security from Simeon's mansion. Long-legged Minari was the only res-cuer left; her two comrades had taken bullets. Seycia saw her crouched behind a black motor vehicle that was parked nearby, watching for an opportunity to free her as she had Miko. Seycia hoped her captors hadn't seen her take cover there. Why had this girl come to save them? They'd only met that morning. She had no idea why she would risk her life for them . . .

Seycia saw Minari peer out from behind the vehicle, watching the backup security guards barrel through the plaza. She shot an arrow, straight and true, and hit the guard holding down Seycia's legs. He fired back at her with his gun, but his aim was crooked as he clutched his bloody shoulder. Seycia kicked him in the face as Minari let another arrow loose, incapacitating one of the two men holding Seycia's arms. Seycia knew she had only seconds before the other, uninjured guards would apprehend her—and kill Minari. As Minari approached with her dagger drawn, Seycia hissed, "You have to go after him. Leave me."

Minari was quick to bow her head in agreement and sent one last arrow flying through the rain. She struck one of the approaching backup guards in the knee, but by the time her shot landed she was already gone. She dashed back into the woods, up a tree, and out of sight.

"Shoot her down!" General Simeon squawked from his hiding place behind the gong.

Simeon's reinforcements fired off a round into the trees, and Seycia held her breath. She listened for a scream, or the sound of a body falling, but she didn't hear anything.

"Don't let them get away!" Simeon shouted, scrambling to his feet. He pointed at his security force, splitting them down the middle. "You go after them. The rest of you, stay with me. We've already called the Savage so we'd best get on with it."

Seycia shuddered as the guards yanked her to her feet and led her toward the very edge of the pit. She forced herself to imagine Miko taking shelter somewhere while Minari caught up to him. She couldn't bear to picture the opposite. Not now. Not after everything she'd done to save him. She gazed up to the sky and wondered if she had ever seen a night so black. It made her think of an enormous crow that had attached itself to the heavens and was hovering above her, waiting for a carrion feast.

"Sister Seycia," General Simeon said as he approached her. Rain pelted his jacket as he reached into his breast pocket. Seycia stifled a cynical laugh—at any other moment, she would have thought he was about to pull a gun on her. Now, she would have welcomed it.

From his pocket, Simeon produced Seycia's fang, still tied to its worn, leather cord. She seethed as he held it out over her head. "May this serve to remind you of your place, as you wait for death to claim you."

With that, he placed the fang over her head. He turned his two tightly pulled cheeks upward into what might have been a murderous grin, quite pleased with himself. Seycia was still as a stone as she felt the weight of her only weapon, now useless, fall against her breast. All around them, the stricken crowd fell silent. Subdued. They knew there wouldn't be any more surprises—and she did, too.

"Our fate in his hands!" Simeon crowed, holding his arms out to the sea of spectators.

"Our fate in his hands," the crowd murmured.

Seycia felt as though the ground had dropped from beneath her feet as Simeon's guards clamped a shackle to her ankle, attached to a heavy iron weight.

A rope ladder was temporarily set against the muddy side of the pit. Seycia hoped, for a moment, that she would be dropped into its depths with some semblance of dignity, when a heavy boot made contact with her back. She tumbled into the mud at the bottom of the pit, facedown. Spitting out dirt, she scrambled toward the rope ladder, but someone had already pulled it back out. She sank to her knees in the freezing shallow water, twisting her bound wrists to no avail.

The rain came in deafening torrents, but she could still hear the faint echo of Simeon's blessing from up above: ". . . We come to you, great Keeper of Life, in supplication. We know why you send the Savage. We know how he hungers. We are here to satiate him."

Then, he stepped to the edge of the pit and leaned over. Seycia squinted through the rain at his monstrous face and realized she'd lost the strength to glare at him, to make him fear he'd underestimated her. She just stared, vacant and resigned.

"May your flesh appease the wicked one. May your blood protect the earth," he concluded his speech. "May your sacrifice be remembered."

A foul grin spread across his face as he pulled the veil back over his head.

"Her sacrifice shall be remembered," the audience echoed.

The gong rang out again, and Seycia felt numb all over, as though the very sound had ushered in a cold front. She could hear the Khronasans start to hum in unison. She huddled against the muddy wall of the pit as the raindrops assaulted her.

She shrieked to the heavens as the frigid water began creeping past her hips. Her legs felt heavy and stiff. Her body was starting to freeze, but her rage distracted her. The furious cries to the night went on, and the thunder joined in her mournful song.

She lost track of the minutes as the merciless rain pounded against her skull, and she felt water at the nape of her neck. She struggled against the weight on her foot and howled with a mouthful of water. Suddenly, she was warm all over, as if someone had swaddled her in blankets like a tiny baby. For the first time, the weight of responsibility lifted from her weary shoulders. The blustering wind rocked her limp body back and forth, the way she was sure her mother once had. She felt as though she had been cupped in two strong, trusting hands. How nice it was to be so small, to let someone else take control.

She grew warmer and warmer still, now only faintly aware of the water rising above her lips. Dreamlike images burned behind her eyelids. She knew she must have once recognized the faces that danced before her in golden bursts of light, but she could not place them now.

Then, a fire erupted inside her chest, like there was something inside her trying to claw its way out. *Breathe, breathe . . . you have to breathe now.* Her lungs began to spasm as her eyes snapped open. She choked on a mouthful of water and jerked her head toward the surface to no avail.

At that moment, the water level rose, as though someone had just thrown a weight in. She opened her eyes underwater and saw a whirlpool forming around her, surrounding her with spastic circles. At the bottom of the pit she spotted two glowing yellow orbs, slowly, menacingly moving in her direction. She stared at them, hypnotized. She'd forgotten where she was, or what was about to happen. Her mind and body were focused on only one thing: to breathe. To live.

Then, as though nature had read her thoughts, she was hoisted out of the pit, like the water had just spat her out. Joy and relief surged across her body as she rose into the air. *Someone had come back to save her.*

She gasped for breath, but something was wrong. She felt an extraordinary pressure against her breast, like her whole body was being squeezed by an enormous fist. She tried to open her eyes, but she couldn't. She parted her lips to scream, but no sound came out.

Her heart hung heavy in her chest and slowed down . . . down . . . down. There was no more fear, no more pulse. She felt as if she'd been forced through an impossibly tiny opening, swallowed up by darkness thicker than the most palpable black smoke. As the world fell away, she realized:

This wasn't a rescue. This was the end. The Savage had taken its reward.

CHAPTER SIX

HABEN SWUNG HIMSELF out of the passageway with one bony arm, cradling his lifeless prey in the other. This time, instead of the desert, he'd emerged at the mouth of an enormous cavern of craggy black rock. It formed an archway, underneath which flowed the River of Past Lives, thick and slow, like tar.

He pulled a breath and was struck by how quickly his body was twisting back into its humanlike shape. The Savage was already leaving him. He couldn't remember a time he'd regained full lucidity before consuming the sacrifice. But then again, he'd never been offered a sacrifice so soon after just having had one. Everything about it was strange.

There was a small boat made of silver stone, moored along the bank of the River of Past Lives. One of the other demons must have left it there, but it was his for the taking now. He trudged toward the riverbank, shaking rainwater from his ragged black robe. He did not regard the young woman in his arms. He didn't think he had ever looked his victims in the face before, though he couldn't be sure. This new awareness made him uncomfortable. He thought for a moment that maybe he preferred the control of the Savage.

He reached the rowboat, but just before stepping in, he stopped cold. He felt a peculiar sensation, like an electric prick against his arm. He paused and flinched. There it was again.

He peered down at the girl. Her hand was draped against the crease of his elbow, right where he'd felt the pain. He moved her wrist aside and cringed. Her flesh was still warm. She had literally burned him with her mortal heat. *So freshly dead.*

Unable to stop himself, he looked into her face. Raindrops clung to her long black eyelashes. She was utterly human, so full of color and warmth, even in death. He was transfixed by the glow of her amber skin that had so recently seen the sun. He couldn't remember the last time he had looked at a mortal so closely. There was something familiar about her, too, and he wondered if he'd seen her before . . . *But where?* A sigh escaped his lips. Her fate was a shame, but there was nothing to be done now. He tossed her into the boat.

He boarded next, and the wispy, ghostlike hands of the Soulless emerged from the river to shove the boat out to the current.

As the stone vessel drifted along, Haben had the chilling, certain sense that he was being watched—just like he had the day before. But this time, there was no mysterious winged creature in the sky. There were no other demons on the riverbank. Was it the girl? He glanced at her from the corner of his eye. She was splayed motionless behind him, her hair spread out around her like a black crown. She lay on her back in a thin, drenched dress that looked like it had been stained with bloody handprints. He couldn't help but notice the shape of her underneath her tattered, filthy clothing. At least the Khronasans hadn't left him another child, as he'd feared. But she was still young. He wondered what she'd done to deserve this.

He tore his gaze from the girl's unmoving body. This was no time for sentimental regret. The sacrifice was over. And even though the Savage had left him, the hunger pangs hadn't. He stared down into the inky river, gritting his teeth, wondering how long he'd be able to hold out—then he wondered what wondering was even worth. After all, she'd been given to him. And she was already dead.

At the back of the boat, Seycia's hand twitched feebly. Starting at the tips of her toes, life and awareness blossomed through her veins. She pulled a shallow breath. Her first thought materialized: *I survived* . . . But how?

She opened only one eye at first, almost afraid to believe it, and stifled a gasp as she spotted the figure seated in front of her. Shrouded in a black hooded cloak, it held perfectly still with a crooked, hunched posture. Was it a man? A woman? *A demon?* Its shoulders rose and fell. It was breathing, but otherwise it didn't move. Its stillness was terrifying.

She glanced over the edge of the boat at the misty river and swallowed a shriek as she watched a translucent hand emerge from the water to nudge the boat along. She squeezed her eyes shut, and two truths took hold: the figure hunched in front of her was probably not human, and even though she'd survived the pit, she was definitely not in Khronasa anymore.

The boat sailed toward a rocky black archway, the river beyond it concealed in shadow. Seycia's pulse quickened. How would she defend herself in the vacuum of pitch blackness? She always used to have a weapon; she never used to be afraid—

Her breath caught in her throat. She did have a weapon. Simeon had returned it to her—she remembered now. The fang's cord was tucked safely down the front of her dress. She stealthily pulled it out as the boat approached the tunnel's gaping maw.

Darkness closed in on all sides of her. It was deathly silent aside from the *drip-drop* of water from rocky cliffs she couldn't see. Then, a glimmer of light shone up ahead—a soft glow, tinted a phosphorescent shade of green, oscillating against a black canvas. Soon, at least a dozen more bursts of green light shone forth.

As the boat sailed closer to the first patch of light, Seycia realized that it was pouring from the entrance to another, smaller cave. The same could be said for the next one they passed. In fact, the entire tunnel was filled with tiny emerald passages to unknown points beyond, like a winding road lined with lanterns.

She peered up at her captor again, who still had not moved. Seycia slowly positioned her fang between her second and third fingers, comforted by the smoothness of it against her skin. If the dark creature turned around, if it threatened her in any way, she would be ready.

As they floated past the pools of green light, Seycia became aware of sluggish, shadowy movement on the riverbank. She squinted and could make out at least a dozen huddled figures, swaying from side to side. They looked nearly human, though she couldn't see their faces. Each of them was clad in dark, tattered robes. None of them spoke, though some moaned low in their throats and thrashed in slow motion against the rocks. Finally, one of them turned, revealing a bright white face that almost glowed through the darkness and two huge milky-white eyes. Its face had all the attributes of a human, but there was something not quite right about it. It looked right at her, though it didn't seem to focus on her. It opened its mouth, almost excitedly, baring its teeth. Then it rolled its eyes back into its head and turned from her. She ducked back behind the edge of the rowboat, shaken.

These were demons. There could be no doubt about that. And there was also no doubt that the creature who had taken her prisoner, the silent figure at the front of the boat, was the subject of all the most frightening tales from her childhood: the Savage. She felt her fang slip through her fingers as her palms perspired. This wouldn't be like fighting off General Simeon. The Savage was a demon. She wished with all her might that she had drowned in the pit after all.

Seycia felt the boat slide onto a rocky bank. She shut her eyes, feigning death as her mind raced, repositioning the fang between her fingers. She decided she would rather try to fight than play dead and surrender. She felt the demon rise from the boat without a sound, and she cracked one eye half open. His back faced her as he dragged the boat farther onto the riverbank. This could be her only opportunity.

She flung herself out of the boat and lunged at the demon's back. But just before her fang made contact with the side of his pallid, exposed throat, he turned. It happened in half a breath. He whirled around, her eyes met his, and she was, for a moment, too shocked to finish what she'd started.

He had a face like any other man's, with a flicker of youth behind his weary gaze. She wasn't sure what she'd been expecting, but he was staggeringly humanlike, aside from the caverns of emaciation below his tired green eyes and sharp cheekbones. Her aim was misguided. She sliced at him crookedly and swiped his white hand with the razor-sharp tip of the fang.

He cried out, blinded by pain, then gaped at her. He had just realized what she already knew: If she'd been dead when he abducted her, she certainly wasn't anymore.

He clung to the place he'd been struck, eyes ablaze with panic, as though he didn't understand what had just happened.

He yanked his hand away from the injury and stared at his palm, covered in dark red blood. She watched as his face flashed with shock, then fear, then fury. She backed away from him as he peered at the fang tucked between her fingers.

He opened his mouth, attempting to speak. "I-I . . ." But no words came forth.

Seycia caught sight of the Savage's tongue, black as coal—just like the old song. She brandished the fang, masking her dread.

"G-g . . ." he stammered, uncomfortable, as if he'd lost the muscle memory of speech. "G-give." He stretched out his tattooed arm toward Seycia and opened his bony palm. She took a step backward, calculating her next move.

"Give. Me," he said in a tense whisper, clearer this time.

Seycia watched as the teeth in his mouth expanded from his gums, doubling in size, a jaw that could have belonged to a ferocious wild dog. He'd tear the skin clean off her bones.

With barely a thought, without even considering where she'd go, Seycia spun around and bolted down the riverbank, a bloodthirsty growl at her back as the demon chased her. As she took off running, she immediately noticed how labored her breathing was—as if the air here wasn't made for her. It was thin and difficult to draw, like she'd ventured too high up a mountain. And that wasn't the only terrifying change. Her hand, gripping the fang as she ran, was starting to shake and lose feeling. She stifled a gasp as the cold, numb sensation spread past her wrist, toward her forearm. She fumbled with the fang and forced it into her opposite hand, which she still had control over . . . for now.

She scampered down the slippery pathway lining the river, frantically scanning the tunnel for an escape route. The darkness seemed even denser now that she was running for her life.

The green light flickering from the caves was her only guide. *The caves . . .*

She took a running leap, jumped up onto a low cliff, and scrambled inside the nearest cave. She heard a hideous snarl from behind her as she hoisted herself over the ledge, clutching her chest as she struggled to breathe. She felt sensation slipping from her legs, and the numbness spread to the tips of her toes. Her feet grew heavy, and her heart swelled with horror. She'd need to run faster if she wanted to find shelter before she completely lost control of her body.

As she clambered through the cave's entrance, she was enveloped by a pulsating green glow, which emanated from the rock itself. The entire space glittered, as though she were inside a jewel. A dark tunnel forked off from the green cave, and she took the shadowy passage. Up ahead, she noticed a faint white light, shining like a beacon, and sprinted toward it, deciding somehow that it was her portal back to the world of the living, away from these monsters. Surely it had to be daylight, she thought, if only to calm her twisted nerves.

She burst forth toward the blinding light, stretching out her hands to touch what she was unable to see. After a moment, she was able to take in her surroundings. Dismayed, she knew immediately that this was not the mortal world. It was only a bright white cave, lined with crystalline walls that sparkled like fresh snow. But it felt peaceful, clean . . . maybe even safe?

She ran a few paces before she skidded to a stop and stared at the sight before her, stunned. The mouth of the cave, which but a second before had been at her back, was now facing her. She turned and bolted forward, hoping sheer speed would keep it from happening again, but this time she ran straight into the rocky wall and smacked her temple.

She had walked right into a trap. The cave would not let her pass. She shuddered, suddenly realizing she could no longer feel the entire right side of her body, and she thrashed on the ground with a terrified yelp. Furious footsteps echoed from the tunnel behind her as the Savage approached. Her heart pounded so loudly she swore he could hear it. She mustered all the strength she could and forced herself to her feet, favoring her left side. She'd escape her fate or die trying. It was all she could do.

She tried to exit the white cave one more time, giving herself ample space to spring across the length of the floor, wondering if she could trick the cave if her feet didn't touch the ground. It was a feeble attempt, but she managed to jump.

This time, the whole space revolved so the ceiling was where the floor had been. The pointy stalactites that hung above her only seconds ago now jutted from the ground. And she was falling right toward them. She threw her weight against the wall in the split second she had before they would impale her.

She screeched, bracing for impact against the jagged wall of the cave, but went cold with horror when she realized she couldn't even feel it. She tumbled to the ground and tried to stand, but no longer could. Helpless, she watched as the demon emerged at the entryway, baring his nightmarish teeth. His thick cloak had fused to the skin on his shoulders, as though his arms had become two huge black wings. She tried to grasp the fang, but she'd lost control over her hands. It fell to the floor.

"Give," he said again. His voice was more than an octave lower now, a deep, shaky growl. He finally sounded like the monster he was.

Seycia maintained fierce eye contact, the only strength she could summon, as he took another step toward her. But instead of reaching out, he approached one of the stalagmites beside her.

He grasped it with both hands and yanked it upward with a guttural snarl. Seycia watched in terror as the stalagmite broke away from the ground. Did he intend to stab her with it, to slash her to pieces?

Heavy black smoke billowed from the place the stalagmite had stood, filling the entire cave with clouds of ash. She choked as she tried to draw a breath, but she no longer could. There was no clean air, and she felt as though her muscles were melting. It was as if all connections between her body and mind had been cut, and the little consciousness she had left grew hollow and dark. She stared straight ahead into nothingness.

Haben didn't like the way the girl's vacant, paralyzed eyes looked through him. He pressed her eyelids down. There, that was better. He plucked the fang off the ground.

The swelling in his jaw contracted, and he felt skin against his fingers instead of scales as he rubbed his shoulder. As his rage subsided, his humanlike features returned.

He turned the fang over in his hand and examined its deadly contours, managing a slight grin. He recognized it at once, now that he could see it up close. The fang had come from a Creeback. Haben had never encountered a Creeback when it was preparing to attack, but he knew all immortal creatures were vulnerable to its bite. Dohv had created the Creebacks at the dawn of time to protect himself from deviant demons in his employ. Little wonder it had cut Haben and made him bleed when she attacked him. His immortal flesh always healed right away when he encountered injury. Haben wondered how a mortal girl could have come to possess a thing like that. He knew Dohv sometimes sent his Creebacks through the Veil to wreak havoc on the humans and keep them in line. To kill one would be an enormous feat. Had *she* killed it? And, stranger still, why hadn't she died when she crossed the Veil? *Who was she?*

He stared into her expressionless face and shuddered when he realized he *had* seen her before. This was the girl who had caught his eye at the pit, the night he took the boy victim. She was the reason he'd become distracted and shown his face. The thing she'd been holding was the Creeback's fang, and he'd been attracted to it because it didn't belong in her world—it belonged in *his*.

He kept his gaze fixed on her as she hovered between life and death. She thought she was so clever, so powerful. But without her weapon, she was no different than the rest of the mortal fools he had consumed. A spasm of hunger shot through him, and he doubled over with a snarl. *She hurt you. She deserves what's coming. Don't let her go to waste.*

He crouched down beside her and held the fang between his fingers. He felt his jaw twisting again; the Savage was ready to take its hard-won reward. His vision blurred as he allowed the darkness to overtake his body.

He caught himself smiling wickedly as he stroked the girl's cheek with the smooth side of the fang. He'd use her own weapon to slice her to bits. He looked her over, wondering where to begin. He clasped a hand around her smooth, slender neck, positioning it just so. He'd cut her from ear to ear first. He would eat slowly. He would truly enjoy this one.

He pulled the fang across her flesh in a methodical, straight line, but the wound closed itself as quickly as he made the incision. He balked, examining her skin with horrified fascination. How could she possibly self-heal? She was a human; there was no question of that. How did she have that capability? And, even stranger, why hadn't *he* healed when she'd cut him with the fang? The bloody half-moon gash on his hand remained. He touched it and winced. It still stung.

Which was the true weapon, the girl or the fang? His body slowly returned to its humanlike state as he forced himself to take a moment and think. He picked up the fang and held it to his own skin, making a quick slice against his palm. His mouth hung agape as he watched his skin fuse back together. The fang was useless in his own hand. *The weapon is the girl.* For some reason, the fang was deadly in her hand, and hers alone.

Haben backed away from her, thinking fast. He now had a way to wound immortals. A world of possibility opened itself to him. With such a weapon, he could finally confront Dohv. He might even be able to fight for freedom from his curse. He had never dreamed of being able to do such a thing.

He spun to face the unconscious girl, weighing his options. He certainly couldn't kill her. He had to keep her in the Underworld, but she wouldn't survive much longer as a mortal, and she'd be useless to him as a corpse. He'd have to turn her into something else . . .

He'd have to make her a demon.

He crouched down and hoisted the girl's body onto his shoulders. He barreled through the tunnels as quickly as he could, devising his plan with each step.

He wasn't sure if demons ever created new demons, or if they even could. But he vaguely recalled the ritual Dohv performed whenever he wished to make a new immortal slave . . . the same rites that had been performed on him all those years ago. Dohv always started by pulling his victim's discarded identity from the River of Past Lives. He would breathe consciousness back into the Soulless, and the demon would take the form of whomever they had been in their last life. Haben knew he was already going against the rules: the girl wasn't a Soulless from the river. She wasn't dead. He'd have to improvise as he went along.

He knew he would need to find some vegetation beyond the cave network. He also knew there should be ample sunlight, and that he needed to be close to the sea. But he would have to do it fast. His plan would be worthless the instant her soul slipped from her body. Dohv knew how to recover a soul after it had passed on. But Haben didn't have the slightest clue.

He emerged from the cave network at a spot he knew was close to the Shore of Awakening. All newborn immortals awoke in the sea there, within the womb of the Underworld, after undergoing transformation.

He stepped onto the white sand, relieved to find that they were entirely alone. He pressed a finger to her neck for a pulse. It was faint as a whisper. He would need to act right away.

Haben remembered three things occurring when Dohv restored his body and turned him into a demon. He remembered sunlight, first of all. He had felt warm all over as he opened his heavy eyelids to a blistering, bright violet light from above. Then he remembered being forced to swallow something. Someone had pried his lips apart and placed a small leaf onto his tongue. The last thing he remembered was cool seawater. He floated there until his consciousness was complete again. Dohv then pulled him from the water, and his new life as a demon had begun.

He laid the girl in the sunlight, which was the first step. He scanned the landscape for any kind of vegetation he could feed her. There was a clump of weeds growing beside a gnarled stalk of black driftwood across the beach. He sprinted toward it, glancing backward every few seconds to make sure the girl had not moved.

The weeds were stiff, with tiny spikes jutting from the edges of each slender leaf. He uprooted the weed in his fist and ran back to the spot where she lay.

The sunlight was restoring color to her skin as he kneeled in the sand and pressed his fingertips to her jaw. He pried open her mouth and placed the spiky leaf on her tongue. He stared at her for a moment, frustrated. Why wouldn't she swallow it? He shook her angrily.

"Girl?"

She gave no sign of response.

He turned toward the turquoise sea behind them and gathered water into his palms. He held his hands over her mouth and let a few drops slip from between his fingers onto her tongue. She choked and sputtered before managing to swallow the leaf.

Minutes passed. She was still as a stone. He nudged her shoulder and stared into her vacant face. He breathed a sigh. He had been too late. The fang would be useless . . . and so would he.

He listened to the gentle crash of the waves behind him, staring at the fang in his palm, the tip still stained with his blood. He slumped into the sand and tossed it behind him.

Then . . . a sound. A strange, shallow gasping sound, like a crippled bird trying to beat its wings. He braced himself for disappointment but couldn't help but look at the girl.

To his shock, her fingers and feet were twitching. He inched toward her to get a closer look. Her chest rose and fell in short, panicked hiccups. All the hair on her arms stood on end as a bead of sweat crept down her forehead.

Fascinated, Haben took hold of her wrist to feel for a pulse again. The second he touched her, she sprang to a sitting position. Her arms were pinned at her sides, stiff as boards. Haben watched, amazed and horrified, as her eyelids snapped open to reveal two white orbs where her eyes should have been. She stared right through him, and he somehow felt even colder than he already was. She lurched and warped herself into a contorted knot, kicking up sand. A dribble of blood fell from her nose as she clawed for her hair. But she couldn't seem to grasp what she was reaching for, as though she didn't have control over her spastic hands.

"Girl . . . ?" He reached out to touch her again.

She swung at him and released a terrible scream. He glanced around, hoping nobody had heard her. When he peered upward, he was startled to find that the mysterious winged creature who had been watching him the day before was back in its orbit. It circled lower this time, past the crooked black fissure in the violet sky. He could see it was a bald bird with a flat, snubby nose and two fleshy, webbed feet. He'd never known Dohv to own a creature like that, but to whom else could it possibly belong?

He froze, flooded with panic. Whatever the creature was, he could not allow it to see any more than it had.

Seycia shrieked again, clutching her chest. Haben leaped on top of her, pinning her arms down with one hand while clasping the other over her mouth. She bit down on his hand as the bald bird continued circling overhead. This needed to end. Now.

He heaved her body over his shoulder and stormed toward the water as she dug her nails into his flesh. He pried her off him and threw her into the sea with a grunt.

Her body hit the water with a loud crash, and within an instant, she was still again. She surfaced seconds later and bobbed along the waves, motionless as a doll. Haben breathed a sigh and drank in the silence. Now that she was in the water, he had little to do but wait. She was becoming *something*, that was certain. Whatever that *something* was, he couldn't be sure.

Haben realized he no longer had the girl's weapon. He scanned the seashore, glad to see he had not tossed the fang very far. He picked it up, pocketed it in his robe, and glanced up at the sky one more time.

The bald bird was retreating now. It let loose a raspy *caw, caw!* as it drifted out of sight, as if to warn Haben that this would not be the last time they would see each other.

Haben drew an unsteady breath. After eons of predictability, the unknown he had encountered so far that day had shaken him to the bone. He shuddered to imagine what else might be in store.

CHAPTER SEVEN

MIKO WATCHED THE sun crawl out from underneath the gray clouds blanketing Khronasa's morning sky. The rain had stopped. And Seycia was gone.

He breathed a solemn sigh as he rose from the place where he sat, a weathered, terra-cotta rooftop, and tried to imagine her soul traveling home to the Forest of Laida. He pictured a huge, ancient tree not unlike the one planted right outside their cabin that held out its branches like a warm embrace, welcoming her spirit home. It would be silent and peaceful there. Her suffering was over, but he had to survive now. It was what she'd wanted. He allowed himself very few tears.

He had spent the night hopping from rooftop to rooftop after realizing that the wilderness was crawling with Simeon's guards. He tried not to stay in one place too long. He'd been crouched behind a deteriorating brick chimney for about an hour; it was time to move on. But he couldn't go back to the woods.

He wondered what happened to the girl who had rescued him, with the dagger and the long, matted hair. He'd heard gunshots after he made his escape. She hadn't come after him.

He wondered if he'd ever find out who she was. He wished he could thank her, or ask why she'd done it at all.

He skipped from one slippery rooftop to the next, soundlessly as a cat. The buildings in Khronasa's city center stood close together in claustrophobic clusters, as though inviting neighbors to spy on one another.

After a few minutes, he came upon a dilapidated building with a shattered attic window. He climbed inside. If the building was abandoned, he could hide there for a bit.

The attic was bare, aside from a leather-bound book in the cobwebbed corner and a moldy, tattered chair. He settled down in the chair and pulled his knees to his chest, suddenly feeling as though he'd collided with a wall as exhaustion slipped over his body. But he couldn't allow himself to sleep. Not just yet. Hiding in plain sight was probably a better plan than taking to the woods, but it required him to stay vigilant. Seycia would have taken turns with him keeping watch, so he could get some sleep, but now he was on his own.

Miko bent down and grabbed the leather-bound book from the floor. He needed something to keep himself awake and occupied.

Inside were words in a language he could not read and, to his surprise, photographs. He had never seen any up close, but he knew they existed. There were photographs of Coalition Army defectors posted around Khronasa, and he'd glanced at them whenever he and Seycia ventured into town for the sacrificial ceremonies. Seycia had explained that the Coalition, in addition to guns and motor vehicles, also had special image-capturing devices.

The book was full of photos of important-looking men dressed sharply in tight jackets and black boots. Some held guns. All gazed up from the page through their dark, vacant, glasses with the smug hint of a smile. Miko couldn't read the captions, but he knew the men in the photos were probably all movers and shakers in the emperor's regime.

He paused for a moment, wondering who might have owned a book like this. Who had lived in this building? Where were they now? Maybe they'd been Khronasan turncoats—families who chose loyalty to their occupiers over the preservation of their people. It would make sense that they would own a book cataloging the most important Coalition leaders and their histories. But why was their window smashed in and why were all their belongings gone? Maybe, Miko thought dryly, they weren't as loyal as the Coalition thought.

Miko thumbed through the pages and came across a portrait of none other than General Simeon. It was an older photo, likely taken after the Coalition's rise from underground, but before Simeon had come to Khronasa. The general's face was clean and free of scars. In it, Simeon exited a shiny, sleek black motor vehicle—for important Coalition officials only.

As though afraid to make eye contact with Simeon's portrait, Miko quickly flipped the page to a photo of a broad-shouldered, lean, middle-aged man with white-blond hair and bright blue eyes that seemed to detach from the page to follow his every move. He wasn't wearing glasses or goggles like the rest of the Coalition. There was something special about him. But that wasn't the only thing that struck Miko about the photo: above the fireplace hung a *severed human head*, in the same spot where Miko's father had once mounted a boar's head in their own home. Miko's stomach turned and he slammed the book shut.

He sat in silence, wondering who the sinister blue-eyed man in the photo could be. Who would have such things in his house? He closed his eyes, trying to commit every contour of the man's face to memory. If he ever encountered him, he wanted to know.

He glanced out the window. He knew that if he wanted to steal a few chicken eggs or a loaf of freshly baked bread, the time was now, before morning. He could come back here and set up a shelter once he had food. He had been completely unprepared for his flight. He had no food, no water, and no warm clothing. He didn't even have his poisoned darts—they were back in their cabin on the hill. He'd have to make new ones.

He put the book back where he had found it, then padded carefully across the rickety floor of the attic, toward the ladder that would take him to the ground floor. He was fairly certain the house was abandoned. He hadn't heard a single sound.

His suspicions were confirmed as he climbed down the ladder and scanned the ransacked kitchen. The only sign of life was a lone cockroach scurrying underneath a crusty pot on the stove.

There was a rucksack on the ground, half-packed, and blood spatters marred the once pristine white tile floor. Miko drew a sharp breath as he examined the grisly scene. The family had been on their way out. But they had not been fast enough.

Miko picked up the rucksack delicately, as though afraid to disturb its departed owner. There were two jackets inside—one made of rubber to keep out the rain, and one made of wool. He would take both jackets and the rucksack.

As he took stock of the other items on the counter, glittering white caught his eye. He moved aside a grimy towel to reveal a smooth chunk of white marble. He turned it over and stared at it, fascinated, as he made out a clawlike hand carved into the stone. It was a shard of marble from the temple ruins in the forest.

He wrapped the shard in the wool jacket for safekeeping and placed it at the bottom of his rucksack. He would carry it with him, even if it could not give him food, warmth, or shelter.

He made his way toward the front door, carefully stepping around the dried blood splatters on the ground. He peered out the cracked window to make sure nobody was on the road.

The front door swung crookedly on its busted hinges as he tiptoed outside and drew a gulp of cool air. Wary, he stepped out onto the rain-soaked cobblestone street.

He was quite unsure of his location. He could navigate the forest with his eyes closed, but he had never wandered alone through the heavily populated streets of Khronasa. A labyrinth of ancient concrete structures towered above him, and lamps lined every street corner, exposing all the shadowy hiding spots. He wasn't sure where he'd go next, but he knew the entire place was dangerous. There were plenty of deadly creatures that lurked outside their cabin on the hill, but the people who lived in the city scared him far more.

The streetlamps flickered in the early morning light, buzzing like flies attracted to overripe fruit. This particular street was lined with tall townhouses similar to the abandoned one he had hidden in. They were all the same, constructed of unfinished dark wood with triangular red rooftops. He wondered how he would ever tell his house apart from his neighbor's if he lived there.

He came to an intersection and turned right, scouring the block for any sign of resources to steal. He was hoping to come across a market of some kind, but the area didn't look very promising.

Crunch. He heard a footstep in the dried leaves a few paces behind him. He whirled around, nervously patting his pocket for his darts . . . until he remembered he didn't have them. Nobody was there. The dim streetlamps were his only companions. He crept along the slick cobblestone street all the more silently.

About half a block down, he came upon a house with a wreath made of fruit hanging on its door. He made a beeline for it. *How stupid, what a waste*, he thought as he hopped up the front steps of the building, *using fruit as a decoration*. He touched an apple hanging at the bottom of the wreath and dug his fingernail into its skin, producing a trickle of sticky juice. *Real fruit!* He grinned and began to pry the wreath from the door.

A dog snarled from the other side of the door as Miko yanked the wreath away, stumbling as it fell on top of him. Then an angry male voice rang out from inside the house, followed by the distinct sound of a shotgun being cocked. Miko froze and his heart raced. But before he could stand to make a break for it, a hefty pair of arms snagged him from behind, and someone clamped a hand over his mouth.

Miko squirmed and kicked and dropped the wreath as he was whisked away. Whoever his captor was, he was strong enough to lift him off the ground. Miko's blood ran cold as visions of men mounted atop mantels flooded his head. He bit the hand that covered his mouth and thrashed to no avail, yelping as he felt his shoulder dislodge from its socket.

Whoever had apprehended him dragged him into an alleyway and waited a moment before speaking. "I'll let you go now. But you need to promise to be quiet. No screaming," a man's voice whispered.

Miko nodded, blinking back tears, and the man released him. He clutched his injured arm.

"Here. Let me fix that," the man added gruffly.

He placed a steady hand on Miko's shoulder and twisted his arm. Miko choked back another scream as he felt his bone lock back into place. He stumbled backward, getting a good look at the man who'd come between him and his food. He was tall and built, with a head of thinning red hair and a red beard to match—a striking complement to his bronzed, leathery skin. He reminded Miko of an aging red fox. The man studied him, and Miko shrank beneath his gaze. He knew at once that the man recognized him from the ceremony . . .

"What do you think you're doing, wandering around the city like you own the place? Don't you know there's a price on your head?" he growled.

Miko swallowed hard, but said nothing.

"And why were you trying to steal one of those wreaths? They're poisoned!"

"They are?"

"Everyone knows about the wreaths. Stupid little thieves like you get what's coming to them."

"Well, I don't live in the city," Miko explained sheepishly. "So I guess I never heard about the wreaths."

The man stared at Miko with a frustrated scowl fixed on his face. Finally, he spoke again.

"My name is Ezara. A group of us went out lookin' for you after that fiasco at the ceremony, hoping we might find you alive."

"Why?" was all Miko could think to say. Was Ezara working with the girl who'd saved him? Did he have the answers? And if he did, that meant he wouldn't hurt him . . . *right?*

"There are folks who think what you did was big. Important. Nobody's ever escaped the pit before." Then he added, "I also used to hunt with your father. Back in the old days."

"But I didn't *do* anything. I mean, I ran. But someone freed me," Miko corrected him. "Do you know who that girl was?"

"Can't say I do," Ezara said quickly, avoiding Miko's gaze. Miko wondered if he was lying. "Anyway, if you're hungry, I can take you to my mother, and she'll fix you something. But then you need to get out of this city—unless you're trying to wind up like your sister. Then by all means, frolic in plain sight."

Miko wanted to ask more questions, particularly about his father, but he was distracted by the rumbling in his stomach. He gazed up at Ezara with weary eyes.

"How far is your mother's house?" he asked.

"We're close—but keep your mouth shut. Not another word till we're behind closed doors."

Miko nodded and followed him out of the alleyway. He wasn't entirely sure he could trust this surly stranger. But in a place where people hung wreaths of poisoned fruit on their doors, he knew he could use a bit of guidance . . . and food, if Ezara was telling the truth.

They turned a corner and passed a dozen Coalition soldiers, dressed in their red uniforms and black boots, marching in formation. Miko stared at the cobblestones as he shuffled along but if Ezara was anxious, he didn't show it. He took a casual step in front of Miko, shielding him from the soldier's view, then offered them a friendly salute. The troops marched on, and Miko exhaled with relief.

"This way," Ezara whispered once the soldiers were out of sight. "City patrol units walk in big groups to look intimidating, but half of those guns aren't even loaded."

"Really?"

"No, I made that up," Ezara replied with a cynical laugh. "But wouldn't that be funny?" Miko returned Ezara's chuckle politely, but he wondered if Ezara was just the slightest bit . . . well, off. Was he actually sent out to look for him, or did he have another motive?

Miko shivered as they turned onto a darker street—one with no lights to guide them. The houses there were smaller and older. The cobblestones ended, giving way to a twisted, muddy path. This was the foot of the hill, where the oldest homes in Khronasa stood. He'd often wondered if any of them were even occupied.

Ezara led Miko to the door of a crooked two-story house, painted a faded blue color. Years ago, someone must have tried to make its exterior look cheerful. Ezara produced a key from his tattered leather coat and unlocked the rusty padlock on the front door. Miko was getting nervous. Seycia would not have wanted him to go into this house. Ezara was a stranger, even if he had indeed known their father.

Ezara stepped through the door, but Miko stayed behind on the front walkway. "Come on, get inside," he grunted.

"I-I think . . . maybe I'll go hunt for food instead." Miko backed away.

"Oh, come off it. We're trying to help you. Don't be an idiot."

"It's just . . . I think I should hunt—" Miko was about to take off running down the street, back toward the forest, when a second voice called out from behind the dark doorway.

"Ezara, did you find him?"

It was a woman's voice, rough and crinkled with age but with a gentleness that stopped Miko in his tracks.

"I did, but I can't get him inside the damn house," Ezara grumbled.

"Well, not like that you won't," the woman replied. It was as if Miko could hear the serene smile on her face. She appeared at the door. She was indeed elderly but held a steady gaze with her big dark eyes. One of them was clouded over by a cataract. Her snow-white hair was woven into a long braid that reached her waist, and she wore a deerskin overcoat and a vest made of fur. Miko suspected the family had hunted for the hides themselves. And if they hunted, they were not to be feared. The Coalition hadn't bought their loyalty. Miko stepped forward to get a closer look at her.

"This is my mother, Belicia. She'll make you something to eat if you come into the house like a sensible person," Ezara said as he stepped inside behind Belicia. He turned to her. "Is the tea ready?"

"On the fire," Belicia answered. She looked to Miko as Ezara disappeared into the house. "What's your name?"

"Miko," he responded, growing warm with embarrassment. "Sorry I didn't come in before. It's just . . . I—"

"I understand. It's good not to trust strangers. It's how you stay safe," she said. "But sometimes we need strangers to help us when we're on our own."

"How do I know you won't turn me in?"

"I suppose you can't," she replied gently. "Tell you what. We'll leave this door open for you—"

"Like hell we will! You know they're out looking for him!" Ezara snapped from inside.

"We'll leave this door open for you. And if you decide you want to come in for some tea, you may." She ignored Ezara and gave Miko a small, crooked smile. She was missing one of her front teeth.

"All right," Miko answered, shuffling just a few steps closer to the door.

Before Belicia ducked inside, she turned to him and said, "I'm very sorry for what happened to your sister. And I'm sorry about Ezara. He's been out all night."

Ezara gave a tired grumble from inside as he lit a lamp. Belicia turned and joined Ezara in the kitchen, leaving Miko to make his decision. The kitchen looked so warm, so inviting . . .

"I almost ate the fruit from one of those wreaths, but Ezara stopped me," Miko said, more to himself than to Belicia. Ezara had protected him and then offered him food and shelter. He could have dragged him away to the authorities right then and there, but he hadn't.

"So he did," Belicia said.

A moment later, Miko stepped through the front door and into the welcoming glow of the oil lamps lighting the kitchen.

A small fireplace was situated straight ahead, and a black iron teakettle hovered low above the roaring flames. Ezara was already seated at a handcrafted wooden table on a stool, sipping a mug of tea, foggy with steam. Six lanterns hung from a rope strung across the rafters, from one end of the room to the other, evenly illuminating the kitchen with soft, golden light.

Ezara got up from the table and slammed the door shut behind Miko.

"That's about enough of that," he muttered, sitting back down, as Belicia crossed to the fireplace and poured Miko a mug of tea.

"Please, sit," she offered, and he did, across from Ezara.

Belicia slid the mug in front of Miko, and he grabbed for it with trembling hands, took a slow sip, and sighed happily. The tea was minty and smooth, and it calmed his nervous stomach. He noticed Ezara watching him intently, as though expecting him to pull a dagger from his belt at any second. But before he could think to say anything—

"Do you like cheese? Sausage, maybe?" Belicia opened the ice box on the other side of the room.

"I like everything," Miko replied, louder than he'd meant to.

Belicia laughed and grasped a knife that was hanging from the wall. She cut a block of yellow cheese into generous slices. Ezara was still watching Miko. He swallowed a long gulp of his tea, feeling as though he shouldn't return eye contact.

"We need to make that last, you know," Ezara said as Belicia prepared Miko's plate.

"So says he who had a second helping at supper last night." Belicia cast a wry smile in Miko's direction. Miko decided he not only trusted Belicia, but he liked her, too.

Belicia placed the plate of sausage and cheese in front of him. Miko felt Ezara's condescending eyes as he shoveled food into his mouth, but he didn't care one bit. Once he was satisfied, he lifted his gaze to Ezara, ready to ask more questions.

"How—er . . ." Miko swallowed a mouthful of cheese, and then continued. "How did you know my father? What was he like?"

Ezara leaned back in his chair and pursed his lips. "Oskar and I were hunting partners. Our cabins weren't far from one another. Did he ever tell you about the day we slaughtered the Black Beast?"

"My sister, Seycia, knew all about it." Miko felt a twinge of cold sorrow as he spoke his sister's name. "I was really young when our parents died, but she was eleven summers."

"I was there the day he killed it. This creature, it appeared out of nowhere in our forest one day, ripping apart flocks of sheep in the middle of the night. It killed a neighbor boy, too. Awful few days we spent trying to catch it. It was the strangest-looking thing we'd ever seen—black and scaly, like a huge lizard, at least twice the size of you. And it moved *fast*. I'd never seen something slither around like that. The worst thing about it was that mouth full of fangs. They could cut through flesh like butter. A nasty sight—"

"My sister had one of those fangs," Miko said, riveted. "My father kept one of its teeth when he killed it. She got it when he died." He added after a moment, "How'd he do it? Kill it, I mean."

"Oskar shot it full of arrows from a distance and then, when it slowed down, he sliced its head clean off with his ax. Then he dug out one of the fangs. Just like that, with his hand and a dagger." Ezara made a twisting motion with his wrist as if he were extracting the fang himself. "Your father was the superstitious type. He thought the beast had come from the Underworld.

There were a lot of superstitious types, people who traded their finest possessions for a piece of that ugly thing."

"Did you take any of it?" Miko asked. Ezara scoffed and took a long swig of his tea.

"No, not me. I don't exactly believe in worlds beyond and all that nonsense, you know?"

Out of the corner of his eye, Miko saw Belicia stop cleaning the kettle at the fireplace. She stood up straight and raised her eyebrows in Ezara's direction. But she said nothing.

"So you don't believe in the Forest of Laida? Or Dohv?" Miko asked. "My sister told me there was proof all of that was real."

"Rumors of proof. From hundreds of years ago," Ezara corrected him. "Listen, if there's an afterlife, if something happens to my soul when my body gives way, I'll find out about it when I get there." He shrugged and then looked over at Miko's empty plate. "Well, he's all done," he called out to Belicia. "Shall I lead him to the edge of the woods? That's far enough, right? Or should I take him across the bay?"

Miko froze, not understanding. Were they kicking him out?

"No, Ezara," Belicia said, stepping into the light. "The people need him. You heard what High Priest Jenli said—"

"I heard him, but I don't agree with him," Ezara barked. "I said if we found the kid that we'd feed him. What did you think, that we'd keep the poor bastard? Like a pet?"

Miko shrunk in his chair, uncomfortable. Ezara cast him an apologetic look.

"Sorry. But you'll lead Simeon's troops straight to our door if you stay."

"I-I understand," Miko said, though his crestfallen face betrayed him. He liked the warm lamplight, and being with Belicia, whom he'd only just met but was already fond of.

"They won't come looking for him here," Belicia argued. "There's no reason to suspect us. Half the neighborhood figures I'm a harmless old hag who's lost my wits."

"Well, so do I."

Miko didn't know what to say. Ezara shoved away from the table and yanked his boots back on. "If he stays, then I go. I won't be anywhere near this place when Simeon's flunkies come knocking."

"They won't."

Ezara grabbed a bow and a quiver of arrows from the corner by the fireplace. He sneered at his mother. "You want to keep him? Fine. I'll be off."

"Good. Glad you're finally getting out to do some hunting for once."

"Wait. I'm sorry. I'll go—" Miko said, starting to feel bad, but Ezara slammed the door in his face. He was gone. The cabin was silent.

"Don't worry," Belicia muttered. "He's perfected his dramatic exits, but he always comes home."

A moment passed as Miko took another sip of his tea. "Does Ezara really not believe in the Underworld or any of that?"

"I don't know what Ezara believes anymore," Belicia replied, a hint of sadness in her voice. "He's nervous, as you can probably tell. He's nervous all the time."

Miko gave a slow, understanding nod.

"It's been a hard seven years. My son and I . . . we've seen some awful things. He's become everything the Coalition wants us to be: obedient, afraid to ask for help, afraid to help oneself."

"Because he doesn't believe anything's coming after this," Miko thought aloud. "If he doesn't believe in the Forest of Laida, then he doesn't believe he'll ever come back. That's why he's so afraid. If he dies, it's all over."

Belicia fell silent, taking this in. Miko added, "He's not loyal to the Coalition, is he?"

"How could he ever be? He's seen too many friends die," she answered as she sat down across the table from Miko. "Here. Why don't you let me hang your wet things by the fire?"

Miko stood, peeling his damp shirt from his skin. Almost trancelike, he heard himself say, "Have you ever seen General Simeon up close? Have you ever seen how small and skinny he is? People treat him like he's some kind of god, but I'll bet he's the easiest person to kill. He might have bodyguards and all that, but he's just a man."

He handed his tunic to Belicia, and it took him a moment to realize that she was frozen to the spot.

She bent down to his level and whispered, "I don't know you well, but I know that I don't want you killed. Don't ever let anybody else hear you say something like that."

She clutched his shirt to her chest as though it were a shield against his words. He knew she was right, but he couldn't hold back what he wanted to say next. "All I'm saying is . . . If I don't support him, and if you don't support him, then there has to be others who don't either. And if all those people feel that way, they should be able to kill him. He's just one person," Miko said.

Belicia cleared her throat, wrung out his jacket, and laid it by the fire.

"Would you like a little more tea, Miko? There's still some left—"

"I don't want tea! I want someone to *do something!*" His voice cracked as he choked back a sob.

"Shh. Come now. You're very tired." She gently pushed his ragged bangs from his forehead. "Why don't you have a rest upstairs? There's a bed. It's warm."

He drew in a shaky breath, clenching his fists. After a moment, he finally nodded.

"All right," he said, and then looked over at his empty plate. "But do you think . . . maybe . . . I could have a little more sausage first?"

"I don't see why not." Belicia smiled at him and crossed back to the icebox.

A hiatus elapsed between the two of them—utter stillness aside from the *clink-clink* of the knife against the plate. Miko piped up again, more softly this time. "He's just a man," he said as Belicia handed him his plate. "Men die every day."

"Then let's say a prayer the Savage sends a tornado to blow his roof off," Belicia replied, trying her best to lighten Miko's load.

But nothing would lighten his load. It was too late for that. In the place where he felt the most emptiness, a seed had been planted. The idea that was taking root would fill up the whole void if he let it. He was ready to risk everything if it meant he'd have his revenge. A vision took hold, in his mind's eye: One day, he would be the one to hit that gong in the plaza. He would summon the Savage. And the screams from the pit would be General Simeon's.

CHAPTER EIGHT

SEYCIA AWOKE TO a soft, delicate hum reverberating between her ears, feeling weightless, as though her body were filled with nothing but air. She tasted blood on her tongue. Her head lolled from side to side as she finally opened her eyes.

She shuddered as she took in her surroundings: She was underwater, hovering beneath the waves of a turquoise sea. Her body did not surface, nor did it sink. It was suspended in the water, with no gravity to control it. She peered at the sand below. It was pure white, sparkling in the violet sunlight seeping through the water. No vegetation sprouted from the ocean floor, no creatures swam about. It was strange, she thought. No body of water on Earth was uninhabited like this.

And then she remembered: this was not Earth. She recalled the final moments before she had lost consciousness. She had been in a cave with no way out. The Savage was chasing her. She was supposed to have died in the pit, but she was still alive.

She opened her mouth to scream but instead, without even realizing it, she drew in a breath. She froze, stunned. She had breathed underwater. She was sure of it. She opened her mouth once more, and it happened again.

With equal parts fascination and terror, she slowly began to swim. The water was warm, and the current did not fight her as she touched her toes to the sand below and settled there on both her feet. She found she could walk quite easily along the white ocean floor. She skipped and floated upward—a languid, effervescent dance. She was delighted, awestruck. She bent backward, grabbed her ankles, and pushed herself into a spin, circling 'round and 'round. She was ousted from her dreamlike state seconds later when a hand clenched her scalp and yanked her out of the water. She spat out seawater as she was tossed onto dry sand, under the glaring sun. She lay on her side and pulled her knees to her chest.

The demon hovered over her, watching her writhe on the ground. "Girl," he said.

She rolled onto her back and squinted up at him, shielding her gaze from the harsh sunlight. He no longer looked like the monstrous Savage, but the human in the dark robe who had startled her on the riverbank.

"Can . . . can . . ." He struggled to speak. "Can you see?"

She wasn't sure she'd heard him correctly. *Can you see?* She didn't reply.

"Can. You. See?" he repeated.

Seycia slowly rose to a sitting position. She hadn't been sure up until that moment that the demon could speak in full sentences. She looked into his face. His eyes appeared intensely green against the white pallor of his skin.

"Y-yes," she said.

She scanned the beach. The violet sun hung low in the hazy sky. The ocean behind her was clear and bright blue, and there was a huge black rock formation looming in front of her—the entrance to another cave. She felt as if she'd never seen colors quite like these before. Not on Earth. They seemed more vivid. More *alive*, somehow.

"Good," the demon said, interrupting her thoughts. "Sometimes . . . there is blindness."

She didn't like the way he peered down at her. She felt peeled apart by his gaze, as though she were the subject of some experiment. She slowly straightened her wobbly legs and rose to her feet. At eye level, she felt stronger. She noticed her wrist, which had been broken and burning with pain, had completely healed. Her ribs no longer ached as she breathed, and the long bloody scrape on her shoulder was gone. Her body was entirely clean and free of scars.

As she stared at her arms and legs in amazement, the demon reached into his pocket and pulled out her fang. She lunged for it, but he held it back.

"Name?" he asked flatly.

She didn't answer him, still grappling for her weapon.

"Name," he repeated.

"Seycia." Realizing then that the two of them had been easily conversing, she thought to ask, "You speak Khronasan?"

"We all speak the same, down here. Tongue of the dead."

"So . . . I'm dead?" she stammered.

He didn't reply. He didn't so much as look at her as he stuffed her fang into his pocket. Seycia scowled as she reached for it.

"Give that back."

"When you understand."

"Understand what?" she snapped. "What have you done to me?"

A quiet hiatus fell between them. She wondered if he'd forgotten what she'd asked him or if he'd even heard her. She thought of running again, but she needed answers first.

"I said, what have you—"

"You know who I am?"

She nodded coldly. "You're the Savage."

"I have a name. Just as you do." He glared at her.

"But you're a demon."

"Haben," he muttered. She wasn't sure she'd heard him at first.

"Is . . . is that a name? Your name?"

He nodded, then added, "You're afraid."

"No. I'm not."

"You should be."

Haben took the fang out of his pocket again and dangled it before her. She hated the way her precious weapon looked in his bony fingers. "I changed you. Because you're going to help me. With this."

"You *changed* me?"

He nodded. She glanced at her arms and legs and touched her face, starting to understand. She didn't *feel* different, but she knew she was. She remembered the way she'd struggled to breathe before, how she couldn't control her stiff, numb body . . .

"I'm a . . . demon?" she asked him, though she already knew the answer.

His silence confirmed it, and fury erupted inside of her. He had no right. She would be in the Underworld forever now. She would never go home. Never be with Miko again. She cast him a loathsome glare. "I'm not helping you with anything. Go ahead and keep the fang. Do what you want. But I won't stay."

"No. This doesn't work. Not without you," he said, methodically palming the fang. "It's cursed. Only you can kill with it. I tried. I can't. Where did you get it?"

"From my father."

"Did *he* curse it?"

"I-I don't know." She thought for a moment, then added, "But only my brother and I have ever used it."

"Then just your family. They have the power?"

"What *power*? I don't know what you're talking about, and even if there *was* a curse, I wouldn't tell you how to break it." She glowered at him, stepping closer now. "I'm not going to kill for you. Give it back."

"It's mine." He threw the cord over his neck and stared her down. "And so are you."

At that, Seycia vaulted toward him with all her strength and kicked him in the gut as hard as she could. He buckled with a groan but didn't go down. No matter. Seycia saw her opportunity to snag the fang from around his neck. Just as she was about to grab it, he snatched her wrist in his freezing cold hand and twisted it sideways, twice over. She stifled an agonized howl. He was much, much stronger than he looked.

He stared hawkishly into her desperate face as she averted her eyes. She wouldn't let him see her in pain. He yanked her in even closer. She felt the shaky rise and fall of his chest against hers as he hissed into her ear. "Look at me."

She slowly raised her eyes to his.

"We will have problems," he said. "*You* will have problems. If you don't listen."

Like hell she would. She shoved her free elbow directly into his sallow face. He let go of her wrist to cradle his eye, and Seycia gasped as she watched her limp, fractured arm heal on its own, her bones cracking like a roaring fire. Her hand was numb for the briefest of seconds. And that was when he grabbed her again—before she could even think of running—seized her shoulders, and threw her to the ground.

She watched in horror as his jaw loosened and his teeth started to expand. She had pushed him over the edge again—she'd triggered the Savage. She knew he couldn't hurt her—not permanently anyway—even with that mouth of enormous, razor-sharp teeth. But she didn't want to feel what he could do.

"You will stay with me." His voice had become a low, fearsome growl. "You will use my weapon when I tell you to. *Only* when I tell you to."

"It's . . . mine," she struggled to say.

She managed to kick him, square between his legs, and leaped to her feet with a laugh. An easy target. He was more humanlike than she'd thought. This time, she was able to pull the fang off his neck before he recovered. She tore off, her weapon back in her hand, and bolted down the beach with a speed she'd never possessed on Earth. Maybe she had never been so frightened, or maybe it was one of her new immortal traits. Either way, she'd be long gone soon enough . . . Until the sand beneath her feet suddenly quivered.

She stumbled, forced to slow down. It felt like an impending earthquake. She stopped and gazed out at the ocean. Then she saw it: an enormous tsunami wave forming on the horizon, building in strength and size by the second, careening right toward her. The wave crashed down around her and pulled her out to the open water as though it had a mind of its own. She didn't even have a second to panic or catch her breath. She was on her way . . . But where?

The seawater spat Seycia out into a rocky, dark tunnel. She was certainly glad she could breathe underwater now. She pulled herself to her feet, shivering, as clouds of her own breath floated in the air before her.

Seconds later, another mighty cascade of water filled the tunnel, and she jumped to the side to avoid being battered by it. Haben came staggering out of its wake, angrily shaking off his robe. He cast a frosty stare in her direction.

"Maybe now you'll learn to be afraid," he said. "We've been summoned. Dohv knows about you."

"You mean he knows about *you,* and what you did to me." He gave no reply as he started walking ahead of her. "Dohv is Lord of the Underworld," she went on.

"Mm." It was as if she could hear his eyes rolling.

"So he'll punish you for what you've done. I know you broke a rule. You've probably broken a lot of them," she rambled with a scowl.

He bristled, then asked, "Where's my weapon?"

She held it up and narrowed her eyes at him. "Suppose I show it to him?"

Haben shrugged. "Be my guest. If one of us is caught with that thing and sent to Antenor, better you than me." He brushed past her down the black tunnel.

"Sent to . . . ? Wait, stop!" What kind of trap was he leading her into? She sped up and met his pace. He stared straight ahead, as though he had completely forgotten that she was beside him.

"*Where* is Dohv going to send me if he sees this?" She held up the fang.

"Quiet." He nudged past her and kept walking.

"What is Antenor?" she asked in a whisper.

"Where the traitors go."

Seycia shuddered and hung back a few paces, weighing his words. *Traitors.* What happened to traitors here? She didn't dare imagine. But *he* was the traitor, not her. She'd only just gotten here. She would explain everything to Dohv. With any luck, the Keeper of Life would show her mercy and send her home. Or, if not, he might at least let her soul rest in the Forest of Laida. Anything would be better than an eternal life she didn't ask for.

They approached a barrier of water at the tunnel's edge. As Seycia stepped closer, she realized it was the same dark river of ghostly figures she had encountered earlier. She saw wispy fingertips crest the surface of the water and grimaced, hoping they wouldn't have to wade through it.

"The Soulless can't do anything to you unless Dohv tells them to," Haben muttered, watching her hesitate.

To her relief, the rocky surface beneath their feet shifted forward, creating a bridge. Haben crossed it first. Seycia followed.

"What are they?" she asked, once they'd passed over. "The Soulless?"

"Mortal souls live many lives. Each time they die, they shed those lives. Dohv keeps their shadows in the river so he doesn't accidentally create the same person again someday. He has a copy of every mortal who's ever lived."

She shivered as she pictured the sheer number of them. Even the longest river she'd seen in Khronasa, the one that flowed through the denser, rainy parts of the forest, couldn't compare.

She could now see that the river was part of a huge round moat, encircling two glimmering towers of obsidian stone that emerged imposingly before her. She stepped off the bridge onto a smooth, mirrorlike black floor and shuffled along as though it were ice she might slip on.

They approached the enormous silver gate of Dohv's palace, where two tall columns of blue fire stood guard on either side. Seycia shivered, as though she sensed the flames were alive, watching them. Beside them stood a dozen silent humanlike figures, tall as trees, dressed in dark, tattered robes. She wasn't even sure they were sentient beings until they opened their mouths and spoke, in unison: "Proceed." Their voices were deep and ancient, as though they'd been speaking that word, and only that word, for thousands of years. The massive gate swung open with a dull, heavy creak that was loud as thunder. But before the two of them could enter, a cold, high-pitched voice echoed across the barren courtyard.

"Who is *that*?"

Seycia watched as a small figure strode out of the palace and made its way toward the gate.

"I didn't think you'd have *company*."

Seycia could see now that it was a boy, slightly younger than Miko—a boy demon. His flesh had been drained of all color, just like Haben's, but instead of wearing a long black robe, he was shirtless. Two dark shapes that looked like claws were tattooed onto both of his shoulders as though a ghastly reptile was about to come crawling up over his back. She swallowed hard. The fang was in plain sight. She dropped it down the front of her collar, still unsure whether she was going to tell Dohv about it.

"Zane, Dohv's errand boy. Don't say anything to him," Haben whispered through clenched teeth. Seycia nodded.

"Hello? I asked you a question," Zane said with a huff as he came closer. "Who. Is. That? She looks . . . wrong."

Seycia stiffened. *Wrong?*

"That's Dohv's business," Haben muttered.

"She's a human," Zane's breath caught as he realized it, examining Seycia closely. "Look at her face. Look at all that color." He broke into gales of laughter and pressed his palms to two iron serpent claws jutting out of the gate, letting them in. "Dohv is going to *love* this."

Zane led them through two huge double doors made of the same black, translucent glass as the towers above. Etchings were carved on the surface of the doors. Men, women, and demons alike were depicted strewn about a war-torn, parched landscape, mouths hanging open, mid-scream, as they cast their eyes to the heavens. Seycia was suddenly less enthusiastic about their audience with the Keeper of Life. She didn't want to meet whatever creature lived behind those doors.

She caught the boy demon's eye as he turned to guide them inside. He cast a smirk in her direction. She swore he'd just seen the fang, but how? She crossed her arms over the spot where it hung against her breast.

She and Haben followed Zane down a narrow corridor, harshly lit with jets of pale white light shooting down from above as if stars, shining too brightly and too closely, had been affixed to the ceiling.

She peered over at Zane, marching on his tiny bare feet in front of them. *All that color*, he'd said. She glanced at her hands. It was true. She looked strange compared to the two bone-white demons—her amber flesh still had warmth to it, as though she'd just been in the sun. Had something gone wrong during her transformation?

The three of them made their way up a smooth stone staircase the color of pewter. Shafts of blue fire a hundred strong shot up from the floor as they approached the landing. Zane skipped like the excited child he resembled through the fiery stalks, toward a granite throne at the center of the room.

A colossal figure sat there, frozen like a towering statue, wearing a robe that seemed to be made of clouds of swirling black smoke. As she inched closer, Seycia realized the clouds had *faces*—human faces. They wore the smoke like a mask, obscuring their expressions. These were the Soulless, Seycia realized, pulled from the river. She shuddered. She gazed up to glimpse the face of the seated figure; the robe's hood concealed it completely. But she knew. This was Dohv.

Zane jumped up onto the rocky throne and perched on the armrest, right beside the haunting figure, and smiled at her. His teeth were alarmingly white. Haben took a few small steps forward, clasping his hands together behind his back. He made no attempt to communicate with Seycia. She swallowed hard.

What was more dangerous: To tell Dohv about the fang and Haben's plan? Or to heed Haben's warning and do nothing?

A pounding sensation obliterated her head, as though her skull had been split in half by a heavy object. Had she decided to speak just then, she couldn't have. She opened her mouth to scream, but no sound came out. Her vision clouded. Images doubled . . . tripled . . . All she could see was a strange swirl of scintillating silver before her eyes, like a coil of crushed minerals, and then she heard the voice . . .

"You've been most careless with your gifts, Haben. Most careless indeed." The words echoed inside her ears as though they had been spoken across a huge cavern. She knew that the voice belonged to Dohv. She felt nauseous, shaky . . .

"Th-there was—" Haben stuttered. "There was . . . an error. I encountered an error." His voice might as well have been a hundred worlds away.

"I do not consider your duties difficult enough to warrant errors. You are a messenger. You remind the mortals to fear us. No more, no less."

"But she wasn't dead," Haben whispered, his weak voice laced with agony. Seycia was surprised he was able to speak at all. She couldn't have opened her mouth if she wanted to.

"And instead of killing her, you transformed her on the Shore of Awakening and thought I would not hear of it? You must know I am always watching those waters." After a tense moment, Dohv spoke again, *"Are you not starving?"*

"Always," Haben answered. "But . . . she just wouldn't die—"

Dohv laughed as Seycia's aching head pulsed with each burst of sound. *"And this is she?"*

Dohv directed his attention toward her, and her vision cleared. He rose from his granite throne, and as he moved, the Soulless floated along with him. The magical fabric oscillated like waves of murky water as he shrank down in size to her level.

"A pretty thing," he remarked. She couldn't see his eyes, but she knew he was staring right at her. She shivered. *"I imagine you thought you'd give yourself some company, Haben? Seems the only logical explanation. I scarcely believe the girl 'just wouldn't die.'"*

Seycia squinted, trying desperately to make out any recognizable features beneath Dohv's hood as he approached her, but there was nothing but darkness. He reached a leathery, bone-thin finger toward her. His flesh was charred and brown, as though he had been pulled from a gruesome fire. His fingernail, long and pointed, came within an inch of her cheek.

Zane giggled from his place on the throne. The room was silent aside from his childish snicker and the hiss of the fire stalks surrounding them. Dohv was thinking. Seycia found she was able to open her mouth, and she spoke:

"He-he wanted to—" Seycia began in a raspy whisper. "He was going to . . ."

Haben couldn't move his head, but she saw his horrified eyes rivet to hers. His gaze sent a shudder through her. There was something he feared that she didn't understand. Something she knew she ought to fear, too. She stopped speaking, but she already had Dohv's attention. Her jaw clenched all on its own as he reapproached her.

"You speak out of turn. If you are to be a part of my world, you must wait to be addressed by me. But please. Continue. What did he want?"

"He . . . he wanted . . ." Seycia glanced back at Haben, whose petrified stare was now fixed to the floor. "Company, like you said. It must be hard to be alone here."

Dohv sighed with disgust and floated across the glossy black floor, sinking back into his throne. Zane bounced up and down, restless, waiting for the verdict.

"You know full well only I decide who becomes immortal and who remains a part of the river." Dohv accused Haben, *"You trod upon my authority when you gave this insignificant creature eternal life."*

"That was not my intention," Haben replied, trying his best to keep his tone steady.

"Come forth, Haben."

Seycia watched as he shuffled toward Dohv's throne. He exhaled heavily, as if he knew what was coming, as if it had happened before. Seycia tried to follow him but found her body was still frozen to the floor. Zane squirmed with excitement. Something was about to happen.

"You say you are always starving. I believe you. But I also believe you have forgotten what it truly is to suffer."

Seycia felt her heartbeat accelerate against the fang underneath her collar. She tried to ignore it, realizing Dohv might be able to read her mind and would know she was hiding something if she focused on it. Dohv pointed an atrophied finger at Haben's chest, and he doubled over, wailing in agony. Seycia could feel his scream, as though the sound had burrowed beneath her flesh. Zane clapped his hands.

"You have forgotten what fear feels like. You have forgotten to fear me." Dohv stood from his throne and forced Haben to his knees. He held out his hand with fingers spread like a huge, hungry brown spider, and placed his palm on top of Haben's head, clamping his spindly fingers around his skull.

"Regenesis is a privilege. From today, if you bleed, you shall bleed eternally. Your wounds will not heal."

A bloodcurdling shriek followed, coupled with wretched gagging noises as Haben fought for his breath. He convulsed on the floor, twitching against the electric current emanating from Dohv's fingers.

Let him scream, Seycia thought, at first. *He deserves to be punished.* But the screams didn't stop. Dohv kept squeezing his head tighter and tighter, and she swore she could hear the Keeper of Life laughing. Seycia understood Haben's terror, then. The look he'd given her. Dohv wasn't going to help her. He wasn't going to help *anyone.* He enjoyed this, and if she ever stepped out of line, he'd enjoy doing it to her, too. The pit of her stomach twisted.

No more . . . Seycia pleaded in her head, as if Dohv would even care to hear her. *Please, please, no more . . .*

At long last, Dohv released Haben and tossed him to the floor like a used rag. Haben buried his face into his robe, away from her, but Seycia could tell he was in tears by the way his hunched shoulders seized. She finally felt sensation in her arms and legs again and immediately broke free, running toward the spot where he lay. She wasn't sure why she was rushing to his side. It just seemed like what she ought to do.

"Stop," he gasped. She froze.

Zane chuckled, casting a pearly grin in Seycia's direction. She imagined dislodging every one of those perfect teeth from his jaw as she felt Dohv's voice beat against her head again. *"I shall call you forth when I have a task for you. Till then, keep away from the Veil. I will not call you again after that, unless you yourself have a crime to answer for."*

She looked up at Dohv, feeling the fang's cool surface against her skin as she drew sharp, nervous breaths. She could sense he was staring right at her, studying her. She heard him chuckle and she trembled as the sound shook her body. Did he know about her weapon? Would she be tortured next? *"I can already see immortality will not suit your fragile soul,"* he said.

"I wouldn't have chosen you myself. But I'll find a use for you, in time. Now, take him away."

A frigid glare fell across Seycia's face. *Fragile soul?* After all she'd been through, what seemed *fragile* about her? But Dohv said no more. He did not move, as though he had once again become a ghostly statue. Their audience with the great Lord of the Underworld had come to an end. She didn't even have a second to indulge in her relief when Zane snapped at her—

"You heard the Keeper of Life. Get him out of here!"

Seycia cautiously touched Haben's shoulder. He swatted her away with a groan.

"We need to leave . . ." she whispered.

"Don't touch me," he hissed as he drew himself to his knees.

Seycia fought the urge to gasp as he lifted his head. The veins beneath his skin, spreading from the crown of his head to the edges of his temples, turned black as ink and protruded from his flesh like a network of tree roots. The marks pulsed as they darkened, then slowly started to fade. But Seycia could tell by the way Haben winced and clenched his teeth he was still in unbearable pain.

He finally stood and turned away from her, pulling the hood of his cloak up over his head, staring at the floor. Seycia was careful to not so much as even look at him as the two of them exited the throne room, back the way they came.

They silently made their way through the main corridor toward the front doors of the palace. Haben leaned his weight into one of the huge etched panels and limped out of Dohv's lair with Seycia trailing behind him. The door closed with a resounding thud. The tall guardians outside stood at attention in perfect unison and glanced in their direction, moving as one. But they said nothing.

Seycia followed Haben to the rocky bridge across the River of Past Lives, where they waited for the stone slab to creep across the dark water. It moved sluggishly, as though the very landscape wanted to torture Haben just a few seconds more.

"What happens now?" Seycia dared to ask.

He didn't reply. She did not ask again.

The two of them crossed the bridge together, and Seycia thought the adjoining tunnel seemed even darker than before. Haben hobbled past her into the depths of the cave beyond. She wasn't sure if she should follow him or make her own way.

Up ahead, the cave forked off in two separate directions, both tunnels equally pitch black. Seycia watched as Haben took the tunnel to his right and disappeared into the shadows. She was free of him now, just like that. She could come and go as she pleased. Her heart skipped a beat as she vanished down the tunnel to the left.

But she paused after only a few paces. What if she found herself in trouble by taking the wrong path? There were laws in this world, and she'd seen what the punishment was for breaking them. Haben would at least be able to provide her with information before she ventured out on her own. She weighed which risk was greater: to accidentally break a cardinal rule in the Underworld and be tortured, or to be Haben's indentured assassin with the fang? Considering she still had the fang and could do as she pleased with it, the latter seemed safer for the time being.

She spun around and hurried after Haben. The palpable blackness enveloped her. This tunnel was smaller; she could feel it. She breathed deeply, forcing herself to relax in the tight space. The darkness dwarfed her and crushed her all at once.

She walked and listened, stretching out her arms into nothingness. All was quiet. A leak in the cave's ceiling, dripping slowly, was the only sound. She knew the tunnel had to lead *somewhere*. She'd have to reach daylight eventually.

Then she heard him. Strained, ragged breathing echoed through the cavern. She could just make out his outline a few feet in front of her. She pursued the sound of Haben's labored breathing for what felt like hours, losing all sense of time and space in the tunnel. She only knew that she would emerge whenever he did. He had to know she was there, but he didn't say a word. Finally, he led her to a reddish pool of light. As they drew closer to it, Seycia realized it was not the light that was red, but the sand directly outside the tunnel.

They emerged onto a vast, crimson expanse of desert. The sun was setting, and the sky was painted with glorious streaks of dusty violet and orange as blue darkness bled across the horizon. She was struck by the color of the rising moon, the same shade of red as the ground beneath her feet.

She looked down at the footprints Haben's feet had made in the sand. Had she seen the tracks anywhere on Earth, she never would have guessed that they had come from a demon's foot. Her footprints, beside his, were identical, if not a bit smaller.

A lone, gnarled tree with faded white bark sprouted from the sand up ahead, a black, blemished chunk of volcanic rock situated right below it. Haben slowed as he neared the parched oasis. He sank down upon the stone, drew his legs beneath his robe, and huddled there. The two of them were the only creatures in the desert, as far as the eye could see. It was a lonely place.

Seycia stood as still as she could, afraid to disturb him. She felt bad for following him. This was a private moment, and she was intruding. She slowly crouched to a sitting position and turned her back to him. She would allow him some peace. She used to ask Miko to do the same for her when the pressure of her fears weighed too heavily upon her. She would ask him to turn his back so she could have a moment to gather herself together. He never complained, and he never turned around until she asked him to.

Miko. She would be trapped here forever. She couldn't protect him anymore. She felt a bleak pang in her chest as she finally accepted it. But there had to be a way to confirm his safety from here, to look in on him. How was Haben able to cross into the mortal world? She thought she might like to see General Simeon as well. She would sacrifice the very tree of her soul in the Forest of Laida for the chance to witness his death someday.

The Forest of Laida. A bolt of realization shot through her, and she sprang to her feet with wide eyes. Haben hadn't mentioned it, but it had to exist—it just had to. It was the most important pillar of her faith. If the Forest of Laida were real, she would find a tree there for each and every soul on Earth. It was where souls replenished themselves between mortal lives. Even if someone cut General Simeon's throat in his sleep, his spirit would just come back for another life someday, a life that would be as foul as the one he was already living. Unless he never came back.

Seycia turned and was startled to find Haben staring directly at her. She wondered how long he had been gazing at the back of her head, waiting for her to face him. He didn't look angry. He just looked tired.

"You know," she began softly, enticing him to listen to her. "You might have been right about the fang. About a curse, or something. It's done things I don't understand. My father told me it was a powerful weapon."

"Hmm," was all Haben said in return.

"I was young when he died. So I never knew."

"Ask the question you want to ask me," he said through clenched teeth.

"How do you get to the Forest of Laida?" she asked, almost dreading the answer.

"You don't," he replied.

"But it exists?" He was silent. "Where is it?"

"What do you want with the Great Forest?"

"I want to help us both." The words tumbled from her lips before she even had time to think it through. She didn't know much about him, but she knew she'd have to appeal to him in some way to get answers. Her plan took shape as she waited for his reply.

Haben scoffed before speaking again. "There is nothing *in* the Great Forest."

"Except for everybody's soul."

He exhaled impatiently as she inched closer to where he sat.

"The rulers of the city I came from are terrible, cruel people."

"I know. I've seen your city."

"Then you've seen General Simeon," she went on. "He killed my parents. He's the reason I'm here, with you. And he's after my brother." Seycia gathered herself before revealing her aim, knowing she would only have Haben's attention for so long. "I want to go to the Forest of Laida, find Simeon's tree, and destroy it."

Haben stared at her for what felt like a lifetime. Then a small, scornful smile crawled across his face. Seycia wasn't sure what to make of it.

"You would destroy someone's soul?" he asked, incredulous.

"Why not? It's a bad soul. It doesn't deserve to come back again."

"You think souls are either good or bad," Haben said. It wasn't a question. Seycia shrugged.

"What about your soul? What do you suppose has become of *your* tree, since Dohv turned you into a demon?"

The question startled him, as if he'd never thought of it before. He replied slowly, "Still there. I think."

"If you show me how to get to the Forest of Laida, if you help me, then I'll find your tree and destroy yours, too."

"I'm already immortal. It doesn't matter if I can't be reincarnated," he argued.

Seycia grew impatient with him. Didn't he see?

"Without a tree, your soul would be homeless, wouldn't it? Your soul would finally die," she explained slowly.

"Then I'd go to limbo."

"Fine, and where is limbo?"

"Not Earth, not Underworld. It's Darkest Death. You cease to be." Seycia watched him carefully as the words stuck in his throat and he exhaled a shaky breath. *You cease to be.*

He shared a look with Seycia, and she knew he finally understood. She would give him his rest—or the closest thing to it.

"If you really wanted to help me, you'd kill me with that thing right now," he muttered, eyes fixed on the fang around her neck.

"I could. But I won't. You can't make me do it, and I need something in return. It's called a favor—not sure if you recall. It's a human thing." She thumbed the fang as she held her gaze on him. "Besides, you owe me. For what you did to me."

He fell silent, and then, to her surprise, said, "That is true."

She studied his face, as though looking for some sign that an apology was coming. But his weary eyes were impossible to read. After a moment, he spoke again. "Dohv doesn't let anyone enter the forest."

"Has anyone ever tried?"

He reflected for a moment. "There was a demon. Lorsa. He told anyone who would listen that he wanted to go visit the tree of his mother's soul. Many, many years ago. He walked straight east, and passed through a canyon there." He pointed toward where the sun's final rays shone. "Nobody's seen him since."

"East?" Seycia repeated. "The sun sets in the west."

"Not here."

Seycia was once again reminded how far from home she really was. She didn't think she'd ever consider the Underworld her home, immortal though she now was. After a moment, she spoke again. "Do you think he found the forest?"

"No. There are traps all over. Dohv can't be everywhere at once, so certain important places signal to him when something's gone wrong. Like you saw on the beach. He has a way of watching us."

"Well, we have something Lorsa didn't have," she said. "We have a weapon."

Haben stared at the daggerlike tooth as it rose and fell with Seycia's steady breath.

"That thing," he explained, "is a Creeback's fang."

"What are Creebacks?"

"Demon killers."

She nodded as she stared at it, finally beginning to grasp the tremendous power her father had passed down to her. "If something goes wrong and we can't find what we're looking for, I'll use this to end your life myself," she said. "But I won't even think about it until I know we've done everything we can to get to the forest."

"I've never gone past the canyon," he admitted, more quietly now. Her face fell, but he quickly continued. "But if you swear you'll keep your promise, that you'll end this for me, then yes. I'll take you there."

"To the Forest of Laida."

"That isn't what we call it here. You should know that, if you want to fit in. It's the Great Forest." Then, he added, "And we'll go there, if we can find it. But I make no promises."

She smiled then, careful to make it quick and modest. She caught him studying her, as though nobody had looked at him that way before.

"Before we go, I'd like to see my brother."

"Your brother?"

"I want to look in on him. Can you show me how?"

He hesitated. "Dohv told you to stay away from the Veil. The passageways are for messengers only."

"What if I just looked, without going all the way in?"

He knit his brow, and Seycia swore she saw his face soften the smallest bit before he said, "Quickly."

He pointed to a shimmering black crater in the sand not far from where they stood. Seycia darted over to the passageway but slowed down before she peered inside, suddenly afraid of what she might see. She glanced at Haben, who gestured for her to step closer.

"Tell it what you wish to see."

She swallowed hard and crouched to the ground. Her own reflection in the Veil stared back at her as she whispered to it, "Khronasa. My brother."

A blinding yellow light took hold of her vision. She felt as though she were being pulled to the core of the earth, that her entire body was being stretched, even though she was standing still. Then an image appeared, wavering like a mirage on a hot summer day. There were the rusty red roofs of her city, guarded by green hilltops that had started to fade to brown in the recent drought. There was her home.

As she moved her eyes, the image moved with her. She scanned the streets, and she was drawn like a magnet to one particular neighborhood at the foot of the hill, where a crooked blue house stood. Was Miko inside, still alive? She prayed that he was. All she needed was one small glimpse of him to fan the flames inside of her. Then, she'd be ready to go.

CHAPTER NINE

MIKO HEARD THE motorcade just before sunrise. He had slept all day and through the night on a makeshift bed on the second floor of Belicia and Ezara's house, unaware of how exhausted he'd been. Hours later, an unusual noise drifted in from the open window and woke him—a deep growl, but not from an animal. He crept toward the window and surveyed the scene below.

A sleek black vehicle, one of the Coalition's putrid-smelling grease-powered machines, rolled along the street like a stalking reaper in the night, with two tiny flags mounted above its headlights. The driver turned the corner, and the vehicle disappeared. Seconds later, three identical vehicles followed. Miko leaped to his feet and clambered out the window, hoisting himself onto the dirty terra-cotta shingles just above his head. He would get a better view from the roof.

Now settled atop the house, he watched the motorcade snake around the block, crawling through Khronasa's sleeping streets. He couldn't see inside the windows. They were tinted a dull, hazy black.

He noticed he was not alone in his sudden wakefulness. Dozens of other Khronasans materialized from their houses to inspect the noisy disturbance.

The dark parade slowed near the central plaza, right by the pit still filled with dirty, tepid water. Miko watched as a group of about twenty sleepy townspeople anxiously moved toward the spot. The cars stopped. Miko held his breath.

The doors of the first vehicle opened, and two tall, hulking men with enormous machine guns emerged from either side.

Then a third man stepped out from the back seat. He had a slight build but boasted broad shoulders and was wearing a long black overcoat. It was hard to make out his face, but Miko noted his neat, white-blond hair that shone in the early sunlight and he could tell he wasn't wearing glasses or goggles. *Could it be?* Was this the man he'd seen in the book?

The spectators in the square immediately kneeled when they saw him. Who in the world was he? Nobody kneeled for General Simeon that way.

Every person in the crowd showed their respect, save for one man who had a long gray beard and was holding a dog's leash. The dog growled and fidgeted, and the elderly man seemed more concerned with calming his pet than honoring this revered guest.

All had taken notice.

The fair-haired Coalition man stepped closer to the pair of them. He crossed his arms but said nothing. The old man smacked his dog and threw himself to his knees, but it was too late. The offense had already been committed.

One of the bodyguards raised his machine gun from his shoulder, and Miko fought the urge to shield his eyes, knowing what was coming.

A barrage of machine-gun fire blasted across the vacant silence, cracking like a thousand whips. If anyone nearby had still been asleep, they were certainly awake now.

The old man crumpled to the ground, dead, and the dog collapsed beside him into a puddle of its own blood. Miko tasted bile in his throat, frozen to the spot as if he'd been standing right beside them.

He focused his gaze on the blond Coalition official. He thought of the photo in the book again, of the preserved head mounted atop the mantel and the serene face of the man seated beneath it. The resemblance, even from a distance, was startling.

"Did you see it?" The urgent whisper nearly made Miko lose his footing on the roof.

He peered down at the window and spotted the top of Belicia's white hair as she craned her neck to look up at him.

"I saw it," he replied. "I'm coming down now."

Belicia stepped away from the window to make room for him to climb back inside. His palms were sweaty as he clung to the shutters, swung his legs back over the edge, and slumped down onto the bed. Belicia remained at the window, surveying the street below.

"I heard gunshots," she said.

"They shot a man and his dog."

"*Who* shot a man and his dog?"

"I don't know. There were two shooters. They were driving, and they were protecting this third man. A whole lot of people ran out of their houses to follow the cars, and one of the people didn't kneel when the blond man came out so they shot him—and his dog," he explained flatly.

"What did the blond man look like?"

"I don't know. Blond. He didn't wear glasses."

Miko's mind raced as he grew cold all over and pulled his knees to his chest, unable to wipe clean the image he'd seen. Silence fell between the two of them as he released a shaky exhale.

"Is there anything I can get for you? Breakfast, maybe?" Belicia asked after a moment. She seemed eager to change the subject.

"If you have a knife and some old wood, I'll take that," he replied, happy to have something else to talk about. "Not to eat. I need to make more of my darts."

"Strychnos darts?" she asked with a sly grin.

"How'd you know?"

"I used to make them when I was younger. My parents weren't too fond of them because our dogs would get into the poison. But they were the first weapon I ever made. I could certainly get you some supplies."

"What other weapons did you make?" Miko asked. A glimmer appeared in her cloudy eye.

"My father was a blacksmith, and he taught me to make iron spears. When I was fifteen, he and I made a crossbow together. I'll admit most of the craftsmanship was thanks to him, but I made good use of it," she reminisced with a faraway smile.

"I wish I knew a blacksmith who'd teach me to make things like that. Seycia and I live up on the hill and don't really talk to other people." He paused, then corrected himself with a frown. "*Lived* in on the hill. We don't anymore. I mean, I don't."

"That's all right. No need to rush into past tenses," she said.

"What was Khronasa like back then?" Miko asked after a moment.

"I think it was . . . exciting," she answered. "We built the temple. We started constructing the city, the marketplace. People painted murals; they made instruments and played music. I think, after the War of the Veil ended, people were finally just happy to be alive again."

"You survived the war?" Miko was all the more intrigued now.

"Oh, no, I wasn't even born yet. My father was there for the end. But he spoke very little about it."

"How long did it last?"

"According to my father, the first fires of the war were set over two hundred years ago. After that, the bombs just kept falling and the cities kept decaying till nobody could keep score anymore," she said.

Miko couldn't wrap his head around such an infinite battlefield. "Why didn't they just stop when they saw they'd destroyed everything?"

"I wish I knew. I suppose it had been a long time coming."

"Because people didn't want to be wrong about what happens to us after we die," he said steadily, as if he wanted her to know that he, a mature thinker who was almost twelve summers old, understood their complex history.

"I suppose it all started that way. But the world got a taste for blood." She shrugged with a cynical sigh. "Luckily, by the time you were born, we had long since begun to rebuild. We had our faith. We had a little piece of earth to call our own. With each passing generation, the echoes of war grew more and more distant."

"Until now," Miko said with a grimace.

A moment passed before Belicia leaned in and whispered, "Why don't you go have a look under your bed?"

Miko shot her a questioning look.

"Go on," she said. "There's something I want you to see."

Miko lowered himself to his knees and peered beneath the wobbly frame of the bed. He caught sight of a small wooden crate and pulled it out. A cloud of dust floated into the air as he presented it to Belicia. He fought back a sneeze.

"Open it."

He opened the box and inhaled sharply as he looked inside. He glanced over at Belicia as though asking her permission to lift the item out. She gave him a gentle nod. He reached inside and produced a heavy, black iron crossbow, complete with a pouch of deathly sharp arrows.

"Is this the one you and your father made?" he asked in wonder, holding it up to the light.

"It is," she replied, gazing at the weapon, wistful. "Ezara doesn't know we still have this. We were supposed to have surrendered all weapons years ago, but I couldn't let it go."

"It's . . . heavy." Miko loaded an arrow into the bow and cradled it in his arms.

"There's one more thing." Belicia pointed to the box.

Miko carefully placed the crossbow onto the bed and reached back into the box. His fingers touched something soft and velvety—a drawstring bag made of deerskin. He untied it and reached a hand inside. His fingers brushed something cold, something made of metal. He knew what it was; he didn't even have to look. His breath caught as he slowly pulled the revolver from the pouch.

"You . . . you can't have . . ." he stammered. "Nobody has these."

"So they say. But this old loon still has a few tricks up her sleeve," she said, quite pleased with herself.

"Have you ever used it?" Miko's voice faltered as he tried to mask his nervous excitement.

"No. My brother found it years ago in the woods. It had probably been dropped by a Coalition soldier during the occupation. Then he passed it on to me when he died. I was the only one who knew he had it. And now you're the only one who knows I have it."

"Ezara doesn't know?"

"Ezara . . . Well, you've seen how Ezara is," she said. "My son wants to lie low. That's his way of coping. I wouldn't want to impose *my* way."

"What's your way?"

"I'm not afraid to think that one day we may need that gun."

"I think that's what I think too," Miko said after a moment and inched closer to her. Then, he added, "I know there are other people who want to fight. I need to find the girl who freed me. Do you know her?"

"Minari," was all Belicia said.

"Minari? That's her name? Where is she?"

Belicia was silent. Miko dared to ask, "Is she still alive?"

"I'll tell you everything as soon as I'm able to. I promise."

He stared hard into her dark eyes, obscured by hazy clouds of age. He longed to know everything she knew.

"For a long time, I've worried about the children in Khronasa," she went on, returning his intense gaze. "I've wondered, because you'd never seen a better world, if you'd know how to create one. But if there are more like you, perhaps we will someday."

"Gather 'round, gather 'round everyone," General Simeon barked, storming across the gilded foyer of his mansion. "Hurry up."

His staff poured in from the labyrinth of hallways and staircases that branched off from the palatial, open space. Three cooks from the kitchen shuffled across the sparkling quartz tile, wearing grease-stained aprons. They tittered anxiously, on edge—because Simeon was, too.

Once he had everyone's attention, he stood on the bottom stair and cleared his throat. He favored the group standing to his left as he spoke, as if he could somehow hide the hideous stitches on the right side of his face.

"I've just received word that His Imperial Majesty Emperor Caius has arrived in our fair city, and that he will be making a visit here momentarily."

His staff exploded with nervous whispers. He immediately shushed them. "Listen to me, and listen well. I hired you because I believed you were all discreet. Loyal. Today, you must prove that to me." He bore his gaze into the faces of his servants, making sure he had their full attention. "The way we do things in Khronasa is different than the other Coalition territories. Specifically, I am referring to our sacrifices. Emperor Caius is not aware of our traditions here. And I intend to keep it that way. If anyone so much as breathes a word about it to the Emperor or his staff, your family will be hanging from the trees by nightfall and you'll be next in line for the pit."

Chilling silence fell across the foyer. A few servants nodded. Two of the maids clutched each other's hands.

One of the cooks removed his hair net and kneeled in front of Simeon. "Our fate in his hands," he whispered. Simeon saluted him and bade him rise.

"Excellency?" a voice piped from the back of the room. Simeon locked eyes with his valet, a stout young man whose hair had started thinning prematurely. "Forgive me, but do you know *why* the emperor is visiting our city today? It just seems sudden."

Simeon's gaze darkened. Of course, he'd been wondering the same thing. He had as much information as the rest of them. But he couldn't allow his underlings to sow seeds of doubt. Not when the emperor was about to arrive.

"Of course *I* know. But I'm the only one who needs to," he replied with a scowl, then crossed the foyer to the front door. "Line up," he shouted to his staff. "We'd best be outside to greet him."

Simeon led the group out to the front courtyard through a pair of bulletproof glass doors as a motorcade of sleek black cars approached the main gate. His staff formed a semicircle in the driveway, shoulder to shoulder, and donned their protective eyewear in the sun. Simeon stood between two of his bodyguards and clenched his hands behind his back to keep himself steady. Everything had happened so quickly. He felt scattered, unprepared. Were there any signs of his betrayal around the house? After all, he was guilty of more than just hosting sacrifices. *No,* he assured himself. *Everything is in the shrine. The shrine is locked. And nobody enters the shrine.* Still, he couldn't help but curse himself for the risks he'd taken over the years. He never thought the emperor would come to his home. He had only ever seen him once, at his military orientation nearly ten years ago.

The motorcade pulled up the driveway, single file, but one car, all the way at the end of the line, drove toward a dirt pathway that led to the mansion's back entryway. Simeon noted this curiosity but said nothing. He kept his gaze fixed straight ahead as the driver of the first vehicle opened the door and flashed a salute. Simeon and his staff returned the gesture.

"Our fate in his hands," the driver shouted.

"Our fate in his hands," Simeon and his household echoed.

The driver opened the back door of the car, and Emperor Caius stepped out onto the pavement. His presence was steady in an unsettling way, like a stealthy animal that could pounce at any moment. Simeon gazed at him, fascinated. He had not seen him for nearly a decade, but he hadn't changed a bit. He'd barely aged. The sheen of his platinum-blond hair matched the sparkle of his impeccably polished black boots. Flanked by two bodyguards twice his size, he made his way toward Simeon.

"It is our honor to welcome you to Khronasa, Your Imperial Majesty." Simeon bowed his head, staring at Caius's priceless boots through his dark, tinted glasses before allowing himself eye contact.

"And it is a privilege to visit your city," Caius replied. His voice was smooth and soft, as though forcing everyone to listen closely.

Simeon lifted his head with a confident smile as he met the emperor's sharp blue eyes. "Please, come inside."

"Excellent. We have much to discuss." Caius glanced at Simeon's stitched-up face.

Simeon felt his eyes on him. His skin grew hot. But Caius made no mention of it.

Two servants opened the huge glass doors with a heavy creak and Emperor Caius followed Simeon into the house. "Perhaps you'd like to take breakfast in the solarium? There's a lovely view of the ocean."

"That sounds like a good place to start," Emperor Caius replied as Simeon led him up the stairs and down another hallway.

Then something strange happened. Caius nodded to his security detail, and Simeon watched with curiosity as Caius's bodyguards led Simeon's guards in the opposite direction—away from the solarium. Only one of Caius's security guards remained, a stoic, older gentleman with salt-and-pepper hair. Instead of a machine gun, he carried a small pistol in a holster on his belt.

"I'll see you later, outside," Caius whispered. Then he, too, spun around in the other direction, following his security detail, leaving Simeon alone with the salt-and-pepper bodyguard.

"E-excuse me? Your Imperial Majesty?" What was the meaning of this?

But Caius did not look back, nor did he say another word. After an uneasy moment, the salt-and-pepper guard faced Simeon and said, "The solarium, then?"

Simeon led the stranger around the corner and through the entrance to an enclosed, sun-drenched patio, overlooking the seashore.

Inside the room sat a shriveled, elderly gentleman in a silver wheelchair. Simeon's breath caught as he opened the door and approached. The strange, silent bodyguard by his side finally spoke: "General Simeon, His Imperial Majesty Emperor Caius."

"But I thought I just met the—"

"No, sir. *This* is the emperor."

Simeon gaped at the slight, bald man perched in the wheelchair, freckled with brown flecks of age, like an ancient moon covered in craters. He wore a pair of gold-rimmed spectacles that were twice as thick as his own. It was obvious why he'd been posing behind a decoy all these years, but Simeon couldn't help how personally he took the deception.

"I apologize. I know this must be a shock," the real Emperor Caius croaked, struggling to breathe as he chuckled. "I'm afraid I'm no longer the portrait of strength everyone's come to expect, so we put a different one on display. I'm sorry I haven't introduced myself before today."

Simeon sized up the salt-and-pepper-haired bodyguard, still standing close by.

"Ah, don't mind Emil. We're old, old friends," Caius said.

Simeon replied with a distant nod. He watched as Caius wheeled himself toward the glass-paneled wall that faced the ocean. He stared out at the water for a moment, but said nothing. Simeon swallowed hard in the silence that followed.

"I received word yesterday that there was an attack on your security force. A very *public* attack."

Simeon's mind raced as he wrung his sweaty hands. Did the emperor know why there had been a crowd gathered that night? Had he come because he already knew Simeon was practicing the Offenses?

"There was. An attack. But only one of my men was killed. The rest are recovering and should be back to work soon," Simeon said, maybe a little too brightly.

"And what of this injury to your face?" Emperor Caius pointed right at it. Simeon's cheeks burned, and the wound burned, too. "Who did this to you?"

"It's . . . quite a long story, sir." Simeon stared at his feet. "A thief broke into my chambers."

A long moment passed. Caius wheeled himself away from the glass, deep in thought, before speaking again. "You're struggling to keep this territory in line."

"I am not, Your Imperial Majesty. I'm perfectly—"

"You're losing your grip on these people. You've had a sterling reputation in this region for years. I don't know what's changed, but I see right through your blatant half-truths about what happened here," the emperor hissed. "I don't suppose you heard about Ellita?"

"Ellita, sir?" Simeon asked, of the territory south of his. "Did something happen there?"

Caius wheeled himself back toward Simeon. "The Ellitans were practicing the Offenses, and their general went soft on punishment. He had them pay *fines*. Can you imagine? He let them gather together and worship the old gods whenever they pleased, as long as they kept it behind closed doors. He was relieved of his duties . . . when we executed him at parliament."

"I-I see," was all Simeon could say.

"The Coalition must stand against religious fanaticism as one. If one of us softens, if one of us is *hiding something*, we all bear the consequences," Caius continued. "Which is why I've come here: to make an inspection."

"O-of course, sir. I can take you anywhere you'd like in our city—"

"I am here to inspect *you*, General Simeon."

Simeon's blood ran cold as Caius gazed, unblinking, at his wound.

"I'm going to ask you, one more time, exactly what happened to your men, and to your face."

"I didn't see who shot down my men," Simeon began, keeping his voice as even as possible. "I don't know why we were targeted in that moment. And I don't know why I was attacked in my chambers. Perhaps there are religious fanatics who have recently relocated here from Ellita. That seems like a logical explanation, given the timing. Sir."

"That's the answer you want to give me?" Caius pursed his dry lips, staring Simeon down. Simeon shrugged, feeling two inches tall.

"It's the only answer I have."

"Very well," the emperor muttered, gesturing to his bodyguard at the door. "Pity our conversation was so short. If we need to have another, I assure you it will end quite differently. Best of luck to you, general."

Emil opened the door and cut Simeon a glance, indicating that he was to exit first. Simeon bowed low to the emperor, and he realized his knees were shaking. "My fate is in your hands," he whispered, then swept out of the room. Emil shut the door behind him, waiting till everyone had cleared so His Imperial Majesty could exit unseen. Simeon exhaled as though he'd been holding his breath throughout the entire exchange.

Out in the hallway, he encountered the emperor's handsome young decoy, coming down the stairs behind a sweet-faced servant girl. Simeon saluted the "emperor" as they made their way back to the foyer together.

"Leaving so soon?" General Simeon asked the decoy, insinuating his meeting with the real emperor had come to an end.

"We have a number of other cities on our schedule this week. I'm afraid we must be strict about time," the decoy easily lied. "But it's been a pleasure touring your home."

As they crossed the entryway, General Simeon froze, as though he'd just been struck by a bullet. His gaze riveted to an ornate table by the front window, where a vase of red flowers usually sat. In its place was a heavy granite statue of Dohv, glittering in the sunlight—one of the relics he himself had stolen from the temple ruins. He went numb with horror. Someone had *put it there*, hoping the emperor would see it. Someone had been in his shrine. His heart hammered in his chest, praying the decoy wouldn't notice the statue as they strolled past. But he knew it was no use. It was on full display, impossible to ignore.

The decoy met Simeon's eye, and Simeon crumbled beneath his knowing gaze. *What to do, what to do?* And yet, just as he had when he noticed his injury, the handsome decoy flashed him a polite smile and said nothing. Simeon's head spun as he bowed to the decoy and held the front door open for him.

"My fate is in your hands," Simeon said to him, slowly, meant as more than a farewell.

The decoy nodded and joined his security team outside. The sound of the door shutting behind him sent a shudder through Simeon's paralyzed body.

As soon as the coast was clear and he was alone in the foyer, Simeon snagged the statue and bolted up the stairs, two at a time, cradling the heavy stone underneath his arm.

He ducked around a corner, waiting for two maids to pass, then made a break for his study at the end of the corridor.

He caught his breath as he entered the room, dreading what, or whom, he might find inside. He was alone, but there was a gaping hole in the door to his closet, his shrine, as though it had been hacked apart by an ax. He wailed, his suspicions confirmed, and dropped the statue to the floor. He paced in a circle, heart in his throat, hot with rage. He peered down at the bloodstains on his priceless carpet from the night Seycia had attacked him. Someone had scrubbed them down to a pale pinkish-brown, but still his eye was drawn to them.

How had all of this happened? Had he not prayed to Dohv every night for the past seven years, asking for protection? Had Dohv not been listening? For the first time, he feared he could not serve two masters at once.

He examined the broken pieces of his door and pulled a breath. Who on his staff had betrayed him? Emperor Caius was right—he *was* losing his grip on his people. Something was giving them strength. *Hope.* He needed to hunt that hope, wherever it dared to grow, and weed it out.

There was a knock at his door, followed by the voice of one of his security guards. "Excellency? Are you all right in there?" He must have heard him cry out. Simeon steeled himself and marched out into the hallway, careful to close the study door behind him.

"Gil," he addressed the guard. "Please gather the members of my household and put a bullet through the back of each head."

Gil blinked, unsure whether he'd heard him correctly. Simeon suddenly wondered whether he could even trust his personal security detail. He eyed Gil's rifle, then stared into the man's stony, unsmiling face. If Gil had wanted to destroy him, he could have done it a long time ago. This crime had been committed by someone weaker. A coward.

"Everybody, sir?" Gil asked after a tense moment. "My squadron as well?"

"I'll leave them to you. If you suspect anyone's loyalty, if you smell cowardice . . ."

"Y-yes, Excellency. Our fate in his hands," Gil replied in a hoarse voice, and spun back down the hall.

Simeon returned to his study and took a seat by the window, still broken from the night of the attack and shoddily repaired with a plank of wood. He settled in, trembling with fury, and waited for the sound of gunfire down below.

Only bold, swift choices would save him now. The people could not doubt his strength again. He would have to do far better than his last attempt at the sacrifice.

Next time, nobody would escape.

CHAPTER TEN

IT WAS NIGHT now. A dark blue embrace enveloped the Underworld, and the pale red moon hung low in the sky. The sand below Haben's feet appeared almost crystalline in the darkness. Nighttime brought about a multitude of new colors he rarely ever saw. He preferred to spend his nights inside the cave network. Though he never slept, the hibernation was a human comfort he still held on to.

Seycia hadn't wanted to waste any time. She had been completely silent since pulling her eyes from the passageway hours ago. The only thing she said to him was, "We need to be going now."

So they walked. He figured they would reach the canyon by dawn. She had been so quiet the entire time. He thought he might say something to her but couldn't think of anything. He couldn't remember the last time he had interacted with another demon like this. He almost felt like a man again, wondering what he should say to the silent girl beside him.

Finally, she spoke. "My brother is alive."

"Oh. That's good, then," Haben replied. It was probably what he ought to say.

"But the emperor is in Khronasa. I saw him driving in."

Haben paused before realizing he was supposed to ask her further questions. "And . . . what does that mean?"

"He's never come to Khronasa before. I don't know what it means, but I don't like it."

"Oh. I'm sorry for that," Haben said.

Seycia gave him a sideways glance. She seemed puzzled by his flat, polite responses. But was this not what he was supposed to say?

"We'll need to destroy two trees instead of just one, once we get to the forest. Emperor Caius could just replace Simeon if he dies. But without Emperor Caius, the whole Coalition will collapse. Khronasa will be free. So we'll need to find Simeon's tree and the emperor's—"

"And mine. Three trees."

"Of course. Yes, three trees."

After a moment, he said, "You make it sound easy."

"I didn't say that."

"You made it sound that way. 'Khronasa will be free.' Just like that." A quiet hiatus fell between them before he continued, "This thing you're trying to do, it's never been done before. By anyone."

"It's the only thing I *can* do."

He didn't like the sharp tone of her voice. He wasn't even sure what he was trying to tell her, but whatever it was, she didn't want to hear it. She was plenty brave enough. Maybe a little bit too brave.

"I should tell you . . . about Antenor," he said in a low voice. There. *That* was what he wanted to tell her.

"The place where the traitors go?"

He nodded in the darkness, clenching his fists. The mere mention of the place made his heart stammer.

"That's why you don't want to go to the forest? Because you're afraid of Antenor?" she asked him.

"And you should be too," he hissed. "What you saw in Dohv's palace? That was nothing. Nothing compared to what's in Antenor."

"I'd rather not know about it," she said.

"But—"

"If you don't want to go any farther, just point me in the direction of the canyon, and I'll take it from here."

He gritted his teeth, exasperated. "I just want you to know what could happen. If Dohv finds out what we're doing. I told you, he has a way of watching us. You never know what he's seen until it's too late."

Seycia spun to face him, face drawn, arms crossed. "You think I'm in over my head. But you're not from where I'm from and you don't know what I've been up against long before we ever met. Telling me about the consequences won't stop me. So save your breath."

He choked on the words he wanted to say next. He couldn't imagine her, small as she was, being broken and tortured and pushed past the breaking point of her body.

"I just don't want you to . . . to—"

"To what? Get captured? Tortured? If I can't escape it, then I don't want to know."

Frustrated, he turned from her. It was no use trying to protect her, if that was even what he'd been trying to do. She *was* in over her head, and he was the one stupid enough to follow her. After all, Dohv had taken regenesis away from him: he could no longer self-heal. Why was he helping her? She'd lead him straight to the thing he feared the most. He stopped in his tracks and whirled around in the other direction, heading back the way they came, back to the familiarity of his misery. At least it wasn't Antenor.

"Fine, go back," she snapped. "Don't forget—I'm the only one who can kill you."

It pained him to ignore her, but he walked on. He was safe now, back in the comfortable vacuum of silence. He heard nothing but his own footsteps. He wondered for a moment if he'd worry about her tomorrow, when she reached the canyon. Or the day after that, if she managed to find answers there and continued toward the forest. He decided he wouldn't worry. Why would he? He'd known her a day. What was a day compared to the years he'd spent worrying only about himself?

More footsteps, more silence. He cleared his throat, as though he were about to say something. He had nothing to say and there was nobody to say it to, but for some reason he wanted to speak. He'd only spoken every half century or so since his arrival, but after a whole day of using speech, he'd gotten used to it again. Once she was gone, who was he supposed to talk to? The other demons, decrepit and hateful, as beaten down as he was? He breathed a conflicted sigh. The loneliness was heavy and sudden.

He hadn't even realized that he'd walked in a circle and was heading back toward the canyon. She hadn't gone far. He picked up his pace and within a few moments he was right behind her again.

They acknowledged one another but said nothing as he lagged behind a few steps, allowing her to take the lead. He watched the way she swung her arms at her sides as she walked, with determination, as though she held a sword in each hand. She had something real and pure to fight for. There was someone left in the mortal world for whom she would risk everything. He wondered what that was like. He feared he didn't have the same strength she did.

"I think I'll need to rest once we get to the canyon," she finally said. "Only for a short while. But I haven't slept in two days."

"You're tired?" he asked, confused.

"I told you. I haven't slept in two days."

"We don't sleep."

"But don't you ever get tired?"

"Tired enough to sit down after walking a long way, maybe. But not to sleep."

Seycia absorbed this and frowned. "Do you think I look *wrong*, like that boy Zane said?"

"Zane was just trying to cause trouble."

"But he's right, isn't he? I'm different." She paused and pursed her lips. "I still don't understand how I got here in the first place. You know—alive. I was sure I felt my heart stop completely. There was so much darkness. But maybe . . . Right as I crossed over, my heart started beating again. Has that ever happened before, to anyone else?"

He shook his head. What was she getting at?

"And you've never transformed anyone before, have you?"

He was silent.

"So you haven't."

"I did everything I was supposed to do," he said. "If I hadn't, you'd be dead or blind or deformed or who knows what else."

"Then what's wrong with me?"

"Nothing. You're a demon. The way you look doesn't matter."

"You just don't want to admit you might have made a mistake," she said.

"I don't have the answers you're looking for, so stop asking," he snapped back. "Nothing about you makes sense, but here you are. If you want an explanation, it's probably got something to do with however you got that Creeback's tooth."

"I told you, my father gave it to me."

"After he put some sort of curse on it."

"For the last time, I don't know anything about that."

"Well, I know even less than you do."

Exasperated silence fell between them, but both stayed the course.

"You told Dohv you're always starving," she said, gently changing the subject. "Is that true? Are you starving right now?"

"Right now, it's bearable. Other times, it's not."

"And what would happen to you in Antenor? Would your punishment worsen?"

"If I went to Antenor, I'd *beg* to be starving."

After a tense pause, Seycia asked, "What happens there?"

"I've never seen it. But all the demons know." He shivered before he continued, "There's a frozen lake, and underneath the ice are all the demons who've betrayed Dohv. First, he breaks every bone in your body and chains you into place. Then he lowers you into the lake, the ice freezes around you, and that's where you stay."

Seycia nodded, swallowing hard. He watched as she chewed the corner of her lip, forced into silence.

A cool breeze whipped across the desert and ruffled Seycia's tangle of black hair in all directions. She reached behind her and tied her hair into a knot as she walked. Two of her fingers became twisted in the knot, and she grunted as she tried to tug them free. For some reason, this made him want to laugh, but he wasn't sure he still knew how.

A few moments before dawn, Seycia felt the soft sand beneath her feet give way to patches of pebbles. Up ahead lay an expanse of flat white stone that seemed to lead straight to the edge of a cliff.

"Is that the canyon?" she asked Haben.

He slowed his pace and nodded.

"Are there any other demons here? Are we alone?"

"They're probably all back in the cave network. This is territory we don't usually go to."

They approached the precipice of the gorge. The journey down to the bottom of the canyon seemed easy enough, with plenty of rocks for leverage. It was like a deep, empty lake. But it was quiet. Too quiet.

"So why did Lorsa come to the canyon? Why was this his first step?"

"He said something about a passage on the other side that would lead to the forest, but that's all I ever heard," he answered. "The only thing I know for sure is that he never came back."

A sudden *ca-caw!* pierced the early morning sky. Seycia scanned the clouds. She caught sight of a strange bald bird drifting through the fog, sailing on huge, fleshy wings.

"What is that?" Seycia marveled at the odd, winged creature.

"It's been following me. Since yesterday. I don't know why. I don't like it."

"Does it belong to Dohv?"

"It must," he breathed, then glanced down to the bottom of the gorge. "We can't go down there. Not while it's still watching us—"

"Wait . . ." Seycia pointed to the sky.

The creature made a wide turn across the horizon. It flew into the distance, back the way it came, the heavy flap of its wings inaudible now. Soon, the only trace of it was a final, muted *ca-caw!*

"Maybe it wasn't looking for us after all," Seycia said.

"It's new. I don't trust new things."

A pause fell between them as they weighed their next move. "We have two choices," he went on. "We turn around, or we start climbing down right now before that thing comes back."

"Well then," she said as she swung her legs over the ledge. "Are you coming?"

He shuffled toward the ledge, then paused to glance over at her. "I can't heal anymore," he reminded her in a hoarse voice. "I'll have to go slow."

She nodded, and they made their way down the rocky white wall of the canyon. She went ahead of him, carefully testing the stability of each foothold before beckoning him to follow. As they approached the bottom, Seycia scanned the area below for any signs of life. All was still.

She hopped down from the lowest rock and hit the sandy ground with a gentle thud. Haben followed seconds later with equal silence. Seycia poised the fang between her fingers in that old, comfortable clawlike position. No matter where she was, holding it made her feel brave.

The canyon floor was a long stretch of pale white pebbles. They would be able to cross it within an hour or so. But why was this canyon even significant? Where was this passage to the forest that Lorsa had mentioned? Haben had no idea what the next step was.

He nudged her, interrupting her thoughts. He pointed at a rock ledge not far in the distance. Something, *someone* was dangling off the cliff, bound together by some sort of black rope. The unfortunate, squirming creature reminded Seycia of a fly caught in a spider's web.

"Lorsa," Haben murmured. "He's still down here."

Seycia looked at the pathetic, twitching figure again. Patches of bloated white flesh bulged through the thick cords that bound him. It was hard to tell that it was a demon, let alone *which* demon.

"We'll talk to him," she resolved.

But before she could take another step, a high-pitched, ragged howl echoed across the canyon. The two of them spun around in all directions but couldn't find the source of the awful sound. Seconds later, they heard it again, only louder.

"Whatever it is, don't let it see you. You have the weapon," Haben whispered to her.

"Right," she replied. "If you're able to distract it, then I can—"

She swallowed her words as the two of them spotted the disfigured shadow that had just come hobbling into the sunlight. Seycia couldn't help but gasp as the creature approached. It was some sort of unholy union of man and insect, standing erect on two legs, staggering along thanks to its enormous hunched back. It was covered in scales and bleeding sores and its eyes were two huge, mirrorlike orbs. Seycia could see her own reflection in them, even at a distance.

"Then *maybe* . . . I can kill it." Seycia nervously finished her thought.

"We should find out if it's useful first," Haben hissed, as the creature took another jerky, menacing step toward them.

It opened its mouth and snarled, revealing rows of jagged brown teeth that looked like sharp splinters of petrified wood. As it barreled toward them, preparing to attack, Seycia shouted at Haben, "Not useful! Distract it and wait for me!"

"To do what?"

But she didn't answer. She scampered onto the rock face and hid beneath a sloping, craggy stone. Haben made sure she was fully concealed, then picked up a rock and threw it across the canyon. It struck the monster in the shin as it approached. It cried, flung itself to the ground, and raced forward on all four legs, doubling its speed. Haben veered to the side, steering the beast from the place Seycia was hiding.

She gestured at him to climb up. As the repulsive insect closed in on him, he jumped onto the rock face. The monster followed.

Haben climbed farther and shot Seycia a furious glare.

"Not yet," she mouthed. She was well aware of his fear. She knew he couldn't heal anymore. But she also knew if she didn't strike at just the right moment, they'd both end up like Lorsa, dangling off the cliff.

Haben's fingers were slipping from the rock he clung to, and he looked at Seycia, nearly at eye level now. "Come on," he seethed at her through clenched teeth as the beast growled behind him.

Finally, she yanked a rock free from beneath her and tossed it over Haben's shoulder. It landed with a loud thud behind the monster, who swung around in a frenzy, looking for the source of the sound. Seycia drew a sharp breath and leaped onto the creature's hunched back. It was every bit as foul as she thought it would be—slimy, scaly, and stinking of rotting flesh. But she held on tight; she'd show Dohv what a "fragile soul" looked like.

Before the beast could register what was happening, Seycia tore the fang from her breast and plunged it deep into one of its eyes. The creature released an earsplitting scream as an inky, dark red liquid gushed from its eye socket. It fell from the rock face with Seycia still clinging to its back.

As they hit the ground, Seycia slashed its throat with the fang in one swift movement. Its blood drained across the crystalline floor of the canyon as it twitched and moaned in gut-wrenching agony. Haben hopped down from the ledge and stood beside Seycia. As she watched the creature draw its last breath, she realized her arms were covered with its blood.

She bent over to wipe them clean on her skirt but was horrified when the blood would not come off. Her arms were permanently stained. She frantically rubbed them against a nearby stone and cast Haben a stricken look.

"No. Oh no . . ." She stared at her arms, spattered with dark red spots. "If Dohv ever sees me again, he'll know I killed it. He'll know it was me."

"I warned you, he has his ways of knowing," Haben replied flatly. They stared at each other for a long moment. "That is," he continued, "if he *does* ever see you again. Maybe he won't."

She shook her head in despair.

Haben made a cautious move in her direction. "We'll find something to cover it up," he said. "That's the easy part. Then we can get on with it and destroy those trees. What did you say their names were? General Simeon? And your emperor?"

"Emperor Caius," she muttered, still clawing at her stained skin.

"Right—just think of them and what you're here to do," he went on. She stared at him in surprise. Was this encouragement? It seemed like it.

"Now, let's ask Lorsa where that passage is. We might not have much time," he said.

"Fine. Let's talk to Lorsa," she agreed after a moment.

Haben led the way back up the rock face streaked with the monster's blood, toward the place where Lorsa's body hung. They crept around the stains and pulled themselves onto a higher ledge. Seycia couldn't help but notice how easily Haben climbed—his sudden lack of physical pain. It was the first time since their meeting that he wasn't hunched over and clutching his chest.

As they drew closer, Seycia could see that the black cord binding Lorsa was actually a horrendous daisy chain of scarab beetles, linking their legs together. He hung upside down by his feet as they gnawed at him and clung to his skin.

"Are you the demon they call Lorsa?" Seycia shouted to the twitching body.

"*Unnhharghh*," the demon cried.

"He can't speak," Haben whispered. "We need to cut him down."

"Only if he has answers. Otherwise he's just another pair of eyes that saw us here," Seycia argued, then she called out to the demon. "We're sorry you're hurting. We can set you free, if you can tell us how you get to the Great Forest."

A few seconds elapsed, and the squirming body held perfectly still. Lorsa made a labored grunting noise as though he was trying to clear his throat. Finally, he uttered, "B-Blue . . . Blue Mountain. S-side with no shadows."

Seycia's heart leaped. "And then what?"

He groaned and thrashed again.

"Let's cut him loose now," Haben said. But Seycia did not reply. She was fixated on a small cavern not far from the spot they were perched, eyes narrowed.

"Do you hear that?" She pointed at the hole in the rock.

An unnerving chattering sound emanated from the cavern, growing louder and louder with each passing second. Then, a shiny black ooze seeped from the hole—no, not ooze. It wasn't liquid, she realized. It was a million tiny scarab beetles, fused together in one ghastly pack.

"Go. Find us a place to hide. I know what to do," she hissed at Haben.

He hopped off the ledge. "What . . . ?"

"You'll see." She took a running leap and sprang off the cliff. She careened onto Lorsa's dangling body and clung to it with all her strength, then whipped the fang off her neck. The scarabs swarmed over her body, biting and chewing as she carved away at Lorsa's bindings. The insects were swarming downward too, right toward Haben. He bolted across the gorge, desperately searching for another place to hide. They were running out of options . . .

Up on the cliff, Seycia gave one last, powerful slice with the fang and felt the chain of scarabs coming loose. She held her breath—the stink of them was unbearable. She and Lorsa tumbled to the canyon floor below as the ropes gave way. She braced herself for the impact and felt her bones twist back into place seconds after she hit the ground. She scrambled to her feet, woozy. It would be a while before she was used to that.

Lorsa wailed and scratched at his puckered, blistered skin. Seycia looked out at the sea of scarabs surrounding them. If her last-minute plan was successful, she would know it any second now.

"Seycia," Haben called out from the opposite cliffside. He stood at the entrance to a small cave. The beetles swarmed closer and closer by the second. If there was any hope of escaping, she needed to join him, now.

All of a sudden, the entire drove of scarabs changed course. They turned from Haben, targeting Lorsa, still on the ground. Her plan was working—they'd heard him fall. They knew their prisoner was free. Seycia vaulted back up the rock face, out of the way, and peered down at Lorsa with a sigh.

"I'm sorry," she whispered.

She watched as the demon she had just set free was devoured by blackness. His accompanying scream wound around her heart. She knew she had used him, and she felt awful. But to dwell on it would only delay her. She hopped across the rocks to the place where Haben stood waiting.

"Help me move this." He pointed toward a large stone at the side of the cave. "There are more coming."

Seycia looked up on the cliff. More scarabs were indeed pouring out of the hole. Her diversion wouldn't last long. They began shoving the boulder across the sand to cover the cave's entrance.

"Pull it from inside now," she cried.

They both dove inside the dark cave and dragged the boulder toward them. Seycia could hear the chattering of the beetles just outside the cave's entrance. As they sealed off the cave and the last sliver of sunlight disappeared, the boulder crushed a rogue insect as it tried to squirm inside. They'd made it with barely a second to spare.

The cave was pitch black now, filled with nothing but the echo of their heavy breathing. She collapsed against the cool, stone wall and banished the terror from her body with a long exhale.

"You set him free then put him up as bait," Haben whispered in the blackness, "Lorsa."

"I had no choice," she muttered.

"There might have been another way."

"I'm sorry. I didn't know you cared about him," she said after a moment.

"It's not that. I hardly know him. I just thought . . . Never mind."

They were silent for a moment, barely daring to move, before Seycia kneeled and started feeling around in the darkness. They could start a fire if there was something to burn. She could use her fang as a flint.

"What are you doing?" Haben hissed. "We don't know what's in here."

"Then we need to be able to see it." She stopped short when she felt something dry and wooden against her fingertips.

She cautiously pulled it toward her and ran her hands along its surface. It was a long stick. Perfect. Before Haben could protest, she struck the fang against the wall, the sparks caught hold of the stick she had in her hand, and the space began to fill with light.

"Looks like an ordinary cave to me," Seycia said as she shone her torch around.

"Where did you learn to do that?" He pointed at the flame.

"At home, of course. Everyone knows how."

He settled on the ground once they saw it was free of traps and scarabs. "Where I came from, you could start a fire by pressing a button."

"Where did you come from?"

Where did you come from? Haben froze as he heard her say it. It was a loaded question. He wasn't sure she would understand. But before he could think of how he might answer her, a horrific spasm of hunger washed over him. He cried out and yanked his knees to his chest. Seycia jumped at the sudden shift in his behavior. He groaned and turned away from her.

"What's happening?" She reached out for him. He swatted her hand away and huddled against the wall. He wasn't sure what had triggered it this time. Was it just hunger, or something more—something she'd said?

He wished they weren't alone in such a small space together. He longed to hide. He glanced up at Seycia, who was staring at him in the flickering firelight. *Should have taken her. Should have shredded the pretty skin right off her bones instead of changing her. Why, why, why?* He rocked back and forth and moaned low in his throat.

"What makes it better?" she asked him. Her voice sounded far, far away.

He couldn't answer. He growled against his knee and dug his teeth into his skin. They felt larger. He felt his body changing.

"Stop, stop . . ." He heard her voice again, closer now. His vision was hazy, but it looked as though she was hovering right above him. "You've been all right. You've been all right this whole day. I need your help. Please. Come back to me."

He huddled against the wall of the cave, overcome with dizziness, and buried his face in his palms. She touched his hand. He snarled at her, but she only held on tighter, slowly prying his shaking hands from his head.

"I need your help. Please," she said again. Her voice was clearer now.

He felt cold sweat on his brow as he slowly opened his eyes. She sat directly in front of him.

"There," she said. "You're getting better. I can see it."

He replied with a disoriented nod.

"Why does that happen? Is it because you're starving?"

"It's . . . it's because of a lot of things," he responded, his voice ragged. "Sometimes it's hunger. Sometimes it's anger—" He drew in a sharp breath and added, "Comes and goes."

"So you were angry, just now."

He shook his head. It would be impossible to explain what set him off. He didn't even fully understand it. She'd asked him a question. What was it? It was something about that question . . .

"When we were in the canyon, when we were running before, you didn't seem like you were in pain. You said you're always hurting, that you're always hungry, but—"

"I suppose it helps to be distracted," he said.

He lifted his head and looked at her. The tingling sensation in his jaw subsided.

"So . . . what was it like where you came from, where you could push a button for fire? You never finished telling me," she urged him on.

There. That had been her question. He collected himself. "It was a long, long time ago," he began, his voice low and hoarse. "We built machines to do everything for us. Fire was the least of it."

He sensed the only way to keep the Savage at bay was to keep talking. He ignored his galvanizing heartbeat as he continued. "But it might have been better, if we'd never had them. There were things that weren't meant for us. Power we weren't supposed to have."

He clenched his teeth and stared at the ground. He felt his stomach lurch. He'd said more than he wanted to say.

"You were alive for the War of the Veil, weren't you?"

A heavy pause fell between them.

"I'm sorry," she said.

"No one's sorrier than me," he said. He shuddered and bit down on his tongue.

"What was your family like?" Seycia asked. "Your friends?"

"I don't remember."

"You don't? I remember mine perfectly."

"Over time, you'll remember less and less."

"How old were you . . . when you died?"

"We stopped counting once we came of age. But the thing that happened to me . . . I was a young man, when it happened. I wasn't alive for long."

"Neither was I," Seycia replied. "I would have celebrated my nineteenth summer this year. I mean, if you can call it celebrating. Usually Miko and I would just bake bread. Go for a swim."

They settled into another sad silence. The torch was growing smaller, and Seycia scanned the floor for more discarded sticks. Haben lay his head against the wall as the knife of hunger in his gut twisted again. He needed her to keep speaking.

"Your brother? What's he like?" he thought to ask.

"He's smart. Very smart," she said. She spotted another stick a few feet away and rose to grab it. "We've been on our own since he was five, so he knows how to take care of himself. He's a good hunter. Before I . . . before I left him, it was hard for me to accept that he didn't need my help with things anymore. Not as much as he used to anyway. But he'll always seem that way to me."

Seycia lit the torch and the fire bloomed to life.

"I'm sorry," Haben said after a moment. She spun to face him.

"For?"

"What I did. To you. I shouldn't have." The words stuck to his throat. He forced them out one at a time. "When I came here, I was angry. For a long time. I know you are, too. So . . . I'm sorry."

She pursed her lips and stared at him, as though trying to decode his words. "When you say things like that, I can't tell if you mean them. It's almost like you think you're *supposed* to say them."

"I do. Mean them. I'm just trying to get used to it again."

"Get used to what?"

"Saying anything at all," he replied. "It's such a human thing. To speak to someone."

"I still feel very human," she said.

She stared at him imploringly, as though hoping he'd agree with her. Her dark eyes reflected the dancing firelight. The hunger had all but vanished, but in its place he felt a different kind of ache—a small, sweet twinge that grew and washed over him as he breathed. He wrenched his gaze from her and studied his pale feet. He somehow dreaded this feeling even more than the hunger. He could feel his face growing warmer. Maybe it was because the fire was so close to him. Or maybe . . .

The moment collapsed around him when Seycia cleared her throat and shifted away. He exhaled, as if relieved.

"Lorsa said we need to go to the Blue Mountain," she reminded him of their next step. "To the side with no shadows. Is that close by?"

"There's supposed to be a tunnel that takes you there quickly: a matter of hours as opposed to days. Maybe that was the passage Lorsa came here to find," he replied. "But I know the mountain. I can get us there."

"How do you feel?"

"The pain is gone," he answered.

"Good. Tell me when you want to move on, and we'll find a way out of this cave."

She rose to her feet and stretched, scratching at the blood spatters stained onto her arms with a frown. "I guess we're both marked now, aren't we?" She held up her arms with a cynical laugh. He scoffed in return, a little distant. "I'm glad you feel better. And I enjoy distracting you. I get to learn things about you."

He felt his face prickle with heat again. "When you asked me if I knew what happened to my tree when Dohv made me like this . . . why did you assume I hadn't always been this way?"

"Oh." She pursed her lips, surprised. "I'm really not sure. You just seemed human to me, I guess."

You just seemed human. He didn't dare to hope. He might have finally figured out how to curb his starvation, but he wasn't sure he liked this alternative. At least he knew his hunger well. It was an old friend. This new feeling was a stranger, as agonizing as it was invigorating. He would never tell her how beautiful she looked in the shadowy torchlight, tying her hair in a knot and standing on her bare toes. Besides, what good would it do? Even if he "just seemed human," he wasn't what he used to be. He never would be again.

As the sun set outside the cramped cave at the bottom of the gorge, a hideous, scaly creature slithered through the sand, propelling itself forward on its two front feet. Bright white fangs jutted from its lips as it sniffed the ground like a hunting dog.

"Get back here, stupid," Zane grumbled at the Creeback, who was several feet ahead of him, wading through piles of dead scarabs.

"Silence, boy." Dohv's voice echoed in Zane's ears as he turned to see his master gliding silently behind him.

The Creeback gave a screech and stopped where it stood. It gnashed its teeth at the thing it had spotted. Zane sprinted up ahead and caught sight of a figure squirming underneath the pile of beetles.

"There, there he is!" Zane shouted excitedly and then lowered his voice. "Lorsa's down there."

Dohv lifted both of his arms, and the sea of scarabs parted down the middle. Lorsa lay on the ground, convulsing and gasping for breath. He gazed up at his master with pitiful tears in his bulging eyes.

"Quite a commotion at your prison today, I've heard," Dohv said to Lorsa. The demon clutched his temples at Dohv's voice and nodded in response. *"Seems someone triggered the trap. Who cut you down, Lorsa?"*

"S-some . . . some girl. She cut me down with a . . . a tooth, I think? Like that one." He nervously pointed to the Creeback's fangs.

"A girl cut you down, or a demon?"

"She must have been a demon. But she didn't look like one," Lorsa explained, gazing with pleading eyes at the vacant face beneath Dohv's hood.

"Was she alone?"

"No. Someone was with her. I've seen him before. He's the one who's always hungry, he's—"

"Haben," Dohv breathed, his voice quaking with rage.

"He's as stupid as you!" Zane pointed at Lorsa and cackled. "What was he doing all the way out here?"

"Indeed." Dohv loomed over Lorsa and stretched a bony finger toward him. Lorsa trembled and curled into a ball.

"I-I don't know why they were here," he mumbled.

"Come now. The girl set you free, then abandoned you in your helpless state. You owe them nothing."

Lorsa's lip quivered. "They asked me how to get to the Great Forest," he whispered.

Dohv was silent for a moment, then extended a frail, charred hand to Lorsa. *"To your feet, brother."*

Lorsa cautiously took his hand and stood upright on shaky legs. Dohv continued, *"You must tell me everything you heard them say. If you help me find them, I will reward you handsomely. Your transgressions shall be forgiven."*

Lorsa broke into relieved sobs. He could not spill the information fast enough. "Before they cut me down, I heard the girl say they were going to destroy trees in the Great Forest—the trees of a general and . . . some emperor? Then they asked me how to get there. I didn't see where they went. But if I think of anything else, I will tell you straightaway, my lord."

"Destroy the trees?" Dohv absorbed the information.

"I'm sorry, I don't know who this general is or—"

"I do." Dohv heaved a sigh. *"Zane?"*

Zane came to attention and scampered to his master's side.

"Find them. They must never reach the forest." He signaled to the Creeback, who came slithering up to Zane. *"She will help you. She's good company."*

"Can she kill them if she finds them?" Zane asked hopefully.

"Only the girl. But Haben must be brought to me. What I have in store for him will be far worse than death by a Creeback's bite."

Dohv draped his arm around Lorsa's frail shoulders. *"You have saved my empire today, Lorsa. Those particular trees are most valuable to me. Come back to the palace. We will wait for Zane to bring forth the guilty."*

Dohv waved his hand toward the rock face in front of him, and it transformed into a winding staircase. He led Lorsa out of the canyon and into the twilight, then peered over his shoulder at Zane and the Creeback one last time.

"Do not come home until you've tracked them. I will be watching."

CHAPTER ELEVEN

MIKO SAT AT the tiny window of Belicia and Ezara's attic, turning the iron crossbow over and over in his hands. Every contour was flawless. He practiced lifting it up and loading it, trying to get his muscles used to its heft and shape. He hadn't handled the revolver yet, though. He wasn't quite ready for that.

He longed to get out of the house to practice with the crossbow. Maybe in the dead of night, when everyone in the city was asleep.

He eyed a rickety bookshelf in the corner and aimed the crossbow right at the top shelf. It was already full of holes and cracks—what was one more? He squinted and stuck out his tongue, then released the arrow. Joy surged through him as it flew from the bow.

Just as the pointy tip of the arrow made contact with the bookshelf, the attic door creaked open. Miko gave Belicia a sheepish look as she made her way into the room and yanked the arrow from the shelf.

"Sorry. I just wanted to practice," he said.

She handed him the arrow. "Why don't you put that away for a little while? There's somewhere I'd like to take you, and we need to leave soon."

Finally, a chance to get out of the attic! Miko jumped off the bed.

"Where are we going? You sure you don't need me to bring the crossbow? We might need protection."

"No weapons. Not where we're going."

She gazed out the window at the house across the street. Within seconds, someone extinguished all the lights in the windows. "They're on the move. Count with me, Miko."

"Count?"

"Yes. We have to count to one hundred. And then we can follow them."

"Follow them where? What's happening?"

"One. Two. Three. Four . . ." Belicia began.

Miko watched her with a furrowed brow. Why was she counting? "You know, I could bring the gun, too, if—"

Distracted, Belicia lost count and turned to him with an exasperated sigh. "I have to keep counting, or we'll throw the system off. I'm taking you to a special place. You'll be safe, you'll be among friends, but you have to let me finish."

Miko sighed, relenting, and joined her at the window. Together, they chanted, "Thirty-four, thirty-five, thirty-six, thirty-seven . . ."

Once they hit one hundred, Belicia blew out the oil lamps in the attic. She took Miko's hand in the darkness and said, "Be very quiet and follow me."

They crept downstairs and out the front door, into the brisk night air, and walked silently together behind the little house. They traipsed through the backyard, overgrown with weeds and littered with scraps of rusted metal. Belicia pointed to a little dirt path that led to the woods beyond.

Miko knew better than to badger her with questions. He could sense her nervous vigilance, like a deer trying to avoid a hunter. On the pathway, he spotted three others in the distance. They were probably all headed to the same secret place, whatever it was. Miko's pulse jumped with excitement. In all his years living in the woods, he had never witnessed this clandestine parade into the night.

Finally, they reached a small clearing, and Belicia pointed to a ladder sticking out of the muddy earth. Miko approached it and looked closer. The ladder jutted up from a dark hole in the ground, lined with concrete.

"Are we going . . . down there?" he asked.

She hushed him and gestured that he go first. He was nervous now. She said he would be among friends, but he had always been taught that even friends could become traitors given the right circumstances. Belicia nudged him on the shoulder. He swallowed hard and, after a moment, decided to let curiosity win this round. He climbed down the ladder.

An animated chorus of whispers enveloped him as he descended. The little underground shelter was filled with flickering amber light. Khronasan townspeople gathered 'round, seated on small, individual woven mats on the floor. As he entered, he couldn't help but feel as though everybody was staring at him. He even saw someone point in his direction.

He ignored the strange greeting and focused instead on the ornate murals that covered the concrete chamber from floor to ceiling. They were perfectly preserved, as though someone came by to touch them up every few days. Candles lined the perimeter of the room. The light danced across the paintings, as though bringing them to life.

Wide-eyed, he turned in a full circle, taking a long look at each of the murals. The first was a fabulous flood of green and blue. A huge azure mountain towered above a valley of healthy grass and wildflowers, and the sky was a dusty lavender color. He had never imagined such a colorful world. The second panel was a figure he recognized: Dohv, flanked by fire-breathing, pale-skinned demons on either side. A black river snaked across the mural's background and, when he looked closely, he could have sworn that crushed gemstones had been mixed in with the paint. The color shimmered in the dim candlelight.

He was disappointed to realize he didn't recognize the figures in the next painting. There were three women, standing back to back. Their violet hair wound together and created a swirl of clouds above them. A bloodred sun hung above the three identical sisters, and they caressed its rays with their outstretched hands. He couldn't tell if the sun was shining down on them or if they were the ones holding it up in the sky.

Then, Miko turned to the back of the room. On a table made from fallen tree stalks, heavy with leaves, lay a motionless man with red flowers covering his eyes. It took Miko a moment to realize that this was the man he'd seen shot from his window. The body of his faithful dog lay at his feet, as though he were sleeping at the end of his bed. Miko felt his sorrow materialize, sticking in his throat. Most of the time, Coalition officials were sent to collect the bodies to keep the villagers from organizing funerals. But the old man's family must have saved his before the Coalition could get their hands on it.

There was one final painting above the man and his dog: an enormous expanse of glorious green trees set against that same lavender sky. Miko understood. They were going to pray for this man's deliverance to the Forest of Laida. His next thought was of Seycia, and the knot in his throat tightened. If only he had known this place existed, he could have given her a proper farewell.

"Come sit with us," Belicia whispered as she guided him over to a mat on the ground. Someone had given him his own to sit on, woven from strips of soft deerskin.

"We're going to pray for him, aren't we?" Miko gestured to the man on the bier.

"I suppose it's like praying," she said. "But I think what we're doing here, more than praying, is celebrating the continuation of Sanzo's journey. That was his name, Sanzo. The dog was named Luli."

From the back of the chamber came the sweet sound of two wooden flutes playing in harmony. Miko couldn't remember the last time he had heard music at all. He peered up at the glorious murals surrounding him. What was a world without color, without music? Who would ever want to destroy such beautiful things?

Then, he gazed at the people around him. They embraced and held each other's hands, offering what little comfort they could. *Family must feel like this*, he thought. He imagined his own parents would have been there if they could have. He wondered what Seycia would have thought of this place. In a room full of people, he was suddenly, achingly alone.

A man seated a few rows in front of Miko rose to his feet. He wore a long robe, dyed blue, and his face was streaked with diagonal lines of red face paint. His head was shaved so Miko couldn't tell if he'd gone gray or not, but his dark brown eyes looked tired and weary. He had to have been at least Belicia's age.

"That's High Priest Jenli," Belicia whispered as the robed man soundlessly moved past them, toward Sanzo's body. "He hides by day as a carpenter in the city."

Just as High Priest Jenli was about to murmur a prayer over Sanzo's body, a soft clang echoed across the chamber and two latecomers climbed down the ladder. First came a grandfatherly man with a beard. Miko noticed he was having trouble grasping the ladder because he only had three fingers on one of his hands.

Miko gasped when he saw the person who emerged behind him. It was her, the girl with the long legs who had rescued him from the pit. What had Belicia said her name was? Minari? He spun to face Belicia with wide eyes.

"She's alive," he whispered. Belicia nodded.

"She's here to see you."

Miko felt as if everyone in the room had stopped speaking as he stood and Minari approached him. She looked young, maybe three or four summers younger than Seycia, but she carried herself with unshakable poise. He wasn't sure what to say to her, or what he should do. He thought he might embrace her, but there was something almost holy and untouchable about her.

"I'm sorry I couldn't save you both," she said to him, eyes cast to the ground. Her lilting accent was peculiar, but he liked it.

"I-I know you tried," he answered. For some reason he wanted to cry.

"Minari," she said, and bowed her head to him.

"Miko."

"I know."

The question he longed to ask more than anything fell from his lips. "Why did you come to the pit to save us? People died. *You* could have died."

"Because I was supposed to," she replied with a faraway look in her eye. "Actually, I thought at first that it was your sister I was supposed to save. But then I understood: it was you. When the universe whispers, it doesn't lie. Your sister led me to you, but you were the one who was meant to live."

"I-I don't understand. You didn't even know my sister."

"She came to me in a dream and then she came to my door the next day."

Miko's head spun, and he backed away from his strange rescuer, suddenly apprehensive. What was she talking about?

"Friends, let us sit," High Priest Jenli addressed the room. He stood in front of the mural of the three women with lavender hair and gestured that Minari join him. She put her hand on Miko's shoulder, as though to guide him along with her, but he planted his feet. He was grateful to her, and glad to have met her, but what she'd just said made him nervous. If she asked him to speak in front of all these people, what would he say?

Minari read his body language and gave him an understanding nod. She left him with Belicia and stood beside High Priest Jenli as the room quieted.

"Who is she?" Miko whispered to Belicia as they settled back down onto their woven mats.

"A young oracle from Ellita. Her uncle Ortius rescued her last year when her family was targeted," Belicia pointed to the man with three fingers. "She can hear the rhythm of the universe better than anyone I've ever known. She's still learning to interpret it. But if Minari has a vision, we pay attention."

"Like the one she had about me?" Miko shivered as he spoke.

"Don't be afraid. We would never ask you to do anything you did not wish to do."

"My friends, on Sanzo's behalf, I thank you for joining us tonight," High Priest Jenli began. Miko noticed Minari was staring right at him, and he averted his eyes. "May his tree soon blossom anew and bring his soul back to us."

Then, the priest's gaze intensified and he lowered his voice. "Now, while we mean dear Sanzo no disrespect, I feel we must use this opportunity to decide, together, how we are going to proceed after the last sacrifice. I'm sure you have all noticed our new guest tonight."

Miko heard everyone in the room shift. He felt their eyes on him.

"Miko, welcome," Jenli bowed his head to him. "We feel deeply for the loss of your sister. But your survival also gives us hope—the kind of hope we have not felt for many years."

Miko wasn't sure what to do except nod.

"When Minari told us we had to find a way to rescue you and your sister, we were sure it would be a suicide mission. But you made it out alive when the Coalition had guns, and all we had were arrows and daggers. This tells us something about General Simeon's stability. He is growing weak, but we are getting stronger. In your name, and in your sister's name, we will continue to fight."

Miko drew his knees to his chest, uneasy. He wanted his people to fight, but he wasn't sure he wanted them to fight in his name. He wasn't anyone special. Minari was the special one. She'd saved him. All he did was run.

The high priest studied him, and Miko sensed he'd read the discomfort on his face. He hadn't meant to insult him. Not in the least bit. He just didn't know what he was supposed to do or say.

"My son, we look forward to hearing from you when you're ready," Jenli said to him, and once again bowed his head. "The rest of us will plan our next move against the Coalition. Rumor has it, Simeon executed many members of his staff today, if not all of them. We do not yet know why. But this tells us there is something he is afraid of."

"He's afraid of *us*," a man's voice crowed from the back of the room. A chorus of raucous cheers followed, and the crowd started scheming among themselves. Excited, nervous tittering filled the air.

Minari sat down beside Miko and took his hand. She leaned in close and murmured into his ear, "I'm sorry. Nobody meant to frighten you."

"I'm not frightened," Miko quickly replied. He certainly didn't want Minari to think that he was. "I just want to know why this is happening."

"I told you. Your sister came to me in a dream."

"But what did she *do*, in the dream?"

Minari reflected. Her expression was composed and steady, like calm water. She turned to him and whispered, "She stood beneath a tree, holding the hand of a child. It was night, and the tree was burning. She turned around, she looked at me, and she said: *this is the Lasting Light.*"

Miko shuddered. Something about the way Minari described it made it feel so real, as if it were more than just a dream she'd had.

"But I wasn't even in the dream. It was about Seycia."

"She was holding someone's hand. It had to be you. When I found out she had a brother, and that he was being sent to the pit, I knew."

"So . . . what's the 'Lasting Light'?" he asked after a moment. "Is it a person?"

"I don't know."

"Is it me?"

Silence passed between them. He felt his pulse quicken. Finally, she stood and answered: "If you want it to be."

He watched as she navigated the crowd on her long graceful legs, almost floating, and approached Sanzo's body on the bier. She kissed his forehead. Miko turned to Belicia on his other side, wondering if she'd heard the exchange, but she was deep in conversation with another man her age.

"At least forty of them," Miko heard the man whisper. "Maids, cooks, and even a few security guards, from what I've heard."

"Tragic," Belicia said. "But that could also mean his forces are weaker." Miko knew they were discussing the latest news from Simeon's mansion.

He thought of Belicia's crossbow. Of her gun. She said nobody else knew she had it. She was probably protecting Ezara by keeping it a secret. But Miko had nobody to protect. If he could join the fight, if he could use those weapons, then he'd feel worthy of this strange new title Minari had just bestowed upon him. *No*, he suddenly realized. She hadn't bestowed it upon him. She'd given him a choice.

Miko was surprised when he stood up and approached High Priest Jenli. He hadn't thought at all about what he'd say to him, but he felt as though someone had lit a fuse inside of him and that if he didn't do something, right then, he might explode. What if this was the reason he'd survived? He wasn't sure what any of it meant, but he felt its importance in his bones.

Jenli cast Miko a curious glance as he came forth, keeping his posture straight, trying to look taller than he was. "I think I want to talk now," he said, then looked out at the crowd.

"Be sure about this, my son," Jenli cautioned him, and bent down to his level. "You are young."

"So is Minari. But she seems all right."

"Minari is strong. A true fighter."

"So am I."

Jenli nodded and put his arm around Miko. He turned to address the room, but before he could speak, the cover to the hatch creaked open again—louder this time, and with more urgency. A teenaged Khronasan boy holding a bow and a quiver of arrows leaped down the ladder.

"Raiders in the woods! Raiders in the woods!"

Pandemonium set in. The strongest among them shoved their way toward the exit. Miko heard Belicia yelp as a man stomped on her fingers. Miko sprang over and gave her his hand, helping her up, when a terrified woman bolted past and knocked her down again.

"Silence!" Jenli shouted from the back of the room. Not everyone obeyed at first. "Listen to me unless you want to be trapped in here and shot."

Now, the chamber was quiet. He continued, "We cannot all leave at once. A crowd will attract their attention." He turned to the teenage lookout, still perched on the ladder. "Do they know our position?"

"Not yet. I agree. File out separately," the young man replied.

"We'll start with Miko and Minari, followed by the elders and anyone else who moves slowly. You are to pause halfway home and hide in the woods so you're not followed to your houses. Are we clear?" Jenli was firm but measured as he held back the tide of panicked villagers.

"We will go last," Minari spoke up. "Let the elders get out first."

"You know we can't do that."

Minari sighed, reluctant, and joined Miko at the front of the hatch.

Belicia squeezed Miko's hand, and he squeezed back. She whispered as she let go, "Don't wait for me."

He swallowed hard and followed Minari to the ladder. If only he'd disobeyed Belicia and taken the crossbow. He glanced up at Minari as she stealthily lifted the cover of the hatch, wondering if she was armed. Belicia had said they didn't take weapons here, that it was meant to be a peaceful place, but he hoped Minari was the exception to that rule.

The teenage sentry filed out behind them and closed the manhole. He readied an arrow in his bow and peered through the shadowy trees. *That* was who would defend them. Miko was glad to have protection, but he worried about everyone else. Wasn't Jenli worth saving? Wasn't Belicia? Would the rest of them make it home?

"This way," the young lookout mouthed, leading Minari and Miko off the path. They wove through the trees in the darkness—the moon up above was a little more than a slender white crescent. But the night was still and empty. Miko was relieved when he didn't hear any voices, or worse, gunshots.

They walked south, back toward the hazy yellow lights of the city, taking cover every few paces. As they crouched behind a mossy boulder, Miko pulled a deep breath as his racing heart finally slowed. They would reach Belicia's crooked blue house soon. He knew Minari and High Priest Jenli would want him to run inside, lock the door, and wait for Belicia, but he wondered if he ought to grab the gun or the crossbow and help escort the others home.

As their sentry gestured for them to follow him out from behind the rock, two gunshots tore through the silent forest. Miko clutched his ringing ears. It sounded loud enough to wake the whole city. He dove back behind the boulder. Minari shoved him to the ground and held him there.

"Don't. Move," she whispered, as if he could have with her pressing down on him like that. He didn't realize she was so strong.

Heavy boots stomped through the leaves, creeping closer and closer. Miko's breath burned in his chest as he dared himself to exhale. This was it. He'd pushed his luck too many times. Now here he was, without a weapon of his own, inches from the enemy.

He and Minari exchanged a silent glance. Did she know what to do? He peered over at the young sentry, primed to fire his arrow. Miko's eyes widened when he noticed he only had two more in his quiver. He'd felt so safe with them just moments before, but now he was all too aware that they weren't much older than he was. They were children, lost in the woods, and the wolves were closing in.

As the footsteps slowed down, snapping dried twigs one by one, Miko heard a man's voice cry out from the main path: "Hey! Where are you?"

The Coalition soldiers stood stock still, and Minari gripped Miko so tightly he could barely feel his arm.

Another voice answered the first: "Over here, come on." Miko recognized it. Belicia. What were they doing, raising their voices like that? They'd be killed on the spot!

As the Coalition soldiers whirled around and bolted away from their hiding place, Miko knew . . . Belicia must have spotted them and done it on purpose. Minari loosened her grip on his arm, but she didn't let go. Miko expelled a shaky breath as he glanced over his shoulder, toward the place where the voices had come from.

"Run," Minari whispered. And they were about to—but a gunshot rang out, louder than firecrackers.

All Miko could hear for a moment was a high-pitched hum echoing between his ears. He thought for a second he'd gone deaf, until he heard another two rounds. Then, silence. The loudest silence he could remember.

The three of them were motionless for an eternal, terror-stricken moment. But nothing else happened. The woods were empty again. They slowly crept out from behind the rock. Minari was still holding on to Miko's arm, clenching his shirt in her fist.

As they wound back toward the main path to follow it into the city, Miko spotted two figures on the ground, back from where they'd just come. He couldn't leave them. He wrenched Minari's hand off his arm and sprinted toward the spot where they lay.

"Miko—" she hissed in the darkness as he ran.

He slowed to a stop as their faces came into view, then tried to hold Minari back as she approached him. He didn't want her to see . . .

Belicia's lifeless, cloudy eyes stared up to the heavens. He found himself reaching out to her, but he withdrew with a stifled sob. She was already gone.

Beside Belicia lay Minari's uncle, Ortius. He was facedown, but Miko could see the three fingers of his left hand. Minari covered her mouth to muffle a scream as she peered over Miko's shoulder and saw him there. Their lookout caught up a moment later, again readying his arrow, but he lowered his weapon when he caught sight of the scene.

"We need to take them," Miko whispered.

"I'm sorry," their lookout replied. "We can't slow down. I'll tell the others. Someone will come."

Miko glanced over his shoulder and saw the tears in Minari's eyes. Before that moment he could have never imagined her crying.

But she said nothing. She only nodded and followed the lookout back to the path. Miko trailed behind her. He could hear her fighting to keep her tears inside.

They reached the city limits, and Minari finally spoke: "You need to go back to Belicia's house and stay inside. It's safe there."

"Where will you stay?"

She thought about it and then replied, "With you. To keep watch."

Belicia had left the front door padlock open, in case Ezara returned. But the house was dark and quiet as the first sign of dawn crested the hilltop outside. Miko wondered if he'd ever see Ezara again.

Their lookout gave a silent nod of farewell and raced back into the woods to guard the next group of villagers on their way home. Miko let Minari into the cold, empty house.

He lit the oil lamps in the kitchen as Minari glanced around. "She has a son. Is he here?"

"I haven't seen him."

Minari sat down at the table as Miko finished lighting the lamps. Then, he sat down across from her.

"You all right?" she asked him.

"I don't know," he murmured. She nodded, and they shared a long, silent moment. Miko was the first to break it.

"I have a plan. I know how to kill General Simeon."

Minari glanced up at him and shook her head. "You're needed in other ways. Just let them look to you. Don't join the fight."

"Why not? You did."

She was quiet, then narrowed her eyes at him. "How?"

"How would I kill him?" She nodded. "First, we need to steal the gong, from the sacrifice. Whoever controls the gong controls the Savage. We get that, and we've got Simeon."

"But how would you steal it? It's kept somewhere on his property. How are we supposed to get past security?"

"I have a gun," Miko replied. She shrank back, and her eyes flashed disbelief. "I swear. Belicia gave it to me."

"Show me," she said.

"Get a group together, tonight, who can help us break into Simeon's mansion. *Then* I'll show it to you."

Minari scoffed, but Miko could tell she was thinking it over.

"We need to do something." He looked her in the eye. "For Belicia. And your uncle."

She wore a bronze ring on the middle finger of her right hand, and she twisted it 'round and 'round as she chewed her lip.

"The people I can bring . . . They are serious. They'll make a plan. But when they do, that's the plan we have to stick to. They're in charge, not you."

"Fine."

"Lock the door and stay upstairs. Do not leave the house again till it's dark. We'll meet at the temple ruins after sundown."

She hopped off her stool and bowed her head to Miko. He bowed his back.

"You better not be lying about that gun," she muttered, sailing toward the door. Then, her gaze softened as she glanced over her shoulder. "Try to get some sleep. Belicia would've told you that."

She was perfectly framed by the dim, dawn light that was starting to permeate the cracks of their little house. She reminded Miko of one of the murals in the underground temple, so serene. As she turned out the door, he thought he might like to paint her someday, on a wall somewhere . . . but not underground, not in the temple. Someplace outdoors, where everybody could see it whenever they wanted to.

Miko tried to sleep as he settled into bed, but he was restless. Every time he shut his eyes, his ears would start ringing again and all he could think of was Belicia's lifeless gaze, cast to the sky. Every time he pictured it, it felt like seeing it for the first time.

Finally, he sat up. He dove beneath the cot for the box containing the crossbow and the revolver. Carefully, he lifted the gun and pointed the barrel into the mattress as he fiddled with the chamber. *Click.* Miko jumped at the sound; the gun's chamber hung ajar. He leaned in closer and counted six spaces for bullets inside the clip. Two of the six were empty.

Four bullets. He wasn't sure how many bullets he'd assumed would be inside, but he had at least hoped there would be enough for a few practice rounds. *Practice for what?* He dared to think of it. He lay the gun down on the bed and stared at it, as though willing it to submit to him, to make him its master.

He didn't realize how long he had been sitting there, meditating on the revolver, until the room began to grow dark again. It had almost been a whole day. He hadn't grown hungry; he hadn't slept. As the sun sank below the city rooftops, he finally sat up and closed the revolver's chamber. *Snap.* He placed it back in its deerskin pouch and slipped it into his rucksack. He shoved the crossbow inside as well. The gun carried no guarantees, though it certainly gave him courage.

He tiptoed into the kitchen, where a generous hunk of sausage had been left out on the cutting board beside Belicia's carving knife. The hair on his neck prickled. He knew, for sure, that he hadn't left it there. He heard a tired grunt in the darkness behind him, and he picked up the knife and whirled around.

"That's mine, you know," a voice grumbled. Ezara sat in the far corner of the room, whittling a wooden spear with a sharp dagger.

"You're back," Miko breathed. He put the knife down.

"I came to check on my mother. Thought she might be out somewhere, with you." A pang hit Miko's chest.

"N-no," he whispered. "We were out. Together. But—"

He couldn't bring himself to say it.

"What happened? Where the hell did you go?"

"I'm sorry," Miko choked out. "I-I don't know why she did it."

"Did what?" Ezara rose to his feet, trembling. But Miko couldn't bear to answer. He watched the truth break across Ezara's face. He flipped his sharp dagger around and pointed it at Miko's chest. Miko shrank back and bolted for the door.

"This is your fault, you little shit!" Ezara's voice cracked as he chased after him, still brandishing his blade. "She died for you, and you're nothing! *Nothing!*"

He jumped between Miko and the doorway, blocking his exit, swiping at him with his dagger. Tears poured down his rough, leathery face. "Where you going now, huh? How many more of us are going to die for you?"

Miko leaped to the side to avoid Ezara's blade and in one swift motion, pulled his knapsack to his chest, opened it, and snatched the revolver out of the bag.

He pointed it with a steady wrist, right between Ezara's eyes. He could hardly believe he'd done it so fast.

"Wh-where did you get *that*?" Ezara breathed.

"Your mother. She wanted me to have it." Miko responded, surprised by the depth of his own voice. "There are only four bullets, though. I'd hate to waste any of them." He slung the bag back on his shoulder but kept the gun fixed on Ezara. He backed away, toward the door.

"You pull that thing on Simeon's guards and you'll be gunned down before you can figure out what to do with it."

"No worse than what you just tried to do," Miko fired back. "Now, move. I need to go."

Miko pulled back the safety and Ezara went pale. He shifted to the side with a disbelieving stare, allowing Miko to pass.

Miko felt for the latch behind him and pried it open. He inched out the door backward, facing Ezara, who had still not dropped his dagger. He did not move his finger from the trigger. He took another step back. He was outside now.

Before he shut the door and headed down the path, he said to Ezara, "I'm sorry. My mother died, too."

Ezara opened his mouth to reply, but no words came forth. Miko shut the door and turned his back.

He shuffled down the road a few paces, listening for movement from inside the house, but none came. Ezara had let him go. He was weary with regret, having just delivered such devastating news to him. But he had to move fast or he'd miss the rendezvous.

He took the same trail to the woods they had the night before, through the unkempt yard of the little blue house. He had hoped he might run into a few others on the path, headed in the same direction. But he was alone.

As he got closer to the site of the temple ruins, he heard whispers. He ducked behind a grove of trees and peered at the shimmering white rubble. He counted five people, and Minari was one of them. He also recognized their lookout from the night before. *Only five people?* How many had Minari approached? He made his way over to them. The other three villagers were burly middle-aged men wearing dark fur vests, with their long black hair knotted against the back of their necks. They had warrior's tattoos on their arms: dark, intricate spirals carved into their flesh to represent the two realms—Earth and Underworld.

The old warriors kneeled before Miko as he approached, and he shook his head. "Please don't do that," he said. Ezara's words echoed in his head. *How many more of us are going to die for you?*

"All right, Miko. Let's see that gun." Minari stalked toward him. He nodded and opened his bag.

"I also have a crossbow. It's a good one," he said. He lifted both weapons out. Minari and the warriors gaped at the revolver. One of the older men reached out to touch it, but his partner pushed his hand away.

"I'd like to have a go with that one, if you don't mind," the teenage lookout said, pointing at the crossbow. "We weren't properly introduced last night. I'm Ardash."

"Ardash. Sure. You can try it," he handed it to him. "As long as I get the gun."

"You can hang onto it, but don't use it," Minari warned him.

"What's the point of having it if I can't—"

"Miko, we have to listen to the elders. They have a plan."

Miko looked to the warriors, then back at Minari. "To steal the gong. Right?"

"What we need to do first is evaluate the property," the tallest of the three warriors spoke in a gruff monotone. "We don't have the manpower to do anything more. Not tonight."

Miko grimaced. He didn't want to evaluate. He wanted to use his weapons. This was for Belicia. Seycia, too. This was to prove he wasn't *nothing*.

"Last night, I heard Simeon killed most of the people who worked for him. That could mean less security at the mansion."

"We cannot know any of this for sure," the tall warrior replied.

Nobody else argued with him. Miko sighed. This seemed to be the plan that everyone had agreed upon before he arrived.

"Sun's down," Minari said after a moment. "We need to head out."

Ardash nodded and picked up the crossbow, testing its weight in his arms before securing it to his back. The three older warriors took the lead, and motioned for the rest of the team to follow. Miko was the smallest in their troop by far. In single file, they made their way down the path toward the red rooftops of the city beyond.

Miko padded along the quiet streets, watching the houses increase in size with each passing block. Seycia would have sooner let him swim in the swamp where the alligators lurked than allow him to venture this far into the city. He thought of the wreath of poisoned fruit he had encountered. What other traps could be laid in the darkness?

Minari glanced at him over her shoulder and gave him a reassuring smile. Did he look nervous? He hadn't meant to.

As they approached General Simeon's property, Miko spotted an enormous barricade of tall evergreen trees surrounding the perimeter of the mansion. Ardash stopped after a few paces, peering ahead at the gates. There was a Coalition guard keeping watch—but *only one.*

"See? There aren't as many people guarding him," Miko whispered excitedly, pointing to the gates. "We could get to the mansion."

"But what's inside the mansion?" Ardash frowned.

"Let's walk the perimeter and make note of areas we could breach," the tall warrior said, leading them into the thicket of evergreen.

But Miko already saw a way onto the property. He surveyed the trees surrounding the mansion. Evergreens were harder to climb than ordinary trees, but he had done it before. He turned the gun over in his palm, staring down the muzzle . . . then broke away from the group.

"Hey! Hey, Miko! Where are you going?" Minari hissed in the darkness.

"Stand watch," he replied over his shoulder.

He flung himself up the trunk of one of the evergreen trees and started to shinny upward.

"Get him!" Ardash cried. But Minari held him back.

"If this is what he thinks he's meant to do, let's see him do it," Miko heard her whisper from down below. He wasn't sure if Minari's faith gave him courage or if it made him even more anxious.

Miko peered at them through the branches as they watched, holding their breath. Now that he was in the trees, he realized they weren't quite as close to the property as he would have liked. The trees stood against a lower wrought iron fence that boasted razor-sharp spikes. He would need to climb to the top of the tree and survey the property to find the best place to jump out and over the fence.

"I'll only be a few minutes," he whispered to Minari from up above, then disappeared between the boughs.

The needles pierced his palms as he made his way up, but he was numb to all of it. Before long, he reached the highest limb that could possibly support his body weight. He teetered out onto the boughs and saw, directly below the next tree, a spacious solarium with glass walls on the top floor of the mansion. Its roof was made of sturdy bricks, punctuated by rectangular skylights. He dared to believe his luck—if he could just hop into the tree beside this one. It wasn't too far . . .

He leaned back on the branch, about to burst forth toward the neighboring tree, but he stopped short. *This is too easy.* Seycia would have told him that. There was no way the mansion was really so exposed, that it could be so simple to hop onto the roof.

He tore off a branch and broke it into three pieces, and tossed one to the ground. It landed without a sound. Then he took the second piece and threw it at the roof of the solarium . . . where it burned to a crisp in midair. Miko stared, shaken, but not surprised. There was an invisible fence around the perimeter of the roof. *Of course.*

But how high does the fence go? That was the question. If he could somehow hop over it, wherever it was . . .

He aimed his final branch up and over the spot where he'd seen the electric spark. It sailed high into the air, in an arc, and came down onto the roof of the solarium unharmed.

He would have to force his body into the same trajectory. A timid voice in the back of his head told him to turn around, that it wasn't too late to join Minari and the others. But they were hiding. And he hadn't come this far to do the same. Not when he could finally defend himself.

With that, he leaped forward and sprang into the neighboring tree like a fearless squirrel. He felt blood smear his palms as he clung to the sharp pine boughs. He snapped off a twig and threw it at the invisible fence one last time, watching closely as it smoldered in the wind. Keeping his eyes locked on the spot, he sucked in a great breath of air and jumped as high as his tired young muscles would allow. He fought the urge to shut his eyes as he tumbled toward the solarium. Just a little farther . . .

A horrible, electric hum filled his ears as he sailed through the air, followed by an explosion of pain on the left side of his head. He felt blood cascade into his eye, hot and sticky. He couldn't see or hear a thing as he landed with a thud onto the roof of the solarium.

He lolled his heavy head from side to side, faintly aware of a pulse, of breath in his lungs, of being alive. He rubbed his eye, fearing the worst, but the blood wasn't coming from his eye socket. It was pouring from a gash just above his left ear.

He blinked his vision back into focus, touched the tip of his left ear, and swallowed a horrified yelp. It was split down the middle. He must have nicked the invisible fence. He drew a shallow, nervous breath and rose to a sitting position, holding as still as possible, assuring himself that nobody had heard him land on the roof. The room below was silent. After a moment, he tore off a bit of his shirt and tied it tightly around his ear, gritting his teeth through the pain.

He pulled the revolver out of his knapsack, then looked up into the sky at the blanket of stars above. He pictured a million tiny guns all hanging in the heavens, pointed at the earth, ready to rain down fire at any moment. Anyone could be next.

Anyone can be killed. This would be his mantra. He repeated it in his head, over and over—*anyone can be killed, anyone can be killed*—as he heard muffled footsteps from the solarium below.

He crawled over to a skylight overlooking the room and saw two figures enter. He angled his bloodied face against the skylight to get a better look, and stifled a gasp.

There was General Simeon, flanked by a bodyguard holstering a heavy machine gun. They exchanged a few words, as though the bodyguard were briefing him about something. General Simeon nodded, listening, and went to the corner of the room to prepare a drink.

Miko watched, vibrating with exhilaration and terror. Forget stealing the gong, forget the Savage. *He* could kill him. Right here, right now. This was why Minari had her vision. This was why he had survived. His heart surged as he pulled out the revolver and cradled it in his palm.

He watched as Simeon mixed a drink at the bar, listening to his bodyguard chatter on. It was the ideal moment. Miko's fingers writhed against the trigger, slippery with sweat. Four bullets. If he aimed perfectly, he could even get the two of them. *Anyone can be killed. Anyone can be killed.* The barrel of the gun kissed the glass skylight. *Anyone can be killed. Anyone can be killed—*

It was as if a hand that was not his own pulled the trigger. The gun's recoil was much more powerful than he'd imagined. His wrist jerked to the side as the bullet shattered the glass and lodged itself into the tile floor of the solarium, creating a dark crater right beside General Simeon's feet. He and the bodyguard gazed up in shock, and Miko was sure they had both seen his face. He readied the revolver for a second shot.

But before he could fire, the bodyguard jumped onto the table and aimed his machine gun straight through the skylight.

Miko leaped out of the way as bullets from the semiautomatic burst through the glass like a geyser.

He ran to the edge of the roof and launched himself into the sky, blinded by terror and deaf to reason. It was less than a second later, as he sailed through the air, that he remembered the invisible fence. His blood ran cold as he plummeted toward the ground, hearing an ominous electric hum. He squeezed his eyes shut. His final thought was of Seycia . . . of Seycia and how he had failed her. *Don't try to be a hero*, she'd said, *live a little longer so you can become one when you're older.* He hadn't listened. He hadn't listened . . .

Pain sliced through him on all sides, as though he'd been split into pieces. Somehow, he felt as if he were still falling, even though he knew he would have to had hit the ground by now. He imagined bits of his broken body floating through the endless night sky, like ash after a deadly fire.

Then he opened his eyes and found himself on the cold, hard gravel of the mansion's walkway, unable to move—though he could see a puddle of blood seeping from underneath his legs. The backs of both his knees had been seared by the electric fence. Three Coalition soldiers encircled him from above like a pack of vultures.

A voice that sounded very, very far away barked, "You're in the custody of His Imperial Majesty Emperor Caius. State your name."

But he couldn't. No words came out. It was as though he were watching the ordeal from outside his body. The guards lifted him high over their heads and carried him off. He couldn't fight. He couldn't move. He wondered how he was even breathing.

Just beyond the property, Miko spotted five figures weaving into the shadows. It was Minari and the rest of their crew. *They'll come back for me*, he thought, *they have to.*

But as he felt himself being carried inside the gates, a terrible realization struck him. He'd just proven to them that he wasn't the Lasting Light. The person they wanted him to be would have succeeded. Ezara was right: he was nothing. He watched the woods, praying a storm of arrows would burst from the treetops. But nothing happened.

They wouldn't be back. He was on his own.

CHAPTER TWELVE

SEYCIA WAS SURPRISED to wake up. She was sure she hadn't been sleeping. Or had she? It hadn't felt like a deep sleep, if it had happened at all. Haben had said that demons didn't need to sleep. She stretched her neck and rubbed her eyes, realizing she was still on the cool, damp floor of the cave. Only a thin beam of light infiltrated the space, from the opening they'd covered with the stone hours before.

She eyed the corner of the cave, where Haben was leaning against a rock, staring straight ahead into the darkness. He turned to her.

"I was waiting. I asked if you wanted to go and you said nothing. I wondered if you'd died," he said.

A quiet laugh escaped her lips, before she realized he was serious. "Oh. I fell asleep, I think."

"We don't sleep."

"I know you said that, but maybe I might need to sometimes," she said as she rose to her feet.

He picked a stick off the ground and thrust it toward her. "Here. Make some fire. We should go."

She took the stick from him but paused before striking her flint. "I really think . . . I know you don't believe me, but—"

"You're not still human," he interrupted, like he'd known exactly what she wanted to say.

"It's just—"

"You can't be injured. You saw for yourself."

"But I sleep. And I'm not like you—"

"You mean you don't turn into a monster?"

"Well . . . I *don't*."

Haben sighed then spun away from her, walking toward the dark tunnel up ahead.

"Hey, wait for the light," she shouted. But he didn't.

She struck the flint against the wall and caught the sparks against her torchwood. She held it in front of her and made her way to the spot where he was waiting for her, farther down the passageway. He fixed his sunken eyes on her, and she felt a sudden chill, as though a ghost had passed through her body. She drew back, but he inched closer.

"You're hoping," he said in a tense whisper, "that you'll be able to escape this. Because you're still human. Because I made a mistake. Right?"

She didn't respond, but her silence confirmed it.

"That hope is going to destroy you down here."

"Why would you say something like that?" she asked, an ache in her voice.

"I forced you into this life. If I could, I'd undo it. But I can't. All I can do is help you learn to survive."

The searing anger she'd first felt for him reared its furious head. "You think I don't know how to do that? Survive?"

His voice softened. "If you have nothing, Dohv can't take anything from you."

She exhaled a shaky breath. He was right. She'd seen what Dohv was capable of, how he'd prey upon any weakness she dared to show . . .

"There will be consequences for destroying the trees," Haben continued. "And you'll be facing them alone. I'll have left you by then."

She nodded, struck by the sudden emptiness she felt. *I'll have left you by then.* She'd almost forgotten about that part.

"I want you to be prepared for what's coming."

He held his gaze on her, and she felt her fury subside. He hadn't meant to sound so cruel, and she understood what he was trying to do—to force her to look at what he'd become, at the years of torment on his face—but she wasn't looking at his scars. She was looking just beyond them. She took in every hollow of his tired face, searching for even the smallest surviving shred of the man he used to be. He wanted her to understand that someday she would be just like him. But she wished *he* would understand that he was still so much like *her.* There were traces of mortality left in him, she was sure of it. She glanced at his hands, white and frail. Once, long ago, she imagined he had held the hand of his mother . . . or a girl . . . or maybe a child of his own. There was so much she wished she knew about him. She was certain somehow that he hadn't forgotten anything about his past. Every memory was etched into his flesh. Just like her own.

"I understand what could happen, even if we make it," she whispered. "But we're still going, aren't we?"

He nodded.

"It doesn't mean I'm not afraid, though," she said. "It doesn't mean that at all."

She faced him and placed a gentle hand on his arm. He flinched, but she tightened her grip.

"I promise you'll escape this. I'm going to help you."

His eyes darted back and forth like an anxious wild animal. It took him a moment to return her gaze. For some reason, she wanted to stay locked to that exact spot as long as she possibly could.

He finally shifted away from her and she turned, shining her torch up ahead into the blackness. It was only then she remembered that she had no idea where they were going next.

"So, this Blue Mountain . . ." she said as she took a few cautious paces forward.

"We'll see where this passage leads and follow the River of Past Lives to the east. The river runs underneath the mountain."

"Then we look for the side with no shadows. Whatever that means."

He nodded, then glanced in her direction. She hadn't noticed she'd been bracing herself with her arms and was staring anxiously at her feet.

"You don't like the caves, do you?"

"They just seem smaller than they really are," she replied. Was she uneasy because of the cave, or something else?

"Well, it won't be long." He pointed straight ahead. "That's our way out. You can feel the cooler air."

"I can't feel anything."

"You haven't lived in a cave for the past two hundred years."

She let loose a low laugh as they walked together in silence for a few tense moments. The *drip-drop* sounds echoing across the cave sounded even louder now. Why was his silence suddenly so heavy to her? What was it that she saw behind his exhausted eyes that had held her transfixed for that moment? And why had the thought of losing him forever to limbo struck such a nerve in her, despite the promise she'd made?

Back in Khronasa, it had only been her and Miko. Nobody else had ever penetrated their intense family bond, and she dared not trust anyone but herself. She'd built a fortress around her life. She'd never let anyone touch her, nor touched them back in return. But she had touched *him*. She had wanted to, and each time it was deliberate. What was it about this man that made things different? *He's not a man*, she reminded herself.

She stole a glance at him. He was a shadow of someone who was once a man. That much could be said. When she reached out to touch him, it was that person she wished she could touch.

"Stop," he whispered. She whirled around to face him.

"Stop what? I'm not doing—" she stammered. Her cheeks burned as though she feared he'd just read her thoughts.

"Stop. Listen."

"I-I don't hear anything," she said, relieved, feeling foolish. But only for a moment. She realized it had been a long time since she'd heard a single *drip-drop* echo through the tunnel. It was dead silent.

"Exactly," he said. "Do you feel that?"

It took her a few seconds to understand what he meant. She could feel the air flowing from the other end of the rocky corridor now, but it was bitterly cold. Her breath formed little clouds in the flickering torchlight. She inched a few paces ahead of him, wary.

"Do you think we need to turn around?"

He didn't reply, and in that silence she swore she could hear soft footsteps and the sound of someone breathing. Not just one person—several, all doing it at the exact same time.

"Haben—?"

She'd only had her back to him for the briefest of seconds, but that was all it took. She spun back around and found him hunched over, shivering, arms clenched tightly around his chest. His eyes were vacant and glassy, staring straight through her. Seycia jumped.

"What's happening?"

"Run," he hissed.

Then, she saw it: a cluster of ghostly, swirling Soulless had gathered around his feet. They moved in circles up the length of his body, wrapping him in their black vapor like a spider's prey.

"Laida, stop screaming! I can't think when you scream like that!" he shrieked just before the Soulless covered up his mouth and one of them slipped down his throat.

Seycia's breath caught and she took off running. What had he just said? Who was he talking to? She didn't want to find out . . .

But before she could think of what to do next, she went rigid with cold, shivering so violently she could no longer run. She could feel the Soulless swarming around her, and a flash of blinding light forced her to her knees. She crumbled against the wall, unable to breathe, unable to think. A strange murkiness took hold, as though a heavy curtain was being pulled over her eyes. She whirled around, colliding with the cold, clammy cave walls. Her pulse raced; her throat closed up. They'd walked right into a trap . . .

But then, a sweet calm washed over her, and her heart swelled as she heard a voice sing in the darkness:

How lucky am I, how blessed are we
To have a child who grew from a good tree
She never cries, she never pouts
She never lies, she never shouts
She makes us proud, how lucky are we
To have a child who grew from a good tree

The woman who sang it brought tears to Seycia's eyes. She knew the voice immediately, and she knew it well. The darkness around her started to clear as she whispered, "Mama?"

She was home. Everything was just as she'd left it seven summers ago. She bounded around her family's spacious old cabin, petting her father's fur pelts that hung on the wall, smelling the stew cooking over the fire. And that's where she saw her, standing at the hearth. She was lovely as ever, with those same long eyelashes she remembered, and freckles on her nose. She fixed her warm hazel eyes on Seycia as she approached.

"Mama," Seycia said again, and the woman touched her forehead to hers. They held hands for a long moment as joy flooded Seycia to the tips of her toes.

"Stay with me," her mother whispered, running her fingers through Seycia's tangled black hair.

Seycia nodded. Of course. Why would she ever leave? Her mother's gentle fingers against her scalp lulled her into a soothing trance. It had been so long since she'd felt this way. So safe. So perfectly happy.

She didn't notice that her mother had plucked a knife from the cutting board with her other hand. Seycia's eyes began to flutter closed, but then she caught the silvery edge of the knife reflecting in the firelight. She didn't even have a second to scream before her mother clenched her hair in her fist, and Seycia found herself face-to-face with the knife.

"Let me go! Help!" Seycia shrieked as the entity pretending to be her mother pointed the knife right at Seycia's eye, as though she intended to cut it out.

Thrust from her trance, Seycia dodged the knife in the nick of time. With a devastated wail, she shoved the imposter into the fire and took off running. She should have known, she should have known. This was all the stuff of dreams. Too beautiful to be true.

"Please. I want us to be together," the entity cried as it rose from the fire, still in her mother's voice. Her clothes smoldered, and her flesh blackened and peeled as the fire rippled across her body. But she didn't flinch, as though she couldn't feel it.

"Don't leave me. I've been alone for so long."

Seycia swallowed her tears as she gazed at her mother's burning figure. Why did it feel so real? Who was doing this to her?

She glanced around the cabin, desperate to escape. She pulled for the door, but it was locked tight. She opened a window, but there was nothing on the other side but damp, dark stone, blocking her exit. And that's when she remembered: this was the Underworld. She was in a cave. And she wasn't the only one who needed a rescue.

"Haben!"

She listened for a reply as the burning imposter stalked toward her, still clutching the knife. "Haben!" she shouted again. "Can you hear me?"

She peered over her mother's shoulder, at the fire in the hearth. She noticed a black hole on the other side of the flames, rotating in dark, cloudy circles, and she bolted toward it. The Soulless had created this world for her. And she'd have to pass through them if she wanted to escape it. She held a hand to the fire. It was hot and painful, to be sure. But it didn't burn her skin the way it had her mother's imposter.

"Seycia! You can't leave me!" her mother screeched, barreling toward her with the knife drawn. Seycia spun around, drew a breath, and ran headfirst through the fire and into the black portal behind it.

The scorching pain was brief. For Seycia, it was nothing compared to the horror that followed as she passed through the Soulless and ruptured their illusion. Voices screamed words too heinous to ever repeat as all the rage she'd ever bottled up exploded to the surface. It was as if every evil humanity had ever committed were playing out behind her eyes. She wanted to scream all those horrible words right back. She wanted to kill with her bare hands. But she forced herself to put one foot in front of the other. She knew she had to fight through them.

She awoke on the other side, back in the cave—at least, it felt like waking up. Breathless from the ordeal, she discovered that she hadn't actually moved. She was right where she'd left Haben, but now she was surrounded by a dozen shriveled, humanoid demons, holding torches, who clung to each other as they breathed as one.

One of them pointed a sharp arrowhead directly at her eye.

She unleashed a terrified howl and kicked the shrunken demon to the ground. She pulled out her fang as she fought her way past the rest of them. She gasped when she realized not a single one had eyes—just empty, blood-crusted sockets beneath the hoods of their robes.

She lowered the fang as her terror gave way to sadness. She shoved them out of her way, but she didn't strike them with her weapon. It didn't seem right, to kill any of them. All these pitiful creatures had was each other.

She bolted back down the tunnel, heart thundering in her chest. Had Haben escaped? Was she too late?

She peered around the pitch-black cavern, but it was impossible to see anything. "Haben!" she cried into the darkness. There was no reply. Maybe she hadn't reached him yet? She kept running.

She could hear the blind vagabonds breathing in unison, right behind her, chasing her down the tunnel. How were they able to move so quickly? She ran as fast as she could on her trembling legs.

She barreled through the cave with a burst of reckless hysteria, tears streaming down her cheeks, and suddenly she felt as though the tunnel was getting smaller. Yes, it was. The walls were closing in on her with every step she took. Her stomach turned inside out and she thought she might be sick. *Never getting out! Never getting out!*

At that moment, she lost her footing and fell down, through a hole in the cave's floor. Down, down, down she tumbled through a space that was even tighter than the passage she'd just fallen from but with smooth, slippery walls. She could hardly breathe she was falling so fast.

Seconds later, she plunged into a deep, dark body of water. She snapped open her eyes below the surface and swallowed a scream with a mouthful of water. She'd been tossed from the tunnel into the River of Past Lives.

The Soulless floated in circles all around her. There had to be hundreds upon thousands of them. *Every mortal that's ever lived.* That's what Haben had said. She swam upward and braced herself for another encounter. She heard those horrible voices again and felt that same unbridled rage taking hold as the Soulless slipped past her, cold and slick like eels. She gritted her teeth and fought through them, clawing her way toward daylight.

As she breached the surface and finally tasted fresh air, a hand seized her ankle.

"Argh!" she screamed and jerked about like a fish on a hook, trying to shake the culprit loose. It didn't matter that she could breathe underwater. There were forces here that she couldn't control. There were millions of Soulless . . . and only one of her.

"Seycia," Haben sputtered from behind her, coming up for air. His grip on her foot loosened.

She fought against the heavy current to face him. She had no words left. She was catatonic.

Haben grabbed her by the shoulders and guided her toward the shore, where she pulled herself up onto the rocky ledge and drew her shaky knees to her chest. He swung himself onto the rock next to her. Her weak stomach finally got the better of her, and she became sick, heaving into the river. Haben shot her a shocked, sideways glance.

"I'll bet . . ." She coughed. "I'll bet demons don't do *that* either."

"No. You're . . . right about that."

She felt his hand brush her shoulder before he steadied his grip to keep her from rocking back and forth. A moment passed before she was able to raise her head and meet his stricken gaze.

"Who were those people?"

"Not people. Demons. They use the Soulless to lure others into their circle."

"What did the Soulless show you?" Seycia asked after a moment. He shook his head but offered no reply. "You called out a name, you said—"

"I don't remember."

"You don't? I do. I was with my mother. And she was—"

"I said I don't remember," he interrupted her, quick as a knife. "None of it was real anyway."

She surrendered to silence. He would say no more. The two of them watched the ebb and flow of the ghostly river for a moment. It was calming, somehow. She thought she might take his hand. She wasn't sure why—it just seemed like a thing she ought to do. But she didn't.

"I'm glad we both found a way out," was all she could think to say.

He gave a slow nod in response, then rose to his feet. "That's the Blue Mountain," he said, pointing to the east.

A silver-blue peak of ancient volcanic rock, older than time itself, dominated the distant skyline. The setting sun framed the mountain with a halo of dusty pink clouds. A few final rays of sunlight shone through the colorful mist, as though reaching out to touch the last remaining moments of the fading day. Just beyond the mountain peak, Seycia spotted a deep, dark crack in the sky, as though someone had slashed the clouds with a sharp object.

"And that?" she asked Haben, pointing to the black fissure.

"That's where the humans breached the Veil."

Seycia's breath caught, even though somehow she'd suspected that's what it was. The mortals had left a permanent scar on this world—a world they were never meant to see. She stared at it, wondering if the people who created it ever once considered the consequences.

"This is an awful place," Seycia said after a moment, returning her gaze to the mountain. "But sometimes it doesn't look that way, does it?"

He shook his head, taking in the view. Then, to her surprise, he offered his hand to help her to her feet. She cautiously took it and felt his fingers close around hers. His touch, which had felt so cold when they first met, was warmer now. She noted the curious change as she stood. She couldn't help the thing she wanted to say next . . .

"Listen," she began, before they could set off again. "I want us to . . . I want *you* to consider a different outcome. When all this is over. I know I said I'd help you. And I will. But . . ."

His face fell, and he let go of her hand. "What are you saying?"

"If I destroy your tree. Or if I . . . if I end it for you some other way." She couldn't even say the words. *If I kill you.* "I'm starting to wonder if I can do it. I've never killed anyone before."

"You killed that thing in the gorge."

"That was different, it wasn't a person."

"Lorsa used to be. A person."

"He can't die. I didn't kill him."

"You may as well have."

Seycia studied him. His dark grimace was like a shadow across his face. "I came with you because I knew you'd do the job. You were ruthless enough to destroy someone's soul. I liked that. Don't let me down."

"But I'm not. Ruthless. At least, I don't want to be," she said, realizing it for the first time. "Killing someone who might kill you first is different than just . . . you know."

"Do I? If you won't help me, then I don't see a reason to go on like this."

"All I'm asking is for you to consider whether you really want to—"

But she was unable to utter another word. A monstrous Creeback burst from the river, toward the cliff, and lunged right toward her. It happened so fast that she didn't even realize she was back in the water . . . until it was too late.

Haben saw it coming before she did, but he didn't have a second to warn her. The Creeback snarled and snagged Seycia's leg in its terrifying jaws. Haben blanched at the size and strength of it, at the way it thrust its tremendous body onto the cliff with only its two front feet. He grappled for Seycia's hand as the demon killer swooped back down into the river with its prey in tow. All was silent except for the rush of the current below.

"Seycia!" he called out, but he knew she wouldn't answer. His gut twisted.

He glanced down into the water, then at the opposite riverbank. There stood Zane, with his fiendish, pearly white grin. They'd been tracked. Haben felt as though a freezing hand had closed around his throat.

He knew he should run. He could probably escape if he bolted off the cliff at that very moment. But instead, he dove headfirst into the river. He swore he could hear Zane's maniacal cackle as he plummeted into the water.

The hoards of Soulless made it nearly impossible to see underwater. He opened his eyes wide and swam with every scrap of strength he had. He knew he had to stay focused and keep moving or he'd be drawn in by their horrible, all-consuming ugliness. The river was deeper than he'd imagined. All across the riverbed, underwater rock formations rose up like statuesque giants.

He spotted her at the entrance to a watery cave, struggling against the Creeback. Her blood emptied in dark, gruesome swirls, leaving her body with the current. This was a wound she wouldn't recover from. There was no cure for a Creeback's bite. But he'd be damned if he left her underwater that way. He realized then how close he was to death himself. He could so easily surrender to the Creeback and let it kill him, too. But he couldn't; he was the only one who could save Seycia. He thought of the argument they'd had just moments before. Maybe he understood now . . .

He approached the Creeback, and it glared at him with a hideous grunt. Haben eyed the fang hanging around Seycia's neck. Could a Creeback's fang kill another Creeback? He propelled his body onto Seycia's and snatched the fang. The Creeback gnashed its enormous teeth at him and, in doing so, let go of Seycia's leg.

Haben shoved the fang into Seycia's limp fist and guided her arm toward the Creeback's neck. But the monster was too quick. It whirled around and slashed Haben with the razor-sharp scales lining its thick, reptilian tail. He grasped his chest where he'd been sliced, clenching his teeth as the awful ache rippled through his body. He felt blood against his palm, but he averted his eyes. He couldn't look at the cut. He couldn't slow down, not yet.

He threw the fang over his own neck and grabbed Seycia around the waist in one rapid motion. He caught sight of her leg. He wished he hadn't. Her calf and knee were gnawed to the bone. Blood, blood, blood . . . so much blood. He had forgotten what it was like to fear for someone's life. There was nothing in the future, and the past didn't matter. There were only the few precious moments he had left to take action.

He shook her with all his might when he realized she wasn't breathing underwater. No reaction. The Creeback gurgled and growled, spitting a violent typhoon of water in their direction. He had to get her out of the river. Even if Dohv was waiting for him at the water's edge, he wouldn't let her be lost this way.

He spied a rock shaped like a jagged, open circle. Soulless passed through the ring with ease, one after the other. He shot toward it, the Creeback in hot pursuit. It was at least three times the size of him. It would have to work. It would have to, it would have to . . .

He pressed Seycia's body against his and crashed through the rocky ring. He felt the Creeback's tongue brush the bottom of his foot, and he shivered with horror before a mighty, furious howl filled the underwater chamber. Haben whirled around, clinging to Seycia's pale, motionless body. The Creeback was wedged inside the circle, thrashing in agony as it watched its prey escape.

Zane was still standing on the opposite shore, doubled over in fits of laughter, as Haben shot to the surface, pulling Seycia's body along.

"Why don't you take a bite? Get one last meal before Dohv comes for you," Zane hollered with a spiteful cackle as Haben pulled Seycia up onto the cliff.

But all he could hear was the rush of his own blood in his ears as he stared into the gray void of Seycia's face. Her leg was turning a sickly blue color as the infection spread like wildfire. Haben fumbled with Seycia's fang, eyeing her shredded flesh, dreading the thing he knew he had to try.

He snapped the fang off its cord and tied the string around her thigh as tight as he could. He would need to do it quickly, before the infection spread . . . before Dohv came. Then she could hide. She could hide and recover. She could reach the Great Forest. He'd be gone, but she could keep going. He placed the fang into Seycia's lifeless hand, clamping her limp fingers around it with his own, and lowered it to her skin.

"I'm sorry," he said, pushing her matted hair out of her face. He pressed the tip of the fang to her leg, forcing his eyes open, keeping his hand steady . . .

CA-CAW!

The sound was so close it shook a dozen rocks loose from the cliffside. Ears ringing, frozen to the spot, Haben dropped the fang. The colossal bald bird flapped its fleshy wings right above him, creating a riptide in the river below. It had finally caught up with them. The bird stared right into his eyes and cried out again, as though it were trying to tell him something. As though it wanted him to stop what he was doing, immediately, and listen.

Haben heard Zane yelp from the other side of the river, "No, no, no!" There was something about the creature that caused the boy demon to panic. Haben wondered if it had come to help him somehow.

Zane jumped into the river, trying to swim to the opposite bank, but he was too small and weak against the forceful current. As Zane was swept downstream with a furious howl, the creature jerked its fleshy head toward the east, then looked back at Haben. It was as if it were saying, *Follow me.*

The bird took off, still glancing over its shoulder at Haben. *Well, are you coming?*

Haben weighed his choices, head spinning. If he stayed here, Dohv would soon arrive. Even if he decided to trust this strange creature, could he get to safety before Seycia's body gave way to the infection? He peered down at her and noticed the infection hadn't spread past the place where he held her, across the waist.

The bird cried out once again, and Haben made his decision. He raced down the riverbank as fast as he could with Seycia in his arms, following the creature as it sailed below the clouds, guiding him along. He didn't know where they would end up, or whether it would be safe. But there was something about the way the bird gazed into his eyes, something so soulful and humanlike, that he decided he could trust it. Maybe it hadn't been spying on him. Maybe it had come to watch over them for a reason. He had to hope.

As he ran, he glanced down at Seycia with a sunken heart. If she surrendered to Darkest Death before they reached their destination, wherever that was, no torture Dohv could devise could break him any further.

If you have nothing, Dohv can't take anything from you. He'd said so himself, to her, not long ago. He took the cold, dead weight of her hand in his and wished more than anything that he'd listened to his own advice.

CHAPTER THIRTEEN

"GIL, AM I glad to see you," Simeon breathed as Gil, who had so fearlessly defended him the night before, entered his bedroom with his semiautomatic slung over his shoulder.

"I haven't slept a wink," Simeon said in a hoarse voice, sitting on the edge of his bed as his most trusted bodyguard approached. "I know it sounds foolish but . . . maybe if you stood outside my door—"

"I was already there, your Excellency," Gil bowed his bald head, buffed like fine silver. "You can rest easy."

"That's a relief."

"How are you this morning?"

"I'll be fine, of course, lack of sleep aside. He was just a boy," Simeon said with a grumble and rose to his feet. "I fear, however, that we'll need extra security. I don't think we have quite enough people on staff."

"That's what I wish to discuss with you," Gil replied. "We've had several volunteers as of this morning, villagers with military experience who wanted to help defend the grounds. With your permission, of course."

"You'll keep a close eye on them? Make sure they're not here to finish what that idiot started?"

"On my honor. They seem like good recruits. Not *everyone* in the city has turned against you, your Excellency. It's just being made to look that way."

"W-what do you mean 'it's just being made to look that way'?" Simeon snapped. Gil cast him a troubled frown.

"So you haven't seen."

Gil made his way to the bay window at the far end of the room, the one that faced the front gates, and pulled the curtains open. An enormous crowd of Khronasan villagers had gathered outside the gate to the mansion, and the scant remaining security force held them back. But the Khronasans weren't fighting or causing any disruption. They weren't breaking any laws. They simply stood there, staring up at the mansion as if to say, *Your days here are numbered.* Simeon shivered and backed away from the window.

"Is this because of the incident during the emperor's visit? You know that was a setup, don't you?"

"Of course, your Excellency. But I don't think it's because of that. I'm being told it's because of the boy."

The general ripped the curtains shut. "That boy's father and sister did . . . this." His mangled face burned with humiliation as he gestured to it. "Did you know that?"

"I did not, your Excellency."

"He's being held in the prison, underground. He'll be executed at sundown. It's already been arranged."

"You're going to kill him, sir?" Gil asked, wary. "With all these people gathered in support of him?"

"Why are they gathered in the first place? This is ludicrous. He's just a kid. What about all the other children they've watched us toss into the pit without question?"

"Well, that's just the thing. He escaped the pit. He fought back."

"And he lost."

"Even so. It seems he's given the people hope."

"That they'll do what, overthrow me?" Simeon chuckled, but Gil did not.

"Your Excellency, it's not my place to advise you. Not in the least bit. But if you kill the boy, you'll make a martyr out of him. You'll have a mutiny on your hands, and these people will make sure you go down with the ship."

Simeon approached the window and peered through the space between the curtains at the crowd below. From this distance, none of them seemed to blink. He'd barely managed to keep the secrets of his household contained. If these people weren't afraid of him anymore, evidence of his offenses could easily reach the emperor. Unless, of course, they decided to tear him down themselves. With a shudder, he turned back to Gil, clearing his throat to hide his distress.

"Well, how else am I supposed to keep these lunatics in line?"

"There might be another way," Gil lowered his voice. "You could redeem yourself if you let the boy go and put an end to the sacrifices. Resign as general. Apologize and go into exile."

Simeon stared at him for a long, tense moment, as though he wanted Gil to wonder if he were considering it . . . then laughed in his face with an offended snort. "Why would I ever do that? *Go into exile?* Please. This isn't about redemption, Gil. This is about reminding these swine who's in control."

"Of course, your Excellency. It was only a suggestion."

"One I didn't ask for," Simeon spat. He waved off Gil, impatiently. "Leave me. I have to think in peace."

"By all means, sir." Gil gave a sturdy salute. "Our fate in his hands."

"Let's hope it is," Simeon muttered.

Gil exited the room, leaving him in silence.

Simeon quickly pulled on his housecoat and made his way out of the bedroom, down the hall, and toward his study. He hadn't set foot inside the room since the break-in, and he'd barred anyone else in the household from entering. He'd been too shaken to even think of approaching the shrine. But he needed the kind of guidance only a god could provide. He would have to go back down there.

He had covered the broken door to the shrine with a heavy tapestry, and he breathed a sigh before moving it aside to unlock it. He glanced at the hole in the door with a grimace. Part of him wished he'd learned who the culprit was before he executed the lot of them, even though it would have led to the same fate.

As he ventured down the stairs, he was relieved to discover that all of his other artifacts were intact. Only the statue had been stolen that day. But whomever had taken it had glimpsed everything else. His skin turned to gooseflesh; he felt violated and exposed.

He searched for the box where he stashed his pouch of sacred bones, and he found the little wooden chest unharmed, safely tucked away in a far corner of the room.

He unrolled the prayer carpet across the cold, concrete floor, arranged the Creeback bones into a neat triangle, and kissed them. A cold breeze swept through the room as he closed his eyes and whispered, "Praise be to Dohv, revered Keeper of Life and Lord of the Underworld. I am troubled and in desperate need of your guidance. Despite our bargain, despite my promises to you, an attempt was made on my life last night. I do not blame you, my lord, but if you can help me, I will spend eternity in your debt. If I execute the criminal, my people may rise up against me. But if I do not, I will be viewed by those who respect me as a man of weak will. Please, lord. Send me a sign. What do I do?"

At that moment, the temperature in the room plummeted. Simeon shivered in the bitter cold. His shivering grew more violent with each passing second, and a nervous lump formed in his throat. Something was happening . . .

"M-my lord?" Simeon whispered, before he doubled over in blinding pain and his eyes rolled toward the back of his head. All he saw was blackness. He twitched and seized as a deep voice flooded his mind, rattling his frail, mortal body.

"Kill the boy," Dohv said.

Simeon coughed and gagged, unable to breathe. But he was sure he had heard it. Seconds later, vision returned to him, and he pulled a deep gulp of air. The room was once again a pleasant, moderate temperature, and he huddled on the floor, stunned, unable to move for a long moment. Dohv had never spoken to him before, and his instructions had been unmistakably clear. But how would he do it?

Gil had warned him that a formal execution could backfire, that the people could make a martyr of the boy. He didn't want to fuel a full-blown revolt. But what if he could make it look like an accident? If the boy died but he wasn't to blame, not only would the people's symbol be gone, but he might also be able to dodge the resulting outrage.

Simeon staggered to his feet. Forget Gil. Dohv had demands, and it was Simeon's duty to oblige. He placed the sacred bones back into their pouch and marched up the stairs, two at a time.

He tore through his liquor cabinet in the study, searching for a very specific bottle. He'd had the concoction mixed for him by the Coalition's weapons division, years ago. He'd meant for it to be a last-resort suicide method for himself, but today there was a much better use for it. He spotted the tiny blue-green bottle made of sea glass all the way at the back of the top shelf. He grabbed for it, shoved it into his jacket pocket, and sailed out the door.

As he stormed across the mansion's manicured lawn, toward the entrance to the compound's underground prison, Simeon stole a glance at the front gate, where the crowd of Khronasans was still waiting. Waiting . . . for what? To catch a glimpse of him? For the perfect moment to strike? He heard a crunch in the gravel behind him and whirled around to see Gil at his back.

"Move quickly," Gil murmured in his low, husky baritone. "Don't let them see you."

Simeon nodded and continued toward the prison. Gil followed, keeping his rifle balanced just so against his forearm.

Simeon pushed through the heavy double doors of the concrete entryway and descended the staircase into the prison. He reached a dark corridor at the foot of the stairs, housing prison cells on either side. The entire place reeked of human waste and impending death. Simeon drew in a sharp breath and covered his mouth. He'd forgotten about the stench. He hadn't visited this place in some time. He reached into his pocket and grazed the little glass bottle, just to make sure it was still there.

The security detail at the front of the hall stood and saluted him. "Our fate in his hands," the three men said in unison.

Enough with the fanfare. "I want to see him," Simeon replied with a curt hiss.

"Here are the items he had on him when we apprehended him, your Excellency, if you wish to inspect them," one of the prison guards said, holding out Miko's rucksack. Simeon stopped and snagged the bag. "His cell is the third on the left."

With a terse nod, Simeon rummaged through the rucksack. Inside was an ancient, heavy revolver. He laughed. The boy thought he'd be a match for their artillery with *this*? It was an antique at best! But still . . . he had to wonder where he'd gotten it from.

There was one more item inside the sack, all the way at the bottom. He reached inside and pulled out a marble slab about the length of his palm, covered in intricate carvings, like the demolished temple in the forest. He'd never seen such a perfect piece of it intact. He was about to stuff it into the pocket of his coat . . . but the eyes of all the guards were on him. He couldn't afford another slip. With a sigh, he left it on the patrolman's table and took the gun with him.

He approached Miko's cell. Young morning light struggled through the tiny window, illuminating the spot where the boy sat, motionless, legs folded to his chest.

"There's only one reason I allowed you to live through the night." Simeon cradled the revolver in his hand and revealed it to him. "I'll show you mercy if you tell me who you got this from and what they're planning," he lied.

"You killed them," the boy said coolly. "So I really don't know."

Simeon leaned in closer, glancing at an empty tin pitcher just outside Miko's cell. "You, there," Simeon shouted at one of the security guards. "Refill this, would you?"

A guard approached and took the pitcher from General Simeon.

"Get the boy some water."

As the guard rushed off with the pitcher, Simeon turned back to Miko. He hadn't budged. He glared daggers through Simeon, sitting still as a stone.

"You protect these people, but they abandoned you. They let you go off on your own, knowing you'd fail," Simeon lowered his voice, hoping he might reach the boy where his insecurities hid. But his expression only hardened.

The guard returned with the tin pitcher, and Simeon turned for the briefest of moments, just long enough to dump the entire bottle of poison into the water. He locked eyes with the guard for a split second—a silent contract. Simeon placed the pitcher in front of Miko's cell, where he'd easily be able to reach it through the bars.

"Go on. Drink. I can have a meal brought to you as well."

"If I help you."

"You're catching on," Simeon snarled, and his heart raced as Miko reached through the bars, pulled the small pitcher into his cell, and took a long gulp.

He coughed, smacked his lips, then said, "Well, I won't. Even if I tell you what you want to know, you'll kill me anyway."

But Simeon just laughed. He'd already taken the bait. Now it was just a matter of how much information he could extract before the poison took hold. He had no idea how long it would be.

"You'll regret it though, when people find out," Miko said, with a chill in his voice that made Simeon's hair stand on end. It was as if he already knew everything. "I'm the Lasting Light. If you kill me, Khronasa will burn to the ground. And you'll burn for eternity in the Underworld."

Simeon's breath caught as he met the boy's sinister gaze. What was he talking about? Was this a side effect of the poison? Or something else . . . ?

"There are demons all around you," the boy went on, inching closer to the bars. "They're here, right now. You just don't know it. And they'll finish what I started."

Simeon felt clammy with cold sweat. *He's just playing a game with you. Don't listen to his lies.* And yet . . . was it possible that this boy, this so-called Lasting Light, was not of this world? Dohv had singled him out, after all. Did they share a common enemy? Or, he panicked, maybe Dohv *wanted* the bloodshed that would follow. What would happen after the boy was dead? Which way was up? He felt like he was losing his mind.

Simeon backed away, laughing to mask his dread. Either way, it was too late. He'd already poisoned him . . .

"Tell me, have you ever even heard of the Lasting Light?" Simeon asked with a cruel snicker, putting on a brave face. "I certainly haven't."

He saw Miko's lips quiver just the smallest bit. Perhaps he'd finally hit a nerve.

"I must say, it *is* a decent strategy: convince a boy he's a god so he won't be afraid to do your dirty work. Do you believe everything your people tell you?"

Miko swallowed hard, but he kept that same stoic look on his face. Simeon pocketed the boy's revolver, then spun down the hall, back the way he came.

"May this be the last time our paths cross," Simeon hissed over his shoulder.

To his back, with that same steadiness, Miko replied, "It won't be."

Simeon shuddered as he stormed out of the prison. The boy sounded so sure. He had no idea what he'd just tangled with. *You'll burn for eternity in the Underworld.* His voice rang in Simeon's ears.

As he made his way toward the exit, he swiped the temple shard off the patrolman's table while he had his back turned. Dohv needed to know he still had his unwavering loyalty, just in case the boy was right. As Simeon dropped the shard into his pocket, the patrolman spun back around to face him. Had he noticed?

"Our fate in his hands," the young man said, offering a salute.

Simeon was slow to answer. His other master was calling. Finally, he choked out, "Our fate in his hands," and returned the salute.

His gut twisted as he met Gil at the door, who shut it behind them with a loud bang. He had no idea if his troubles would end when the boy's life did . . . or if they'd only just begun.

Miko exhaled and finally relaxed his tense posture on the floor of his cell. He never thought he'd have the courage, let alone the moment, to say everything he'd wanted to say to General Simeon. He hadn't expected him to get so nervous, either. But Miko wasn't sure if he could believe his own words. And as he thought about what Simeon had just said, he felt the doubt inside of him grow.

Had Minari, Belicia, and the rest of them used him? Had they made him believe he was special so he'd risk his life for them? *No. It's not possible.* Hadn't Belicia risked *her* life to save his?

Suddenly, Miko gasped as an ungodly ache surged across his body. The sickness struck him like a bolt of electricity and made him wonder if he was reliving the shock of colliding with the fence. He didn't even realize he'd just fallen to the ground. He felt weak all over, unable to hold himself up—as if his body and mind had stopped communicating. His head throbbed like there was a monster inside. He curled up against the wall with a groan. The filthy stone stank of mold, sweat, and a sour smell he didn't want to try to identify. But the stone was cool, and his body was scorching hot.

Miko's aching legs twitched, involuntarily. He winced when he aggravated the spot where he'd been sliced by the electric fence. It felt like he'd been cut straight across the backs of his knees with an invisible knife.

He wanted to cry out, but his throat was scratchy and raw, and in his mouth was a taste like old, toxic rust. What was happening? *What was in that water?*

His chest burned as he struggled to pull a shaky breath. The edges of everything faded, and his eyelids felt heavy as stones. He couldn't see. He couldn't hear. He couldn't think.

He surrendered to the emptiness. And the world vanished like smoke.

CHAPTER FOURTEEN

NIGHT FELL, AND Seycia could tell Haben was still walking. The base of the Blue Mountain loomed straight ahead, like a dark wall they were about to collide with. He'd carried her the whole way. Seycia felt as if she were hovering inches above her frozen, aching body. She couldn't move, couldn't speak, but through her sliver of consciousness she was able to tell what had happened. She knew she'd been hurt. She knew she'd been pulled from the river. And she knew how afraid Haben was.

Seycia felt him stop walking. There was nowhere left to go but up the mountain. The mysterious creature that had led them there swooped down from the summit and, to Seycia's surprise, landed in the rocky, black mud, right in front of them. It bent its neck, as though it wanted Haben to climb on. It was offering them a way up the mountain. Seycia still wasn't sure this creature was on their side, but she sensed Haben trusted it—or otherwise he had no choice but to trust it.

She felt Haben slide onto the strange, fleshy animal's neck, still holding her steady. She caught his eye as he stole a glance at her. She saw fear there . . . and a hundred other emotions she couldn't identify. She glanced down at his arm, locked around her waist. He was clinging to her so hard he'd started shaking.

They sailed in circles up and around the mountain. She wished she could say something to him, but she was completely paralyzed, unable to control any part of her body aside from her eyes. She longed to close them, but she was terrified she might never open them again if she did.

She focused on the mountain peak as it came into view: a mammoth heap of petrified cerulean lava, frozen since the beginning of time itself. Near its summit, a particularly huge tree had sprung forth, thrusting out from the cliffside, as though its other half had been enveloped by the volcanic rock. As they drew nearer, she noticed there was a small, irregularly shaped capsule hanging by two cords from one of the tree limbs, swaying in the breeze.

The bird slowed down and edged closer to the tree. The thing swinging from the branch looked like a lavender-blue chrysalis, and a gentle, warm light pulsed from within, as though some kind of glowing insect were asleep inside. Upon closer inspection, she noticed that the entire pouch was made of fine, colorful hairs. The cocoon and the tree itself were much larger than she had thought at a distance, large enough to be somebody's home. But whose?

The bird flew right up to the side of it and hovered in midair, releasing another one of its earsplitting cries. Seycia felt Haben flinch beside her, and he turned to gaze into her vacant face. She longed to shout, "I'm here, I'm alive, don't give up on me yet." She hoped he knew.

A patch at the front of the chrysalis quivered and slid upward like a vertical door. Three shapeless figures appeared there, silhouetted in the pale glow from inside. It was too dark to make out who or what they were. They raised their arms out toward them, stretching their long, bony fingertips like branches of an old, brittle tree. Their hands reminded her of

Dohv's and just seeing them made her shudder. What if this was another trap?

Suddenly, Seycia felt her body rise into the air without a sound, levitating toward the outstretched arms of the three figures. Haben grabbed for her, nearly toppling off the creature's back. She felt him catch on to the ends of her hair in his fist.

A faint, silvery voice called out, *"Stop! He can't hear you that way. He's a demon!"*

The voice was female, neither young nor old, but had a cool, refreshing, pear-shaped tone. Had one of the figures in the doorway just spoken?

"Can you hear me now, Haben?" another voice called out, sturdier and deeper.

"I hear you," Seycia heard him reply in an uneasy whisper. He was still clinging on to her hair as she floated in the space between.

"Let her go. She will not survive much longer if you don't."

"Who are you?" he asked.

"We'll show you if you let her go," the silvery voice said.

The third figure still hadn't spoken.

"You'll help her?" Seycia felt him wind her hair around his fingers as he stared at the doorway, weighing his options.

"You must let us help her," the deeper voice said.

Seycia wasn't sure why, but there was something so steady and trustworthy about that voice. She felt sure, at the core of her being, that they would be protected. She wondered if Haben could feel it, too. Seconds later, he let her go. She floated toward the waiting arms of the three shadows at the door. At their touch, Seycia felt her pain start to melt away and a sweet, numbing sensation spread across her body.

As they caught her in their arms, she was finally close enough to see them. All three were women, but their ages were impossible to determine. Lavender hair sprouted from their heads, woven into long braids coiled around their ears like a soft, thick crown. It looked exactly like the hair their home was made of.

The woman in the center had the loveliest face, angular and slender, with enormous turquoise eyes. Seycia swore she could see the waves of the ocean each time she blinked.

The woman to the right had an almost wooden texture to her brown, leathered skin and yellow eyes that looked like two bright autumn leaves on a tree.

The final woman on the far left, the silent one, was the strangest and most striking of all. She averted her shining black eyes and her snow-white hands trembled. The tips of her fingers were charred and black, as though she'd been badly burned. Her lips were an ever-changing whirl of red and gold, like a smoldering fire spread across her face.

Each of them wore long-sleeved gowns draped across their thin, fragile figures, and the translucent robes camouflaged with everything they touched. They reminded her of three ancient willow trees bathed in early morning dew.

The bald bird made a tired, gurgling noise in the back of its throat—Haben's cue to disembark. Seycia saw him cautiously crawl off its neck, and the three figures stepped aside to let him into their hanging hut.

"Come inside," the wooden-complexioned sister said to Haben. She'd been the one with the firmer, more confident voice. "Please excuse us. It's been some time since we've had company. We did not mean to alarm you. We were trying to communicate with you at the bottom of the mountain until we remembered demons aren't blessed with our telepathy."

The three of them turned at the exact same moment and carried Seycia inside. Haben followed. The timid woman turned around for a closer look at them. Seycia was transfixed by her fiery mouth as she raised her lips in what was, perhaps, meant to be an inviting smile.

The inside of the pod was much bigger than it appeared, and a thick layer of fine, silver sand covered the floor of the chrysalis. There were three lofts connected by ladders constructed of what Seycia was sure now was the goddesses' hair. Crystals, herbs, fungi, and flowers of every shape, size, and color dangled from the ceiling. The light source hung at the top of the hut, like a tiny indoor star hovering in midair.

A huge tower of tiny glass marbles dominated the entire wall on the far side of the hut, from floor to ceiling. Upside down in the women's arms, it took Seycia a moment to realize what the structure was: a crystalline replica of Dohv's palace, each glass piece wedged perfectly against the ones beside it, like an enormous, three-dimensional puzzle.

"I'm sorry," the sister with the huge turquoise eyes mumbled as she brushed past Haben. She suddenly seemed anxious, as if in a hurry.

As her other two sisters carefully lay Seycia's body into a nest of glossy black feathers, she shuffled over to the glass palace and pushed a new crystal fragment into the edge of the sculpture. Her fingers trembled, as if she were not in control of herself.

"I'm sorry," she said again to Haben, as she worked. "I have to. One of us always has to. There is great pain, if we refuse. But my sisters are helping your friend."

The quiet, nervous sister with the fiery lips crouched beside Seycia and cut off her ragged dress with one swift swipe of her finger. She hadn't even made contact with the fabric. Seycia shivered, still unable to move, as she looked into the goddess's glistening obsidian eyes. There was something wild and wounded about her gaze.

"What are you doing to her?" Seycia heard Haben ask as the remaining two sisters hovered over her, examining her wounds. They didn't answer for a moment. "I said, what are you—?"

"Shh." The wooden-complexioned sister shot him a glance. "We'll heal her. And you." She gestured to his tattered robe and the gash on his chest from the Creeback's tail. "But my sister must concentrate. Be still."

Seycia felt the black-eyed goddess place her hands on her shoulders, and a warm, electric current coursed through her body. Her eyelids grew heavy and started to droop, but in her twilight sleep, she could see her silent caretaker collecting various crystals and herbs from the ceiling. Seycia watched, fascinated, as she parted her molten red lips and spat into a small silver bowl of yellow fungi. She then ground it up with her blackened fingertips and applied it like a salve to Seycia's wound. Another soothing current pulsed across her body, in time with her heartbeat, as the goddess made contact with her skin. She wiggled her toes and breathed a heavy sigh. To her relief, she was starting to regain control over her body.

The goddess then moved Seycia onto her side and plucked four long, lavender hairs from her own head and tied them together. She strung a razor-thin crystal needle with the hair, and used it as thread to stitch up Seycia's wound. Seycia flinched as she felt the needle brush her skin, but there was no pain as it pierced her. The hair glimmered and quivered as it fused to her flesh, as if it were alive.

Finally, she heard the goddess make a sound: A low, satisfied *hmmph* from deep within her chest. She seemed content with her handiwork. She pressed her palm against Seycia's forehead, and Seycia couldn't fight the heavy haze that descended before her eyes. Her heartbeat thudded steadily in her ears, now the only sound she could hear.

Before she gave herself over to the sweetest sleep she'd ever known, she could make out the blurry shape of her caretaker, hovering over her, and Haben, standing right behind her. She hoped he wasn't afraid anymore. She knew they were safe. She thought it might be the first time she'd truly been safe in her whole life. As she drifted into a deep slumber, she slowly managed to smile.

Haben inched forward, careful not to disrupt the silent black-eyed goddess, and peered down at Seycia's peaceful face. He unclenched his fists and pulled a long breath. "She'll wake up, won't she?"

"When she's ready. Her body is recovering," the wooden-complexioned sister replied.

Haben turned to face her and in a reverent whisper, asked, "Who are you?"

"We haven't any names, I'm afraid," she answered, moving closer to him. "And we only appear this way to you because this is how you perceive sentient beings. We're the heartbeat of a much, much larger beast, born the day this world was born."

"You're gods," he breathed as he realized it. "But I thought Dohv was the only—"

"Dohv has banished us."

Haben caught her wounded stare, and it was as though she'd invited him to share in her pain. He could feel it. He inched closer to her. "I have to be able to call you something."

"On Earth, they started calling us Meri, Irem, and Remi. I think I do like that. The place your friend came from . . . Her people called us that. I would be Meri. That would be my sister, Remi." She pointed to the vibrant, blue-eyed sister still hard at work on the glass palace, then turned to the silent sister. "And she's Irem."

Haben locked eyes with Irem, who lifted her head, sensing she'd been mentioned.

"Thank you. For helping her," he said to Irem. She grumbled softly in reply, then started braiding Seycia's hair as she slept with her long, twig-like fingers.

"Irem doesn't speak?" he asked Meri.

"Irem *can't* speak," she explained with a frown. "No thanks to our brother. Who it seems you've been acquainted with." Meri gestured to the black tattoos encircling Haben's arms. He shrank back, pulling the sleeves of his robe.

"Thank you, for what you've done," he said. "But . . . because you're Dohv's sisters, I can't be sure if . . . I-I don't—"

"We're no fonder of him than you are," she reassured him. "Only those for whom Dohv has no regard or those who are trying to escape him come to this corner of our world."

At that moment, a frigid breeze swept through the little hanging hut, and the entire room swayed back and forth like a tiny rowboat on the ocean. Remi unleashed a devastated howl as she tried to save the perfect sculpture she was so close to completing. The light source above flickered. Haben clung to the plush, stringy wall for support.

The glass palace toppled to the floor and shattered, like a thousand little bells ringing all at once. Remi huddled in the corner and wept. As the glass on the floor disintegrated into a fine dust, Haben understood the meaning of the sand beneath his feet. This had happened, many, many times before.

"It's all right," Meri said as the cocoon stopped rocking and light slowly returned to the room. "We'll make a new one. We always do."

"Because you have to."

She looked at him in weary solidarity. "This was Dohv's bidding. We never leave the mountain." Then, she added, "It may sound foolish, but we still have hope we'll finish the sculpture someday. If we do, it will be a sign that our brother's powers have weakened. And maybe, on that day, we can finally leave this place."

"I didn't know he could do this," Haben said. "Not to other gods."

"The four of us were born of equal power, but he found a way to harvest it as your world grew more violent. Irem is perfectly clairvoyant, and she saw how dangerous he would one day become. She couldn't bear the horrible visions, so she spoke out against him."

"And he made sure she wouldn't speak again."

Meri nodded with a sigh. "It's as if Dohv cut the cord between her mind and her lips. The words make little sense, even when she tries to communicate telepathically, with us. She sees all, but she can never explain what she sees. It destroys her."

Meri shuffled over to the far corner of the room where the glass palace had stood just moments before. A brand new stack of crystal shards appeared out of thin air, neatly set against the wall, as though some invisible messenger had delivered them. Meri touched Remi's shoulder and beckoned her to stand. Meri then began the useless task all over again, assembling the glass pieces from the ground up.

"It's thanks to Irem that you're here with us," she went on as she worked. "She was the one who sent Norryn to follow you."

"And Norryn is . . . that?" Haben pointed out the door where the bald bird was hovering, peering inside. He met the creature's eye, and it gave an odd, scratchy cooing sound in return. He still wasn't sure what to make of it.

"Dohv created the Creebacks. We created a race of creatures to help us sail the skies. Dohv had them killed when we were banished," Meri explained. "Norryn is the only one left. He's also the only being that Irem can still communicate with. One morning, not long ago, she came to us in a frenzy of broken words. It seemed she'd had a premonition, and it had to do with you. So she sent Norryn to find you."

"What did she see?" he asked, and shivered. Why him?

"Nobody knows but Norryn. He'll listen but he won't reply. So we can only guess."

Haben nodded, unsettled, and then glanced at Seycia. He swore her flesh was not as pale as it had been only moments before. Yet he hadn't noticed, until then, that she was completely naked. Somehow, her body hadn't given him pause while Irem was repairing her wound. But now he was fixated upon the curve of her bare hip as she lay with her back to him, huddled deep in the nest of black feathers. He looked at Irem, who was staring straight at him. He swallowed hard, unable to return her gaze.

"Then Irem knows why we've come here," he said after a moment.

"She does. But we don't. And we'd like to," Remi piped up. It was as though she had forgotten that she'd just been weeping. She floated inches off the floor; her feet never touched the ground. Her eyes were effervescent, her face inquisitive. She kneeled and picked up the silver pot of ground fungi with one hand and tugged at the sleeve of his robe with the other. "But first, we'll need you to take that off so we can heal you."

He took a step back. "You need me to . . . what?"

"You were attacked by a Creeback. Not as badly as your friend, but the infection's going to spread if we don't get to work," Remi insisted, forcing him to turn around.

She untied the coarse black cord around his waist, and he took a moment before slowly lifting his robe. The rough fabric clung to his raw, bleeding flesh, and he winced as he pulled it off, clenching his teeth.

He stared at his feet and twisted his toes in the sand on the floor. He didn't dare look at the face of the woman staring at his emaciated, naked body. Even if she wasn't exactly a *woman*. Whatever she was, it didn't matter. He was sure nobody had ever seen him without his robes, not even once. Not since he became what he'd become.

His body had been something so different during his mortal years. It was an instrument, a machine built for solving puzzles and jumping to great heights . . . for giving pleasure . . . for receiving it . . . for *living*. Now, it was nothing but a constant open wound. He felt sick with foolishness for his thoughts about Seycia, for the way he'd allowed himself to feel. He felt as if all the hope was seeping out of him through the gash on his chest. There was nothing he could give her. Nothing like *that* . . .

"So," Remi said. Haben drew in a sharp breath, startled by the closeness of her voice. "You didn't answer me. Why *have* you come?"

A cooling sensation spread across his chest as Remi applied the salve to his cut, though he couldn't be sure if the feeling had come from the balm or from Remi's hand itself.

"We've come to escape Dohv," he half lied.

Irem ripped her focus from Seycia and glared at him. She made a frustrated grunt in her throat. Somehow, she knew the whole story. Haben broke her stare, nervous. What would they do if they knew the truth? He'd only just met them. He couldn't even guess.

"That's clearly not all," Meri chimed in as she continued working on the crystal sculpture. "Though it's impressive you've outrun Dohv as long as you have."

"Thanks to this, perhaps?" Remi asked. She was holding Seycia's fang. She'd fished it out of the pocket of his robe. His breath caught as she handed it to him.

"She had it on her when she arrived here. It's killed everything we've come up against."

"How did a mortal girl wind up with a Creeback's tooth?" Remi asked.

"And how did a mortal girl wind up *here*?" Meri added, a sudden darkness to her voice.

"She's not mortal. Not anymore."

"I assure you, she's not a demon," Meri said.

She left her post at the sculpture and touched Remi on the shoulder. Remi tossed Haben his robe and shuffled over to the glass palace to take Meri's place.

"If she's not a demon, then what is she?" Haben asked Meri, pulling the robe back over his head.

"It's difficult to say, but one look at her and it's obvious. She's not like you." She glanced at Seycia, and then at him, with a frown. "Something must have gone wrong."

It was just as Seycia had said all along. He hadn't wanted to admit it then, but now someone else was confirming it.

"When I brought her to our world, she wasn't dead. I thought she was, but—"

"Her heart was still beating when you transformed her?"

He nodded.

"A demon is a mortal whose identity is resurrected from of the River of Past Lives, whose soul is restored," Meri explained. "A demon is always dead first."

"If she's not a demon, then what is she?" A moment passed between them as Meri pursed her leathery lips in thought.

"Some kind of immortal human, I suppose," she finally said.

"Are there many of those?"

"She's the only one I've ever seen."

Irem held out Seycia's arm, still stained with splatters of dark demon blood. She let her charred fingertips dance across the surface of her forearm, and the blotches magnetized to her frail hand. She sent them swirling in all directions and, before long, she had transformed the ugly marks into a lovely, delicate vine curling up Seycia's arm. Haben saw Irem smile.

"I fear for her, if Dohv ever gets her in his clutches," Meri went on with a frown. "You demons are built to live through the pain he wields. But she might be vulnerable."

"She has regenesis. I've seen it."

"It might not be enough. His power runs deep."

He took this in with a grim nod. He felt Meri studying him. "You say you came all this way to escape Dohv. But I sense there's more. You wish to escape everything."

An ancient emotion stirred inside of him as he longed to tell Meri all that had happened. He felt it all the way through, warming the parts of him that still felt so cold. She'd seen him, *understood him.*

"We wish to reach the Great Forest," he whispered.

"And what will you do there?"

"I want to . . ." He swallowed hard. For the first time, he realized: "I don't know what I want. But Seycia . . ." He gazed down at her. "Seycia needs to find the trees of the people who hurt her family and—"

He hesitated, and Irem sat straight up. He shuddered, as though he'd been pierced by the electrifying power of her thoughts. She was trying to communicate with him, but he couldn't interpret it.

"Whatever it is, Irem already knows," Meri said.

"And I don't think she likes it," he added.

Irem brushed Seycia's hair out of her face before rising to her feet. She gave Haben a long, penetrating stare before hobbling off toward a ladder leading to the second floor.

"Where's she going?"

Remi looked up from her work, but neither sister answered him. Nobody could be sure. All three of them watched as Irem rummaged around upstairs, grunting to herself. Then she teetered back down, holding an item in her hand. It was a large green leaf, folded in half.

Remi shrieked when she saw what Irem was holding. "That's mine," she hollered like a child, but she couldn't do anything to stop her sister. She was frozen to the spot, bound by their curse to remain at the crystal sculpture.

"You know it never belonged to either of us," Meri hissed at her.

Haben looked on in confusion as Irem approached him and presented the leaf. But before she relinquished it, she held his gaze and gritted her teeth. He saw her pale skin growing redder and redder as her entire body tensed, as though she were on the brink of an explosion.

She sputtered and stammered, chewing her glowing lips. Finally, she opened her mouth.

"B-bad." That was all she said at first. She seemed satisfied with this first word and continued: "Trees."

Bad trees. Haben, Remi, and Meri exchanged a look. They'd all heard it. Irem, exhausted now, handed the leaf to Haben.

"I didn't think the trees were either good or bad," Haben whispered to all three sisters. Had Seycia been right all along?

"The trees are Irem's children. She can say what she likes of them."

Haben looked to Meri in surprise, then to Irem. She paid him no mind, gently stroking Seycia's decorated arm with the black tip of her finger. Did Irem know they intended to destroy her children? How could she allow it?

Meri went on, "Those trees, those souls . . . they were borne of something awful—a truly awful thing that happened to Irem over and over again. Dohv tortured her the most severely," Meri explained with a tacit frown. Haben's stomach turned.

"You were mortal once, so you must understand. All people inherit dark intentions. This is because of my brother's crime. But they also inherit the light of Irem's love. A mortal soul is forever torn between the two," Haben absorbed her words. He'd always felt that darkness, but he'd felt the urge to be good, too—in his last life, and in this one.

"When a soul chooses darkness," Meri continued, "it goes bad. But it can always choose to turn back toward Irem's love. Sadly, there are souls that have turned toward darkness for too many lives. They have broken Irem's heart. I don't believe she knows how to love them anymore."

"Do you know which ones they are?" He was too afraid to ask, *Am I one of them?*

"Only Irem knows."

He peered over at Irem, whose crestfallen stare seemed to confirm all that Meri had said. He approached, and kneeled to her level. She floated upward, gazing down at him, and he bowed his head to her. "We've come to destroy those bad trees. But only with your permission."

She gave a single nod. She had, of course, known all along. He stood, pulled a breath, and finally examined the gift she'd given him.

As he opened the folded leaf, Haben heard Remi mutter, "I hope you give that back, when you're done with it. I use it to find the pretty trees in the forest."

Meri shot Remi a warning glance. "When was the last time you even went to the forest?"

"I'll use it again when we're free," Remi replied, a wistful ache in her voice.

The leaf appeared ordinary at first, aside from its size. Meri ducked in closer to Haben, watching him examine it. "Touch it," she whispered.

He pressed his fingertip to its surface, and the veins came alive with color. Bead-like droplets of light formed tiny, sparkling clusters along the edges of the leaf. The clusters became shapes. The shapes became trees. It was a map of the forest.

But then, something strange happened. The beads of light broke apart, as though someone had struck the surface of the map. The tiny sparks grew hot to the touch as they scattered to the edges, and Haben nearly dropped the leaf. It felt like cupping fire in his hands.

"I'm sorry . . . I don't think it works," he said, quickly and carefully placing the leaf on the ground.

Remi leaped up from her place at the glass palace and lunged for it. "That can't be. It's always worked for us—"

But as soon as she stood, she was compelled by the curse to sit back down and work. She narrowed her eyes at Meri as she plucked a glass fragment and shoved it into the wall. "It's your turn, you know."

Meri ignored her and picked the leaf up off the floor. She cradled it in her palm. "She *is* right. The map always works for us. But we are not demons. Rather . . ." She paused before finishing her thought. "We're not demons serving a sentence."

A tense moment passed before Haben spoke again. "So, it's me?"

In the silence that followed, Seycia stirred in the nest of black feathers. She rolled onto her side and made a delicate noise in her throat. He felt as though a dam had broken in his chest. She would wake up soon. And he would have to tell her that she would have to go to the forest without him.

"The Great Forest is the holiest place in the entire universe," Meri spoke again. "Only the cleanest and purest of immortal souls can enter. I suppose the thing you were sentenced for is still holding you back. It's strange. You did not seem this way to me."

"What do you mean?"

"When the two of you arrived, when I saw you . . . I thought you were as human as she was until I got a closer look at you. There's a warmth I feel. It surrounds you."

He laughed without realizing it, and then cut her an ice-cold glance. "You don't know me. You don't know why Dohv made me this way."

"Oh, but we do."

He stiffened and fought the urge to gasp aloud. She knew what he'd done—who he once was. *But of course she did.* All the horror he'd suppressed since the day of his death came flooding back.

Meri closed her crinkled brown eyelids and leaned against the plush rope ladder, suddenly looking very tired and very, very old. "You could be a clean soul again, I think. But it would require you to become the opposite of what Dohv made you."

"We don't have time for that," he shot back, louder than he'd intended. "She has to go now."

"Oh, but I think you're nearly there." Meri regarded him with a confident, serene look. She folded up the leaf and handed it back to him. He took it, cautious, and found it was no longer hot to the touch.

"All you need to do, I think, is earn her forgiveness. You must atone for what you did in life. You destroyed the future. *Her* future."

His gut twisted, and he felt as though all the blood in his loathsome body was being stirred into a whirlpool.

"She doesn't know about any of that," he muttered.

"Did you plan tell her?" Meri's gaze bore into him.

"No." If she learned what he'd done, and if she truly believed there were good souls and bad ones, he knew what would happen. She'd go on to the forest by herself, and he would lose her forever.

A still, gloomy moment passed. All was silent aside from the delicate clink of glass against glass as Remi worked, and Seycia's steady breath as she slept. Seconds ago, he'd longed for her to open her eyes again. Now, he wished she'd stay asleep, just a little while longer, just until he made a decision.

"I . . . I need to be alone," he said, and started climbing the soft, woven ladder to the second story.

"She'll be awake soon," Remi called after him. "She'll want to talk to you."

"Fine."

He reached the topmost floor of the hut and found he was so close to the floating light source that he could have held it in his hand. A hole in the side of the cocoon gave him a view of the Blue Mountain, spread like a waterfall below him, and the entire Underworld beneath that, bathed in crimson moonlight.

He hadn't even noticed that he was still clutching the leaf until he felt a cramp in his fist. He dared to open it again, and the beads of light gathered at his touch. But as soon as they appeared, they burned up and scattered like ashes. He snapped it shut, then peered down to the first floor, and saw Irem staring straight at him with a strange, knowing look on her face. It wasn't a smile. It wasn't a frown. But the look was somehow encouraging. He turned away.

Silence filled the little house as the sisters communicated telepathically with one another down below. The only sound was the rhythmic *creeeak creeeak* of the cords the house hung from as it swung in the breeze.

He looked out the hole in the wall at the foggy River of Past Lives, curling around the base of the mountain. The rush of the river lulled him into a hypnotic half-sleep. *Creeeak creeeak.* It was as if all the terror and adrenaline of the past day had hit its peak and his body had no choice but to let go, even if his mind was racing.

He hadn't even heard her coming. She'd been so quiet. He had no idea how long he'd been staring, trancelike, at the river. The light above him had gone out. It was dark now. When had that happened?

"Look at my leg," Seycia said, the hint of a laugh in her voice.

She pointed to the lavender stitches that had now dissolved into her skin. Irem had put the Creeback's fang on a cord made of her hair and hung it back around Seycia's neck. She was dressed in a robe made of the same silvery, translucent material as the sisters' clothing. It melted against her shape. He caught himself staring, and he knew there was no conceivable way he could let her go on without him. Not when they'd come this far together. Not if there was a way to stay with her.

"They're everything, the whole universe. Had you ever met them before?"

But it was as if he hadn't heard her. His ears were filled with the thundering of his own heart. All he could think of was the shameful truth he knew he'd have to tell her. She sidled up to him but he was stiff and paralyzed, unable to respond to her closeness, to her voice.

"I'm sorry for what I said to you before I got pulled into the water," she began. "When we get to the forest, I'll find your tree and I'll destroy it. I made you a promise, and I keep my promises."

"It doesn't matter anymore," he muttered. He picked up the leaf and unfolded it. She gazed at the beads of light, spinning in frantic circles like a flock of confused birds. He felt her eyes on him as he put the leaf down and stared at his feet, too afraid to meet her gaze.

"What is this? I don't understand—"

"They gave it to me. It's a map of the forest."

"But what's wrong with it?"

"It's me. It won't work as long as I'm near it. Meri says only clean souls can enter the forest."

It took Seycia a moment to understand what he was telling her. "You . . . can't come with me?"

"Do you want me to?"

"Of course I do. We've gotten this far because we did it together." He could see the despair in her eyes.

"There's something I could do, something Meri thought might help."

She nodded, then whispered, "Please. I don't want to do this without you."

He inhaled a shaky breath. "I'm going to tell you something, and it's going to sound terrible. You probably won't understand, but I'm asking you to try."

She nodded, but he couldn't look at her. He kept his eyes fixed on the river below, watching the hundreds upon thousands of Soulless drifting along the current, unaware of the lives that had been snatched from them ages ago. Lost lives *he* was responsible for.

"I'll start by saying I'm sorry, instead of finishing with it," he said. "So you know before you hear everything."

CHAPTER FIFTEEN

"WHEN I WAS young, when I was alive . . . I was alone, just like you."

Seycia tried to hold his gaze as he spoke, but he still couldn't look at her.

"The world I came from was an exciting place once: there were new discoveries every day, people all across the world could connect with each other at the push of a button. And my father . . . he was one of the dream makers. The things he made saved people's lives. He changed the whole world. But he didn't even know my name."

"What about your mother?" Seycia asked.

"By the time I was born, she was out of his life. But she died. I was young when it happened," he went on, detached, as though he were reciting the words. "There was a cure for almost every disease, but after she left my father, we were poor. Nobody would help her."

"I'm sorry . . ." She offered her hand to him, but he didn't notice. Or if he had, he didn't take it.

"My father and I finally met, and he paid for my education. I never saw him, I hardly knew him . . . but I knew all about his work. He built things that had touched the stars. He convinced world leaders to stop poisoning the earth. To me, he was a god. It was all right that he didn't have time for me. He was saving the world. And whatever he did next, I wanted to be a part of it."

"Your father breached the Veil, didn't he?" Seycia whispered.

"No. I did."

Seycia's breath caught, but she didn't shrink back. Somehow, she'd known he was coming to this when he began his story. He watched her for a reaction, but all she did was nod. A moment passed between them before he spoke again.

"But that was later," he choked out. "I studied for years until I worked up the courage to ask him for a job. He gave me one . . . provided I could show I'd earned it.

"I led a team whose job it was to dig a tunnel, a thousand miles beneath the earth. It would be a historic achievement. No one had ever ventured so deep.

"We started digging, working out of an underground hatch for months at a time. The deeper we went, the stranger things became. First we heard sounds: voices, in a language no one had ever heard before, echoing across the heart of the earth. Nobody knew what it meant. And then, one day, our instruments stopped working. We could go no farther. We'd hit the Veil.

"I think I knew what was beyond the blackness, even though we didn't have proof yet. This was uncharted territory—a world beyond our own. A place that might finally answer life's greatest question: Where do we go when we die?

"I knew there would be consequences, if we broke through the Veil, if we found proof of an afterlife. I wondered if we were ever meant to discover this world in the first place.

"But I told my father, anyway. And I told him I would be the one to break through to the other side."

"What about the war? Is that when it started?" Seycia offered after a moment.

"You could say that's when the trouble began."

Finally, he looked into her eyes. Seycia could feel by the way he held her gaze that he was about to tell her something important. Something that hurt.

"As we worked to breach the Veil, we found a language expert to help us understand what we were hearing. She hoped one day we might even learn to speak to the dead. She wanted to break through just as much as I did. She truly believed in what we were doing. I wondered what was driving her. There were a lot of things I wondered about her. Her name was Laida."

The name struck Seycia in the deepest part of her. Her eyes widened, and she felt her heart pound.

"From the moment I met her, she was under my skin. I tried to keep my distance, not to come on too strong. But whenever I'd see her . . ." Haben went quiet and withdrew from Seycia. "One day, she told me she had discovered what the voices were saying. 'Hello,' from one side of the Veil, and 'Goodbye,' from the other."

"Souls leaving and returning to the forest . . ." Seycia whispered. He nodded.

"She cried, realizing what it meant: souls were coming and going from our world. She told me she'd taken the assignment because she hoped one day she'd be able to speak to someone she'd lost. Her sister. Someone had killed her."

"Oh . . . that's awful." Seycia thought of Miko, and wondered how young Laida had been when it happened.

"I wish I'd asked her more about it. I cared for her, I really did. Looking back, I know she was always hurting. I should have tried harder to reach her. There were so many things I should have done."

He breathed a lonely sigh before he went on.

"Meanwhile, we were getting closer and closer to breaching the Veil. We'd never seen anything like it on Earth before. Not quite stone, not quite vapor. Denser than steel. We worked every day, we didn't rest. I couldn't let the world think I was some kind of fraud. I couldn't let my *father* think I was.

"We learned we could rupture the Veil by creating an explosion among the elements that made up the human form. Laida was there the day we made the discovery. She held my hand, and we watched the fissure open. It was just a small crack, but it was enough to see to the other side."

"What was the first thing you saw?" Seycia asked, spellbound.

"The river. And the Soulless in it," he said. "We watched for a full day—Laida, me, and the rest of my team—looking down on the Underworld from up above. As the hours passed, the fissure rotated, and new places came into view. The last one we saw, as the sun came up, was the Great Forest."

Seycia drew a breath. "So you *have* seen it."

"Only from the other side. I've never been there." Then, he added in a hoarse voice, "When you see the forest . . . it calls to you. It's like listening to the most beautiful song you've ever heard, and it goes on and on forever."

"Did you know what it meant, when you saw it?"

"I can't explain it . . . but I did. I felt it instantly, all the way through me. It was like a memory of home. I knew that was where we'd come from."

He pulled a breath, and his gaze darkened. "That night, two things happened. Laida and I . . . we made our feelings known. Then, a few hours later, she left the safety of the hatch and went to the rupture site. By the time I found her, she'd walked right up to the Veil, tears coming down her face. It was like she was in a dream, she wouldn't listen when I told her to stay away."

Seycia held her breath.

"She didn't jump. She tried, but she couldn't. The veil wouldn't let her pass."

Silence took hold of them. Haben cleared his throat with a shudder. "The next day, my father stood by my side and we told the world what we'd found. We had proof now. I'd never been so proud. I'd never seen him so happy.

"But right away, things went wrong. We found out the explosion we created to tear the Veil caused tremors all over the earth. Hundreds were killed. People were scared, with good reason. And that wasn't the only thing they were scared of.

"There were beliefs—strong, ancient beliefs—that the world had before. What we'd found was about to change everything. People rioted. Cities were in crisis. I ignored the guilt I felt. The *fear* I suddenly had.

"I went back to the hatch to escape the news that night. To see Laida. But when I came back, she was dead."

Seycia bowed her head, even though she'd sensed that was what he was about to say.

"In the letter Laida left for me, she said ... Well, she wondered whether it was better not to know what was beyond this life. Fear holds us back from death. But she decided she wasn't afraid anymore. I knew for sure then: we'd made a horrible mistake.

"I was grieving, I was a ghost. But I knew I couldn't waste time. I told my father we needed to shut the project down and seal off the rupture. More people were going to die. This was more than humanity could handle. We'd already seen it. And it was going to get worse."

"But he wouldn't let you."

Haben nodded, then added with a cold laugh, "As consolation, he offered to name one of our discoveries after her. Laida."

Of course. Seycia felt a pang in her chest. That's how the mortals had come to know it.

"The next time I tried to enter the hatch, I wasn't allowed. My father didn't care about me, or Laida, or any of the people we'd hurt. He'd used me to make history. I'd *let him* use me.

"The months went by, and factions formed. Leaving home was dangerous. People fought openly, on the streets. Especially after dark.

"There was a group I'd heard of, a dangerous, secret network, who was rumored to be planning an attack on the rupture site. They were followers of another religion, a religion we'd just proved obsolete, and they were devastated. I didn't think their beliefs were worth killing for. But they had the resources to destroy the project . . . and I could help them do it.

"I couldn't get in, but I had Laida's old credentials. I gave them access . . . and that was that."

Seycia searched his face. Was he proud? Fearful? Ashamed? But his eyes betrayed no emotion. He looked exhausted and drained. Vacant.

"And that's when the war started?" Seycia urged him to continue.

"My whole team was killed . . . including my father. The hatch was gone. We couldn't access the Veil anymore. After that, the military targeted any person they thought might be associated with this network. And there were quite a few of them." He cast Seycia a wry, tragic smile. "*That's* when the war started."

He looked at her as though he wanted her to return his smile, to indulge his irony, but she was motionless. She felt tears prick her eyes. Somehow she'd never put a human face to this terrible thing that had happened hundreds of years before.

"I thought I'd done the right thing. I didn't understand what I'd caused. How many lives would be lost. I'd looked through a door we were never meant to open, and no matter what I did, I couldn't close it. I only made it worse.

"The war intensified. I thought about Laida. Wondered where she was, whether she was watching me. Cursing my name.

"I went into hiding. I thought about dying, about killing myself, like she did. But I knew it wouldn't help. My soul would be back for another life. And I didn't want one. Not in this world.

"The day the war caught up to me, there was this white flash on the horizon outside the window of my apartment. The odds and ends that defined my worthless life started tumbling all around me as the building collapsed. But what I don't remember is any kind of panic. It felt like waking up from a nightmare. By the time my life was over, I was already dead.

"There's a wash of blankness after that, like somebody turned off the light then switched it back on again. And when it came back . . . here I was."

"Dohv pulled you from the river?"

"He told me I was to be punished. I was the one who broke the sky. And I accepted my sentence, gladly. I deserved it.

"Dohv chose Khronasa as the site of my punishment because it was where Laida was born. I'm reminded of her, every time I cross over—her and everybody else whose death I was responsible for. When I take a sacrifice, they become a part of me. I feel their pain. I take on their suffering. Their fear. That was what Dohv wanted. And it worked, every time. Until now. Until you."

He fell silent. Seycia sat numbly, unsure of what to say or how to say it. She looked up and saw Haben's gaze crumble, as if she'd already told him she could never forgive him.

She reached for his hand, and he was shivering. She noticed her touch had steadied him, and after a quiet moment, she spoke.

"There's one thing you never told me. What did people call you, back then? What was your name?"

He hesitated, as if he might be punished for saying the words aloud. "Emory. *Em.* It was a family name, on my mother's side. Haben was my father's last name. Dohv liked to call me that, reminding me of the part of myself I hated the most."

More silence. Her grip on his hand tightened. He tried to pull away, but she wouldn't let him.

"I don't expect you to forgive me, for any of this," he whispered. "I'm the reason your world became the way it is."

After a moment, Seycia replied, "You're not the same person you were. I think everyone gets to start over. That's why we have the Great Forest," she said, careful not to invoke Laida's name.

"But you believe some of us don't deserve another chance." He pulled away from her, and she went cold.

"General Simeon is different," she argued, but she was having trouble processing it herself.

"How is he different?"

"He just *is.* He's not like you. He would never apologize. He would never feel remorse."

"You don't know that."

Seycia shuddered and met Haben's stare. She couldn't accept his apology, not completely, unless she also accepted that she might be wrong. *Maybe,* she thought, *a monster can be redeemed if he truly wishes to be.* A soul was a soul, born neither good nor bad—it had a *choice.* She looked into his eyes, and she knew it was true. She thought of the way he'd carried her to the mountain, of the terror in his voice when he thought he'd lost her.

"You're a good man," she said, and rested her forehead against his. He tensed in surprise, but he didn't pull away.

"I'm neither of those things."

"I think you are if you want to be."

They held each other's gaze for what felt like a lifetime. Seycia felt her pulse quicken as she rested her head against his, and she wondered what she was supposed to do. She knew what she *wanted* to do. But she wasn't sure she should . . .

Haben broke her stare when he bent down to pick the folded leaf up off the floor. She was glad to be free of the tense moment, but she also wished it hadn't ended.

He unfurled it, and she peered over his shoulder, holding her breath. He paused, as though he were afraid of what might happen, then touched its smooth, green surface with the tip of his finger. Those same beads of light burst forth, but this time they didn't scatter and burn up. They formed shapes . . . trees. Rows and rows of them, in different, sparkling colors, swaying in an invisible breeze. They shared a glance, and she watched exhilaration break across his face.

She laughed aloud and, without thinking about it, she threw her arms around him. His grasp tightened around her body, and she felt warm all over, as though the cold barrier between them was melting away. He held her there, and she found herself once again staring into his face, wondering what to do. It was as if they were both waiting for something, standing at a precipice, daring the other to be the first to jump. She felt like there was a vise around her heart, squeezing tighter and tighter, making it hard to breathe.

He reached out to push her knotted hair away from her eyes, and a soft tingle rushed over her, like blood circulating after hours of numbness. She inched forward and let her lips hover against his for the briefest of seconds. It felt like for-ever before he met her halfway, as though he didn't remember what to do at first. Her cheeks burned. She was horrified . . . What had she done? She had vowed to kill him. How would she explain this?

But before she could pull away, he clutched the back of her head and pressed his mouth closer to hers, parting his lips to feel her more deeply. He traced the shape of her over her glossy, translucent robes, and her breath froze in her throat. She was heavy as a stone, and yet, she was sure she might float away.

It seemed to Seycia that the kiss had lasted a lifetime, though it had probably only been seconds. Only seconds until she heard a high-pitched, frantic grunt from the first floor of the hut. Only seconds until she remembered they weren't alone. She felt Haben reluctantly pry his arms from her, and she smoothed down her robe, trying to shake his touch from her body. She avoided his gaze and glanced at the ladder in the corner instead, where Irem was ascending.

Irem hobbled over with wide, glassy eyes. She tugged on Seycia's arm and pulled her to her feet.

"What is it?" Seycia asked, clasping her hands around Irem's.

"She can't answer, you know," Haben said.

"Shh," she hissed at him and turned back to Irem. "What's happening?"

Seycia locked eyes with Irem, unblinking, and a shudder coursed through her. It was as if Irem were trying to unload something from her mind and pass it to hers. Strange, colorless images flashed before Seycia's eyes in blinding bursts of light. There was blood on a dirty concrete floor. The sound of someone coughing. A boy crying. A boy . . . *Miko*.

"Can you understand her?" Haben whispered, watching her with Irem. But Seycia didn't answer for a long moment.

Irem gurgled in her throat, and Seycia finally broke her gaze. A cloud of fear fell across her face. "Something's happening. It's my brother. But I can't see it."

"How was she able to talk to you?"

"She didn't . . . talk. But she's able to show me things. I think it has something to do with how she healed me. She's a part of me now," she explained, rushed. "Please. We need to find a passageway."

Irem was already climbing back down the ladder. She motioned for the two of them to follow. Seycia made her way down first, but Haben hung back. She peered up at him.

"Are you coming?" she asked.

He nodded, then picked the leaf up off the ground. They exchanged a glance, charged with all that had just transpired between them. Seycia felt her face glow under his stare. As he pocketed the map, they shared a powerful, wordless understanding.

He could follow her anywhere he wanted now. And he would.

CHAPTER SIXTEEN

SEYCIA FELT COLD all over as she climbed down the ladder to the ground floor of the sisters' hut. Why hadn't she insisted on checking in on Miko earlier? She had barely glimpsed him the first and only time Haben had showed her a passageway. What could have happened since then?

She swallowed hard as Irem nudged her toward a shimmering sea-blue panel with jagged edges, hanging like an opaque mirror on the wall. She spotted Remi curled up in the nest of black feathers. Meri was the one working on the sculpture now.

"You don't know what she's seen, do you?" Seycia whispered to Meri.

Meri shook her head. "Best go to the passageway."

She lifted a weathered brown finger, and the blue panel across the room levitated upward to reveal a gaping black hole in the side of the house. No starlight shone through it. It was a window to another world. Irem shuffled toward it and beckoned to her.

Seycia clung to the woven wall, peering into the blackness. Her heart wrenched deep in her chest. She should have been there, watching over Miko—even if watching couldn't save him.

Haben emerged behind her, and together they faced the void.

"What are you waiting for? Go in," Remi urged her, rising from the nest.

"I-I thought I couldn't," she turned to Haben. "You told me only messengers could go in."

"Only messengers *should*," he replied. There was a nervous edge to his voice. "It's better if you have a job to do."

"I have one."

"Whatever's going to happen, you can't stop it. You'll see, you can't help him."

But she ignored him and faced the passageway. Haben cast the sisters a worried glance. Weren't they going to stop her? But the three of them stared back at him, expressionless.

Seycia squeezed her eyes shut and hurled herself into the darkness—into the Veil. She felt Haben seize her arm as the passageway swallowed her up. He had followed her in.

The black void was thick and heavy, an unimaginable pressure on all sides of her. She thought her brain would burst. She felt as though she was screaming but she couldn't hear a sound. She did her best to focus on Miko, to allow the passageway to bring her to his side. She thought of the way he stuck out his tongue as he hammered together planks of wood, of his mischievous grin as he sliced open a fish for dinner, of his laughter when he would splash in the mud after a summer rainstorm as a boy . . .

As quickly as the awful pressure had come, it was gone. Seycia focused her eyes, the blackness fading away with each blink. She had emerged in the middle of a creek, the same one she'd fished in for years, the one she'd played in as a child.

But she couldn't feel the water. She knew it ought to be bitterly cold, but there was no sensation. Haben was beside her, and she cast him an alarmed glance.

"You won't feel anything," he answered the question on her lips, back to his low, anxious mutter. "You shouldn't have come."

He pointed across the creek, through the trees, where she could glimpse Khronasa's dark city streets. She gasped. They were not alone.

Hundreds of gray figures shuffled across the city—peering into windows, following villagers on their way home. It was as though all the color had been sapped from them, even as they passed beneath the streetlamps—like they were deflecting the light.

Seycia shivered as she realized: this was what *they* looked like. She wondered about the villagers the demons were following, whether they'd known them once. She wondered how many years they'd been watching them . . .

"Demons cannot touch anything. They can't affect this world, as much as they wish they could. Only a messenger can," Haben explained as he led her out of the creek and toward the treeline.

"But . . . that's what you are," Seycia said, catching up to him.

"I'm not. The Savage is."

She swallowed hard as they walked on, wondering why the passageway had released them here. Was Miko nearby? She looked around and thought she saw the dim, orange glow of the sunrise, cresting the horizon of her homeland. But she quickly realized . . . it wasn't the sun. It was an enormous wall of fire, spreading across the countryside from the heart of Khronasa's city center. The entire hillside she had once called home was scorched and black. What had happened since she'd been gone?

As she spun in the other direction, she suddenly understood why the passageway had taken them here. She recognized the tall evergreens lining General Simeon's property from when she escaped his mansion. She had seen this place again in a flash of light, in Irem's vision. Miko was here.

"Seycia, wait—" Haben hissed as she took off running—or at least, it was almost like running. She couldn't feel the ground beneath her feet.

She approached the front gates of Simeon's mansion, where a pair of bodyguards marched in sync across the property. They were coming right toward her. Her heart skipped a beat, but she knew what would happen. They passed by without so much as a glance. She breathed a sigh of relief and followed the guards as they approached a small, concrete building just a stone's throw from Simeon's automotive shed. She felt compelled to go inside. She felt sure Irem had also seen this.

"Wait, Seycia," Haben joined her and tried to pull her back. "I don't know why Irem showed you this. She knows you can't—"

But she'd already closed her eyes and passed straight through the wall of the concrete building, following the guards. Her body dissolved into nothingness, indistinguishable from the smoke that hung in the air.

When she emerged on the other side, she immediately knew that yes, Irem *had* shown her this place. It was the entry to a prison beneath the general's mansion.

She raced down the concrete corridor as fast as her feet could carry her, not even sure if Haben had followed. But his warning didn't matter to her. If Miko was here, she had to see him. She turned a corner, then skidded to a stop.

Miko was curled in a ball against the corner of his prison cell. His knees were drawn against his chest, as though he were protecting himself. Seycia wasn't sure if he was alive or dead at first. He was so pale. His lips were a dull shade of blue.

She propelled herself through the rusty iron bars of his cell and fell to her knees at his side. She threw her arms around him, but her touch went straight through his body. She thought she saw him shiver. She gasped—*he was still alive.* But what had happened to him? He was barely breathing. What could she do? She tried to touch him again, but it was no use. Haben was right. Sobs shook her body. But Miko didn't stir.

"Seycia," Haben materialized on the other side of Miko's cell.

"He's going to die."

"We can't stay. I'm sorry. We can't help him from here."

"*You* can help him," Seycia said. "There has to be a way. Irem wouldn't have sent us here if there wasn't. You just don't want to."

He stormed over to her and tugged her to her feet. She wrested his hand away, tears streaming down her face.

"Even if I could control it, how is the Savage supposed to save him?" he snapped, then cast her a softer glance. "I can't do it."

Seycia clenched her teeth to hold her tears back, listening to Miko's infrequent, shallow breaths. The sight of him motionless on the ground was like staring down the sum of all her nightmares. If there was no way to save him, she didn't want to see anymore. She slowly turned from him, heavy with regret, like her pockets were full of stones.

She faced the concrete wall, ready to depart, and whispered, "I understand."

But before she could take another step and pass through, Haben touched her shoulder, guiding her back around. He sighed and then, to her surprise, he took to his knees beside Miko.

"What I meant was . . . I can't do it like this." She caught his eye, and the look he gave her sent a shudder across her body. "I need you to do two things: I need you to trust me. And I need you to stay away."

She gave him a wary nod and drew back, toward the far corner of the cell. "What are you going to do to him?" she breathed.

"If it works, you'll know," he replied in a low, hoarse voice, and inhaled sharply.

Seycia gasped, equal parts terror-stricken and amazed, as Haben doubled over with a furious snarl and his robe fused to his skin. He was calling to the Savage. She watched him seize on the ground, moaning low in his throat. It looked like it hurt. But he was *controlling it*.

Her heart thundered as she watched his face transform. His monstrous teeth expanded from his jaw, and his eyes narrowed with a flicker of light. She recognized the wicked glow she'd seen from the pit that night. Her gut twisted. She hated to admit it, but she was still afraid of the Savage. Very afraid. And what he might do to Miko only deepened her terror.

"H-Haben?" she whispered across the darkness. There was no reply. "Em?"

But he didn't answer to that name, either. She approached him, even though that was what he'd told her not to do. She stood right behind him, not sure whether she should force him to stop. Whatever intentions Haben had, she feared he'd already forgotten them. She knew what the Savage could do.

But as she reached a shaky hand out to grasp his shoulder, she saw the Savage make contact with Miko's body, carefully placing his long black talons against Miko's chest. Seycia held her breath . . . but Miko was unharmed. If the Savage had wanted to tear him open, he could have. Haben was still in control.

She watched, transfixed, as the Savage leaned over Miko so their faces aligned, barely an inch from one another. He opened his mouth, exposing those razor-sharp teeth. She swallowed a scream. She didn't dare move. She didn't even blink.

But she quickly understood what was happening. When Miko exhaled, the Savage drew it in. She watched, awestruck, as color and warmth bloomed across Miko's face. The Savage was pulling the pain and sickness from his body. It went on like this until Miko's breathing deepened and he rolled over onto his side with a contented sigh.

The Savage withdrew, and Seycia fell to her knees at Miko's side. She tried to take his hand, forgetting for a moment that she couldn't. She shed tears of relief as Miko rolled onto his back and stretched out his limbs like a star. She could hear his quiet, peaceful snore, the same one she'd listened to every night before she would allow herself to sleep. She looked at the Savage as he took to the ground, heaving with a humanlike groan.

Haben's face re-emerged, and he grimaced in pain as his bones protruded from his skin and shifted back into place. But even after the transformation was complete, Seycia could see his face was still twisted in anguish. He winced, drawing his knees to chest, as Seycia made her way toward him.

"I'm sorry. I didn't know it hurt so much."

"It's not . . . it's not the . . . " he gasped and doubled over, struggling to speak. "It's not the Savage."

He staggered to his feet, clutching his chest. Seycia saw his lips start to turn blue, and his eyes rolled back. She lunged for him as his knees gave out, and she supported him with her shoulder.

Whatever sickness he'd just pulled out of Miko was tearing through his body. Haben couldn't die, but he could no longer heal himself. Seycia froze in horror, holding him up with all her strength. What had she done to him?

"Give it to someone else," she whispered into his ear. She wasn't sure he even could. But it was the only thing she could think of.

She led him out of Miko's cell as he gagged and trembled, desperately taking stock of their surroundings. She knew they needed to stay hidden; they weren't visible to the human eye, but as soon as Haben became the Savage again, he would be. There were other prisoners being held here, but she couldn't bear the thought of making them suffer, too. She guided Haben around a corner and spotted a young, portly night watchman, slumped over his desk, his cracked protective goggles crookedly fixed atop his head.

"Him," Seycia shook Haben as he fought to keep his eyes open. "Give it to him."

Haben replied with a weak, distant nod, but nothing happened. Seycia wasn't sure if he even had the strength to transform into the Savage again.

He slumped over as a powerful convulsion surged through his body, and Seycia fell to his side with a devastated cry, trying to hold him upright.

This is my fault. He didn't want to. He knew . . .

He fell against her, rocking back and forth, slower and slower, until he was completely still. Seycia shook him, but he didn't respond. She knew he wasn't dead, she could feel his heart beating. But she also knew he still felt all of the pain.

"Get up. You have to get up," she whispered, shaking him harder. Then, she had an idea. Her voice went cold, and she said, "If this is where I leave you, then you're worthless to me."

She heard him groan and she narrowed her eyes. "I never thought you were strong enough," she lied.

He snarled, and his eyes snapped open. She saw that sinister yellow light start to burn behind them, and she jumped back. It was working.

"You'll only ever be remembered for one thing," she spat, hating herself for saying it. But she knew what it would do.

The Savage returned with a low, furious growl, as though he had been disturbed from his sleep. He struggled to draw a full breath and seized in painful, jerky motions, unfurling his grotesque black wings.

"Give it to him," Seycia pointed to the Coalition watchman, reminding the creature of what its master had come here to do.

The Savage staggered forward and bent eye-to-eye with the sleeping man. His breath reeked of old liquor. She prayed he wouldn't wake. She glanced around, making sure nobody could see what they were doing. That nobody could see the Savage.

Then, the creature heaved as deep a sigh as it could muster and breathed out a plume of gray ash. It hovered in the air in front of the guard's face. Seycia watched, holding a shaky hand over her mouth as though she were afraid she might accidentally breathe it in herself.

After what felt like an eternity, the guard pulled a raspy snore and inhaled the poisonous ash floating inches from his lips. The Savage stumbled, arching his back and rolling his neck as the sickness evaporated. Seycia watched as the Savage began taking Haben's shape again . . . But before the transformation was complete, the heavyset watchman sat straight up, as though he'd been struck by lightning, and clutched his throat with a bloodcurdling howl.

At first, Seycia thought he was screaming because of the pain. And he might have been. But he'd also just spotted the Savage.

The monster loomed over the watchman, teeth bared. Seycia's heart stammered. The Savage might have known well enough to protect Miko, but she didn't think that was the case this time.

Without a second thought, she seized the monster's arm. He whirled around and met her gaze with a murderous growl.

She stood frozen to the spot. She was sure he wouldn't hurt her. *Almost sure.*

The patrolman toppled backward off his chair in a fit of agony, sputtering foam the color of blood. His cries splintered the silence, and chaos exploded across the prison. A pair of armed guards, the same ones Seycia had followed inside, scrambled down the hall. They needed to leave. Now. She couldn't let the Savage do the awful thing it was created to do. She thought of how it would make Haben feel, to know he'd lost control.

She gripped the creature's arm even more tightly and craned her neck to gaze into its contorted serpentine face. "*Emory*," she hissed, as loud as she could.

The other two guards rounded the corner. They shrieked like terrified children at the sight before them. They held perfectly still, and so did Seycia, dreading what would come next. She knew she couldn't physically hold the Savage back . . .

"I-I . . ." she heard a voice croak from over her shoulder. The creature trembled, and she spun to face it. "I'm sorry," she heard Haben's voice as the monster collapsed to its knees and shrank back to its humanlike shape.

But seconds before the Savage vanished, two gunshots rang out. The earsplitting *pop-pop* struck Seycia through the heart—she'd never forget to be afraid of that sound. Haben writhed on the ground, and Seycia gasped when she noticed the sleeve of his robe had been torn. Blood spilled down his shoulder. The Savage had taken the bullet.

Haben clutched the place he'd been shot and gritted his teeth as he stood. He and Seycia shared a bewildered, terrified glance before he whispered, "Help me."

Seycia supported his weight as they shoved their way through the concrete wall of the prison, making their escape. She stared at the bullet lodged in his pale flesh as they raced across General Simeon's front lawn and past the evergreen trees. She felt another stab of guilt as she imagined all the pain he'd just endured. First the poison. Now this.

Haben feebly pointed toward the creek, where they'd first emerged from the passageway.

As they waded into it, Seycia whispered, "I'm sorry. For what I said to you."

"I know," he replied in a ragged whisper.

The riverbed quivered; Seycia couldn't feel it, but she could tell by the ripples in the water all around them. She held tightly to Haben's arm as the force of the passageway pulled them down, through the water, and into darkness. They tumbled backward and upside down, through the intense, murky void of the Veil.

The passageway released them back onto a soft pile of silver sand on the first floor of the sisters' hut. It was a long, breathless moment before either of them moved.

"He's hurt," Seycia cried, brushing sand from Haben's wound as he shakily rose to a seated position.

Remi was the first to approach, and she recoiled when she caught sight of the bullet wound. "That's not a Creeback's bite," she whispered. "This is the wickedness of man. He cannot heal?"

"Dohv took regenesis from him. Can you give it back?"

Remi sighed and shook her head. "He is Dohv's creation, so his body must abide by Dohv's laws. But I will do what I can," she said, and crouched down between them.

She placed a hand over Haben's wound, firmly pressing her palm against the blood. "Can you feel that?" she asked him.

After a moment he exhaled and replied, "Not anymore."

As Remi slowly, carefully got to work extracting the bullet from Haben's flesh with her long fingers, Irem hobbled into the room.

Seycia exchanged a glance with her, and bowed her head in thanks. As Irem gave her a sturdy nod that might have been a look of pride, Seycia realized that this had been a test, to prepare them for what lay ahead. She shivered, then peered back over at Haben. Remi had removed the bullet and was now rubbing a salve into the wound, the same shade of blue as her eyes. But nothing magical happened. The wound stayed open. *This is the wickedness of man.* The sisters' magic had its limitations. Her heart twisted.

"I can't ask you to do this again," Seycia said to Haben as Remi wrapped a gossamer bandage around his shoulder. "This doesn't have to be your fight. Don't go any further if you don't want to."

"I'll be fine," he said, but the anguish in his eyes told a different story. She didn't think she'd ever seen anyone so tired.

"I can still go to the forest and do what I said I'd do. For you," she whispered to him. He gave her a puzzled look, as though he'd forgotten all about their contract.

"No. I'm coming," he replied, and he said no more. Remi fused the hole in his robe back together with a flick of her wrist.

"If you are, then it's time to go," Meri said from behind them, working on the crystal sculpture. She stood to face them, and Remi switched places with her. "Morning light is best to guide you there."

The house swayed in the wind, and Seycia peered out the door to see Norryn circling overhead, making soft, strange clucking noises as he drifted by.

"Norryn has been waiting," Meri went on.

"I don't suppose we can walk?" Haben asked, anxiously glancing out the door at the huge animal ducking and diving around the hut.

"You couldn't possibly walk. You're in the right hemisphere, but you'd get there years from now if you went on foot," Meri said. "Besides, she can communicate with Norryn."

It took Seycia a moment to realize Meri was pointing at her. "Can I? I don't think—"

"You're linked to him now, the same way Irem is. She passed on some of her gifts to you. I suggest you learn to use them."

Irem grunted in agreement from the corner of the room. She hobbled outside and made a jerking motion over her shoulder. Seycia and Haben took that as their cue to follow. Haben clutched his injured arm as he walked, ignoring the sting, trying not to agitate it.

Before they stepped out the door, Haben handed Seycia the leaf from the pocket of his robe, folded into a small square. "You should have this, if you're the one he's listening to."

She let loose a nervous laugh and took it from him. "Let's hope he does."

They stepped out onto the ledge of the swaying chrysalis. Seycia was floored by the majesty of the Blue Mountain in broad daylight. The color of the volcanic rock perfectly complemented the violet sky above the shadowy landscape below—an intricate mosaic of darkness and light, the welcoming places and the horrible places. She noticed Haben squinting off into the distance at a plateau made entirely of ice, like a frozen shelf hanging in the heavens. The top of it was obscured by the darkest clouds she'd ever seen.

"Antenor," he whispered. "I've never seen it before, but that has to be it."

Seycia touched his uninjured arm and gently spun him to face her. "You're sure about this."

A cynical laugh escaped his lips, "I'm not about to let you have all the fun." *Don't ask me again*, his gaze seemed to say.

Seycia swallowed hard, then unfolded the leaf. Meri emerged behind them.

"How do I find just one tree?" Seycia asked her. "There are millions—how does it know?"

She pressed her finger to the map's surface, and a tiny trail of light followed her touch.

"There are many ways to use it," Meri replied. "For you, though, the easiest way might be to write the names."

"Onto the leaf?"

She nodded. "Whatever name you knew them by, as you picture their face. Every tree has had thousands of identities, but they remember every single one. So take your finger . . ."

Seycia held the leaf out in front of her and tentatively raised her finger to it.

"And just write a name. Any name."

Seycia thought hard. She hadn't written anything in years. She squeezed her eyes shut, picturing the alphabet her parents had taught her as a child. She traced a letter onto the surface of the leaf, the first letter of the first name she could think of. O-S-K-A-R. Her father's name. The letters pulsed with light, then disappeared. Nothing else happened. Seycia stared at the leaf, confused.

"Think harder. Imagine this person. Not just what they look like. Remember the way they made you feel," Meri murmured.

Seycia closed her eyes and her father's face emerged in her mind's eye—his kind eyes, round and dark, the color of earth after rain. Just like her own. She remembered the rough texture of his unruly beard, and she pictured the tiny white scar underneath his chin where the beard never grew back. She thought of his reassuring laugh, how hearing it was like being wrapped into the tightest, warmest embrace. She remembered the way he held her mother in his arms as they sat by the fire as a family. The way her mother smiled at him. The love she knew they'd shared. Suddenly, the leaf quivered in her palm, and a spasm of light upon its surface shot off toward the left side. She stifled a gasp as she stared at it.

"Ah, that means you would go left," Meri explained. "It will work perfectly once you're inside the borders of the forest. Just watch it until it tells you to take a different direction." Then she added, "I think you'll do well with it, if you have Irem's gifts."

"Thank you." Seycia returned her smile as she folded the leaf back up. It was still pulsing with light, still zeroing in on the name Seycia had traced into it.

Norryn swooped down toward the door and released an excited cry upon seeing Seycia. He stuck out his boiled-looking, wrinkly head to her, and she stroked it. She hadn't noticed last night, but up close, his flesh looked like a fabric made of millions of tiny, iridescent scales, glimmering in the early morning sunlight. It was smooth to the touch, like stroking a glass surface. Norryn clucked in his throat and closed his black, beady eyes as Seycia patted his neck.

"Is he speaking to you?" Haben asked.

"No. I think he's just happy to see us," Seycia laughed, giving Norryn a final pat.

"Before you go, there's something we must ask of you," Meri said from the doorway behind them.

Seycia turned to her. "Anything."

Meri addressed both of them. "You're the only visitors we've had since our banishment, which means you're the only ones to have come this far unscathed since Dohv's rule began. We would have the power to depose him if we weren't trapped here. But if we've given you the right gifts, you might be able to do what we cannot."

"You want us to confront Dohv?" Haben stared at her, slack-jawed. "I don't think you know what you're asking—"

Meri interrupted him, stern yet serene. "Think of what you have: A map of the Great Forest. A Creeback's fang. Norryn. *And* you've overcome the curse Dohv himself put upon you."

Irem's eyes lit up, as though she'd forgotten something until just that moment. She scrambled over to the tree holding their house aloft and tore a branch from one of its limbs.

They watched Irem peel the twigs off the tree branch, making it as smooth as possible. Then she opened her mouth and breathed a stream of blue and yellow fire against the branch. She let it burn for a moment before blowing out the flame like a candle. She bounded back toward them, holding the stick out to Seycia.

"Thank you." Seycia eyed the stick with reverence as she took it from her.

As their hands touched, a vision flashed behind Seycia's eyes—another message from Irem. She saw burned leaves on the ground, smoldering to blue embers. Smoke the color of sapphire enveloped her, and she swore she could smell it: like sweet jasmine burning over hot coals.

"What are we supposed to do with that?" Haben asked as Seycia withdrew.

"Destroy the trees," she said in an awestruck whisper.

Seycia turned the branch over in her hands, gently, as though it were a fragile thing she might break. It was still hot to the touch all the way through.

"Irem has every confidence in you, and so do I," Meri said. "If Dohv catches you once you complete your mission in the forest, and catch you he shall, you will be able to fight back. I guarantee it."

"But will we win? If we fight back?" Seycia asked.

"The answer to that question is cloudy and dark, for all of us, even Irem. Our future is on a set course right now. We see only *that* course, only those results. But that course could be altered, if something stronger than the march of time emerges. We do not know *what* will change the rhythm of the universe. We only know that it's coming." She looked at Haben before adding, "There was a reason Irem asked Norryn to follow you."

Seycia looked at Irem, hunched over, nervously shifting her gaze between the two of them. How many thousands of years had this magnificent creature been tortured? She wanted to set her free. She wanted to set all of them free.

Norryn nudged Seycia's hip with his blunt, oblong beak. It was time to go. He craned his neck toward the two of them and scooped them both up with ease. Seycia tucked Irem's branch under her arm. She looked over her shoulder at Haben, who was trying to get comfortable against a fold of Norryn's loose skin.

"I trust you not to drop us," he said wryly, rubbing his aching shoulder as she settled in beside him.

"That's the least of my worries."

They both fell silent, and she stared off into the rising sun, climbing higher in the violet sky with each passing minute.

"Ask him to take you west," Meri said to Seycia. "It will be clear which way you should go after that. The light will guide you."

She wasn't sure what Meri was talking about, but like so many things in this world, she knew she had to have faith that she'd understand when she was meant to. She pressed her cheek against the top of Norryn's flat, bald head. She hadn't been told how to communicate with him, but she sensed she wasn't supposed to use words. That wasn't how Irem spoke to him. *East,* she thought. *Take us east. East . . .*

Norryn gave a joyful *ca-caw!* that rang across the mountainside. The loud noise gave her courage. It was like a call to arms, an alarm to wake her and send her on her way.

Norryn flapped his gigantic wings and veered off around the side of the hut. At that moment, Remi burst out of the door, briefly leaving her post to see them off. Seycia gave the three sisters a long, loaded stare as Norryn thrust off and away from the mountain.

She thought she might shout her thanks to them, but they were high in the air before she could get even one word out. But she was sure they knew just how thankful she was. She didn't have to be afraid. She knew they would be watching.

CHAPTER SEVENTEEN

MIKO AWOKE ON the freezing floor of his cell from the deepest sleep he'd ever had.

He didn't remember where he was right away, nor could he understand how he'd managed such a peaceful slumber in this cold, horrible place. He rose to a sitting position and lolled his head from side to side, sifting through his memories. He'd been sick. Worse than that—it had been like collapsing at death's door. He knew that much. But nothing else.

He stretched out his legs, massaging a cramp in his knee, and was shocked to discover he no longer felt any pain where the electric fence had burned him. The wounds were still there: raw and red, crusted with blood. Why couldn't he feel them? And how had his horrible illness literally vanished overnight?

You know how, a voice in the back of his mind whispered. Was this the proof he'd been looking for? His pulse jumped, but Seycia would have told him to think hard about all the possibilities. She'd never wanted him to believe anything blindly. *And yet . . .*

He suddenly realized the air around him smelled like smoke, hot and thick. He crept over to his cell's tiny window and peered outside, where clouds of ash belched down the hill-side. What was happening? When had the city caught fire?

CLANG! Miko jumped at the sound of the prison door opening and closing down the hall. He heard the slow creak of rusty wheels, followed by the stomp of Coalition boots.

From one side of the prison, three Coalition bodyguards marched toward him, clutching their semiautomatics. From the other end, a hunched figure, disguised by shadow, pushed an old wooden cart full of weapons.

Miko stole a glance at the items in the cart as it passed. He spotted Belicia's priceless crossbow among the confiscated weapons, and his heart sank. Not only had he lost her precious heirloom forever, but it also meant Ardash had been captured, or worse, killed. He'd let him have the crossbow the night they snuck onto the general's property. He wondered what had happened to the rest of their group. To Minari.

Then, Miko saw the face of the man pushing the cart, dressed in an ill-fitting Coalition uniform. His despair flashed to fury and burned in his chest. It was Ezara. What was he doing here?

"Hey! *Hey, traitor!*" Miko barked at Ezara through the bars of his cell. "Is this who you are? Did your mother die thinking she could trust you?"

But Ezara said nothing. He just stared at the floor, as though he hadn't heard him. "If she died because of anyone, it was you," Miko hissed in the iciest voice he could muster.

At that moment, one of the three approaching guards reached Miko's rusted holding pen. He peered inside and Miko saw him flinch, as though he was surprised to see him. As though he was surprised to see him *alive*.

But before Miko could react or think of something to say to him, he heard Ezara mutter from the shadows, "Miko, get down."

Miko barely had time to obey. He'd never seen anyone spring to action so fast. Ezara tore a semiautomatic from the cart of weapons, just like the ones the guards were holding. But he was quicker, and they hadn't been expecting a fight. Ezara opened fire before they could let even one round loose. One, two, three—the bodies collapsed. A puddle of blood inched toward Miko's cell as he caught his breath.

Ezara quickly turned the bodies over, examining them till he found what he was looking for: a set of silver keys. There were several of them, and it took Ezara a moment to determine which one would unlock Miko's cell. His hands shook as he fumbled with them, but his voice was calm and steady.

"We've only got a few minutes alone down here. I need you to stay low, move fast, and be my right hand."

Miko nodded in a daze. *Click.* Ezara unlocked the door to his cell and swung it open.

"Ezara?" a girl's voice called out from across the prison. She had a familiar, lilting accent; it was Minari. Miko's heart swelled as he and Ezara raced down the hall.

"On our way," Ezara called out to her, tossing Miko the keys. "Unlock every cell as quickly as you can. Everybody gets out and everybody gets a weapon. But do it fast."

Miko realized Ezara had led him right to Minari's cell. She clasped the bars, and a smile broke past her anxious stare. She had a few bruises and a swollen lip, but otherwise she was unharmed. He exhaled with relief as he found the key that would free her.

She raced past him and made a beeline for the weapons cart, pulling out Belicia's crossbow and an ax.

"What's going on?" Miko asked her, breathless, as he unlocked another cell door. "And why's everything on fire?"

"You really don't know?" She handed the ax to the prisoner Miko had just freed.

"I've been in here."

"The whole city heard about what you did on the general's rooftop," Minari explained. "People started thinking . . . if a boy was brave enough to point a gun at Simeon, then we should be, too."

They ran to the next cell, stopping along the way to grab more weapons.

"Ardash and I got ourselves arrested and went underground as fast as we could so there'd be someone on the inside who could help you escape."

"And Ezara?"

She glanced over at him, finger on the trigger of his semi-automatic, standing guard at the door.

"We were lucky to have him. A lot of Khronasans joined up with the Coalition when the protests started—too scared to be on the losing side. But I don't think that's why Ezara's here."

Miko stole a glance at Ezara as they burst into another cell, where Ardash awaited rescue. He clapped Miko on the shoulder as he passed and Minari handed him Belicia's crossbow.

"Sorry. Won't lose it again, I promise," Ardash held the weapon up to Miko, then flashed a roguish grin.

As Ardash approached Ezara at the end of the hall, Miko heard footsteps up above and his blood ran cold. The door swung open, and Ezara and Ardash fired their weapons in perfect unison—a deadly coordinated dance. The two prison guards who had just tried to enter crumpled to the ground.

A third soldier came barreling down the stairs. He shoved his way through the door, gun pointed. Before Miko could blink, he'd shot Ardash square in the chest, and Ezara fired right back at him. Miko took cover with a knot in his stomach. He heard Minari call out to Ardash, but he didn't reply.

A moment passed among the escaped prisoners as they stared at the bodies on the ground. Ezara picked up the crossbow and tucked it under his arm, then bent over and closed Ardash's eyes. He cast the rest of the group a resolute gaze, as if to say, *Don't stop.*

With heavy hearts, Miko and Minari pushed the cart down the hall as fast as they could. They threw a weapon into every unlocked cell. There were few firearms in the cart. Most were blunt objects or arrows.

"How do we get out?" Miko shouted from the other end of the corridor, unlocking the last of the cells. "They'll see us if we go up through the general's property."

"Simeon built himself a little network of tunnels some years ago, just in case the city ever rose up against him and the idiot had to make a break for it," Ezara explained. "I found it yesterday. It's being used for weapons storage. Nobody ever goes in."

Miko handed the final weapon in the cart to a young man with a shaggy beard. It was an old revolver, much like the one he'd tried to shoot Simeon with.

The man turned the gun over in his hands with a frown. "Hey, Ezara," he shouted. "You'd better teach us to use these things."

"You'll have to learn as you run. Come on," Ezara hollered as he sailed past.

"I didn't get a weapon," Miko whispered to Ezara, rushing to keep up with him.

Ezara sighed, then handed him Belicia's crossbow. "Just remember the first thing I told you: stay low."

Miko nodded, cradling the bow in his arms like a trophy. He was glad to have it back in his hands again. He was glad to have *any* weapon.

"This way," Ezara instructed the group.

The prisoners bolted after him as fast as they could, and Miko was relieved he could no longer feel the pain in his legs. Ezara threw open the door to a closet filled with supplies—batteries, flashlights, lanterns, Coalition uniforms, and bulletproof vests.

"Grab what you can, then follow me," he said.

He yanked a tool from his pocket and began unscrewing a steel panel at the back of the closet. Miko moved to his side to help him lift it away from the wall. Behind it was a concrete staircase leading to an abyss of complete and total darkness. A few of the prisoners flicked on flashlights and lanterns. Minari slammed the closet door behind her and shoved a stool below the doorknob. Ezara led them down into the blackness as the rush of Coalition footsteps filled the hallway. They'd just barely escaped.

Miko stayed up front with Ezara, holding his breath as they crept through the cobwebs in the dark, cramped passageway. A long moment passed between them before he whispered to Ezara, "I thought you were one of them."

Ezara replied with a gruff scoff and peered over at Miko as they walked. "I'm whoever I have to be."

"But why are you doing this?"

Ezara spun to face Miko. "I couldn't let my mother die for nothing."

They exchanged a somber glance. Miko thought Ezara might put a hand on his shoulder, but he didn't. He whirled back around, pressing forward. Miko stared at his bare feet as he padded along the grimy floor.

"Where are we going?" he asked, after a moment.

"There's an exit to the tunnel under the plaza stairs, which is where you'll find General Simeon sitting pretty as we speak, trying to get the rioting under control. Poor bastard emptied his own personal kitchen and started handing out food to the people this morning. He's hoping he can fill 'em up, send them home, and let them forget about the whole thing. The whole thing being *you*. There was a rumor he tried to poison you last night, but here you are. We thought we'd try to take him out before he made another attempt."

"So we're going after Simeon," Miko realized.

"As of now, that's the plan."

Miko's breath caught. He jogged to keep up with Ezara. "And what do we do when we get there?"

Ezara held up his gun with a shrug. "Do our best with what we've got, I guess."

CHAPTER EIGHTEEN

THE RISING SUN chased Norryn's wings across the sky as he carried his passengers east. Dawn had just crested the hilltops. Seycia peered over the edge of Norryn's neck at the world whizzing below them. They flew over fields of sparkling white ice caps; meadows lush with yellow flowers; and deep, turquoise lakes in the most intricate of shapes. She wondered what creatures lurked there, and whether she'd meet them someday. When they were free to go where they pleased, she decided she'd like to see every corner of this beautiful, terrifying world. Norryn huffed, and she realized he'd read her thoughts.

I'll take you with me, she wordlessly replied with a smile, scratching him behind the velvety flap of his ear.

She thought of all the animals she and Miko had encountered throughout their childhood in the wilderness. There was so much they said without a single word. To finally be able to communicate with one was nothing short of pure magic. She peered over at Haben, seated behind her, transfixed on the landscape below. He was still clutching his injured shoulder.

"Don't look down." She gently nudged him. "Here." She handed him the map of the forest, still folded into a tiny square. He took it with a grateful nod, glad to have something else to focus on. She was surprised by how quickly she'd shed her mortal fear of injury; being up in the sky with Norryn didn't scare her at all. But she sensed Haben's nervousness, and she knew how real it was.

He unfurled the leaf as Norryn tore through a wispy cloud, climbing even higher.

"Look," he said, pointing to a strip of light falling across the land directly below them.

The ribbon of sunlight shot through the darkness ahead, pointing to the horizon like an enormous golden arrow. Seycia looked behind them, puzzled. The Blue Mountain was at their backs, casting a huge shadow. The shadow covered everything except for one sliver of light.

"The side with no shadows," Haben said.

"It's a pathway." Seycia's eyes glimmered. That's what Meri and Lorsa had meant. Norryn stayed on course with the sunbeam below.

They were silent for a long moment, watching the golden strip of light fan out as the sunrise caught up with them. There was a strange, sweet smell on the wind, like the scent of ocean air tangled with a warm, invigorating spice from some faraway place.

Seycia closed her eyes. She wasn't sure if it was Irem's blessing or the fact that they were so close to the Great Forest, but she had never felt so wholly connected to the earth before. The light below them, the aroma on the gentle breeze, the warm feel of Norryn's flesh, and the sound of Haben's breath behind her—everything was a part of her, and she was a part of everything. She was a slim fiber woven into the fabric of the universe, perfectly positioned where she ought to be. In this place meant for the dead, she finally felt the weight of life, of connection, of eternity. Nothing was ever lost.

She became aware of Haben's fingers resting against hers. She pressed her palm to his and knew she wasn't alone in this moment of perfect clarity. The forest was calling to them, just as he'd said it would. She breathed the sweet air deeply. She would need to be brave soon. But not just yet.

At that moment, Seycia felt Norryn's course change. They were starting to fly lower. He cried out with an anxious squeak, getting their attention. They were almost there.

The landscape below them had changed. Where before there had been rocky canyons and black cliffs was a stretch of pure white sand twinkling in the early sunlight. Up ahead, the sand gave way to a massive expanse of brilliant green. *Trees.* Those were trees in the sand. They had finally arrived.

She took note of how completely silent everything was. It was just as her father had imagined. The rhythmic beat of Norryn's wings was the only sound. She felt like an intruder. Even breathing made her feel guilty, as though she'd stepped on something fragile and beautiful.

As they approached the treetops, something strange happened. It was as though Norryn couldn't fly any lower, like he'd reached some sort of invisible barrier. He squawked, and an iridescent glow rippled across the sky, like they'd disturbed a pool of still water.

"What's happening?" Seycia whispered aloud, though she knew Haben didn't have the answer. She wasn't sure Norryn did, either.

Norryn cooed in his throat and hovered in place. Haben tapped her on the shoulder, and pointed behind them with an anxious stare.

One of the trees was suddenly towering above the rest. Seycia was sure it hadn't been there a moment before. She spun in the other direction, where another tree directly in front of them creaked and groaned, doubling in size. The mammoth boughs surrounded them, and the two trees created an enclosure, trapping them inside.

What do we do? Seycia transmitted to Norryn, gripping his scruff. *What are they?* But Norryn just cooed again. For some reason, he didn't seem nervous.

A warm tingle shot down Seycia's spine, like an unseen hand had caressed her there, and a mighty breeze swept across the forest. Norryn bobbed up and down in midair. Seycia felt her stomach drop, even though he'd only descended a few feet.

On the wind, there was a deep voice, neither male nor female, as powerful as the breeze itself: "The Spirit Sentries wish to know the purpose of your journey."

Seycia glanced at Haben with wide eyes, and he nodded. He'd heard it, too. She panicked, at a loss for words. The thought had crossed her mind earlier, but now it consumed her: Had they come here to do something evil? Something they could never undo?

Haben held up Irem's map, unsure who he ought to show it to. The voice wasn't coming from the trees, it was all around them. "We were sent here," he said as he presented it.

"The Mother of Man gave this to you?" the voice uttered.

"Irem," Seycia whispered. Haben nodded in agreement.

"We're here to do her bidding," Seycia said. Guilt crept across her skin, hot and cold at the same time. She wondered if the Spirit Sentries—whoever they were—knew she hadn't told them the whole truth.

The voice was silent, and Seycia choked out, "We've received many blessings from her."

Finally, the voice answered, "If you are truly worthy of these blessings, you will do only the thing she has sent you to do. We will be watching."

The two trees pulled back, releasing them from their enmeshed branches, and they shrank down again. It was almost as if she could hear them sigh as the leaves rustled. Another massive gust of wind shook the forest below, and the glimmering barrier beneath Norryn's feet dissolved like melting ice.

"If you find yourself lost, we shall guide you," the voice added, gentler this time.

Then, the wind settled and the voice was heard no more. Norryn clucked and rolled his neck in a circle before continuing downward at a gentle angle. As he sailed on, Seycia turned to Haben with a stricken gaze, shaking her head.

"Why would Irem let us do this?" she whispered.

"Because too many souls choose darkness, in every life. They've hurt her."

"But what if General Simeon isn't one of them? What happens if we destroy a soul that could have redeemed itself? I-I didn't think this through." Her heart was pounding as she thumbed Irem's branch, tucked into her belt.

Haben took a breath, pursuing his lips. "Meri said only Irem knows which souls have betrayed her. She didn't try to stop you, which could mean the trees we're here to destroy are on her list."

"But we don't know for sure."

"No. We don't."

She pulled her knees to her chest and bit down hard on her lip. Norryn dove down until they were level with the tops of the trees, flush with the healthiest, most enormous leaves Seycia had ever seen. The leaves were the same size as the map, with four perfect points at each end. Many of the trees boasted glorious red flowers in heavy, low-hanging clusters.

But the most astounding things were the trunks of the trees. There was, to begin with, the sheer width of them. Seycia thought it would take a full minute to run in a circle around the base of each tree planted in the pristine white sand. The bark of the spirit trees was pale and worn, with layers of darker colors visible in patches where the bark had stripped away over time. As they passed, Seycia was sure she saw them undulate and bend, despite their size, each according to its own rhythm, as though the trees were breathing.

Her heart fluttered. She'd always known they were living things, but she couldn't have imagined what they would look like up close.

"What do you think happens, when a tree dies? *If* it dies. They get replaced, don't they?" she wondered aloud.

"We'll probably find out, once we do what we've come here to do," he replied. She nodded, more than a little wary. Then, he added, "Tell Norryn to bear right."

She turned around and saw he was holding the leaf map. "Where are we going?"

"You'll see. Tell him."

She leaned her cheek against Norryn's ear and transmitted the directions to him. He gave a little gurgle in his chest and then leaned right.

The trees were aligned in perfect rows, one after the other with equal space between. They went on and on and on. Seycia couldn't comprehend the number of them. *As many trees as there are souls on Earth*, she thought. She wondered what the world was like thousands of miles from Khronasa, in the cities these other souls were inhabiting. Were they suffering too?

They traveled for what could have been hours or perhaps minutes. It was difficult to process the passage of time. Seycia's eyes glazed over, as though she'd fallen asleep, as they passed row after row of trees. The forest truly seemed to go on forever. Finally, Haben spoke up again.

"Tell him to find a spot to land."

Seycia looked at him, puzzled. "What are you doing? The Spirit Sentries told us we had to follow Irem's instructions."

"If they wanted to stop us, they would have done it by now," Haben replied. "And I think Irem would allow this."

Seycia studied him, even more confused. "I don't understand."

"Just get him to land," he repeated, squinting at the map. Seycia hesitated, then finally signaled to Norryn, who skidded to a stop in the sand below his webbed feet.

Haben held up Remi's map. "Who is Oskar?"

Seycia held her breath. She'd completely forgotten that she'd written her father's name into the leaf. Haben swung off Norryn's neck and held out his hand to her. She took it, bewildered. Haben walked in front of her, consulting the map and eyeing the tree directly in front of them.

"Seycia, who's Oskar?" he asked again.

"My father."

Her head was swimming; her knees trembled. She could scarcely look at Haben as he led her to the tree—her father's tree.

"General Simeon killed him," she whispered as she approached it. "He was protecting us. H-he tried so hard to . . ." But she couldn't finish her thought.

Haben stopped in front of the tree, glanced at the map, and nodded. This was the one.

Seycia shuffled toward the massive tree trunk, curling her toes in the fine sand beneath her calloused feet. Her face was inches from the bark now. She held up a quivering hand and took a long moment before caressing the tree trunk with the tips of her fingers. The bark was warm and smooth. She pressed her hand against it more firmly now. She felt the pulse of the tree expand and contract beneath her palm, and she gasped. She hadn't even noticed she was on her knees. Tears streamed from her eyes as though they'd been trapped inside of her for a hundred years and were finally breaking free.

She turned to Haben, at a loss. He moved toward her and dropped to her level on the ground. She fell against him.

He murmured to her, "I'm sorry. I-I shouldn't have brought you."

"No, no. Thank you. I'm . . ." She met his gaze. There were unshed tears in his eyes. "I'm not sad for him. I'm sad for what happened. But he's not gone. He's out there somewhere." She slowly rose to her feet, and he stood with her. "I used to dream about seeing him again, seeing his soul in someone else's body. We'd run into each other somewhere, and neither of us would know why, but we'd feel compelled to stop and talk. I thought about that every day."

Haben nodded.

"I promised him I'd take care of our family when he was gone. Miko's all that's left."

Haben reached into the pocket of his robe and pulled out the map. He offered it to Seycia.

She unfolded it steadily, noticing her hands were no longer shaking. She was ready. General Simeon might have taken everything in the world from her, but now she could take it back. If Irem had allowed her to access this holy place, then her intentions had to be right. They just had to be.

She held her fingertip on the surface of the map, staring it down as though it were the face of her victim. She traced an *S* into the veins of the leaf. The tiny beads of light gathered together at the touch of her hand. She pictured General Simeon and his two gruesome scars—one from her, and the other from her father. She remembered the way he'd made her feel, like she was lost in a poisonous fog—unable to breathe, unable to scream. But before she could write a second letter onto the leaf, the earth trembled beneath her feet. She yelped and grabbed on to Haben for support, staggering in the sand. Seconds later, the ground lurched again, even more violently.

Seycia fell against her father's tree, dropping the map as she smacked her head against its trunk. Norryn released a panicked cry and waddled toward her as Seycia peered up at the sky, past the tops of the trees. The clouds bulged and thickened, as though the sky had been covered by a heavy cloak of black ash. Seycia stood and caught Haben's anxious glance. She picked up the map and folded it into the belt of her dress.

"I don't need to ask what that was, do I?" she whispered.

They both knew full well what it was, or rather, *whom*.

Where were the Spirit Sentries? Couldn't they hold him back? *No*, she realized with a shiver, *Dohv was stronger*. He was stronger than Irem and her sisters. He was stronger than everything.

Haben grasped her shoulders and pulled her toward him. "It's me he wants. It's always been me."

"Then go. Hide. Take Norryn and—"

"No, we can't let Dohv come into the forest. If he does, then—"

But he swallowed his words as he caught sight of the clouds. The dark atmosphere was breaking apart into millions of spindly figures, tumbling on the wind. Arms, legs, and faces emerged—it was the Soulless. They linked their limbs together, forming shapes, forming something larger than themselves.

"We can't let Dohv come into the forest," he repeated in a hoarse whisper. "If I hide, he'll come in and find me. And he'll find you, too."

The two of them watched as the discarded lives created what looked like two wheels out of their enmeshed bodies. They turned in circles while the remaining Soulless clung together to form a platform above them. The ghostly chariot rolled silently, ominously, toward the edge of the forest.

"He'll come in. Unless I come out."

With that, Haben started running.

Seycia bolted after him. "Stop! What are you doing?"

He slowed down and turned to her, calm and resigned, as though he'd known all along that it would come to this. "Meri said something I didn't tell you, about what might happen if Dohv ever tried to hurt you. You were right. You're still human. And he could kill you."

Seycia's heart stammered as she stared at him.

"Finish what you started here," he said. "All he really wants is me."

"But what about Antenor?"

Lightning fractured the sky above. The sweet smell of the forest air was gone, replaced by the foul odor of sulfur, of fire, of flesh burning. A dark shadow appeared at the center of the phantom chariot. A passenger.

"Go," Haben said.

He was right. It was the only way. She grasped both his hands in hers and kissed him against his temple, gently, longing to convey everything she felt. He pressed his mouth to hers, abandoning all reason, all fear.

She gave him one final, shattered glance as she pulled away and tore off into the forest. She couldn't bear to stay a second longer. The tears started falling again, and she knew she would never leave if she succumbed to sadness and fear. She longed to look back. She knew she couldn't. She jumped onto Norryn's neck, and he vaulted into the air, cutting through the trees like a pointed arrow with a mind of its own. And then they were gone.

Haben felt a heavy emptiness in his chest, and a familiar, sharp chill spread from the tips of his fingers to the top of his skull. In spite of his dread, he turned around and raced toward the edge of the forest, to the place Dohv was waiting. This was the thing he was meant to do for her all along. He was sure of it. There was a place he was supposed to be, and this was it. Loving her was a consequence of coming to this place, and it was loving her that had helped him get here . . . But there was nothing he could give her. Except for this.

His legs ached as he sprinted between the trees toward the stretch of white sand up ahead. He had never run this fast, not with this body, not in this life. The gaping bullet wound in his shoulder had started to bleed again, through his cloak. He clung to the spot, but he didn't stop moving.

As he reached the place where the first row of trees met the desert beyond, a horrific, high-pitched ringing assaulted his ears. His head throbbed and he tasted cold iron on his tongue. He collapsed to his knees as the shadow of the Soulless chariot fell across the sand, like the entire sky had just tumbled to the ground.

"*You are an unholy creature who has no right to set foot in this place,*" Dohv seethed. His deep, furious voice echoed between Haben's ears. "*You have disobeyed me time and time again. This ends now.*"

With all his strength, Haben lifted his head and peered up at the sky. Dohv stood in the center of the chariot's platform, the husks of the dead holding him aloft. He looked much larger, as though he had expanded to the same size as the murky clouds in the sky.

"*Where is the girl?*"

Haben's breath caught as he spit out a lie. "I left her at the Blue Mountain. She was hurt and slowing me down."

"*True to form that you'd desert her—but I don't believe you.*"

Haben fought to keep his head raised, to appear unaffected, and bore his gaze into the void beneath Dohv's hood, knowing the eyes of his enemy were in the darkness somewhere, staring right back at him.

"Lorsa told me what you and the girl were planning. I know why you've come to my forest."

"It isn't your forest," Haben said.

An excruciating flicker of electricity shot through him, and he gritted his teeth, stifling a gruesome howl. His raw, bleeding shoulder throbbed in time with the rest of his body. And still, he fought to keep his eyes open. *Let him waste time*, he thought. He hoped Seycia was well on her way to Simeon's tree by now.

"Wherever she is, they will find her soon enough." Dohv pointed a spiny finger at his army of Soulless. They broke apart, casting off in separate directions. Dohv then raised his arms to Haben, lifting him off the ground. *"And you will come with me. A creature like you with no use to me has only one place left to go: under the ice."*

Haben hovered in midair, face-to-face with Dohv, whose psychic grip was like an invisible noose around his neck. He sputtered and twisted in anguish, trying desperately to escape, even though he knew he couldn't—and wouldn't.

"She'll join you when we find her."

Haben's vision ran red as blood gathered in his eyes. He ought to have been dead by now, were death available to him. He knew that much. And it was far from over.

Dohv held out his hand, spreading his five grotesque fingers wide. He pressed them against Haben's head, the same way he had before, but this time the force was even stronger. A searing vibration rattled every one of his brittle bones, and he was sure he would combust from the inside out. Then, his body showed him mercy; he felt as though he were being swaddled by layers upon layers of darkness, taking him down, down into nothingness. He felt his entire being flood with relief as everything went black.

Seycia buried her face into Norryn's skin as the Soulless broke to pieces and Dohv disappeared on the horizon. It was done. Haben was gone. She breathed a heavy sigh, and Norryn craned his head over his shoulder to nuzzle her cheek. She stroked his flat, beak-like nose. They were hiding in the lush leaves at the top of Oskar's tree. They hadn't dared to move until Dohv's clouds cleared.

"You all right?" she asked Norryn.

There was no need to ask him aloud, but she was at a dismal loss with nobody to speak to. Norryn rubbed his nose against her head to reassure her. There would be no time to revel in the accomplishment of her goal. As soon as the trees were destroyed, she would be on her way to Antenor. The three sisters were confident she had the power to confront Dohv, and if they believed in her, then she, too, had to believe. She had to believe there was a way to save Haben. But first, there was the matter of the trees. Heart in knots, she pulled the map from the belt of her dress.

She had already inscribed an *S* into the flesh of the leaf. Her fingertips trembled. It was finally time. She pictured the hideous face of her life's greatest enemy and continued writing:

S-I-M-E-O-N.

CHAPTER NINETEEN

MIKO WASN'T SURE how long they'd been in the tunnel, but he knew they ought to be emerging soon. Every now and then, he'd glance over at Ezara, as if he could tell by his furrowed brow whether they were close. He readjusted his grip on the crossbow, fighting a cramp in his shoulder. He glanced over at the shaggy young man with the revolver, examining his gun, chewing his lip. Minutes ago, Ezara had quickly showed them how to use the firearms and reload them, but the man still looked uncertain.

Another tense moment passed in the darkness, silent as a tomb, before Ezara stopped and felt along the wall, as if he was looking for something. Miko watched him, curious, as he once again turned to the group.

"We're about to climb above ground at the southwest corner of the main square. If you're unprepared to fight back, you're more than welcome to hide down here till it's done. But I can't guarantee how long you'll be hiding or who might find you when it's over." Ezara spun to face Miko. "That goes for you, too. If you want to stay—"

"No. I'm coming."

"I thought you might say that."

Ezara led them around the corner and there, on the side of the concrete wall, was a rusty iron ladder.

"The city is full of new recruits who haven't even received proper uniforms yet," Ezara said to the group as he stepped up onto the ladder. "You'll blend in if you act like you're supposed to be there."

The group nodded in the dim light with solemn stares. It was as if everyone knew Ezara's plan was rushed and dangerous beyond belief, but nobody was about to argue with him. He was, after all, the one who'd gotten them all out of the prison. And this could be their only chance to fight back.

"Act as though I'm your squadron leader. Follow my every command. You may see faces you recognize in the crowd. Don't say anything; don't even look at them. If you recognize them, then they probably recognize you, too. Just walk straight ahead to the plaza, where Simeon is."

"And when do we start shooting?" the shaggy man asked.

"When I tell you to."

"This is horse shit," he spat. "How many people here have ever fired a gun? And how old is *he*, huh?" He pointed an accusatory finger at Miko.

"I'm twelve summers. And *I've* fired a gun," Miko hissed at him. The man's mouth snapped shut.

"I'll bet you're old enough to remember the way Khronasa used to be," Ezara said, not just to the man, but to the whole group. "Maybe we even hunted together in the old days. For years, we've cowered to a psychotic regime of fearmongers, and I don't know about you, but I've never felt entirely comfortable with that. This isn't living, what we've been doing. We all know it."

Silent solidarity fell across the group.

He turned back toward the man. "Of course, feel free to stay down here. If you think you can live with that."

The shaggy young man anxiously fingered the gun in his hand, but didn't say another word. Ezara then turned to Miko and crouched down to his level. "I want you at the back, understand? You're too important."

Miko nodded, readjusting the crossbow in his sweaty palms.

"This is for your parents," Ezara whispered. "Your sister."

Ezara continued up the rusty ladder on the wall, but before he reached the top, he paused and dug into his boot. Miko watched, puzzled, as Ezara fumbled around inside of his shoe and pulled out a tiny golden amulet on a chain. Miko inched closer to get a better look. The amulet was engraved with a picture of a tree. Ezara kissed it and shoved it back into his boot.

"We've got nothing to lose if we get another shot at this, am I right?" He flashed a wry smile, and Miko's heart swelled. *He still believes.*

Ezara unlatched the manhole cover at the top of the ladder and pulled it away with a heavy scrape. Miko felt his pulse galvanize as the roar of revolution filled his ears.

Seycia clung to Norryn's skin till her fists turned white as he rocketed up and around the trees. She felt like she was riding a wild horse that might buck her off any second. She pressed her forehead against his back as he jostled her, instructing him to veer off to the right.

As they turned, Seycia noticed that the clouds up ahead had once again turned a deep, hellish black. She gasped and huddled against Norryn's neck. Were the Soulless back again? The cloud was moving right toward them.

She snapped her eyes to the map in her hands. The bead of light indicating her position was drawing nearer and nearer to the one indicating the tree. Norryn cawed anxiously as he flew.

Seycia became aware of a low, monotonous humming sound, growing louder and louder with each passing second. She glanced over her shoulder, watching as the black cloud above disintegrated and the Soulless broke apart from the mass. She was close enough to see that all of them were holding their mouths agape and humming in unison, a ghostly chorus of dissonant noise. She shuddered. There were millions of them. Maybe more.

"If you can fly faster, now's the time to do it," Seycia whispered into Norryn's ear. He took off as though shot from a cannon.

She gripped the map with all her strength, trying desperately to keep it from blowing away in the wind. Finally, the tiny bead of light signifying their location aligned with the one signifying their destination. Before she could even tell Norryn to slow down, they screeched to a halt and landed. She hadn't noticed how fast her heart was thundering until he'd come to a full stop. He kneeled, allowing her to dismount. She had finally arrived at Simeon's tree.

Miko wordlessly followed his ragtag cohorts, hanging toward the back of the line just as Ezara instructed. He held his head high and marched. Seycia had always told him that if he behaved as though he belonged somewhere, he would. He hoped this was true, especially now, especially as his eyes glazed over in shock at the ghastly state of his city.

Only charred skeletons of the town's major buildings remained. Scattered remnants of the lives of the Khronasans littered the soot-covered streets—plates, cups, shoes, a child's crude wooden doll. As they approached the central plaza, where the sacrificial pit still stood, he heard . . . What was that? Singing?

A cheery-faced choir of Khronasans in Coalition uniforms were gathered on the plaza platform, performing the Coalition's anthem as General Simeon stood toward the back, handing out sacks of food to a queue of townspeople that circled twice around the central square. Armed guards stood watch at every corner. Miko swallowed hard. But of course, he knew Simeon wouldn't let himself be an easy target ever again.

"Our fate in his hands!" A fellow soldier saluted Ezara as they passed. He led a similarly bedraggled group of Khronasans in the opposite direction.

"Our fate in his hands," Ezara returned the greeting.

Miko coughed as he inhaled a cloud of smoke, and the song crescendoed to its climax. Ezara mounted the stairs of the plaza platform and readied his weapon. But Miko froze, glancing at the Coalition guards on every side. If Ezara wasn't a perfectly straight shot, this was going to get ugly quick. Ezara peered at Miko over his shoulder, though the reassuring nod he gave him did little to calm his nerves.

Minari, standing in front of Miko, turned and whispered, "If this goes south, you'd better run to the hills, got it?"

Miko nodded. He felt like a puppet armed with a crossbow, not in control of his own movements. As he shuffled forward, a flicker of realization glowed in his chest. He had powers the rest of these people didn't have. His body could heal in ways theirs could not—at least, that was the way it seemed. How could he let them risk their lives while he stood to the side? It wasn't right.

In that moment, Miko saw that Ezara had reached the plaza platform, with General Simeon in his sights. His finger squeezed the trigger of his semiautomatic, and Minari threw herself to the ground to avoid the crossfire, yanking Miko down with her. Miko spat out dirt as a hurricane of gunfire erupted above them.

Time slowed to a crawl as Miko staggered to his feet and swiped the crossbow off the ground. Minari grabbed for his leg, but he shook her off. He wasn't afraid anymore. He could survive this—he knew it all the way down to his bones.

As he scrambled up the stairs, he saw that General Simeon was still alive, barking orders to his security detail. The other men in their group rushed to Ezara's aid, firing their weapons. Miko took cover behind a marble pillar and hugged the crossbow to his chest, calculating his next move.

Seconds later, the shower of gunfire quieted as Miko's comrades and Simeon's guards both reloaded their weapons. Miko glanced in all directions, looking for Ezara, not spotting him among the dead littering the pristine white tile. He found him on the opposite side, crouched behind a pillar, reloading his gun. Minari had joined them as well—she stood beside Ezara, guarding him with her bow drawn. General Simeon cowered behind a wall of burlap sacks, surrounded by his bodyguards—or what was left of them. Only two remained.

"You would be well advised to drop your weapons," Simeon barked. Miko managed a smug grin. It wouldn't be *that* easy. Simeon had forgotten what it was like to have his enemies fight back.

Miko glanced down at his crossbow with a frown. There wasn't much he could do without a firearm. He could either run and hide . . . or he could get one. He took stock of the dead around him. One of Simeon's fallen bodyguards, not three feet away, still held a handgun in her fist.

"I said, drop your weapons," General Simeon hollered from his pitiful hiding place. He slowly emerged, taking a quarter turn toward the spot where Ezara stood.

Miko knew he could probably grab the pistol before anyone could react. *Probably.* He watched Simeon's guards closely, waiting . . . waiting . . .

At that moment, a man about Ezara's age who had been singing in the choir bolted out from behind another column, toward the weapons of the dead. He'd apparently had the same idea as Miko; he'd just acted sooner. He wasn't armed with anything at all. Simeon's bodyguards aimed and fired at him, giving Miko just enough time to sprint over toward the pistol he had his eye on. Just barely.

Miko snagged the gun out of the dead woman's hand as the foolish Khronasan man fell with a smack against the cold, hard ground. Miko had a firearm now, but he was also out in the center of the platform, exposed, unprotected. In a panic, he threw his arms out into a triangle shape, just as Ezara had shown him, wrapped his finger around the trigger, and squeezed. He'd get them before they could get him.

Though he'd barely gotten his sights, the bullet grazed the side of Simeon's shoulder, slicing his jacket. He whirled around and stared at Miko. A tense, fearsome moment passed between them. Simeon's look said it all. *But I killed you.*

"Hold your fire," Simeon hissed at his guards. "I'll handle this one."

Miko caught sight of Ezara's horrified face and wondered if he should have run after all.

Simeon stormed toward him, accompanied by the same guard who had stood by his side the night Miko snuck onto the roof. He seethed, "Know this, boy. The Keeper of Life wants you dead. Outrun me as many times as you like. But *he* will find you."

Two shots rang out, and Miko saw Ezara emerge from behind the pillar, brandishing his gun. But Simeon's loyal bodyguard moved faster than Ezara's finger. He blocked the shot meant for General Simeon and was already curled in a heap on the ground, a bullet lodged in his stomach.

"Gil . . ." General Simeon gasped, then glared daggers at Ezara. Simeon's last remaining bodyguard, standing behind him, readied his weapon.

"Nooo!" Miko wailed as the bodyguard fired.

Ezara slumped against the white marble pillar, leaving a smear of blood as he slid to the ground. Miko didn't even have a second to mourn his rescuer, his friend, as General Simeon and his bodyguard raced toward him.

Miko stood his ground and aimed the pistol again. He could get General Simeon right in the gut, if he came at him in a straight line and if he did it quickly. But when he pulled the trigger, nothing happened. He yanked aside the cover of the chamber, as Ezara had instructed, and his heart sank. There was no copper inside. It was empty.

Simeon let loose a vicious chuckle as his guard seized Miko, grabbed the gun, and tossed it over his shoulder like a flimsy toy. Simeon approached him as he thrashed against the guard's iron grip and wrapped a firm hand around his throat.

"Anyone who wishes to defend this boy can join that sorry sack of shit on the ground over there," Simeon addressed the remaining Khronasans, pointing to Ezara's body.

Miko spotted Minari inching away from her hiding place, eyes on his crossbow lying on the ground. "Don't," he managed to choke out. Simeon's guard pointed his gun at her. She froze on the spot and raised her shaky hands over her head.

Simeon stared deep into Miko's eyes, crushing his windpipe in his viselike grip. He drew in a weak, stilted breath, savoring it, suddenly fearing it would be his last. He'd wanted so much to believe in the Lasting Light, that he'd been willing to convince himself of anything. He'd made it out alive before, but this felt different. Terror gripped him, tight as the hand that squeezed his throat. He wasn't going to survive this time.

Seycia stared at the towering tree before her, then pulled Irem's branch from her belt. It was still warm to the touch. And she knew why. The branch was filled with fire.

She glanced up at the gathering Soulless, moving closer and closer. She had only seconds, if that. She could feel their ghostly fingertips caressing her shoulders. Gooseflesh prickled across her skin.

She peered at the map. She was standing at the precise location indicated on the flesh of the leaf. The two beads of light were perfectly matched on top of one another. If she moved even one step to the side, one of the flickering lights moved with her in the same direction. This was Simeon's tree. It had to be.

So why was she hesitating? Her breath caught as she clutched Irem's branch in her shaky fist. It was no time to reconsider. If Simeon's soul wished to redeem itself, it should have done so long ago. His time was up.

The ominous hum from the cloud of past lives rattled the branches high above her head, like a chilling foghorn on a stormy bay. An impenetrable cold front encircled her as the Soulless descended, ten, twenty at a time. She had to do it. Now.

Seycia snapped off the top of Irem's branch, and a column of blue and golden flames spouted from the end, the same flame that had come from Irem's mouth. Irem had given this tree its life, then given Seycia the power to take it away. But as the flame grew brighter, her panic swelled. She might still be wrong about this tree. She thought of Haben, of how he'd fought to live a new, better life. Of everything he'd sacrificed. Her heart wrenched. This was all she'd ever wanted. She'd come so far. But Simeon was one of millions of lives this soul might have yet to live. If she made a mistake . . . if she killed a soul that might still have a chance . . .

As her head swam, a fearsome gust of wind swirled around her, kicking up the sand beneath her feet. The encroaching Soulless backed away with a wicked snarl, a thousand strong. Seycia felt that same warm tingle up and down her spine, and Norryn squeaked. The Spirit Sentries had returned, and they were holding the Soulless back for her.

"I don't understand!" her raspy voice cracked as she shouted to them, turning in all directions, unsure of where they were. "I'm going to kill it. Forever. Is that what you want?"

She waited for a reply from the sentries, but none came. She trembled, facing the tree, watching Irem's fire consume the stick. What to do, what to do? She knew every second cost her. And yet . . .

Miko felt a sudden, eerie calm wash over him as General Simeon's hand clasped his throat, tighter and tighter, and his breath grew shorter by the second.

To live was to die. And here he was. His father had gone before him, and his mother. Seycia, too. He felt as though they were all inviting him to come home, home to his tree, home to a place he could finally rest. He was so very tired after all. So, so tired. And yet he fought to keep his eyes open the entire time, returning Simeon's wretched gaze full force. Why, he couldn't be sure. Maybe he felt it was braver. Maybe he wanted to make sure Simeon would never forget him ...

Seycia stared up at the tree, watching its bark expand and contract, still breathing. The Soulless formed a shell of darkness around her as the wind continued to hold them back, but she didn't know how long the Spirit Sentries would wait for her. She held up the torch, watching the flames dance inches from the low-hanging leaves.

Norryn whined behind her—a desperate, plaintive sound, and she spun to face him. They locked eyes, and he made the sound again, moving toward her. And that was when she remembered—Norryn was Irem's voice. He was the only one who understood her. *And Seycia understood Norryn.*

"You're sure?" She asked Norryn—and Irem, too.

She shivered as Norryn cried out again, crippling her with anguish, and it was as though she could feel Irem's heartbreak. This tree, this soul, had caused more pain than Seycia could bear to imagine. Irem knew. Norryn knew. The Spirit Sentries knew. And now, she knew.

She extended Irem's torch toward the lowest hanging limb as it swayed in the fearsome wind, fighting to keep her hand steady. As she watched the glorious blue flame magnetize to the leaves, she whispered, "Don't ever come back."

The thunderous *crack!* that followed sent shock waves across the forest and knocked Seycia off her feet, and she swore, beyond the howling wind, that she heard an inhuman scream pierce the sky. She wanted to scream along with it, but she couldn't move, she couldn't speak.

She scrambled backward with a horrified gasp as the fire devoured the leaves and raced up the tree trunk like a predator chasing its prey. As if it had a mind of its own. The pure, white bark smoldered, glowing blue, then burned a hellish black. The terrifying beauty of the dying tree held her transfixed. Whatever happened next was out of her hands.

Simeon's guard cocked his gun, and the sound echoed across Miko's mind as though it were far, far away. He didn't have the strength for another breath. And somehow, that was all right. The place he was floating toward was warm. The place he was leaving was cold and frightening.

Warm, warm, warm—he felt warmer by the second. Then, suddenly *hot*. Scorching hot. He heard a muffled scream as air rushed back into his lungs. Miko flung his eyes open as Simeon loosened his grip.

He had only seconds to process what he saw before his head hit the marble floor with a sickening thud, but he was sure he'd seen it: a horrible tremor rocked Simeon's body, like he'd been stabbed in the back by a hundred swords. He twitched and howled, clawing at his skin, as though there were something alive inside of it. With a final, bone-chilling cry, his flesh came to pieces as a burst of blue and yellow fire erupted from his chest and spread across every inch of his body. His tinted glasses flew off his face and shattered on the ground.

Miko's mouth hung agape. He understood the warmth he'd felt. It was the fire—this spellbinding, otherworldly fire, reducing his greatest enemy to ash.

Simeon's guard collapsed to his knees in horror. Minari was screaming. The flames still danced before him, but Simeon was gone, as though the ripples of heat in the air had absorbed every inch of his earthly body.

Miko's head swam, pounding with pain, as the wall of fire swirled before him and burned with colors he swore he'd never seen before in his life. And then, she appeared: Beyond the flames, a figure stood, obscured by smoke, with long black hair blowing in all directions like a tornado. It was as if the fire had opened a window to another world, and he could see straight through to the other side. He couldn't make out the figure's face beyond the smoke, but there was something about her. Something that called to him . . .

The figure took a step toward him. Through the fire, Miko saw her place a hand to her heart. Then to her lips. *No . . . it can't be.* His heart leaped in his chest as Seycia finally held out the palm of her hand, as though she were reaching out to touch him.

A hundred nights in their little cabin flashed before his eyes, each one ending the same way. He could almost feel Seycia's hand pressing against his forehead, as if they were home again and she was standing over his hammock, wishing him goodnight.

He tried to lift his head, to shout her name, but he was too weak. He extended a feeble hand toward the fire to return her blessing. It didn't burn him. Or if it had, he didn't feel it.

The smoke cleared as the flames dissipated. Seycia's image evaporated into the hazy air, and he finally glimpsed her face as she held her palm out to him. She met his eye, and he met hers. But the moment was over before it began. She was gone.

Miko uttered her name with all the strength he had left, then gasped aloud and shut his eyes, heavy with tears.

He felt hands gripping his shoulders, carrying him away from the plaza platform, as the otherworldly fire raged behind his eyes, burned into his memory forever. *She'd never left him.*

He wasn't sure what he'd seen, or what it meant, but he knew that much was true. He wasn't alone, and he never would be again.

Seycia backed away from the towering flames as the final embers of Simeon's tree fell through the sky like tiny stars, tumbling toward the earth. One of them landed against her cheek, and she wiped it away like a smoldering tear. She thought she heard a whisper on the wind—*Seycia*. She froze with wide eyes. Was he still with her?

She stifled a cry and reached out to touch the burning tree, singeing her hand.

"I'm here! Miko, can you hear me?"

But there was nothing but smoke and the crackle of collapsing wood.

"Miko . . . please, don't go . . ."

She searched for him, desperate for any sign of his presence, but whatever she'd seen was already gone. Seycia trembled and took a step back as the base of the tree trunk crumbled to ash. Her heart wrenched as she replayed his voice over and over in her head, flooded with joy that seconds later flashed to a sea of sorrow. Had he seen her signal to him? Would she ever get another chance?

Reeling, she glanced at Irem's torch with a frown, noticing that it was much, much shorter now. She couldn't keep it burning. Not when she had more trees to destroy. She extinguished it in the sand, tucked it into her dress, and ran to Norryn, climbing back on top of him.

She wondered why Miko had appeared to her. He must have been there, somehow. It was as though she'd gazed right at him through Simeon's incinerating soul. What had become of Simeon's flesh and blood in those final moments? She couldn't be sure, but his soul had no home now, and without a home, his soul would perish. The deed was done, for better or worse.

She'd almost forgotten about the cloud of Soulless stalking her beyond the treetops, until the heavy wind keeping them at bay suddenly vanished. She froze as horrifying stillness fell across the forest.

"Wait! I-I'm not finished!" she cried. But the invisible sentries were gone. Why had they abandoned her? Had she made a mistake? Hadn't they wanted her to do this?

Norryn looked into her eyes with a low, foreboding growl that seemed to come from the deepest part of him, like a dog warning its master not to come any closer. She didn't know he could make such a sound.

"Just one more. Just the emperor. Then we go after Haben."

Norryn made the same angry, reluctant sound. *No more*, he seemed to say. But Seycia shook her head, ignoring him, as the Soulless descended, black and ruthless. She'd have to find a way to outrun them.

Just go, Seycia transmitted to Norryn, squeezing his ear in her fist. *Please.*

Norryn released a hesitant squawk, but he didn't disobey. He took off into the smoky fog as the chilling choir of the dead rang in Seycia's ears.

Norryn squealed as he dodged a cloud of Soulless, trying to block their path. They were swarming her, trying to confuse them, trying to take Norryn to the ground. She pulled a sharp breath and shuddered: the air around her was thick and moist and rotten smelling. She was literally taking the Soulless into her lungs.

Seycia tried to consult the map, but she couldn't see a thing through the blackness. Her heart thundered as Norryn shot into the sky like a rocket, skimming the treetops. Another heavy mass of Soulless swooped in on either side of them, enmeshing themselves in the center. This swarm, Norryn did not anticipate. He squealed as he collided with the foggy black lattice.

Seycia was blind for a moment, engulfed by the Soulless, unable to breathe. She felt Norryn fall to his side, and she clung to his skin with all her strength as he righted himself. They had nearly flown through the entire pack of them, nearly cleared the hurdle, when out of the darkness . . . *Smack!* They hit a tree. Seycia's body plummeted to the ground on top of Norryn's as he released a stricken *ca-caw!*

Norryn whined on the sandy forest floor and nudged his beak around in the darkness, searching for Seycia. She rolled over onto her side with a groan and lunged for his neck.

She grasped Irem's branch in her belt as she caught her breath. She nudged Norryn to urge him to move forward, but his body vibrated with that same impassioned warning growl. She understood him. She'd understood before, but she hadn't wanted to.

We go no further. This soul is not for you to take.

A sigh escaped her lips, heavy with regret. It pained Seycia to imagine that someone like Emperor Caius could possibly redeem himself, but she had no right to control his destiny. Her heart twisted as she realized she'd wasted her time trying to target a second soul, a soul Irem did not want her to destroy, when Haben's moments were numbered. She could not do two things at the same time, nor was she supposed to. There was somewhere else she was meant to be. She had to go to Antenor.

Norryn read her thoughts and craned his neck to meet her gaze, black eyes stormy with horror.

I can't leave him. We have to go.

With a terrified yelp, Norryn pulled himself upright and gave himself a running start to vault back into the air. But before he could take flight, Seycia felt a sharp tug at her ankle and nearly toppled off Norryn's back. She kicked the Soulless away, but more of them appeared. Norryn bucked and growled as he took to the sky, but the greedy hands kept grabbing for his wings. It was no use. She had to surrender.

Drop me, she silently transmitted to Norryn. No response. She tried again. *Drop me. Let them take me. And meet me in Antenor.*

But Norryn did not obey. She pinched him and this time hissed aloud, "Norryn. Drop me now or I'm jumping."

Still, he would not listen. So Seycia shut her eyes and let go.

Norryn squealed in horror. *Go, go, please go*, she desperately transmitted to him. She was the intended target, and he'd be no use to her if they were both captured.

She felt wind in her face as Norryn heaved his wings and flew off with a devastated cry. She braced herself for the impact as she fell, but none came. Instead, the woven limbs of the Soulless broke her fall and cradled her in a hammock of foul, clammy darkness. She lay as still as possible as they drifted up and away, carrying her with them.

She had no idea what she'd do when she arrived in Antenor, not a clue how she would get Haben to safety if such a way even existed. She pressed her fingers against each of her tools in the blinding fog, naming them. The fang. The map. Irem's branch.

She'd made it this far riding on nothing but split-second choices. It was the only method she had, the only one she knew. And it would have to do in a place she couldn't possibly prepare herself for . . . a place like Antenor.

CHAPTER TWENTY

SEYCIA COULDN'T SEE a thing through the heavy net of intertwined Soulless. A frigid chill spread across her body from the inside out, as though the center of her bones had turned to ice. The tears in her eyes froze.

The Soulless emanated that same ugly, all-consuming darkness, creating a horrible echo chamber of cruel whispers. But this time, the fury they inspired invigorated her. She would need every scrap of that anger to fight what lay ahead.

The web of Soulless broke apart, and she plummeted down through the sky. She landed on her back in a deep, dark hole with gritty black mud at the bottom that stunk like tar. The walls were lined with dense, slick ice. She shivered, reminded of the pit in Khronasa, and pulled herself upright. She watched the Soulless fade into the darkness above her; it was still daytime everywhere else in the Underworld, but it was black as midnight here in Antenor.

She saw only a small circle of night sky above, and the murky clouds refracted an eerie red glow, as if there were a fire burning nearby. There was no sign of the desolate landscape or the frozen lake Haben had told her about. There was nothing to tell her that this was Antenor. But she knew it had to be. She knew Antenor was where Dohv's servants would send her, to punish her for desecrating his forest—just like Haben. Thankfully, she had reinforcements.

She stumbled to her feet against the slick side of the hole and forced herself to think only of her next step. She'd take it moment by moment. The first thing to do was climb out of the pit. The only way out would be Norryn. She closed her eyes and called for him, hoping he could still sense her across the distance. She patted herself down for her tools, reciting them to herself again: *Fang. Map. Irem's fire—*

"It's you," a frosty voice called out in the darkness. Seycia jumped. She wasn't alone.

It was Zane, the boy demon, shackled head to toe with a chain of the same grotesque scarabs that had nearly done her in at the canyon. He struggled to breathe as they coiled around his neck. For a second, she felt bad for him. His dark eyes were enormous and glassy with terror.

"Had a feeling I'd see you here eventually, bitch," he snarled at her.

She didn't feel quite so bad for him anymore.

"And to think," she muttered, plotting as she spoke, "I was considering saving you only seconds ago."

He laughed and gasped in the same breath as the beetles dug into his skin. "How are *you* supposed to save *anyone*? What, with that fang? This is Antenor. We're *all* going under the ice."

"Why would Dohv bring you here? I thought he looked after you."

"Until I got his pet stuck under a rock at the bottom of the river," Zane spat. "Oh, wait. That wasn't *me*. That was you. And Haben. At least you both got what you deserved in the end."

"Dohv betrayed you," she said softly. "You're angry."

"Of course I'm angry! What do *you* care, anyway?"

"Where is Haben?" she dared to ask.

"Dohv took him first. He's already gone to the cliff," Zane replied.

"The cliff?"

"Right, the cliff. Where they lower him. Into the ice."

Seycia silently, desperately called out to Norryn again. Where was he?

The beetles bore into Zane viciously, gnawing on his sallow flesh. He howled and writhed on the muddy ground. Seycia watched him for a moment before she spoke again.

"You know, I can get those things off you," she said, just smugly enough to keep the upper hand.

"Then why don't you?"

"I don't see why I should, all things considered. I'm sure you understand." She glanced upward, scanning the sky for Norryn. Every second cost her.

"You said you could save me," he yelped.

"If I do, it comes at a price. I'm here to destroy your master. And I'm going to need a second set of hands."

Zane cackled and shook his head. "Oh, you're going to destroy my master? Perfect! Good thing you're practically human with no powers whatsoever!"

A shadow fell across the hole in the ground, and Seycia's heart faltered, wondering if the army of Soulless had come back to take her to the cliff. She remembered what Haben had told her: *You're still human. Dohv could kill you.* Whatever she did next, she would need to do it carefully. Flooded with dread, she glanced upward, but it was only Norryn, circling high above. She narrowed her eyes and turned back to Zane, determined now.

"My way out is here," she said. "So I'll be going now. Last chance if you want me to cut you loose."

Zane looked at the sky, then at Seycia. "Dohv can't be beaten. He just can't. What makes you think you're powerful enough?"

"Maybe I'm not. But an army with nothing to fear . . . That's a different story," she said, and then the plan crystalized before her eyes. "We can destroy the thing the demons fear the most. We can destroy Antenor."

"With what?" Zane breathed, and Seycia swore she saw a ray of hope break though his sullen gaze.

"I'll show you if you come with me."

But the boy demon said nothing. Norryn careened downward, catching Seycia's eye. She felt the breeze underneath his wings grow stronger and stronger.

"Wait, wait, I'll come, I'll do it," Zane stammered as he caught sight of Norryn. "Don't go. Cut me loose."

She signaled to Norryn to retreat and drew her fang. Zane backed away, wary, as she pointed it at him.

"Stop it. Just hold still," she said as she hacked into the chain of scarabs. Zane sputtered at the stench of them.

"You know what this thing can do," Seycia said of the fang as she carved away the last of the beetles. "So do exactly as I say unless you want the pointy end stuck between your eyes, understood? If you go against me, you get to choose: the fang or the ice."

Zane shook himself loose and massaged his sore, puckered arms and legs. "Fang or the ice, got it," he repeated.

She wondered if he'd thank her for releasing him but wasn't at all surprised when he didn't. Seconds later, Norryn dove headfirst into the hole, faster than she'd ever seen him fly before. She heard a ferocious, angry screech as she grabbed for Norryn's neck and climbed on. Where had *that* come from? Surely it hadn't been Norryn.

"There are demons standing guard," Zane said as he hopped onto Norryn's back. "That's them. We need to be fast."

Norryn rocketed into the air, straight through the dense layer of fog above them. They were so high that Seycia could see daylight again. Zane clung to Norryn's skin and clenched his teeth in terror.

"Stop. He's not going to drop you," she hissed at him. "Unless I tell him to."

Zane blanched, and Seycia enjoyed a smug smile. She had him right where she needed him—helpless, frightened, and a mile up in the sky.

"The first thing we need to do is get Haben off the cliff. Then, we can take care of Antenor."

Zane shook his head at her. "You're wasting your time trying to save Haben. If you really want to do some damage here, your chance is now, when Dohv is focused on torturing him."

"That's not the plan. I came here to get Haben. But if Antenor burns in the process, even better."

"What do you mean if it *burns*?" Zane asked. She pulled Irem's stick from her belt and held it out to him.

"There's fire inside."

"Fire can't hurt Dohv."

"This isn't ordinary fire. Trust me."

She handed it to him and he flinched, feeling the heat inside. There was a gleam of understanding in his eye as Norryn dipped lower, past the layer of fog, and Antenor's full skyline came into view. Seycia held her breath. The monstrous ice shelf broke off into jagged pieces at the end, sharp as daggers. Hundreds of demons, loyal to their master, stood guard on the lower ledges. Seycia's stomach turned. She wasn't sure of their strength, but the sheer number of them made her hair stand on end.

"We'll need to find a way past all of them," Zane muttered, pointing to the barricade of demons keeping watch. He kept fingering Irem's branch, as though he was pulling strength from it.

"One thing at a time," Seycia whispered.

At the top of the icy plateau, beside a massive, roaring fire, a trio of burly demons lowered a strange-looking, contorted mound on a chain toward a monstrous expanse of frozen water below. She recognized Lorsa among them—once again Dohv's faithful servant. Seycia didn't have to wonder what was at the end of their chain. It didn't look human—it didn't look like *anything* anymore—but she knew. She knew they had Haben. She ignored the unbearable sinking of her heart, trying to keep focused on their plan.

Dohv stood at the center of the ice, watching as the twisted mass of broken limbs inched toward him, bit by painstaking bit.

"Get ready, we're going to grab him," Seycia hissed to Zane.

Norryn hovered a safe distance from the cliff as Dohv pointed toward the ice with a single, gaunt finger. He moved in a slow, precise circle, and the ice melted at his touch, creating a gaping hole in the glacial blackness below: Haben's grave.

She swallowed hard and glanced at his body dangling at the end of the chain. He didn't struggle. He made no sound.

"We wait till he's at the bottom," she whispered aloud, if only to keep herself from leaping off Norryn's back at that very moment. They would have a surface to stand on once he'd reached the ice. It was no use trying to get to him before he hit the ground.

Haben's disfigured body hit the frigid water in the hole Dohv created, and Seycia saw him flinch for the first time. She couldn't bear to imagine how cold that water was. He thrashed and struggled as the water engulfed him. At the top of the cliff, Lorsa's contingent let the end of the chain drop into the hole—another job well done.

But something was wrong. Haben was in the hole now, but nothing happened. Dohv shuffled toward him. He clasped his hand over Haben's head and forced him into the water as Norryn began his gentle, quiet descent toward the ice.

Dohv released a mighty roar as he let go of Haben's head and he bobbed right back to the surface. Livid, he kicked his shapeless body and began to pace.

"He's not frozen," Zane gasped. "They always freeze up right away. I watch every time. I don't know why it's not working . . ."

Seycia's heart leaped. *Now!* she transmitted to Norryn.

She hadn't expected Norryn's miraculous speed or his angle of approach. She clung to his scruff with everything she had, but still, she felt herself slipping. She let go with one hand, and Zane did too, just long enough to snag both of Haben's arms and pull him up onto Norryn's neck. But her grip on Norryn's skin was already weak, and before she could right herself, she toppled over and fell through the fog—toward the ice. She heard Norryn squawk in terror as she tumbled to the earth.

She squeezed her arms against her chest, bracing for impact, and hit the ice, hard as stone and colder than anything her mind knew how to process. As she landed on her back and felt her spine twist back into place, she saw Norryn rocket up and away through the low, hellish atmosphere. The demons keeping watch on the cliff screeched and scrambled in all directions, but she knew they couldn't reach Norryn. He was already soaring far above their heads. She transmitted to him, *Don't turn back.* Haben was safe with Norryn. That was all that mattered. After everything he'd sacrificed, he deserved to be free. To live. If Darkest Death was her fate, if Dohv destroyed whatever was left of her, she would face it, head on—just as he had.

Careful not to slip on the ice, she slowly rose to her feet, and her heart thundered across her whole body as she spun to face Dohv.

It was just the two of them on the ice now, and Dohv expanded in size with each passing second as his anger mounted. She felt his voice coming before she heard it as her vision swam with clouds of silver and her ears rang. She'd forgotten about this part.

"The girl who wouldn't die."

She fought the urge to buckle her knees.

"There was perfect order in my world for thousands of years until you arrived. But I always put things back where they belong. As you have seen. What did you think of my sisters?"

She couldn't answer. She could barely move her jaw.

"You must know that escaping the ice does not mean you have escaped me."

He held both his hands out in front of her, spreading his long fingers wide, as though he was about to claw her face. *"If you feel for this traitor, so too will you feel his pain."*

His fingertips flinched, and he thrust them toward her with a deafening *crack!*—as though he'd struck her with a bolt of invisible electricity.

And yet . . . Seycia felt nothing. Her mind raced. What had happened? Dohv briefly released his psychic grip on her, and she was able to move her arms and her mouth—probably, she thought, so he could watch her suffer. She threw herself down to the ice with a chilling shriek, pretending to convulse and struggle for breath. A glimmer of hope burned inside of her as he reached out his hands a second time. Again, she felt no pain. Something in her was acting as a shield against his power. He couldn't hurt her like he could hurt other demons.

Because he didn't make me.

Understanding surged through her, bright as Irem's fire. Maybe she *did* have the power to confront him. But she couldn't let him know his psychic torture had failed, not until the absolute last second. As she lurched on the ice and curled her body into a tight, shivering knot, she felt for Irem's branch in her belt. But it wasn't there. All the air went out of her lungs. Zane still had it. She had her fang, and the map. But her third, most powerful totem was gone.

Dohv loomed over her and thrust a spindly hand to her chest, and again she heard that same sickening crack. But she was so distracted by having lost Irem's branch that she didn't react right away. She was a split second late, but that was all it took. She heard Dohv scoff in confusion as he backed away.

"How is it that you breathe?" he snarled, and the words wrapped around her head like a vile snake.

She sprang to her feet, ablaze with terror, and tore the fang from underneath her collar. She wasn't sure what she'd do with it, but it was all she had. Dohv laughed and expanded in size. He was double, triple the height he'd been. She felt her entire body go stiff again as he reached out to grasp her in his enormous palm. He held her high in the air, and her breath burned in her chest as she tried to anticipate his next move.

With a furious grunt, Dohv threw her to the ice with the full force of his supernatural strength. She hit the ground headfirst, a dead weight. Her consciousness was dull and fuzzy as her skull throbbed and her bones shifted back into place. She could hear the freezing water as it lapped against the edge of the hole that was meant to be Haben's grave.

Dohv's black cloak of Soulless swirled around his feet as he approached her. She rolled onto her side, desperately trying to blink her vision back into focus.

"That is mine."

She squinted up at Dohv, not understanding at first. He pointed across the ice, where the leaf map lay unfurled on the ground, flickering with golden light. It had flown from her belt when he threw her.

Dohv glided across the ice, soundless as a ghost, and picked it up, reverent. She couldn't see his eyes in the dark void beneath his hood, but she knew the sight of it had captivated him. She struggled to sit up, still clutching her pounding head.

"Did my sisters give you this?" he asked her, voice quaking with rage.

She found he had permitted her to respond. She nodded and said in a steely voice, "You banished them, but you didn't take away their power."

With an earsplitting roar, Dohv charged toward her, picked her up, and threw her across the ice again. It was the only way he could think to hurt her, but it wouldn't do so long as she could self-heal.

"I took all of their power. Make no mistake. And this was not their gift to give you."

Seycia watched as Dohv held the leaf in the palm of his hand, lovingly stroking its surface, like greeting an old friend. But something else caught her eye, just beyond the edge of the frozen lake: a resplendent indigo light bloomed across the horizon. Her vision was still blurry, but she swore the glow was coming from the monstrous ice shelf up above, and that the plateau was somehow *shrinking*. Dohv hadn't noticed. He was still transfixed by the leaf. Before she could think of what to do next, his frantic, nightmarish voice beat against her ears.

"What have you done? You've broken it!"

She was paralyzed, cosmically locked to the ice, as Dohv sailed over and held the leaf out to her. The beads of heavenly light scattered in all directions, the same way they did when Haben first tried to use it. She stared at the blackness underneath Dohv's hood, trying in vain to predict his next move, to read his expression, but there was none. He tossed the leaf to the side with a hideous wail and shamefully shrank down in size.

His shadow fell over her, dark and cold as the ice she lay upon, and he spread his five fingers wide, approaching the crown of her head. She remembered the moment he'd taken regenesis from Haben, the way he'd gripped his head and reduced him to a walking corpse. Would she be vulnerable, too? Was there a way to fight back?

She held her breath as tears pricked her eyes. She couldn't move, she couldn't scream. Dohv's fingertips grazed her temples, emanating electric heat, and she braced herself for contact.

Ca-ca-caw!

Norryn's cry pierced the icy silence. He was little more than a blur across the sky at first, but as he materialized, an ominous, warped splintering sound echoed from the depths of the lake. The earth roiled and shook.

Dohv whirled around, releasing Seycia from his grasp, and unleashed a bloodcurdling howl as a gigantic, freezing waterfall cascaded down toward the ice. Seycia's consciousness cleared as Dohv lost control of her, and she sprang to her feet. The monstrous ice shelf was gone, and the terrifying waterfall was in its place. A flood of frigid water surged toward them. Antenor was collapsing before her eyes, and she had moments, maybe less, to decide what to do.

The demons who had been standing guard on the plateau were now on the ground, closing in on all sides of the frozen lake. She swallowed hard, glancing at them as they encroached, circling her and Dohv. Were they here to save their master? Would they trap her underwater as Antenor fell to pieces? At that moment, Norryn streaked across the sky like a bullet, and Seycia saw Zane on his neck, clutching Irem's glowing torch.

No, she realized; he'd found her an army. He'd melted the ice shelf. And as the enormous, freezing tidal wave crested, she turned to face Dohv. She knew what to do.

"An unclean spirit cannot enter the Great Forest," Seycia said as she picked the map up off the ice and the answers became clear. "You didn't enter the forest to come after us—Haben came to you, and you sent the Soulless after me—but *you* never entered. Because you can't."

Dohv moaned as Seycia pocketed the map. The demon army crept up on him from behind, creating an intimidating fortress. Before him loomed the deluge of melted ice.

Seycia lunged toward Dohv's chest and plunged her fang right in the place she thought his heart might be. She heard the Soulless that made up his cloak shriek as it penetrated them. He stumbled backward in shock, and the demons shoved him toward the hole in the ice. As he teetered on the edge, trying and failing to pull the fang from his otherworldly body, Seycia whispered:

"And, just as you intended, there's only one place for an unclean spirit to go."

Floodwater gushed across the frozen lake, hurdling right toward them. The demons scattered in all directions, taking cover, and Seycia spotted Norryn overhead, about to swoop in for a daring rescue.

"Under the ice."

As Norryn swept up Seycia, the approaching cascade knocked Dohv off his feet and into the frozen grave he himself had carved. Seycia caught her balance on Norryn's back and peered down at the lake with an awestruck gasp.

As Dohv hit the icy water, his cloak of Soulless evaporated into thin air and she glimpsed Dohv's true form for the first time. His skin was hardly skin at all, but a molten swirl of liquid reds and blacks, and his face was like staring into the mouth of an erupting volcano. It was as if he were made entirely of fire. Two vacant black holes, where his eyes should have been, gazed imploringly to the heavens. His mouth was frozen in a horrified *O* as he trembled and lurched, trying to swim away. But his body had already begun dissolving in the water. It hissed with hideous black steam and congealed into a viscous bloodred ooze. Seycia's heart sank when she spotted her fang down below, disappearing beneath the surface with what was left of Dohv.

At that moment, a deafening crackle rumbled across the earth as the floodwater froze in place, becoming one with the lake. The ice fused together over the hole Dohv had fallen into, and in an instant, whatever remained of him was gone. Zane stifled a terrified yelp as his lord sank to his eternal, frozen grave.

She stole a glance over her shoulder at Haben, still chained in place but safely propped against Norryn's shoulder. Zane held Irem's torch, still lit, and Seycia grabbed it from him.

"Sorry, I didn't know how to put it out," he whispered.

Seycia cupped her palm around the flame and squeezed, knowing the fire wouldn't harm her. When she withdrew her hand, only a small, smoky stub remained. She tucked it into her belt, then clambered across Norryn's back to the spot where Haben lay.

A pang of horrible regret hit her as she settled by his side. She hadn't been fast enough. His ankle was twisted twice around his neck, choking him, while his back was bent completely backward. He was folded in on himself in the wrong direction, and his skin was marred with dark patches of black and blue. Dohv must have snapped half the bones in his body.

She fought back a storm of tears as she started untangling the chains from around his broken limbs. She knew it was useless, but it was all she could think to do. She untwisted his ankle from his throat, and he finally released a chilling, bloodcurdling scream. She held him as he shuddered, trying not to grasp him too tightly for fear of making the pain worse. She couldn't even imagine what he was feeling. A mortal in his position would have been long, long dead.

She glanced over at Zane, but he wasn't looking at her. His eyes were fixed on Haben, on the fate he'd so narrowly escaped himself. After a moment, he met Seycia's gaze, and she shook her head. They both knew he wouldn't heal. The only one who could give that power back to him was dead.

Seycia bent over and touched his freezing face. His eyes were vacant and crusted with blood. Tears spilled down her cheeks as she unwound the final length of chain from his shattered body. She tossed it over the side as they left Antenor and crossed a dark, deserted canyon.

What needed to happen next was clear. Seycia had known it the moment she caught sight of Haben dangling from the top of the cliff, twisted into that horrific shape. Only then, she'd had the fang. She could've done the job right then and there. Now, there was only one other option. She touched the final, tiny nub of Irem's branch in her belt. She hoped there would be enough fire.

A memory materialized then—a memory of her mother, shortly after Miko was born. Her mother had been ill. She couldn't stand and could barely speak. Seycia remembered the way her father sat by her bedside in the dim firelight, not saying anything, just holding her mother's hand. Seycia looked after baby Miko. Every few hours, she and her father would switch; Seycia would hold her mother's hand, and her father would care for the baby. The silent dance went on for days. Eventually, someone had come with medicine. But from the start of the sickness till the end of it, nobody had let go of her mother's hand.

As she relived the memory, she took hold of Haben's hand. It was the only thing she could think to do. She could hardly feel a pulse as she supported his wrist against her palm.

Norryn flew back the way they came, chasing the sun across the sky. It would be night again soon. He was making double time, aware of the state of his passengers, but traversing the Underworld was still an arduous flight. Seycia realized she'd barely moved a muscle for hours.

She gazed across the landscape below, looking for the fractured sliver of sunlight at the foot of the Blue Mountain that would lead them back to the Great Forest. She spotted it and steered Norryn on course. Haben hadn't moved for hours and still had not spoken a single word. If not for the labored rise and fall of his chest every minute or so, she would have sworn he was dead.

As a blanket of blue darkness spread across the sky, Norryn dove in for a smooth landing in the sparkling sand that gave way to the Great Forest. The first row of ancient trees loomed before them, welcoming them home. Seycia turned to Zane, who flinched as the forest came into view. He shivered, as though approaching the trees were physically painful.

"I-I don't think I'm allowed in," he whispered, and cast Seycia a nervous glance.

"That's all right. Stay here. If the Spirit Sentries ask, tell them you're with me."

He gave her a questioning look as he hopped off Norryn's back.

"You're safe," she reassured him. "I won't be long." It reminded her of something she might have said to Miko. She gazed at the boy demon, noticing how small he looked.

"Who's going to rule now that Dohv is gone?" Zane asked her.

"Dohv's sisters. I'm sure of it. I think things will be different once they're back."

"And what's going to happen to him?" He pointed at Haben.

She hated with all her heart to say it aloud. So she didn't. "He'll be all right. I know what to do."

Norryn fluttered his wings, and Seycia faced forward, preparing to take to the sky.

"What do I do now that I'm free?" Zane asked before Norryn left the ground. "There's so much time. What do I do now?"

Seycia paused. She had begun to wonder the same thing. What *would* they do now? "Think of why you're here. Why Dohv punished you," she said. "Think of how you can undo it. And maybe one day the forest will let you enter."

Zane seemed satisfied with the answer. He nodded and said nothing more. He watched Seycia take off as the sun sank across the eastern sky, ushering in the first night of an uncertain, brand-new world.

Norryn wove through the trees as Seycia supported Haben's head in her lap, still holding tight to his hand. She prayed he wasn't in pain, though she knew how foolish it sounded. His disjointed bones jutted from his skin in every direction, and his head hung to the side as though his spine was no longer supporting it. She closed her eyes and thought of the way he'd been just hours before. She wanted to remember him that way, not like this.

She thought of the ice in Antenor and how it hadn't frozen around his mangled body. She had said he was a good man. She'd meant it. And she was right.

But he was already broken. She hadn't been there when Dohv's servants splintered his bones to pieces. She had been saving Miko, saving her home. And she'd only finished half of what she'd set out to do: she wasn't able to destroy the emperor's tree. She broke beneath the weight of her choice and choked back a fresh wave of anguished tears. Somehow, she'd thought she could save everybody. She hadn't imagined it any other way, but here it was.

She pulled the map from her belt as Norryn wove his way through the dense treetops. She let go of Haben's hand, just to write the name. She saw his fingers flinch. He released an almost inaudible moan, but she was sure she'd heard it. Her hand danced across the surface of the leaf, writing his full name, the one he'd had in life: Emory Haben. *Em.* She closed her eyes and tried to imagine the man he once was. She pictured his sunken face bright with color and warmth, a body free of scars and Dohv's cruel markings. She envisioned a smile on his face—not the cold, cynical half-grin he often cast in her direction, but something truly hopeful, truly *human.*

The two beads of light on the map flickered in the darkness. One was their position, and one was his tree. She transmitted the directions to Norryn. They were close. He breathed a low, heavy sigh as he flew onward, and she realized she had transmitted her heartache to him as well.

A small, gnarled tree came into view, flanked by two larger neighbors heavy with thick green leaves and crimson flowers. The tree in the middle was shrunken and stunted. Its leaves were dried and brown, and its white bark was peeling all around to reveal a black, sickly looking core. The two points on the map aligned. Seycia tugged Norryn's ear, and he drifted to the ground. The tree seemed desolate and afraid, as though it had been abandoned and left uncared for. It *had* been abandoned, she realized. It hadn't had a soul inside of it for hundreds of years.

Norryn eased to a halt in the sand as Seycia folded up the map. She grasped Haben's hand, longing to forget that she would have to let it go soon. She bent forward and kissed his pale, lifeless face on both sides, barely grazing his skin, so afraid to hurt him. She wished she could think of something to say.

At that moment, he lifted his head, just barely, but the pain was too much. He moaned and collapsed against Norryn's fleshy neck.

"No, no," she whispered to him. "Don't. It's time to rest. That's all you have to do now."

He was finally communicating with her. Why now? Why hadn't she set fire to the tree as soon as they landed?

"Just rest, just rest, just rest," she said, tracing Dohv's barbaric black markings on his arms. "You're safe now, Em."

She finally wrested her hand from his, and he made another frail sound in his throat. But she ignored it. This was right, this was right. There was no other way. She pulled Irem's branch from her belt. It was so tiny now, barely the length of her palm. She snapped off just the tip of it, and a dim flame spouted out. It would have to do.

She threw her legs over the side of Norryn's belly, about to disembark, when Haben's hand swung at her. Before she could stop him, he knocked Irem's branch out of her hand.

Seycia cried out in horror and leaped off Norryn's back to rescue what was left of Irem's gift. She grappled about in the sand, desperately searching for the tiny twig.

"No."

She stopped cold. She knew she'd heard it, but she didn't want to.

He said it again, "No."

She rose to her feet and gazed at him, tearful. "It will be over fast—" she whispered.

"No," he said again, more firmly this time.

"You want this?" she cried out. "For all eternity? You're hurt. Please, please just let me help you."

He struggled to speak his next words. It came out slowly, piece by piece. "Not . . . here. No. Take me . . . to . . . Irem. I saw . . . they fixed you. So—"

"But they can't restore regenesis," she reminded him with a knot in her throat. "I can help you. Right now. I promised you I would."

"No."

They were silent for a long moment. She crouched down one more time, searching for the twig in the sand, squinting in the darkness.

"No," he said with steady finality to his voice.

She looked at him with crestfallen eyes. It was his soul, his body, his decision. She couldn't go against him. She made her way over to Norryn and climbed onto his back, gripping his scruff in her trembling fists. She took Haben's hand, and he finally returned her gaze, however distant.

"Dohv is gone," she whispered, realizing she hadn't even told him.

He gave a weak, contented nod and closed his eyes.

"The world is going to be different. This one, and the one we came from. I'd be lying if I said I didn't want you to see it with me."

He tightened his grip around her hand, and her hollow, sunken heart flooded with warmth, maybe even hope. If he wanted eternal life, a life with her, even through this darkest kind of suffering, that had to be worth something. Now that the three sisters were free of Dohv's punishment, they might be able to help him. At the very least, they had to try.

She laid her head against Norryn's side. *Go home to the mountain*, she said to him. He vaulted into the sky and beat his wings with all the energy inside his enormous body. Seycia felt the cool night wind in her hair, stronger than ever before. Norryn would have them to the Blue Mountain in no time.

Whatever lay ahead, in this world and the world she'd come from, Seycia couldn't begin to predict. The two places were locked in an endless alliance, and it was clear that a change for one would always usher in a change for the other. Today, she had changed the circumstances for *both* worlds. Tomorrow, a new reality would take hold, for everyone, everywhere.

Haben's pulse revived just the smallest bit, and she had to wonder if he, too, was remembering what Meri had said to them on the mountaintop before they left for the forest: *We do not know what will change the rhythm of the universe. We only know that it is coming.*

It was. Perhaps it already had. The future was ripe with possibility, and they would have to decide, and decide wisely, what to do with it.

CHAPTER TWENTY-ONE

MIKO HAD ONLY seen Minari for a brief, frantic moment. She had been there when he finally awoke from his slumber, deep in the underground temple with the colorful painted walls. She had embraced him quickly, asked him if his head was feeling all right, and told him she would see him again in a few hours. Then High Priest Jenli, alive and unscathed, lifted his limp, exhausted body and placed it into . . . What was it? A box? A coffin? He protested in terror as they slid the top of the container over his head.

"Keep still," Minari said from outside the coffin. "This is how you're getting out of Khronasa."

He knew enough to trust her by now, but his head spun with questions. He pressed his mouth against a tiny hole at the bottom of the wooden box and tried his best to breathe normally as the casket moved in a jerky, uncomfortable motion. Why in the world did he need to leave Khronasa in a coffin? And where were they going? Minari said they'd see him soon. Who else was coming with them?

Miko heard a chorus of muffled voices all around him as Jenli, Minari, and a few others carried the casket through the streets of Khronasa. He heard wailing and pleading, and he suddenly understood how perfect their plan was. There were hundreds of other funerals happening all across Khronasa that day, because the riots had finally died down. The entire population was in mourning.

"My condolences for your loss, your holiness," a man said outside the fragile wall of the coffin.

"Thank you. My cousin. We're taking him to sea," Jenli replied.

Miko exhaled with relief. He would not find himself buried underground.

In the darkness of the coffin, he relived the image of General Simeon's incinerated body over and over again, wondering how it had happened. Logic told him someone must have struck a match to his jacket, or one of his cohorts nearby had fired a flaming arrow. But the vision Miko saw beyond the wall of fire, the fleeting glimpse he'd had of Seycia, made him sure it had been something else. He'd barely been conscious at the time, and it was possible his mind was playing tricks on him, but the very core of his being told him not to doubt himself. It was real. But what did it mean?

Hours passed. Miko dripped with sweat and shifted in discomfort to all corners of the casket. He could sense they were on the water now; he felt the ebb and flow of the waves underneath him.

Finally, at sunset, Minari lifted the lid from the coffin, and Miko shot his head out like a cannonball. He was on a rickety wooden sailboat, not a shoreline in sight.

There were more than a dozen people on the boat, Jenli and Minari among them, but he didn't know their names. Some were elders from the ceremony he'd attended at the underground temple. Others were fellow escaped prisoners from Ezara's army. They all stared at him eagerly, as though expecting him to say something.

"Did, uh . . . did you all have to come in coffins too?" was the first thing he could think to ask. A light chuckle rippled across the small crowd.

"No, just you," Jenli replied.

He helped Miko out of the coffin and handed him a luke-warm mug of tea.

He stumbled across the sailboat's deck, unused to the way his legs wobbled on the water. Jenli settled him onto an over-turned crate. All eyes were on him. It was making him nervous. He flinched and sipped his tea, staring at his feet.

"Do you remember what happened, Miko?" he asked.

"General Simeon. He . . . well . . ." Miko couldn't even begin to describe it.

"You remember how he died?"

"He was choking me. And then . . . then he was on fire."

Jenli pursed his lips and guided Miko to his feet. He led him to the side of the boat, away from his rapt audience. Miko clung to the rail for support as the boat rolled over a large wave.

"Miko," he whispered. "Do you know how that happened to General Simeon?"

He didn't answer at first. The boat went over another lurch, and Miko lost his balance, splashing his tea across the deck. He glanced over at Minari on the other side of the boat. They locked eyes, and her stare awakened his confidence. What he'd seen was real. And it mattered.

"I think . . . I saw something. I saw my sister," he whispered.

"Your sister?"

"When General Simeon was on fire, I don't know how, but she was there. Maybe she was the one who did it."

"It wasn't you?"

Miko's first instinct was to shake his head. Of course it wasn't him. He'd been on the brink of death, how could he have done it? *Because you were desperate*, that voice in the back of his mind spoke again. *You don't yet know what you're capable of.* Miko shivered, and he knew it wasn't because of the ocean breeze.

"It was as though you lit him on fire with your eyes. That's what Minari said," Jenli went on. Miko pulled a breath, then nodded.

"I don't know. But it's possible," he finally said.

"In time, I'm sure you'll learn. But we believe in you, Miko. And we believe you can do it again, when you're ready." Jenli leaned in closer, eye-to-eye with him. "You can do it to Emperor Caius."

Jenli clasped his hands, gazing at him with a desperation that burned as brightly as the fire that had brought them there. Not long ago, the look in his eyes would have terrified him. But Miko knew not to be afraid anymore. He had to believe. He *did* believe. After a moment, Miko squeezed Jenli's hand and murmured, "I will."

Jenli touched his dirt-streaked face and bowed his head to him, grateful tears in his eyes. Miko felt as though he were standing taller than he ever had before.

Jenli addressed their fellow passengers: "He's tired and would like to rest. Please save your questions for a few days. We'll make a plan when we reach our destination. When the time is right, the Lasting Light will return to Khronasa. And we will take what's ours."

"Where are we going?" Miko finally thought to ask.

"There's a country on the opposite shore that has been uninhabited since the War of the Veil. But rumor has it there are still some who live there." Jenli paused and gazed at the full moon illuminating a pathway in the water to their destination. "They call it the Poisoned Country. It might have its dangers, but we hope it's safer than Khronasa for someone like you."

Someone like me. But who was he now?

Jenli joined the others at the opposite end of the boat, leaving him alone with his thoughts, his fears, and his thundering heartbeat. He stared down the void of his mysterious and terrifying future, dark as the waves lapping against the side of their little boat.

He looked up and noticed Minari had joined him. She put a steady arm around him and held on tight. Her touch, her presence, flooded him with hope and a thousand other feelings he didn't know how to describe yet.

They'd reach the Poisoned Country soon enough. And when they did, he would have to give the people, *his* people, the light they needed to glimpse their future.

EPILOGUE

"HE CANNOT BREATHE on his own anymore," Meri said, hushed and low, as if the words themselves might pierce Seycia right in the place where she felt the most despair.

Seycia inched up the ladder, following Meri to the top floor of the sisters' hut. They were free to come and go as they pleased, now that Dohv was under the ice in Antenor, but they had fashioned the place that had once been their prison into an infirmary of sorts. Meri and Remi had left and come back several times over the past few days, but Irem hadn't budged. Seycia climbed up to the second floor, where Irem was lying on the ground beside Haben's broken, unconscious body—both of them deep in a celestially induced slumber. Irem's floor-length lavender hair was intricately braided and tied to both of Haben's wrists; she was feeding him power and healing energy from her own body. But it wasn't enough. Seycia could see it—Irem would breathe, and seconds later, Haben's own chest would rise and fall, but just barely. And then there was the horrible sound he made as he exhaled. Seycia gritted her teeth and fought back tears as she heard it, over and over, like an endless death rattle.

"She's been breathing for him. She could do this forever," Meri explained, circling her sister. "And I have no doubt that she would, gentle thing that she is. She feels his suffering. But I don't want her to."

"Neither do I," Seycia replied. "She's suffered enough."

A moment passed between them as Seycia stared at Haben's misshapen form on the ground, watching the frail rise and fall of his battered chest. She longed to hear him speak again, to ask her why she was bothering to worry about him at all, and didn't she have better things to do?

"If Irem stops, if she lets him go, what happens?" Seycia forced herself to ask.

"Imagine suffocation with no end in sight. No release. That will be his fate," Meri replied quickly, as though afraid to prolong the unfortunate news. "You will no doubt want to return to the Great Forest to destroy his tree, as you had planned to do before."

"No, there has to be another way. He didn't want me to. He wants to live," Seycia said, fresh tears brimming in her eyes.

"You must decide, soon, what you wish to do," Meri whispered. "The river has flooded. The Soulless are without a master, and they're hungry for a fight. I fear for the future of this world if someone doesn't take control." She added with a pointed look, "You're one of us now. We need you."

Seycia nodded, but she didn't want another fight. Not just yet.

In the dismal silence that followed, Seycia gazed at Haben and dared herself to look at every single one of his injuries, every cracked and contorted bone, every dark, throbbing bruise where his chains had been. *Don't make him suffer. Let him go. Just let him—*

"Wait." Seycia spun to face Meri. "He's lost regenesis. He can't heal. But I still can."

Seycia kneeled beside Irem and Haben, running her finger along the soft, smooth braid connecting Irem's body to his.

"Take from me whatever he needs to survive. Those parts of me will come back. I can give them to him."

"I understand why you think this would work. And we won't stop you," Meri replied after a moment, with a twinge of unease. "But you know what happens when you take a part of this world into your body. It changes you. I don't know what would happen if he took a part of *your* world into his. You are still human in ways he is not. It could transform him."

"How?"

"I do not know. It's never been done."

Seycia took her place on the ground, on the other side of Haben, and peered up at Meri with a pleading stare. "Make me sleep and give him whatever he needs."

"You will likely feel some pain. Perhaps a great deal of it," Meri warned, crouching down beside her. "Be sure."

"I am. Unless you have a better idea?" Seycia responded with a wry smile. Meri drew a breath, squeezed her shoulder, and placed both her palms against Seycia's eyelids.

"Come, the void. Come, shadow. Come, darkness," Meri whispered.

And darkness came.

THE END

ACKNOWLEDGMENTS

I'd like to extend my gratitude to my loving parents and my husband, Sam, for their endless encouragement, all my Inkshares backers and fellow authors, and the Inkshares Syndicates for supporting the project. Many thanks as well to the entire Inkshares team who work so hard to bring new stories into the world. Big-time gratitude also goes out to the amazing Jennie Stevens and my manager Merideth Bajaña, who both championed this project early on, and to Matt Harry for his developmental edits.

I'm also grateful to Gautham Jothi, Mia Resella, and Audra Arnaudon for reading those early (admittedly very messy) chapters, my terrific, insightful beta readers Stuti Malhotra, Courtney Hope, Hilary Clifford, Emily Coleman, and Lisa Frye, Masha Stepanova for contributing her artwork, David Diperstein and Jess Nurse for their stunning book trailer, Liz Parker for her guidance and support, and Meggyn Watkins for her early edits. It takes a village!

GRAND PATRONS